I0572471

Foolish Is The Heart

Foolish Is The Heart

Brandon walked into a crowded and stuffy conference room in the university's athletic complex. He saw a few familiar faces and nodded at them before finding a seat near the podium. A row of TV cameras on tripods lined the back of the room. He took out his reporter's notebook from the inside pocket of his light brown corduroy sports coat and flipped through it until he reached a blank page. He took a pen out of his pocket, clicking it a few times, and then scribbled some O's on the page to see if it had ink.

"Sir, do you have a news release?" a woman standing next to him asked.

Startled for a moment, Brandon stared at her for a few seconds without speaking. He couldn't help noticing the deep, dark brown eyes and black hair. She had a creamy complexion and was wearing a bright red lipstick. He thought she was stunning.

"No, I don't," he said. "Thank you." She handed him a two-page news release and he glanced down at it.

"My name is Clarice Horton," she said.

Brandon stood up quickly and extended his hand. "I spoke with you yesterday," he said. "I'm Brandon Wilkes."

"It's a pleasure to meet you, Mr. Wilkes," she said. "Do you have any questions?"

"Questions?"

"About the news conference," she said, smiling.

"Uh, no, not right now. Everything looks complete in the release."

"Well, if you have any questions or need to talk to anyone after the news conference, just let me know."

"Thanks."

A few seconds later several university officials walked to the podium. The television camera lights in the back of the room flicked on brightly and everyone began scrambling for a seat. The news conference concerned a two million dollar donation by a national company to help athletes who suffered career-ending injuries. It lasted about twenty minutes as four people read prepared statements and answered several questions.

Brandon glanced around the room for Clarice, finally seeing her with several company officials. He caught her eye from a distance as he was leaving and they smiled briefly at each other.

What They Are Saying About

Foolish is the Heart

Brandon Wilkes is a sports columnist who, at age 45, has never been married, although the opportunities have been there. His dedication to his career, which used to monopolize his time, has earned him widespread respect. Wilkes' kind heart and thoughtful ways have won him many friends. Now his carefree lifestyle is changing. The people in his life—coworkers, a clingy girlfriend, business associates—are all hitting some bumps in the road as Wilkes strives to assist each of them and confront the changes in his own life.

Wilkes is a man who will not allow himself to be pushed into situations that he knows are wrong for him, but he does this in a compassionate matter. With the appearance of Clarice Horton, a beautiful public relations associate, Wilkes may have to rethink what he wants in his life.

The story moves at a steady pace, and the plot takes surprising twists and turns. Well-drawn and interesting characters make the novel a fun read that is difficult to put down.—reviewed by Mary Jo Harrod for *Kentucky Monthly* magazine

Foolish Is The Heart

Michael Embry

A Wings ePress, Inc.
General Fiction

Wings ePress, Inc.

Edited by: Rosalie Franklin
Copy Edited by: Dianne Hamilton
Senior Editor: Dianne Hamilton
Managing Editor: Leslie Hodges
Executive Editor: Lorraine Stephens
Cover Artist: Bev Haynes

All rights reserved

Names, characters and incidents depicted in this book are products of the author's imagination or are used fictitiously. Any resemblance to actual events, locales, organizations, or persons, living or dead, is entirely coincidental and beyond the intent of the author or the publisher.

No part of this book may be reproduced or transmitted in any form or by any means, electronic or mechanical, including photocopying, recording, or by any information storage and retrieval system, without permission in writing from the publisher.

Wings ePress Books
http://www.wings-press.com

Copyright © 2008 by Michael Embry
ISBN 978-1-59705-685-4

Published In the United States Of America

Wings ePress Inc.
3000 N. Rock Road
Newton, KS 67114

Dedication

With love and respect to my parents, Dale Embry and Lorraine Embry; my late in-laws, R.C. and Lou Alice Frederick; and stepmother-in-law, Latichia Frederick.

One

Paintings from local artists dotted the walls along with old and new playbill posters of concerts, speakers and various rallies. Little had changed inside Ezra's Restaurant since it opened a few blocks from the University of Kentucky campus in the 1960s as a hangout for various sorts of hippies, free-thinkers, students, writers, and artists, except for the patrons. As James Taylor's music from the 1970s played softly in the background, nattily-clad lawyers, business people in dark colors, college professors in casual attire and students in faded jeans and expensive preppy shirts partook from the wide variety of vegetarian dishes off the menu in subdued surroundings. None of the furnishings matched and varied in shape and size. Tablecloths splashed different designs and colors in the cramped dining room. A single rose in a slender crystal vase graced the center of each table, about the only constant in the hodgepodge décor.

"Would you care for any dessert?" a young waiter wearing jeans, lime-colored T-shirt and a slightly food-stained long apron asked.

"I could use a little more coffee, please," said Jenny Thomas, glancing up with a smile.

"Same here," said Brandon Wilkes, nodding.

"Let me take your plates," the waiter said.

Jenny looked wistfully at Brandon while the waiter removed the plates and silverware from their table. She brushed her long, black hair back on the sides with her hands. The waiter nervously grinned at both of them before returning to the kitchen.

"I'll be right back with your coffee," he mumbled.

"Thanks for bringing me here for lunch," Jenny said. "This is one of my favorite places in town."

"I like it, too," Brandon said, glancing at the wall across from him. "Great atmosphere."

The waiter returned with a coffee pot, refilled their cups and left without saying a word.

"We've known each other quite a while now," Jenny said, peering over her cup after taking a sip.

"Yes, we have," Brandon said, not giving the remark much thought. "Several years, I guess."

"I mean dating," Jenny said as a soft smile crossed her face.

"I'd say three or four months."

"It's been six months."

"Really? Time flies."

Brandon picked up his cup and slowly took a sip. He set it back down and glanced up at the clock on the wall behind the counter.

"I was wondering if you've ever thought about making a stronger commitment?" she asked, holding her cup with both hands. "I mean, we've been together for quite a while and we apparently like each other. I've had some of my friends ask me about us."

"Really? What do they ask?" Brandon said with a quizzical expression.

"When we're going to get engaged."

"Engaged? Are you serious?" Brandon said with a short laugh.

Jenny's expression suddenly turned from solemn to sad. Tears welled in her eyes. She gazed down at the table.

"I'm sorry," Brandon said, leaning forward and talking slightly above a whisper. "I didn't mean for it to come out that way."

"You don't need to say anything else," Jenny said, refusing to make eye contact. She opened her purse and took out a piece of tissue and wiped the tears from her cheeks.

"It's not what you think. What's wrong with being friends? Why do people have to make formal engagements?"

"Because," she pouted.

"That's not an answer," Brandon said, before picking up his coffee for another sip.

"When people date for as long as we have, they start making plans for the future if they care about each other," she said. "Apparently, you don't care that much about me."

"I didn't say that. I just said I wasn't ready for any commitments."

"Will you ever be ready?

"I don't know. I can't answer that now." Brandon squirmed slowly in his chair. "What's the rush?"

"Brandon, I'm thirty-four," she said, this time piercing directly into his eyes. "I've never been married. I want to have children. I want to have a future with someone. I was hoping you'd feel the same way. I guess I was wrong."

Brandon cleared his throat and glanced at his watch.

"Could I bring you any more coffee?" the waiter said, startling both of them for a second with his sudden appearance next to their table.

"No thanks," Brandon said, glaring at him.

"Would you like your check?"

"Yes, please."

The waiter took their bill out of his apron and placed it next to Brandon.

"You can pay at the counter," he said timidly. "Come back again."

Brandon stared at Jenny as the waiter went to another table.

"Okay, what were we talking about?" he said.

"What were we talking about?" Jenny said, her eyes flaring. "You tell me that you've already forgotten in one minute? I can see that you have no desire to make anything about this relationship permanent."

Jenny pushed her chair back quickly and began to stand up.

"Now wait a minute," Brandon said. "Don't be in such a hurry."

Jenny stood next to the table and brushed several tiny bread crumbs off the front of her gray slacks. She glared at him.

"I'm sorry, Brandon," she said. "I can see that you don't have any plans for us. I thought after all this time that we could have something more in our relationship. Boy was I wrong!"

"I care about you," Brandon said, with sorrow in his eyes. "I really do. I'm just not ready to make any long-term commitments."

"I feel sorry for you, Brandon. I care a lot about you but I can see that I'm not making any headway. I need more than what we have and you're not willing to give more. I wish you the best."

Jenny smiled curtly, picked up her purse, turned quickly and walked out of the restaurant. Brandon sat silently. Couples seated at adjoining tables glanced at him momentarily and went back to their own conversations. Brandon picked up the check and ambled to the counter to pay. He dropped a five-dollar tip at his table as he left the restaurant.

As he stepped out the front door, Brandon looked both ways, thinking he would see Jenny waiting for him as they both worked within walking distance of the restaurant. When there was no sign of her, he put on his sunglasses, turned to his left and walked briskly back in the cool air to the *Kentucky Sports Weekly* office.

Brandon had been a columnist at the magazine for three years, after spending nearly twenty years at newspapers in Nashville, Baltimore, Kansas City and Dallas. He enjoyed the slower pace of the magazine, although deadlines from weekend games proved to be just as stressful in turning out the Monday press runs.

"How was lunch?" Maggie Brown, the receptionist, asked as he walked into the office. Her oversized pink cashmere sweater minimized the appearance of her oversized bosom. Her curly blonde hair was piled high on her head. Brandon didn't know her age, but was sure she was at least forty-five trying to appear thirty-five and failing miserably.

"It was okay," he said glumly.

"What's the matter? Didn't you have lunch with Jenny?"

"Yeah. I guess we broke up," he said while taking a seat next to her desk.

"She was getting serious?" Maggie said, arching her dark-penciled eyebrows.

"How did you know?"

"A woman knows these types of things. You don't go out with someone for as long as you guys have without having some expectations."

"What's wrong being friends?"

"If you just want a friend, buy a dog."

"Maybe I'll have to do that," Brandon said with a laugh.

"Don't you ever plan to get married?" she asked.

"Not in the near future. I've been a bachelor for all my forty-five years and I don't see any reason to change that status now."

"You shouldn't lead these women on then," Maggie said.

"Lead them on? I don't do that."

"Brandon, in the time I've known you, I bet there've been three or four nice women that you've broken up with because you wouldn't get serious them. A girl has to have some kind of idea about the future if she's going to stay with you."

"What about you?" Brandon said. "I don't see you running out trying to get married again."

"Honey, I've been through enough ornery guys to last a lifetime," Maggie said, sitting up straight and shuffling her shoulders. "I know better. It's going to have to be a Prince Charming before I let my heart go again, and I don't think there's one out there. Four marriages are enough."

They both laughed.

"Good point," Brandon said as he got up from the chair. "Any messages for me while I was out?"

"Hmm, let me see," Maggie said as she flipped through a stack of memo sheets. "You had something from a public-relations firm. It's in here somewhere."

"It couldn't be too important," Brandon said.

"Oh, here it is." She handed him the yellow piece of paper.

"The Franklin Agency," Brandon said to himself. "Clarice Horton. Don't know the name."

"She didn't give any details other than something about a news conference coming up."

"Okay. I'll give her a call when I get a chance. I'll talk to you later."

"Don't go breaking any more hearts, lover boy," Maggie said with a teasing grin.

"I'll try not to," Brandon said as he went back to his office. He closed the door and glanced out the window, watching the gentle fall breeze swipe away some of the yellow, orange and red leaves from oaks behind the building. Picking up the phone receiver, he dialed the first four numbers of Jenny's office number, then put the receiver back.

Brandon thought about what Maggie had said about women wanting something more from him than dinner, movies and company. Commitment. He wasn't ready for that. If only Maggie knew about the string of women that he'd known in other cities. Jenny wasn't the first to broach the idea about an engagement or marriage. She was probably the twenty-fifth. Perhaps the fiftieth. He couldn't remember, not that he kept count on cooling relationships. And he didn't end them. They did. After he refused to make something more concrete out of the relationship, it was the women who walked.

Brandon turned his swivel chair back toward his desk. He shook his head and smiled. He was relatively happy, he thought, so why get stressed over this episode in his life? He shrugged his shoulders and looked at the message from Clarice Horton, placed it next to his phone but before he could do anything more, he heard a knock on his door.

"Come in," Brandon said.

"Busy?" Graham Jones said as he peeked through the half-open door.

"Nah. Just going through a few notes. What's up?"

"I just wanted to know when would be a good time to go over the story budget for the next issue."

Graham, tall, reed-thin, and balding, was the publisher of the magazine. Brandon had known him since their college days when they worked on the campus newspaper. Graham started the publication a dozen years ago and had tried to hire Brandon from the start. Brandon finally decided to make the move back to Kentucky after getting burned out covering pro sports in Dallas.

"I can do it in about thirty minutes," Brandon said. "I need to make a few calls and check up on a few things. Do you want to meet in your office or the conference room?"

"We'll do it in the conference room. Perry and Doris will join us. See you at about two then.."

"Okay. Buzz me if I lose track of time."

Brandon shuffled through several sheets of paper and took some notes. Before he knew it, Graham was back at his door.

"Ready?" he asked.

"Sure," Brandon said, picking up his notebook. He stacked several papers next to his phone, covering the message from Clarice Horton. "I'm on my way."

Two

"How about a beer after we get out of here tonight?" Graham asked after the meeting was over as they sat across from each other at the rectangular table.

"That doesn't sound bad," Brandon said as he eased up from his chair. "I could use a little liquid refreshment. This has been a hectic day."

"How so?"

"I'll explain later."

"Let me know when you're ready to leave."

"Okay. I've go a call or two to make and I need to finish up on my column. It shouldn't be another hour or so."

Brandon returned to his office and clicked on the computer and began working on his column. He struggled with it because his thoughts were on Jenny. He could still see the hurt on her face. He was surprised she walked out on him the way she did. It was totally unexpected. He liked her and enjoyed her company, but he certainly wasn't ready to make any long-term commitments. Perhaps he should give her a call and try to make up. But after giving it more thought, which took only a few seconds, he decided against it. He figured she would probably still be upset. Besides, perhaps she would call him and try to make up. Wasn't she the one who brought up the subject and then walked out on him?

Brandon glanced at the time on his computer screen and realized he'd been sitting there for thirty minutes without writing a word. He checked e-mail and found the regular fare of announcements and notes from other staffers. And he didn't bother to respond to any of them. Instead, he went back to his column, a piece about the need for colleges to closely monitor athletes' academic progress, and began typing. Forty-five minutes later, he was finished and stored it in a folder for the copy editors.

He sifted through some of the paperwork on his desk, tossing several news releases in the trash and sorting others in his file bin. He picked up the message from Clarice Horton, studied it for a few seconds, and then decided to call.

"You have reached the voice mail of Clarice Horton. I am not...." Brandon hung up the receiver and wadded up the message and flipped it in the trash.

A moment later, Graham came up to his door and asked if he was about ready to leave. They were at Hastings Tavern, a neighborhood hangout four blocks from the office, in less than ten minutes. They each ordered a frosty mug of light beer. Graham also bought a small pack of pretzels since the bar didn't offer appetizers on its menu.

"So how was your day?" Graham asked after taking a big swallow from the mug.

"It could have been better," Brandon said. "I did finish my column which I had struggled with but I also lost a girlfriend."

"Are you saying Jenny left?" Graham asked. "What happened?"

"Same old story. She wanted a commitment."

"How many times have I heard that?" Graham said with a laugh. "Why don't you wear a sign that says, 'Mr. Non-Commitment' across your chest?"

"I probably should," Brandon said before taking a quick sip from his mug. "Sometimes I don't understand why they can't simply have a friendly relationship."

"I'm sure there are some like that out there but you haven't been fortunate enough to run across them. Or maybe you did and dropped them before you could find out."

"Vicki and Amy didn't seem that way but they dropped me," Brandon said with a shrug. "Do you remember them?"

"I think I recall meeting Vicki. Didn't she have dark hair and a dynamite body?"

"That's her. It would be hard to forget her. Perhaps you didn't meet Amy. She was a blonde. I only went out with her a couple of times."

"You just need to find the right woman and settle down and you wouldn't have to put up this time all the time," Graham said.

"Isn't that called commitment?"

"Yeah, but it takes away a lot of the hassles of dealing with women when you have just one woman."

"I don't know if that makes sense."

"Look at Sheila and I. We've been married for eighteen years. I don't have to worry about all these different women, not that I wouldn't mind it once in awhile," he said with a grin. "Just joking. Sheila is my anchor."

"Sheila's a terrific woman and you're fortunate that you found her but the point is that I don't want a permanent relationship. I like doing things without answering to someone else. I like to come and go as I please. I've been on my own for most of my life."

"I'll just say that married life isn't that bad, if you know what I mean," Graham said with a slight snicker. "And it's a lot safer."

"I won't argue with that but I don't exactly pick up whores off the street."

"I didn't mean it that way," Graham said, almost apologetically. "You've gone out with some mighty fine women."

"I know what you mean. No offense taken. I've known you too long to be offended by your comments."

"So what are you going to do about Jenny?"

"Nothing, I suppose. She was the one who got upset and walked out on me."

"Don't you think she's worth at least a phone call?"

"Too many fish in the sea."

"You don't really mean that," Graham said. "Jenny's a nice woman."

"She is nice but life will go on without her. There were many before her, and hopefully, many will follow."

"You are really set in your ways, my bachelor buddy," Graham said, shaking his head.

After drinking another round of beer, Brandon drove to his apartment on the east side of town, a stylish complex next to a man-made lake. He took off his brown sports coat and hung it in the front foyer closet. Then he slipped off his shoes and tossed bundled mail on a rustic coffee table in the living room. He turned on the CD player at his state-of-the-art media center that covered most of the wall and slipped in a disc by the Mavericks, keeping the volume low.

Strolling into his bedroom he took off his denim shirt and khaki pants and put on a Cleveland Browns' T-shirt and gray gym shorts. He checked his answering machine and saw that he had one call. It was from Jenny. He touched the reply button.

"Hi, Brandon," the message began. "I'm just calling to see if you've given any more thought to our little discussion at lunch. I'm not apologizing for what I said because I meant every word of it. I don't know how you feel about me, but sooner or later you're going to have to make a commitment to someone. If you don't want to make any with me, then don't call me back. I wish you the best. Bye."

Brandon shook his head in disbelief. He reached down and pushed the erase button on the answering machine.

"I guess you won't be hearing any more from me," he said softly.

Back in his kitchen, he took out a prepared salad from the supermarket and put it in a bowl, cut up a tomato on it and poured Italian dressing on it. Then he fixed a glass of iced tea and sat down at the table. The phone rang but he let the answering machine take the call.

"Brandon, this is Jenny again. I guess not hearing from you by now is your answer to me. I think you're a sad and lonely person. I hope you can find happiness somewhere. Good bye."

"What in the world are you talking about, woman?" Brandon said, shaking his head and grinning. "I am happy. You're the unhappy person. Women!"

He finished his dinner and rinsed the dinnerware and put it in the dishwasher. The dishwasher was nearly full so he put in some detergent and turned it on. Back in the living room, he sat down on the couch. The CD had finished playing so he turned on the television and flipped through the channels with the remote. Nothing caught his attention so he turned it off. He saw that it was only nine-fifteen on the DVD clock.

He got up and walked back to his bedroom, stopping on his way to erase Jenny's message. In the bedroom, he picked up Stephen King's new novel that he started a few days earlier and lay down on the bed. He flipped on the nightstand lamp and began reading. The next thing he knew it was one-thirty in the morning. He marked his place in the book, placed it on the nightstand before reaching over and turning out the light. He slept soundly.

Three

"Any messages?" Brandon asked Maggie as he strolled into the office the next morning.

"Hmm, let's see," she said, picking up several pieces of paper. "You have one. Here it is."

She handed him the memo.

"Thanks," he said, taking it without reading it. "Anything going on today?"

"I'd be the last to know," she said. "I'm just a peon around here."

"Now, Mag. You know better than that. What's the matter?"

"I'm just having some problems at home," she said despondently.

"Anything you care to share?"

"No, it'll take care of itself."

"Let me know if I can do anything."

"Thanks, but I think everything will be all right."

Brandon walked down the hallway to his office. He adjusted the blinds to deflect the bright sunshine pouring through the window. Sitting down and clicking on the computer, he looked at the memo, saw that it was from Clarice Horton, picked up the phone and dialed her number. He got her voicemail and hung up.

The phone rang and he picked up the receiver on the second ring.

"Brandon Wilkes speaking."

"Hi."

"Good morning, Jenny," he said as he sat up in his black swivel chair.

"I'm sorry about yesterday."

"There's no need to apologize."

"I thought it over last night and I realize that I'm rushing things with you. I should just take my time and let things happen between us."

"That's a good idea," Brandon said as a smile crossed his face. "There was no sense in trying to change a good thing between us."

"But don't you think that things could change?"

"I hope not," he said with a short laugh. "I thought everything was just fine between us."

"But don't you want anything else from our relationship?"

"I can't think of anything," he said. "I like you just the way you are."

"I like you, too, Brandon, but I still think that our relationship can grow. Don't you?"

"Sure," he said.

"So maybe one of these days you'll make some kind of commitment to me?" she asked coyly.

"I guess that's possible," he said, sensing that she was backing him into a corner again. "But there's no rush."

"Are you afraid of commitments?"

"I didn't say that."

"But you don't want to make any."

"What's wrong being good friends?"

A few seconds of silence passed on the phone that seemed to last a few minutes.

"You're impossible, Brandon!" Jenny said, her voice breaking up as she was about to cry. "I don't know why I waste my time with you. I don't know why I even called you."

"But..."

"You only think about your own feelings."

"But..."

"You don't care for me."

"But…"

"I think you enjoy hurting me."

"But…"

"You're a jerk. Good bye!"

Brandon heard the click and stared at the receiver for a moment. He shook his head slowly and put the receiver back on his desk.

"Anything the matter?" Graham said at the door. "You look like you were hit by a stun gun."

"I just had a weird phone call from Jenny. She apologizes at the beginning and hangs up on me at the end. She even called me a jerk."

"We all know that," Graham said, laughing.

"I'll never figure that woman out," Brandon said.

"Join the club. I've never figured Sheila out and I've known her for twenty years."

"Oh, well, life goes on."

"I stopped by to tell you that a woman from the Franklin Agency called me a few minutes ago about some sort of news conference. She said she'd been trying to reach you."

"Yeah, I've had a couple of calls from her. I called her back. I guess we're playing a little telephone tag."

"Anyway, there's a news conference tomorrow morning at ten at the university, and she was wondering if we would have anyone there. I told her we would. Can you go?"

"No problem," Brandon said. "Did she tell you what it's about?"

"Not really. Something about a fund-raiser. She's going to fax over a fact sheet a little later."

"Sounds good. I'll take care of it."

"See you later," Graham said as he turned and walked two doors down the hall to his office.

Brandon checked his e-mail, most of it news releases, and picked up the morning newspaper, scanning the headlines to see if there was anything of interest to him. He put it down after ten minutes.

The phone rang and he took it after the second ring.

"Brandon Wilkes speaking."

"Oh, hello, Mr. Wilkes," a woman said in a strong, clear voice. "I've been trying to reach you the past few days. I'm Clarice Horton."

"Hi, Ms. Horton. I tried calling you back several times. I think we got involved in some telephone tag."

"Yes, I suppose we did. I talked to Mr. Jones this morning and told him about the news conference tomorrow."

"He told me about it. He said you were going to fax something over about it."

"I'll do that in a few minutes. I just wanted to tell you that this is a big news conference. There's going to be an important announcement. I really think you should attend."

This was a spiel he had heard time and time again from public-relations people. In the news business, they were called flaks. They all seemed to think that whatever they were pushing was the greatest thing since the invention of the wheel.

"I plan to be there," Brandon said dryly.

"Oh, that's wonderful," she said with a touch of excitement. "I don't think you'll regret it."

"I'm looking forward to it," Brandon said, rolling his eyes and knowing he was telling a bald-faced lie. He despised news conferences, especially those that smacked of commercialism. He knew the only reason for them was to control the content of news.

"Please let me know if there's anything you need."

"Just the fax," he said.

"Well, Mr. Wilkes, it's been a pleasure talking to you. I look forward to meeting you in the morning."

"Same here," Brandon said, trying to sound courteous.

A few minutes later Maggie walked into his office with a two-page fax.

"Here's something for you," she said.

"Thanks," Brandon said, taking it from her hand. "How's everything with you now?"

"About the same."

"Why don't you get it off your chest?"

Maggie stood silently for a few seconds, then sat down at the visitor's chair next to his desk and crossed her arms over her chest.

"My son was arrested last night for drugs," she said. "They took him to the juvenile facility."

"Why aren't you there with him?"

"They told me that I should let him stay there a day or so for some counseling. They also said that it may open his eyes about what can happen if you get into trouble."

"I guess that could help," Brandon said. "Is there anything I can do?"

"I don't know what anyone can do," she said as tears began to well up in her eyes. "I feel so helpless. He's my baby boy."

Brandon reached over and patted her hand.

"Have you contacted your ex-husband?"

"It's no use. He's worthless. He's a pothead. He never comes around the house unless he wants something."

"Is this the first time your boy has been in trouble like this?"

"Bobby Lee has never been in trouble. He told me after the police came that he didn't know where the grass came from. It broke my heart to see him crying."

"Did you call an attorney?"

"I don't have a lawyer. I can't afford one of them."

"Perhaps the court will appoint one."

"A social worker told me this morning that someone would be calling me about it. She said not to worry because this is the first time it's ever happen to Bobby Lee. I'm just worried they'll take my baby from me."

"That's not going to happen. I'll call one of my attorney friends and we'll take care of it."

"Thanks, Brandon," Maggie said, wiping tears off her cheeks with her hand. "I haven't told anybody about this."

"Well, it's safe with me," he said. "But I think it would be good if you told Graham."

"Would you mind telling him?"

"If you prefer. You just let me know if there's anything else I can do for you."

Maggie got up from the chair and walked to the doorway and turned around and smiled at Brandon.

"You're a very nice man," she said softly. "Thank you."

Four

Brandon walked into a crowded and stuffy conference room in the university's athletic complex. He saw a few familiar faces and nodded at them before finding a seat near the podium. A row of TV cameras on tripods lined the back of the room. He took out his reporter's notebook from the inside pocket of his light brown corduroy sports coat and flipped through it until he reached a blank page. He took a pen out of his pocket, clicking it a few times, and then scribbled some O's on the page to see if it had ink.

"Sir, do you have a news release?" a woman standing next to him asked.

Startled for a moment, Brandon stared at her for a few seconds without speaking. He couldn't help noticing the deep, dark brown eyes and black hair. She had a creamy complexion and was wearing a bright red lipstick. He thought she was stunning.

"No, I don't," he said. "Thank you." She handed him a two-page news release and he glanced down at it.

"My name is Clarice Horton," she said.

Brandon stood up quickly and extended his hand. "I spoke with you yesterday," he said. "I'm Brandon Wilkes."

"It's a pleasure to meet you, Mr. Wilkes," she said. "Do you have any questions?"

"Questions?"

"About the news conference," she said, smiling.

"Uh, no, not right now. Everything looks complete in the release."

"Well, if you have any questions or need to talk to anyone after the news conference, just let me know."

"Thanks."

A few seconds later several university officials walked to the podium. The television camera lights in the back of the room flicked on brightly and everyone began scrambling for a seat. The news conference concerned a two million dollar donation by a national company to help athletes who suffered career-ending injuries. It lasted about twenty minutes as four people read prepared statements and answered several questions.

Brandon glanced around the room for Clarice, finally seeing her with several company officials. He caught her eye from a distance as he was leaving and they smiled briefly at each other.

Brandon returned to the office after the news conference. Maggie was on the phone. She mouthed a silent "hi" to him as he walked back to his office. He read the news release again, and at the bottom of the second page saw Clarice's office number as a contact for more information. He tried to think of some question to ask her. It was very concise and complete. He drew a blank.

"How was the news conference?" Graham asked as he stood at the doorway.

"It was okay. The university is going to receive two million dollars to help injured athletes."

"Is it the only school in the nation receiving money?"

"I don't know," he said as a smile came on his face. "Great question. I'll have to call Ms. Horton and find out."

"I'll see you later," Graham said as he headed to his office.

Brandon dialed Clarice's number but reached her voicemail. He left his message about the funding and asked for her to call. While waiting, he went through his mail and checked e-mail. The phone rang and he picked it up before Maggie had a chance to answer.

"Brandon Wilkes speaking."

"Mr. Wilkes, this is Flora Pickens from the Franklin Agency. I've got an answer to your question."

Brandon frowned.

"The university is the first in the nation to receive this funding," she said, cold and professionally. "Notre Dame, UCLA and Florida will be next in line during the next couple of months, and then more schools will be added. Does this answer your question?"

"Yes, it does," he said. "I appreciate you getting back with me so promptly."

"Please don't hesitate to call back if you have any more questions. Bye."

Disappointed that he didn't hear from Clarice, he turned and began typing the story on his computer. Thirty minutes later it was finished. He walked to the break room and got a Pepsi from the compact refrigerator in the corner. Maggie came in while he was reading the bulletin board.

"Brandon, there's a woman here to see you," she said.

Brandon looked at her quizzically.

"A woman?" he asked. "What's her name?"

"She didn't say."

Brandon walked up the hall to the front foyer. He turned to the right and seated on the visitor's couch was Jenny. She looked up at him and smiled.

"Hi, Brandon," she said sweetly. "Could we talk for a minute?"

"Uh, sure," he said. "Come on back to my office." She had never dropped in at his office. The only person she had ever met at the magazine was Graham. Maggie flicked her eyebrows a few times and smiled at Brandon as he walked past her desk.

"Have a seat," Brandon said in his office. Jenny sat down next to his desk as he closed the door.

"Brandon, are you ever going to forgive me?" she asked sheepishly. "I know I've been a b-i-t-c-h to you the past few days."

"I guess," he said, slightly shrugging his shoulders.

Jenny crossed her legs in her tight red skirt, bouncing her right leg up and down, catching Brandon's attention for a second and causing him to lose his train of thought.

"I don't like us being mad at each other," she said with sad puppy-dog eyes.

"I agree," he said. "There's no reason for it."

"I'll try not to bring up this stuff about commitment and everything. I know it makes you so uneasy. We can just go on like we did before."

Brandon's phone rang. This time he let it ring three times, letting Maggie answer it for him. A few seconds later, Maggie knocked softly on the door and opened it halfway.

"Brandon, you have a call on line two," she said. "Should I take a message? It sounded somewhat important."

"I'll take it," he said, wanting a break from Jenny. He smiled at Jenny and picked up the phone. "This is Brandon. May I help you?"

"Oh, hi Mr. Wilkes. I just wanted to thank you for attending the news conference. I see where my assistant called you and answered your question. I was wondering if there is anything else we could help you with."

Hearing Clarice's voice made him feel a little uneasy with Jenny sitting only a few feet from him. He squirmed and sat up straight in his chair. He glanced at Jenny and forced a smile.

"I think I got everything I need," he said after clearing his throat. "I appreciate your assistant getting back with me so quickly."

"We have several other things going on at the agency that you may be interested in," she said. "Would you be able to have lunch some day and I could go over them?"

"I would like that," Brandon said without hesitation. Jenny's leg bouncing a little faster and he noticed a perturbed look beginning to cross her face as if she could read his mind.

"When would be a good day for you?" Clarice asked.

"Oh, I'm free most any day," he said.

"How about Friday at noon?"

"Let me check my calendar," Brandon said. He opened it and noticed a lunch date with Jenny that had been set for several weeks. "No problem" as he marked through Jenny's name and wrote in Clarice's.

"I'm looking forward to it, Mr. Wilkes," Clarice said. "I'll see you Friday. You have a nice day."

"You, too."

After he put down the phone, Jenny gave him a stern look.

"Who was that?" she asked.

"Just a PR agency following up on a news conference I attended this morning. No big deal."

"So, what about us?"

"What do you mean?"

"What we were talking about," she said, a touch of anger rising in her voice.

"Oh, sure," he said.

"Sure, what?"

"That everything is okay between us."

"Are you sure?" she asked as a smile began to erase the hard look.

"Why not?" he said cheerfully.

"Oh, Brandon, you're the sweetest man I know. I don't know why you put up with me. I know I can be difficult but that's because I care so much about you. I hope you understand that."

"I do."

"So are we still going to have lunch on Friday?"

Brandon suddenly felt uneasy and wriggled slightly in his chair.

"Oh, I'm sorry," he said. "Something came up and I won't be able to do that. I was going to call you. I hope you don't mind."

Brandon could see that she was disappointed.

"But how about dinner that evening?" he added quickly.

A smile popped back on her face.

"That would be great," she said, bending over and kissing him on the cheek and sitting back down.

"I can pick you up around seven," he said. "I'll let you choose the restaurant."

"I'll give that some thought, "she said as she began to stand up. "I need to be going now. I hope you don't mind me dropping in like this."

"That's okay," he said while getting up from his chair

Brandon walked her to the front door. Before leaving, she kissed him quickly on the mouth.

"Who was that?" Maggie asked dryly from her desk.

"A friend."

"She's sure a friendly friend," she said with a giggle.

"Never mind," he said as he walked past her desk toward his office. "It's a long story."

"I bet it is," she said.

Five

After work Brandon stopped at Hastings for a beer. He enjoyed unwinding there because it was an unpretentious watering hole that drew a mix of people. He knew most of the regulars.

Benny, the bartender, caught a glimpse of Brandon seated on a stool at the curve of the horseshoe-shaped bar and nodded at him that it would be a few seconds before he could bring him a draft beer. Two men seated next to Brandon were discussing the upcoming basketball season and the high expectations they had for the university. A couple of businesswomen were on the other side, talking about a business plan. An overhead TV was turned on to CNN but hardly anyone was paying attention to the daily rundown of Wall Street stocks.

Benny finally came over with a frosted mug of Miller Lite. He was wearing an off-white apron over faded blue jeans and white T-shirt.

"Hi there, Brandon," he said in a raspy voice as he wiped off the bar in front of Brandon with a damp dish cloth before setting the beer on a worn cardboard coaster. "Anything going on?"

"Not much, Benny. How about with you?"

"Same oh, same oh. Nothing changes around here."

"And nothing stays the same."

"I think you've got a point if I think about it long enough," he said with a wink.

"Well, I wouldn't do that because I don't know if it's worth that much thought."

"There was a lady in here to see you a couple of weeks ago," Benny said. "A tall, good-looking blonde. I've seen you with her before but it was a long time ago."

"Didn't leave her name?"

"Nope. She just said that she was in town and thought she'd see if you were here. She used to come here with you."

"That sounds like Mona. I haven't seen her in ages. I wonder what she is up to nowadays?"

"She didn't say. She stayed long enough to have a beer and left."

"It would have been nice to see her. A nice woman."

"I don't think I would have let her go," Benny said.

"She started having wedding plans."

The women next to Brandon overheard and glanced quickly at him and turned their heads back. Another patron across the bar waved his mug at Benny for another beer. Then the phone rang, and more customers came in and Benny was busy the next hour. He managed to get over and refill Brandon's mug.

The woman sitting next to Brandon left. The other one caught his eye and smiled softly.

"Do you mind if I scoot over and sit next to you?" she asked, the smile not leaving her face. "I don't like to sit alone and you look safe enough."

"Sure," Brandon said. "I won't bite."

"I'm Debra," she said, extending her hand.

"Hi, I'm Brandon. It's a pleasure to meet you. Do you live here in town?"

"All my life," she said. "I'm a real-estate agent."

"I bet that keeps you busy."

"I'm on the road all day. I had a big sale today so I was in here celebrating with a good friend from my office."

"Congratulations," Brandon said. He took a sip from his mug.

"Oh, thank you," she said with a bright smile.

Brandon guessed her to be in her mid-thirties. She was dressed professionally in a knee-length dark blue skirt and matching blazer. Her light brown hair was cut short. She had glistening blue eyes and full lips.

"Haven't I seen you before?" she asked.

"I come in here quite often."

"It's not here. I've only been in here a few times. Where do you work?"

"Kentucky Sports Weekly."

"What do you do there?"

"I'm a writer."

"Perhaps that's where I've seen you. Is your picture in the magazine?"

"Sometimes."

"That's an interesting publication," she said.

"We try our best."

"Well, I think I'm going out to get a bite to eat before going home," she said.

"It was nice meeting you," Brandon said.

"Care to join me?" she asked while going through her purse to find money for her bar tab.

"I don't know," Brandon said slightly shrugging his shoulders.

"I'm just going over to Fazoni's for some Italian. I'd like to have some company."

Brandon looked at her for a moment, wondering why she was asking him to dinner after knowing him for only fifteen minutes.

"Well, I haven't eaten, so why not," he said with a smile. "I'll meet you over there."

Debra eased off the stool and headed toward the front door. Brandon noticed her shapely body. Several other men did, too. He took money out of his wallet to cover his beers and tip. He waved at Benny as he left the bar. Benny nodded and took care of another customer.

Debra waited in the parking lot outside Fazoni's when Brandon pulled in his five-year-old Toyota Camry. She was driving a new mid-sized silver BMW sedan. Brandon figured that she must be a pretty good Realtor.

They were seated without any waiting in the restaurant. She ordered a carafe of white wine as they waited for their pasta dinners to arrive.

"It was nice of you to invite me," Brandon said before taking a sip of wine.

"I just don't like to eat alone when I can have some company," she said. "Ever since my husband and I separated, it's been kind of lonely for me."

"Oh," Brandon said, a look of concern creeping on his face. "How long have you been separated?"

"Hmm, about a month," she said. "It seems like ages."

"Have you been married long?"

"About five years," she said. "It's my third."

"I don't want to pry but why did you separate?"

"Because he's so jealous and possessive."

"Oh."

"It drives him nuts to even see me talking to another man. He hardly let me out of his sight. So I got fed up with it and walked."

"Have you heard from him?"

"Almost daily. Sometimes I see his car when I'm showing a house to someone. He manages to find out where I go."

"The guy must be crazy about you."

"I used to be crazy about him, too," she said while lightly flipping the back of her short hair. "It's just that he thinks I'm screwing around on him. The only time I've ever screwed around on a husband was with my second hubby and he was the guy I was with."

"What does your husband do?"

"He's a police officer. He's in the detective section."

"Oh," Brandon said, feeling even more uneasy. He glanced at his watch, wishing that the minutes would pass by quickly so he could make a polite exit.

"He's been on the force for about fifteen years."

"What's his name?"

"David Hatfield."

"I don't know him," Brandon said. "Not that I would or should necessarily. But I do know a few cops."

The waiter came back with their orders. They sat quietly for a few minutes while they ate spaghetti and garlic breadsticks. Brandon caught the image of a man standing next to them as he put a bite of food in his mouth. At first he thought it was the waiter. Then he realized it wasn't when he looked up and saw a tall, stone-faced man looking at Debra.

"David!" she said, surprised by his presence. "What are you doing here?"

"I think I should be asking you that."

Brandon sat quietly, not wanting to say or do anything to provoke an ugly scene in the restaurant. Especially involving himself.

"I'm having dinner," she said brightly. "I'd like you to meet Brandon."

David glared at Brandon for a moment and then back at Debra.

"Hi," Brandon said, somewhat timidly.

David didn't say anything. He unclenched his hands and put them in his pockets.

"I think I'll be going," Brandon said, pursing his lips.

"I think that would be a good idea." David said.

"Oh, don't rush off," Debra said. "You've hardly eaten anything."

"I wasn't that hungry," Brandon said. "I really need to go."

Brandon pushed his chair back from the table and stood up. He took two twenty dollar bills out of his wallet and laid them on the table.

"This should cover dinner," he said.

"Oh, you don't need to do that," Debra said. "It was my invitation."

"That's okay," Brandon said. "My treat."

Brandon looked at David and smiled. "It was nice meeting you," he said before walking away quickly. He turned around as he reached the front entrance and saw David sitting in his chair. Debra was smiling while David looked grim.

After reaching his car, Brandon didn't waste any time starting it and leaving the parking lot. He glanced in his rear-view mirror to make sure that he wasn't being followed by a policeman.

Six

Rain pelted the sidewalk as Brandon ran from his car in the parking lot to the office building. His pant legs were soaked to the knees as he stepped inside the building and closed his small black umbrella. He stomped his feet up and down a few times to shake off the water and walked to Maggie's desk.

"Good morning," he said. "Did you beat the rain?"

"Yes, but just barely, thank goodness," she said. "I didn't have my umbrella with me."

"As you can see, an umbrella didn't do me much good," Brandon said, lifting a leg to his wet pants. "Any messages or anything?"

"Clarice Horton called after you left yesterday."

"I'll call her this morning."

"Graham is out of the office this morning at a meeting."

"Anything important?"

"I don't think so."

"How's your son doing?"

"Bobby Lee is on probation right now at school. He's behaving himself."

"That's good."

"He swears that some boys put pot in his school locker to get him in trouble."

"That wouldn't totally surprise me the way kids are today. Did you tell the authorities?"

"No. I didn't want to cause any more trouble."

"Well, Maggie, you should. Just to have it on the record in case something like this happens again."

"I never thought about that. I'll do it this morning."

"Does Bobby Lee like sports?"

"He loves sports but he's still too little to play. He's the smallest kid in his class."

"I've got a couple tickets for this weekend's game at the university. Would you like to have them?"

"Thanks, but I've got a bridal shower to attend."

"Well, if something comes up and you'd still like to have them, just let me know. There's still two days before the game."

The phone rang and Maggie answered it. Brandon could see that it was a business call and went to his office. He looked outside the window. The rain was coming down even harder as the wind whipped the tree limbs, blowing off some of the leaves.

He dialed Clarice's number and was startled when she answered.

"This is Brandon," he said. "I wasn't expecting you to answer the phone."

"Oh, sometimes they let me answer my phone here," she said with a soft laugh.

"I'm just returning your phone call from yesterday. What can I do for you?"

"I was wondering if we still had that lunch meeting on Friday,"

"I almost forgot about that. Sure. Where do you want to meet?"

"How about Porter's at noon?"

"That's fine with me. I like Porter's. It's one of my favorite restaurants."

"Then I'll see you at noon."

"Okay. I hope you have a nice day."

Brandon put the phone down on the desk and smiled. He was looking forward to having lunch with Clarice. There was something about her that intrigued him, an air of self-confidence about her that made her even more attractive. And he thought that she was a lovely woman.

Walter Pittman, the layout editor, walked to his doorway with a handful of laser prints. He stood there for a second, gently tugging at his gray chest-length beard.

"Available for some proofing?" he asked.

"Sure, Walt," Brandon said. "Does this look like a good issue?"

"About as good as any we've had. But they all seem about the same after awhile."

"I know what you mean. We need to make some changes to add a little pizzazz to the magazine."

"I think so," Walt said while pushing his wire-rimmed glasses up on the bridge of his nose.

"Why don't we get together with Graham in the next week or so and discuss what we can do? We'll bring in some others and see what they have to say."

"Just let me know when you want to do it and I'll have everyone there."

"Good enough," Brandon said while skimming through the page proofs. "I'll run it by Graham this afternoon and get back with you."

As Brandon marked mistakes on the pages with a red felt-tip marker, the phone rang.

It was Jenny.

"Are we going out Friday night?" she asked.

"You name the place."

"I haven't decided yet. Can I let you know tomorrow?"

"You can let me know tomorrow night when I pick you up. Just make sure it's not a place that requires reservations," he said with a laugh.

"I've missed you this week," she said.

"I guess we've both been rather busy."

"Have you missed me?

"Of course I have, Jenny."

"You don't sound like it."

"I've been sitting here proofing pages so I may seem a little distracted."

"So what have you been doing lately?"

"Nothing much. Just sitting at home reading in the evenings."

"You should invite me over. I could keep you busy doing other things," she said coyly.

"I'm sure you could," he said with a chuckle.

"Do you want me to come over tonight?"

At that moment Maggie stepped up to his door and waved to get his attention.

"There's a woman here to see you," Maggie said softly. "Should I send her in?"

Brandon nodded.

"Are you still there, Brandon?" Jenny asked.

"I'm sorry," he said. "I've got someone who just came in the office. Can I call you back?"

"Just don't forget," she said. "Bye."

Brandon stood up as Debra walked into his office wearing a stunningly tight green skirt and V-cut blouse that teasingly revealed cleavage of her ample bosom.

"Good morning, Brandon," she said as she firmly shook his hand.

"Hi Debra. Please have a seat."

Debra sat down and crossed her shapely legs. She laid her umbrella on the floor.

"Can I get you some coffee or a soft drink?" Brandon asked.

"No thanks," she said. "I can only stay for a minute. I'm between showing houses."

"In this weather?"

"I finished showing a house just before it rained. I'm hoping this storm will pass soon."

"So what brings you here?"

"I want to apologize for last night. My husband can be an ass at times. I didn't expect for him to show up at the restaurant like he did."

"That's okay," Brandon said with a slight smile. "I understand. Is everything cool between you and him?"

"Not really," she said. "He wants me to come back and I don't want to right now. I think he needs to learn a lesson."

"I wouldn't be too hard on him."

"He's got to realize that I meet men every day in my work and that doesn't mean I sleep with them."

"I know what you mean," Brandon said with an approving nod.

"I need to be going now," she said glancing down at her diamond-studded watch. "My next appointment's in twenty minutes.'

"I'm glad you dropped by. I hope the weather clears for you."

"Do you think we could see each other again?"

"I go to Hastings once in awhile."

"Perhaps I'll see you there then," she said while picking up her umbrella.

"I'll be looking for you," Brandon said.

Brandon turned around and looked out the window as Debra left his office. The rain had let up to barely a trickle. He watched as she walked to her black BMW, backed out of the parking spot and pulled out on the street. A moment later, he saw a dark blue Crown Victoria ease out of a parking space and leave the parking lot. Brandon thought the driver looked a lot like Debra's husband.

"Geez, now he knows where I work," Brandon said to himself while shaking his head.

Brandon sat down and finished proofing the pages. He took them to Walter's work area, then stopped in the break room, poured a cup of coffee and stirred in a teaspoon of powdered creamer. He returned to his office and checked his computer for e-mail. Walter brought in several more pages to proof, and before Brandon realized it, it was five o'clock.

"Time for a beer before going home?" Graham said at the door.

"When did you get back?" Brandon asked.

"Oh, about two-thirty or so. I had a meeting with some folks from the printers and then we went to lunch."

"Anything exciting?"

"Not unless you call an increase in paper prices exciting."

"No, not exciting at all."

"So, you got time to go to Hastings?"

"Sure. Just let me clean off my desk."

Hastings was crowded when Brandon and Graham arrived. They got a table as two patrons were getting up to leave. Benny waved at them from behind the bar. A few minutes later, Rosie worked her oversized butt through the crowd and brought them two large frosted mugs of beer.

"Can I get you guys anything else?" she asked cheerily despite a weary face. Strands of coal-dark hair straggled about her forehead as she stood next to the table.

"The beers are fine, Rosie," Brandon said. "Keeping you busy?"

"Hell, yes," she blurted out while tugging up bright blue pants around her waist.

At that moment, Benny hollered that he had a couple more orders for her.

"I'd better get going," she said, blowing the wayward strands of hair with her mouth. "The boss is calling."

"Don't work too hard," Graham said with a laugh.

Rosie snarled at him in mock disgust and went back to the bar.

"How did everything go today?" Graham asked Brandon.

"It wasn't too bad. I proofed quite a few pages. The next issue looks pretty good."

"Anything going on tomorrow?"

"I'm having lunch with Clarice Horton over at Porter's. She's got a few story ideas she wants to tell me about."

"Any plans for the weekend?"

"I've got a couple tickets for the football game. I offered them to Maggie for her son."

"Did she accept them?

"No. She's got some other plans."

"Why don't you take the kid?"

"Me?"

"What's wrong with that?"

"Nothing. I just haven't been with a kid in years. I wouldn't know how to treat one."

"You treat them like a child."

"I know that," Brandon said, arching his eyebrows slightly.

"It might be a nice change of pace for you."

"I'll think about it."

Seven

Brandon arrived at Porter's about ten minutes before noon. He went to the bar and ordered a Pepsi. He noticed her reflection in the bar-length mirror when she arrived at the restaurant. Her hair was down to her shoulders and she was wearing an aqua blue dress and a string of tiny pearls. He remembered her being attractive when he met her at the university a few days earlier, but certainly not as beautiful as she appeared now. He turned around in the bar stool and stepped down and walked toward her.

"Hello, Ms. Horton," he said.

"Oh, hi," she said with a radiant smile. "I hope you haven't had to wait long."

"No, I just got here a few minutes ago."

A matronly hostess in a black skirt and white blouse came up and took them to their table. The Tudor-style restaurant was about three-quarters full and would likely be packed by twelve-thirty. It was a favorite spot for business people, especially those wanting to conduct some business during the lunch hour.

A waitress brought them glasses of water and took their orders. Clarice asked for a chef salad with fat-free Ranch dressing. Brandon ordered a steamed vegetable plate.

"Why don't you call me Clarice." she told Brandon. "I think we can forgo the formal titles now."

"Only if you call me Brandon," he said.

"It's a deal."

"What did you think of the news conference?" she asked, her tone turning business-like. "Was it worth the time?"

"I thought it was better than most," Brandon said. "There was some news value to it. Most of the news conferences at the university, most places in fact, are simply vehicles to get a company's name in the newspaper."

"I tend to agree," she said. "We try to keep that in mind when we hold news conferences. Sometimes we succeed and other times we're pressured in having a non-news event."

"You mentioned about having some other things coming up," Brandon said, wanting to hurry up and get through the business end of the conversation.

"Well, it's nothing I can really divulge at this moment other than to tell you that I have two that are sports-related, one with basketball and the other baseball," she said. "It has more to do with capital improvements."

"Well, let me know when you're ready to stage them and we may staff them," he said.

"How long have you been a sportswriter?" she asked.

"Nearly twenty-five years," he said. "Since about the day I graduated from college."

"I bet it's really interesting, going to all the games and meeting the personalities involved."

"It's interesting at times but few games are memorable and most of the athletes and coaches are full of themselves," he said with a chuckle.

"Isn't it that way in most things?" she asked.

"Probably so."

"I bet it's difficult having a family being a sportswriter."

"I think it is," Brandon said. "But I wouldn't have first-hand knowledge because I've never been married."

"Oh," she said. "Forgive me if I'm getting too personal."

"No problem," he said, taking a sip of water. "I just chose never to get married. I've seen what this profession can do to relationships. I also know a few alcoholics who are sportswriters."

The waitress returned with their food. They sat quietly for a few minutes as they ate. There was a soft buzz around them of many people talking business and an occasional table being cleared by a busboy.

Brandon looked at Clarice's left hand and noticed that she wasn't wearing a wedding band. He knew that didn't necessarily mean she wasn't married since many couples didn't wear rings.

"Speaking of professions, how long have you been in public relations?" he asked.

After swallowing some food, Clarice cleared her throat and said, "About eighteen years. I worked for agencies in Chicago, New York and Los Angeles before I came here four years ago."

"What brought you here?"

"My husband's job. He's an engineer at the automotive plant."

"Any children?"

"No kids. Actually my marriage is a casualty of the profession. We divorced about a year ago."

"I'm sorry," Brandon said. "Forgive me for getting too personal."

"That's okay," she said. "He wanted to have children and I didn't. I have some things I'd like to do in my job. He wanted me to quit and start having babies. I guess he was worried about my biological clock running down. He remarried about six months ago and his wife is already expecting so I guess things turned out well for him."

"And you, too?"

"I'm not complaining. Howard and I are still on good terms. We just moved in different directions over the years."

The waitress returned and asked if they wanted any dessert. They both declined but each ordered a cup of coffee.

"Do you plan to stay here?" Brandon asked.

"I'm not so sure," she said. "They've made me a vice president. I wouldn't mind going back to a larger city, perhaps Atlanta. There's more of a challenge in the big cities. I've had a few offers but I'm not ready to make that kind of commitment just yet. How about you?"

"Oh, I think I'm here for the duration," Brandon said with a smile. "I've paid my dues in the rat race. Now I just want to enjoy life and do the things that I want to do."

"I've thought about that, too," she said. "I think the older you get you begin to realize there are things more important than work. I'm just not at the point yet."

"You'll get there before you know it," Brandon said.

Clarice looked at her watch.

"I need to be going," she said. "I've got an appointment with a client at one-thirty. I'm glad that you were able to have lunch today. I enjoyed it."

"Same here," Brandon said as he placed the napkin next to his cup. "Perhaps we can do it again?"

"Yes, I'd like that," Clarice said, smiling brightly.

Brandon motioned for the waitress to bring their bill. He picked it up after she laid it on the side of the table.

"Let me take that," Clarice said. "I invited you."

"I've got it," he said. "Perhaps you can treat next time."

"It's a deal."

Brandon put his American Express on the check and the waitress retrieved it. She returned a few minutes and he signed the receipt. Brandon and Clarice walked out of the restaurant together, pausing out front for a moment, then she walked to the right and he went to the left to their cars.

Brandon turned the ignition in his car and pulled out of the parking lot. It was about a ten-minute drive to his office. His thoughts were on Clarice the entire time. She was a lovely woman, more so now that he got to gaze at her across a table. He was impressed by her demeanor. She seemed to be in control of her life. He also found her to be honest and genuine, at least the first impression. But he knew from experience that first impressions didn't always pan out.

"How was lunch?" Maggie asked as she handed him a note as he walked by her desk.

"It was very nice," he said. "Anything happening?"

"Not really," she said.

"Are you interested in the football tickets?"

"I would love them but I can't take Bobby Lee and I wouldn't let him go by himself or with a friend."

Brandon paused for a moment, looking at the note she gave him while he thought about offering to take Bobby Lee to the game.

"Would you trust him with me?" he asked, slightly arching his eyebrows.

"You would take him?"

"Why not? I haven't been to a game as a spectator in a long time. I think it would be fun taking Bobby Lee with me."

"Oh, Brandon, that would be wonderful. Bobby Lee has never been to a game at the university. He'd be so thrilled."

"The game starts at one-thirty. I'll pick him up around noon."

"I'll have him ready. You're so sweet, Brandon. I could just kiss you."

Graham walked in on them, just in time to hear the word "kiss."

"We'll not have any kissing around here," he said with a laugh. "At least not in public view."

"Brandon is taking Bobby Lee to the football game tomorrow," Maggie said, wiping away a tear with a tissue.

Graham gave a knowing smile to Brandon.

"I think that's great," Graham said. "You'll have a good time."

"It's been awhile since I was around a youngster," Brandon said. "I'm looking forward to it."

Brandon grinned warmly at Maggie and walked down the hall to his office. The note was from Jenny, asking him to call her about their dinner date that evening. He picked up the phone and dialed her number.

"Have you decided where you want to go tonight?" he asked.

"I think I'd like to eat at Porter's," she said.

"Porter's?"

"Yes," she said. "What's wrong with that? I haven't been there in ages."

Brandon paused a moment and coughed lightly.

"I just thought you'd like to try one of the new restaurants on the east side of town," he said. "But Porter's is fine with me. What time do you want me to pick you up?"

"How about seven?"

"Do you want me to make reservations?

"I've already done that," she said with a giggle. "Seven-thirty."

"I'll be at your place at seven."

"Do you think we could go dancing or something after we eat?" she asked.

"I don't want to stay out too late," he said. "I'm going to the football game tomorrow."

"Football game?" she said with a ring of disappointment. "Are you working?"

"I'm taking Maggie's son with me." he said. "I got a couple of tickets this week and decided to take him."

"Why didn't you ask me?" she asked.

"I didn't know you liked football."

"I don't but I would have enjoyed spending the afternoon with you."

"This will be the first time Maggie's boy has ever been to a game at the university. He'll really enjoy it."

"Can't you tell him you'll take him another time and take me instead?"

"Of course not," Brandon said, irritated by her suggestion.

"I'll see you tonight at seven," she said, quickly changing the subject.

"I see you then," he said, slightly shaking his head.

Eight

Jenny greeted Brandon at the front door of her apartment wearing a low-cut white blouse and an ankle-length black skirt that was slit up the side to mid-thigh. She kissed him lightly on the cheek.

"Hi, Brandon," she said, her perfect white teeth glistening in her smile. "I'll be ready to leave in a few minutes. Go and have a seat on the couch."

"Take your time," said Brandon, who had changed his denim shirt to a white dress shirt from work. "I'm a little early and it won't take ten minutes to get there."

Jenny went to the bathroom and finished putting on eyeliner. Brandon sat on the couch, looking around at the Ethan Allen furniture that the apartment was furnished in throughout. While she had a good job at the bank, she came from some money and Brandon was sure that her parents helped her buy the furniture and even contributed on the rent. The apartment included a hot tub on the back patio balcony and the complex had an Olympic-size swimming pool, exercise facility and community building.

"I'm ready," she said, standing at the edge of the living room like a model ready to be judged.

"You look lovely," Brandon said, giving her a quick up and down before settling on her dark eyes. He stood up and walked toward the front door with her.

Jenny took a key from her clutch purse and locked the door behind them. She wrapped her arm around his as they walked to his car.

"Oh, what a beautiful night," she said, glancing up as a few stars were beginning to appear in the clear autumn sky.

"Yes, it is," Brandon said. "This is probably my favorite time of the year. Soon the leaves will be turning and then it'll be absolutely gorgeous."

As they entered Porter's, the same hostess he'd seen at noon greeted them at the door. Brandon gave her his name for the reservation and she escorted them to a table near a dimly-lit corner where there was more privacy. A red candle flickered in the middle of the table.

"It's nice to have you return this evening, Mr. Wilkes," the hostess said. "I hope you enjoy your dinner." She smiled and returned to her post.

"What did she mean by that?" Jenny asked after Brandon helped her get seated.

"Mean what?"

"She said something about you returning."

"Oh, I had a business lunch here today."

"With whom?"

"An executive with a public relations agency. What did you do today?"

"I just processed several loans and did a few things to clear my desk for the weekend."

Jenny ordered a filet mignon and baked potato while Brandon selected vegetarian lasagna. They also ordered a carafe of red wine.

"Any plans for the weekend?" Brandon asked.

"I was hoping to go to a football game," she said, pushing out her lower lip.

"Now you know why I can't take you."

"You could take that kid any time."

"I could take you any time, too."

"So you're saying that kid is as important as me?"

"I didn't say anything like that," Brandon said, as a smile erased from his face. "I just asked him first."

The waitress brought the carafe and poured filled their glasses half full. They each took a sip of the wine.

"This is very good," Jenny said. Brandon nodded approvingly.

"If you can't take me to the football game, can we do something afterward?" she asked.

"I'll be too tired," Brandon said. "I'm not sure what time I'll get the boy back home. I'll probably stop at McDonald's or someplace and get him a bite to eat."

"You could come over to the apartment and we could watch a movie or something."

"I'll think about it but don't count on it."

A few minutes later, their dinners arrived. They continued their small talk while they ate their food and finished the wine.

"So can we do something tonight?" she asked after they were finishing eating. She looked at her watch. "It's only nine-fifteen."

"What would you want to do?"

"I mentioned dancing to you this afternoon."

"That's okay but I don't want to stay out too late. I've got a busy day tomorrow."

"Don't remind me."

"I wish I hadn't."

"There's that new dance club near my apartment," she said. "I think it's called Club Nouveau."

"Okay, we'll go there for a little while but I can't stay long," he said. "Also, I don't like disco."

"It's not a disco club," she said. "They play dance music."

"Well, dance music is disco to me."

"Brandon, sometimes you sound like an old man."

"Sometimes I feel like an old man."

They left the restaurant and drove to the club. There were a lot of people mingling about the parking lot as they pulled in and found a space on the farthest row from the building. Brandon paid a twenty dollar cover charge for each of them at the entrance.

"This had better be good," he said as they walked through the front foyer. The music was already blaring as they approached the main dance room. They found a table near the back wall. The ceiling globe sprinkled light over the dance floor while a strobe light flickered to the driving beat of the songs. The floor was packed with dancers, nearly shoulder to shoulder, as they moved to the frantic beat of the music. A waitress wearing a tight red mini-skirt and low-cut top that exposed half of her bosom took their drink orders. Jenny got a strawberry daiquiri and Brandon asked for a light draft beer. She came back five minutes later with their drinks. It was twelve dollars. Brandon gave her fifteen dollars and told her to keep the change.

"This had better be good," Brandon said to Jenny as he put the glass of beer up to his mouth.

"Oh, quit being such a grouch," she said. "This is fun." She sipped some of her drink through a straw and flashed Brandon a sexy smile.

The music was non-stop, going from one bouncy, bass-driven tune to the next. To Brandon, they all sounded a like.

"Let's dance," Jenny said while taking his hand and pulling him toward the dance floor. Before he could put up any protest, they were dancing in the middle of the throng, their bodies touching everyone around them. After two extended-play songs, Brandon was able to take Jenny's hand and return to their table.

"Whew," he said, wiping several beads of sweat from his forehead. "I'm getting too old for this."

"You were wonderful," Jenny said before sipping some more of her drink.

"Don't they ever play slow songs at these places?"

"Hardly," she said. "Isn't this fun?"

The waitress came by and asked them if they wanted to order more drinks. Brandon declined by shaking his head and she moved on to the next table without a change of expression.

Jenny managed to get Brandon on the dance floor one more time before they left for the evening.

"We need to do this again real soon," Jenny said as he drove her back to her apartment. She reached over and touched his forearm.

"I don't know about soon but perhaps we can do it again," he said, glancing at her momentarily and smiling.

He pulled into her parking lot and turned off the engine and lights.

"Why don't you come up to the apartment for awhile?" she said. "I've got some beer in the fridge."

"It's getting late and I've got to get up early in the morning."

"I won't keep you too late," she said demurely.

"I'll have to take a rain check," he said, forcing a smile.

Jenny quickly scooted over next to him and planted a wet, juicy kiss on his unexpected mouth. She wrapped her arms around him and held him in place before he could gather his bearings. She released her hard kiss and rested her head on his chest.

"You could spend the night," she cooed.

Brandon cleared his throat several times.

"That's a nice invitation but I'll have to take a rain check on that, too."

"What's the matter with you, Brandon? Why are you taking a little brat over me?" she said while sitting erectly.

"I'm not doing that," he said. "It's just that I'm not going to tell a little boy I'm going to do something and then back out."

"But it doesn't bother you to hurt my feelings."

"I'm not trying to hurt your feelings. You happen to be an adult."

Jenny put her hand on the door latch and turned it halfway

"I don't know what to think about you anymore. It seems like you're trying to avoid me."

"How can you say that?" Brandon said. "Didn't we go out tonight?"

"But it seems like I have to ask you. You don't want to spend time with me like you used to."

"I've been busy with work."

"Are you getting tired of me?" she asked, her eyes beginning to well with tears.

"No, that's not it," he said. "I've just had some other things going on."

"I thought we had such a good thing going between us and now it seems that you're backing away."

"I'm not backing away," he said, knowing that he wasn't being totally honest with her. "And can't we just be friends?"

"I want more than that," she said while opening the door. "Apparently, you don't."

"Now Jenny," he said.

She got out of the car, slammed the door and walked briskly to her first-floor apartment. Brandon remained in the car, watching until he saw that she was safely inside her apartment. He backed out of the space and drove home.

While walking up the steps to his front door, he noticed a blue sedan parked a half block down the street. It looked like the David Hatfield's vehicle. A moment later, the lights came on and the car eased away slowly down the street.

Nine

A bright and sunny day greeted Brandon when he left his apartment to pick up Bobby Lee for the football game. While most of the fans would be decked out in blue and white, he wore khaki slacks and a green sweater. He arrived at Maggie's small wood-frame house at quarter to twelve, and Bobby Lee was sitting on the front porch tossing a football up in the air.

A quaint picket fence ran around the front and back yards. The mailbox next to the road was decorated with cloth pullover of orange pumpkins and multi-colored autumn leaves.

As Brandon got out of his car, Bobby Lee stood up on the front steps and gave him a slight smile and a quick wave of his hand. He turned around and cracked open the door.

"Mom, Mr. Wilkes is here!" he yelled. He flipped the football inside the front door. Bobby Lee was wearing a blue-and-white football jersey, jeans and tennis shoes. His hair was trimmed neatly and parted on the side.

"You must be Bobby Lee," Brandon said as he walked toward the front porch.

"Yes, sir," he said, timidly.

Brandon put out his arm and they shook hands.

"I'm Brandon Wilkes."

"I know."

Maggie came to the front porch, wearing a pink chenille robe and her just-washed hair wrapped in a towel.

"Forgive my appearance, Brandon," she said. "I've been running a little late this morning, trying to get Bobby Lee dressed and all."

"Don't worry about it," Brandon said with a grin. "What time do you expect to be back home tonight?"

"The bridal shower shouldn't last past five, so shortly after that. Is that too late?"

"No, that's fine. I just want to make sure you're home when I bring him back."

"I'm old enough to take care of myself," Bobby Lee interjected.

"I know you are, son," Brandon said with a warm smile. "We need to be going now."

"Bobby Lee, you behave and do everything Mr. Wilkes asks of you," Maggie said while wrapping her arms around him and giving him a kiss on the cheek.

Bobby Lee, embarrassed by the affection, backed off. Maggie smiled at Brandon and flicked her eyebrows.

"I will, Mom," Bobby Lee said as he stepped down from the porch and walked alongside side Brandon with his head down to the car.

Brandon unlocked the passenger door for Bobby Lee and went around and got in on the driver's side. He fastened his seat belt, and Bobby Lee reached around and fastened his before Brandon turned the ignition.

Brandon felt a little uneasy driving to the stadium because Bobby Lee didn't have much to say. He just stared out the side window. Brandon tried to initiate conversation but the boy would generally give him one-word answers of yes or no. Brandon decided not to force anything since he knew Bobby Lee was probably uneasy, too. He parked about a quarter-mile from the stadium. They walked to the stadium along with a multitude of fans, many fans still tailgating since the kickoff was almost an hour away.

"Why are those people eating out of the backs of their cars?" Bobby Lee asked.

"That's called tailgating," Brandon said. "That's kind of a tradition at football games. People bring food and eat and talk with other fans."

"I think I'd rather eat in the stadium," Bobby Lee said.

"We'll get something to eat when we get there."

"Do you go to many games?"

"I've been to quite a few. I like football."

"This is the first time I've been to a game," Bobby Lee said. Brandon sensed that the boy was feeling more comfortable as he was beginning to make eye contact.

"That's what your mom told me. I hope you'll enjoy it."

They got in a long line that moved quickly through the turnstile into the stadium, stopping at a concession stand where Brandon bought a hot dog, Coke and bag of potato chips for Bobby Lee and a steaming cup of coffee for himself They made their way out to their seats midway up on the lower level, about at the thirty-five yard line. The stadium was slowly filling up as the teams went through pre-game warm-ups on the field. Bobby Lee's eyes were focused on the field, not missing a thing in front of him. After the teams went back to their locker rooms, the university band came onto the field in high-stepping fashion while playing the school fight song. Most of the fans stood up and clapped, including Bobby Lee.

Throughout the game, Brandon explained to Bobby Lee what plays were being run by each team. Before the end of the game, Bobby Lee was making comments about what plays the home team should execute. It turned out to be a good game for Bobby Lee as the home team won, twenty-four to seventeen on a touchdown in the final three minutes.

On the way out of the stadium, Brandon stopped at a souvenir stand and bought Bobby Lee a blue-and-white baseball cap and pennant.

"Thanks, Mr. Wilkes," Bobby Lee said, with a bright smile as Brandon adjusted the cap on his head.

"I thought you should have a memento of your first game," Brandon said, patting the slender boy gently on the shoulder.

It took more than an hour to get out of the parking lot as a long line of cars were exiting the stadium. Brandon turned on the radio station with the post-game show, to which Bobby Lee listened to attentively.

Brandon stopped at a McDonald's after leaving the stadium, and they went inside to eat. Bobby Lee ordered a Big Mac, fries and chocolate shake while Brandon had a Coke. They talked more about the football game as Bobby Lee devoured his meal quickly.

They arrived at Bobby Lee's house shortly after six. Maggie was already at home and came to the door after they got out of the car.

"Did you have a good time?" she asked Bobby Lee.

"It was great," Bobby Lee gushed enthusiastically. "We won, twenty-four to seventeen. And Mr. Wilkes bought me this cap and pennant."

"Brandon, you didn't have to do all of that," Maggie said. "The game would have been enough."

"I wanted to," Brandon said. "Every person needs some kind of souvenir from their first game."

"I need to go to the bathroom," Bobby Lee said, rushing past Maggie and into the house without waiting for a response.

Brandon and Maggie laughed.

"Did he behave?" Maggie asked.

"No problem at all," Brandon said. "We'll have to do it again sometime."

"This was awfully sweet of you. I don't know how I can ever repay you."

"You don't owe me anything," Brandon said. "I think I enjoyed this afternoon as much as Bobby Lee did."

Bobby Lee came back out on the front porch holding his football. He stood next to Maggie, resting his head on her shoulder with a big grin on his face.

"Well, I need to be running," Brandon said. "I had a good time, Bobby Lee. I hope we can do it again."

"You mean it?" Bobby Lee asked wide-eyed.

"I mean it," Brandon said warmly.

"I can't wait to tell all my friends," Bobby Lee said.

"I'll see you at work Monday," Brandon said to Maggie.

"Again, thank you for taking Bobby Lee to the game. Bye."

"Thanks, Mr. Wilkes," Bobby Lee said.

"You're welcome," said Brandon, who turned and walked to his car. Bobby Lee stood on the front porch and waved as Brandon backed out of the driveway and drove away.

The afternoon was more enjoyable than Brandon imagined it would be. A smile of self-satisfaction crossed his face as he drove down the highway toward Hastings for a beer before going home.

The bar was about three-quarters full, most of them fans who had attended the football game. Noisy chatter filled the air as Brandon found a vacant bar stool near the cash register. Benny, looking frazzled from the non-stop activity, nodded at him and brought him a draft beer a few minutes later.

"Go to the game? Benny asked.

"Yeah," Brandon said. "It was a good one."

Before Benny could say anything, several other patrons raised their hands for service.

Brandon sipped on his beer, gazing around occasionally to see if he knew anyone. Someone tapped him on the shoulder.

"Hi, Brandon. What are you doing here tonight?"

He turned around. It was Debra. She was wearing a blue university sweatshirt and tight jeans.

"I stopped here after the game for a beer. Did you go to the game?"

"No," she said dejectedly. "I wanted to but I had a couple of houses to show this afternoon. I heard it was a great game."

"It was."

"So are you doing anything later?"

"Nope," he said. "I'm going to have a beer or two, then go home and relax. I may watch a little TV or read."

"On a Saturday night?" she asked.

"Saturday is just another day in the week for me," Brandon said with a laugh. "I need my sleep."

Debra moved closer to Brandon, pressing her body against him a couple of times.

"You sound like an old man," she said, teasingly.

"Sometimes I feel like an old man," he said, thinking back to Jenny's remark the night before.

"Why don't you go bar-hopping with me?" she asked seductively. "We could have a lot of fun."

"I'll have to take a rain check on that," he said. He looked around the bar, wondering if her husband could be lurking in the shadows. He didn't want another encounter with him, especially since he was an innocent bystander. It wasn't his intention to get mixed up with a married woman and an irate husband, even if they were separated.

"Well, I can see that I'm not going to convince you," she said. "Perhaps one of these nights we can go out."

"Where is your husband?"

"Who knows?" she said before taking a swallow of beer from a bottle. "He's probably sitting out in the parking lot waiting for me. He follows me everywhere. I don't even think I could pee without him knowing about it."

She laughed heartily while Brandon shook his head in amusement.

"I think I need to be going," he said. "Do you want my seat?"

"Thanks, hon, but I think I'll leave, too," she said.

"You don't need to leave on account of me," Brandon said, not anxious about leaving the bar with her.

"I need an escort to the parking lot," she said, grabbing his arm.

"I think I'll have another beer," he said abruptly. "Why don't you go ahead and go? There's no need to wait for me."

"If you're having another beer, then I will too," she said, smiling broadly. "I'll get this round. Hey Benny, bring me and Brandon another beer."

Benny nodded at her and brought the beers over a minute later.

Halfway through his beer, a man came over to Debra and started chatting with her. From the tone of the conversation, Brandon guessed that it was another real-estate agent.

Brandon used the opportunity to go the restroom. When finished, he noticed that Debra was laughing with the man. Brandon ducked out the back exit of the bar and went to his car. He looked for David Hatfield's blue sedan, but didn't spot it anywhere. He breathed a sigh of relief, got into his car and drove home.

Ten

Brandon lay in bed Sunday morning with his eyes open, trying to decide whether to stay there and get more sleep or get up and start the day. He glanced at the digital clock on the nightstand. It was quarter to seven. Bright sunshine was coming through the blinds. It would be easy to rollover and go back to sleep but he opted to get out of bed.

Wearing only his blue boxer shorts, he reached out the front door and picked up the Sunday newspaper that was only a few feet away. There wasn't a sound outside except for a few black birds pecking for food in the front lawn. In the distance he could see a couple of walkers going through their morning routine of a fast pace and arms swinging up and down.

He put the newspaper on the kitchen table and went over to start the coffee maker. He put in a couple slices of wheat bread into the toaster and took out a bottle of margarine and jar of apple jelly from the refrigerator. In less than three minutes, he had his toast on a plate and a hot cup of coffee. Sitting down at the table, he opened the newspaper. He casually skimmed through the sections when the phone rang.

Brandon wondered who would be calling this time of the morning, especially on a Sunday. That hadn't happened since he'd quit working for newspapers.

"This is Brandon," he said after clicking on the cordless phone.

"Good morning, sweetheart!" harkened Jenny's cheerful voice.

"Good morning," Brandon said. "What are you doing calling so early?"

"Aren't you glad to hear from me?" she asked.

"That's not it. I just didn't expect to be getting a call this time of the day. What's going on?"

"I was wondering if you'd like to do something today," she said. "I thought I'd call you early before you got busy and left for the day."

"I really didn't have any plans. I'd like to stay around the apartment today."

"Let's do something," she said with a slight plea in her tone.

"I really would like to relax today," he said. "After the football game yesterday, I'm sort of bushed now."

"How about if we went on a picnic at the park?" she asked. "That wouldn't be too much."

Brandon gazed down at the newspaper and saw a small item about a car accident in which several people were injured. The name Clarice Horton nearly jumped off the page. The story said she was in a car that was struck at an intersection. She and four others were taken to St. Peter's Hospital and kept overnight for observation.

"Are you listening to me?" Jenny asked.

"Uh, sure," he said. "You mentioned a picnic."

"So, would you like to go on a picnic?"

"No, I've got some other plans," he blurted out without thinking.

"I thought you said you didn't have any plans and that you planned to stay home all day," she said.

"Something just came up," he said. "I've got to be going. Talk to you later. Bye."

Jenny slammed the phone down on the receiver.

Brandon looked up St. Peter's Hospital in the telephone book and quickly dialed patient information. All the receptionist would tell him was that Clarice was in good condition.

Brandon hurried back to his bedroom and quickly dressed in khaki pants and a blue chambray shirt. He went to the bathroom, brushed his teeth and ran a comb through his thinning hair a few times and headed out the front door.

While driving over to the hospital, he wondered what he was doing. *This woman hardly knows me. What am I going to say to her?* But he continued to drive on to the hospital in the light traffic.

He found out from the information desk that Clarice was in room 403. He took an elevator up to her floor. Her room was two doors away from the elevator. The door was partially open and he knocked softly.

"Yes?" the voice inside said.

Brandon peeked timidly inside. Clarice was standing next to her bed, already dressed and packing a few items in a plastic carryall.

"Brandon," she said, with a puzzled look. "What are you doing here?"

He was thinking the same thing as a sheepish smile crossed his face.

"I saw your name in the newspaper this morning and came over to see how you're doing," he said.

"I think I'll survive," she said, forcing a smile on her bruised face. "I wasn't so sure last night."

"The paper didn't say much about the extent of injuries so that's why I came over," he said. "I'm glad to see that it's not too serious."

"I was lucky. My girlfriend suffered a broken leg and another friend will probably have to undergo plastic surgery on her face. I just got a few cuts and bruises. More than anything, I'm sore all over."

"Can I do anything for you?" Brandon asked.

"Not really," she said. "I'm getting ready to go home. I've got these few things to pack, and then I have to check out and call a taxi."

"Can I take you home?" he asked.

"You don't need to do that. I don't know how long I'll be here."

"It's not any trouble. I don't have any plans today."

As she moved into the light, Brandon could see that her right eye was nearly swollen shut and her hair slightly matted against the side of her head.

"Okay," she said. "But give me a few minutes to get cleaned up. I hate for you to see me this way."

"Under the circumstances, I understand completely," he said with a light laugh. "I'll go down to the visitor's area and wait for you."

"Thanks," she said. "I hope I won't be too long."

There were several other visitors in the waiting area. One obese man was dead to the world, snoring up a storm. An older couple sat patiently and erect, almost as if needing permission to move. Brandon picked up a few periodicals and began flipping through the pages. Before he realized it, Clarice was standing at the entrance. She had combed through her hair, giving it some bounce, and applied makeup to hide some of the black and blue on her face.

"I'm ready," she said with a tired sigh.

Brandon got up and they headed to the elevator.

"I need to stop at the business office on the first floor," she said.

Brandon took the bag she was carrying while she signed out of the hospital.

After she was finished, he went to the parking garage for his car and picked her up at the front entrance.

"This is awfully nice of you," she said, as Brandon drove away from the hospital. "I really didn't expect this."

Brandon glanced at her and smiled.

"Did they notify any family?" he asked.

"Only Howard," she said. "He dropped in for a few minutes last night. He left after he knew I was all right. I'm sure his new wife didn't appreciate his visit."

"Is she the jealous type?"

"I don't know about that but being practically a newly wed, I don't think I'd want my spouse visiting an ex," she said.

"Can I stop and get you anything before we get to your house?" Brandon asked.

"I can't think of anything."

About twenty minutes later, Brandon pulled into the driveway of her two-story brick home. It had four columns along the front and an attached three-car garage.

She opened the passenger door when he stopped.

"Can I help you with anything?" he asked.

"You've helped me enough all ready," she said. "This was very kind of you to visit and bring me home."

"It was no trouble at all," he said with a boyish grin.

"Perhaps I can repay you with lunch again," she said.

"There's no payment," Brandon said, while thinking that he'd like to see her again.

"No, I want to do it," she said while slowly getting out of the car. "I'll check my calendar after I get back to work and call you. Okay?"

"All right," he said. "Just take it easy the next few days."

"I don't plan to go back to work until this face looks normal again," she said with a laugh. "Thanks again."

Clarice closed the door and walked at a snail's pace to the front door. Brandon waited until she was inside the house before he left. He looked down at the clock on the dashboard and saw that it was only eleven o'clock.

On the way back home, he wondered if he had done the right thing in going to the hospital. He hardly knew her. Sure, he thought she was attractive and intelligent, but did that justify his actions? He shrugged his shoulders and smiled.

When he got home, the answering machine was blinking. He clicked on the playback button.

"How dare you hang up on me like you did!" Jenny's irate voice bellowed out. "You can be so thoughtless and cruel. I don't know if I ever want to see you again. Good bye!"

Brandon grinned and shook his head. He turned off the coffee pot and removed the plate and stale toast from the table. He glanced back over the story about the accident. It didn't provide any details other than someone apparently running a red light at an intersection. Brandon was glad he went to the hospital and knowing first-hand that Clarice was not seriously injured. The only question rumbling through his head was why he went to see her at the hospital. He shook his head again.

Eleven

Brandon tried all week to call Clarice at her home but there was no answer, not even an answering machine. He drove by her house on two evenings after work, but the only lights appeared to be ones for security. He called the hospital after a couple of days to see if she had been re-admitted but she hadn't.

When Friday rolled around, he got in his car and traveled to Athens, Georgia, to cover the next day's football game. He wasn't especially keen on flying, and would usually drive to game sites if they were within a day's drive. For longer trips, such as to the West Coast, he would take an airplane and swear all the way that it would be the last time he'd fly.

He went out to eat with some other sportswriters, mostly from Kentucky, after he arrived. They ate late since most of the other writers had to file advance stories for Saturday's newspapers. Brandon had the luxury of not having to worry about that, only the game story the following day, and he spent most of the time relaxing in his motel room. He brought James Joyce's *Ulysses* on the trip, knowing full well he wouldn't make much of a dent in the seven hundred-plus pages but at least get started on the masterpiece.

He met his friends at Pudgy's Bar and Grill, a few blocks from the motel, at nine-thirty Most of the talk was centered on the next day's game, but there also was the usual shop talk and gossip. Brandon was glad that he was away from the daily newspaper atmosphere where office politics and professional jealousies ran rampant. He and Graham were good friends, both trusting of each other, and there wasn't a fear that the other would say or do anything to hurt the other.

Brandon sat between to Buck Odoms of the Lexington *Journal-Register* and Bev McKenzie of the *Atlanta Post*. McKenzie was a transplanted Kentuckian who had formerly worked in Lexington. She always tried to spend time with the Kentucky writers when they were in the state covering games. While she was making a good salary in Atlanta, she would always talk about returning to Kentucky to work. Most people doubted that would happen because the newspapers didn't pay as well as the one in Atlanta.

After eating their meals, the group broke up around midnight. A few went back to the motel bar for a nightcap. Bev, dressed casually in tan pants and white blouse, joined the four men at the bar. They ordered a pitcher of beer and sat in the corner, away from the jukebox. There weren't many people in the bar. An aging waitress, wearing a skirt too short and too tight for her pudgy body, stood next to the bar and chatted with the bartender as he cleaned mugs and glasses.

Within thirty minutes, only Brandon and Bev were left from their group. Brandon would have left but Bev refilled his mug while he was away at the men's room.

"Why do you still make these trips?" Bev asked, while swishing a strand of blonde hair away from her face.

"I enjoy getting away from Lexington once in awhile," he said. "I also like my trips to Georgia."

"Doesn't it get to be a grind?"

"Not really, because I pick and choose where I want to go. You sound like you're getting a little burned out."

"I suppose I might be," she said with a sigh. "I'm in my late thirties now. Okay, I'm thirty-eight, to be exact. This does wear on you after awhile."

"That was about the age when I started getting tired of all the travel and games. I started wanting something else in my life. I knew that I wouldn't be fulfilled watching ball games all the time."

"I'm feeling the same way," she said. "I don't know how much longer I can do this. But it scares me to think that I might not be doing it. There's a great fear of the unknown for me."

"I think we all have that, Bev," Brandon said with a sleepy smile. "I know I did."

"But you're still writing sports so it can't be that bad."

"I enjoy what I'm doing but I still look at it as a transition for other things I'd like to do before they put me six-feet under."

"You don't have to get morbid," she said with a laugh.

"But seriously, I think life should be an adventure and we should experience as much of it as we can," he said. "Remember the old Schlitz beer commercial about grabbing all the gusto you can? That's so true."

"How old are you?" asked Bev, who was a little groggy-eyed from the drinking.

"I just turned forty-five a few months ago."

"Well you certainly don't look it," she said. "You've aged well."

"And you have, too," he said with a nod.

"Have you ever been married?"

"Never."

"Ever thought about it?"

"Once or twice, but then I came to my senses," he said, chuckling. "How about you?"

"Twice."

"Thought about it twice?"

"No, I've been married twice. This profession is a bitch on marriages."

"I agree," he said while nodding his head. "I would even say the same for relationships, especially for people like you at daily newspapers."

Brandon poured the remaining beer in the pitcher, giving them each about half a mug.

"Cheers," he said, raising his mug.

"Cheers," she said, tapping hers against his.

It was getting close to one in the morning. The waitress was clearing off some of the tables while only two patrons stood at the bar. The jukebox was silent.

"You're sure a sweet guy," Bev said.

"And you're sweet, too," Brandon said, smiling.

"I bet you've broken a lot of hearts," she said, her words beginning to slur a little. "I'm sure many a woman has been attracted to you."

"They're lined up outside my apartment each night," said Brandon, playing along with her.

Bev puckered her full lips and smiled.

"Are you going to be able to drive home?" Brandon asked, realizing that she was in no condition to get behind the wheel of her car.

"Is that an invitation?" she asked, seductively.

"To drive you home?" he said after clearing his throat.

"To let me spend the night with you."

"That would be nice but I think we both need our sleep since we've got the game to cover."

"I'm sure we could find time for some sleep," Bev said.

She looked at him and winked.

"Why don't you let me get a cab for you?"

"Are you serious?"

"Yes, Bev, I really don't believe you should be driving tonight."

"And you don't want to sleep with me?"

"Not tonight."

"I don't believe you," she said, rolling her eyes.

"It's nothing personal."

"Are you gay or something?"

"No, I'm not gay," he said shaking his head. "I just don't think it would be a good idea."

Without any notice she reached over and kissed Brandon passionately on the mouth. He was stunned for a moment, by the booze and the kiss, before opening his eyes and backing off.

"Oh, that was sweet," she said. "You sure know how to kiss."

"You kiss well, too," he said. "I think it's about time we left."

"To your room?"

"And you to a taxi."

"Oh, Brandon, don't be this way," she said with a hurt look. "It will be our secret. I won't tell anyone."

"I'm sorry, Bev, but not tonight."

"Is there someone back home?"

Brandon paused for a moment, then thought about Clarice.

"Yes," he said.

"Then why didn't you say so?" she said. "I don't want to mess around with another woman's man."

They got up from their table and walked out to the foyer. Brandon asked the front-desk clerk to call for a taxi. Within five minutes, an orange taxi pulled out in front of the brightly-lit building. Brandon walked Bev to the vehicle and opened the back door for her.

"I had a nice time," she said.

"Same here," Brandon said. "I'll see you at the game a little later."

Bev kissed him again, this time quickly and got into the cab. Brandon smiled, then walked around to the driver's side and handed him a twenty to take her home.

Brandon walked slowly to his room. It was nearly one-thirty. He was tired but wasn't ready to go to sleep. He took off his clothes and went into the bathroom and brushed his teeth. Pulling back the covers on his bed, he picked up *Ulysses* and began reading. When he looked at the clock again, it was three-fifteen. He put down the book and turned off the light next to his bed.

While laying in the dark room, he thought about Clarice and why he hadn't heard from her. He knew there was really no reason for her to call him because she hardly knew him. But he wanted to get to know her better. He decided that he'd give her house a call before he left for the game that afternoon.

He also thought about the evening with Bev and if he was he a fool for not taking her to bed with him. There had been many opportunities during his career, especially while on the road, to mess around with women. Quite a few of his fellow sports writers had girlfriends in other cities.

Before Brandon knew it, the sun was shining through the curtains that he had forgotten to close when he went to bed. It was only seven o'clock. He got up and pulled them closed, but couldn't fall back asleep. He finally got up, took a long shower and got dressed before going downstairs for breakfast. He saw Buck sitting at a table and joined him.

"Hey, Brandon," he said. "What time did you get to bed last night?"

"A little after one," he said. "Why?"

"We could see the eyes Bev was giving you," he said with a laugh.

"Really?"

"She usually tries to screw someone from Kentucky every time we come down here."

"I don't know what to say," Brandon said.

The waitress came over and poured him a cup of coffee and took his order for oatmeal, toast and orange juice. Buck was already devouring a stack of pancakes and several eggs over easy.

"So what happened?"

"We talked for awhile, then I got a taxi for her. She wasn't in any condition to drive."

"She hit on me a couple years ago," Buck said. "It was tempting but I backed off, too. She got pissed at me."

"I wouldn't say that she got mad at me or anything but she wasn't happy about it," Brandon said, then took a sip of coffee.

After finishing breakfast, they returned to their rooms. Brandon opened *Ulysses*, reading about seventy-five pages before getting a telephone call from Buck. Several guys were taking a taxi to the football stadium and he wanted to know if Brandon wanted to come along. They would be down in the lobby in twenty minutes. Brandon joined them, and they arrived at the stadium two hours before kickoff.

After finding his assigned seat, Brandon left his notebook, and mingled with the other sportswriters, some he'd known for more than fifteen years. Bev showed up thirty minutes later, making eye contact with him but expressionless.

After a few minutes, Brandon walked over to her seat, situated on the front row and near the middle of the press box.

"Hi," he said. "Is everything okay?"

"I'm fine, Brandon," she said tersely. "Is there something you want?"

"I just wanted to say hi," he said.

"Okay, you said hi," she said. "Now go."

Brandon looked at her for a moment, and then went back to his seat to read game notes. The press box was filling quickly with media and university staff. The teams were on the field going through warm-ups.

Brandon remembered that he was going to call Clarice. That would have to wait until he returned home Sunday.

Twelve

Brandon returned to the motel after the game instead of going to dinner with several of the sportswriters. He walked across the street for Chinese carryout and ate in his room. After finishing dinner, he read about twenty-five pages from *Ulysses* and went to bed around eleven. He got up at six the next morning, showered and dressed, and was on the road by seven. He got back to Lexington around six that evening.

It was raining when he arrived in Lexington. He made a dash from the car to his apartment, nearly slipping on the wet black pavement. The answering machine light was blinking as he turned on the living room light. He took his suitcase back to the bedroom and set it next to his bed. He felt like diving into the bed and resting after the long drive but went back into the living room to check his messages.

There were three consecutive messages from Jenny, the last one accusing him of ignoring her. Debra called to say that she would be at Hastings on Saturday night. And the last was from Clarice, apologizing for not calling him sooner about her condition. She had left town to spend a few days at her parents' home in Florida while she recuperated from the accident. She was back in town and planned to return to work on Monday.

Brandon picked up the telephone directory and found a "C. Horton." He called the number and after three rings, she answered. Brandon froze for a moment, unsure what to say.

"Hello," she said in a business-like tone. "Hello?"

"Is this Clarice Horton?"

"Yes, it is"

"This is Brandon. I just returned from Athens, Georgia, and saw that you had called."

"Oh, hi Brandon. It's good to hear from you."

"I'm glad that you're feeling better."

"I'm still a little sore but most of the bruises have cleared up and the swellings have gone down. What were you doing in Georgia?"

"I covered a football game."

"I should have known that," she said. "I'm sorry."

"When did you get back?"

"About four this afternoon. It was quite a change in the weather. It must have been eighty in Tampa, where my parents live, and then to come home to the cold rain and temperature in the fifties. I wasn't prepared for it."

"Me either," Brandon said with a chuckle. "So you're going back to work in the morning?"

"I plan to. I hate to see all the work that's piled up the past week."

"Have you eaten tonight?" he said, closing his eyes tightly.

"Well, no," she said. "I was getting ready to find something in the refrigerator or open up a can of soup."

"Would you care to join me for something? We could find a place on your side of town."

Clarice hesitated a moment. "That would be nice," she said, cheerfully. "I don't feel like dirtying up any dishes. Where would you like to meet?"

"How about Lone Star Cafe?" he said.

"That's sounds great. I can be there in about forty-five minutes."

"I'd be happy to drive by your house and pick you up."

"That's okay," she said. "I'm only about five minutes from there. I'll see you around seven."

Brandon arrived a few minutes late at the restaurant. Clarice was already seated at a table. A soft light from the hanging lamp over the table accentuated her delicate features. She almost seemed to glow as Brandon approached the table.

"Sorry I'm late," he said. "Traffic was moving slower than usual because of the rain."

"I only got here about five minutes ago."

"You sure look good," Brandon said, quickly adding, "I mean from the accident. You can't tell that you were injured."

"Makeup can do wonders on the face," she said with a smile. "I've still got some nasty bruises on my legs and back. I think I'll live, though."

"Do you have any big news conferences this week?" Brandon asked.

"I don't believe so. I've got a few meetings with clients. We're also doing a market survey for a firm out of Boston."

They both ordered a draft beer from the waiter and decided to share a combination plate of mozzarella sticks, fried zucchini and potato skins for an appetizer.

"So, do you have a busy week ahead?" she asked.

"Not really," he said. "I have my column to write and some editing to handle. It should be a routine week."

"Do you go out much after work?"

"What do you mean?"

"Do you go to movies, theater, and things like that?"

"I see an occasional movie," he said. "Mostly, I rent videos. I think movies are too expensive. What are they now, seven dollars a ticket?"

"Some places they're eight dollars," she said. "I don't mind if it's a good movie."

"But when you spend three dollars for popcorn and two dollars and fifty cents for a soft drink, that stuff can add up," he said.

"I guess," she said with a smile.

"I bet I sound cheap," Brandon said with a sheepish grin.

"A little," she said.

"I probably am to some extent," he said. "I remember when I could go to a movie and get snacks for two dollars."

"Was that during the silent-film era?" she teased.

"Looking back, it seems like it should have been that long ago," he said with a chuckle. "I guess it was nearly forty years ago."

"And a loaf of bread probably cost twenty cents, gasoline was twenty-five cents a gallon, and cigarettes were thirty cents a pack," she said with a grin. "Do they still cost the same?"

"Point taken," he said.

"So what do you like to do if it's not spending exorbitant amounts for a movie?"

"I like the outdoors," he said. "I also enjoy going to concerts."

"Symphony orchestra?"

"Sometimes," he said. "What about you?"

"I love the Lexington Symphony Orchestra," she said. "I'm a season-ticket holder."

"Anything else?"

"I love plays and musicals," she said. "I also have season tickets to the Broadway series at the Opera House."

The waiter returned with their appetizer. They both ordered veggie burger platters and another mug of beer. More customers began to show up, gradually taking the tables around them. A George Strait love song played softly in the background.

"Do you go out much?" he asked.

"Not as much as I'd like. I know I spend too much time at work. I need to slow down a little. That's probably what broke up my marriage."

"Married long?" he said, then taking a swallow of beer.

"About ten years," she said. "He was a homebody and I was a workaholic. That doesn't seem to mix. And you've never been married?"

"No," he said. "I've had a few close calls. I just didn't think my profession and marriage would be a good combination."

"Any regrets?"

"Not really. I like my independence. How about you?"

"About marriage?"

"Yes," he said. "Do you regret getting married?"

"I don't think so," she said. "Howard and I were very close the first few years and had a wonderful time. So I don't regret that time. After we started drifting apart, it became more difficult. But we still managed to remain friends even though we had little in common."

"I guess that's good."

"It really is," she said. "We still talk on the phone occasionally. His wife is a bit on the jealous side but I can understand that."

They finished their food and ordered coffee. A minute after their coffee arrived, she yawned.

"Excuse me," she said, blushing lightly.

"That's okay," he said with a laugh. "It's been a long week, and a long day."

"Yes, I am a bit tired," she said.

Brandon asked the waiter for the check and paid for it with his credit card. They got up and headed to the front door. Brandon walked behind her. He noticed her tight jeans revealed shapely hips. She also wore a simple, long-sleeved white blouse and a single-strand gold necklace that glimmered in the light.

"I had a nice time, Brandon," she said at the front foyer before going outside in the rain. "Thanks for asking me out this evening."

"Thank you for accepting," he said. "Perhaps we can do it again?"

"Perhaps," she said with a smile.

She shook his hand softly, opened the door and walked swiftly to her car while holding an umbrella. Brandon waited until she was inside her car before he dashed to his vehicle.

While driving home, Brandon wondered if she would go out with him again. He wasn't sure about her answer about going out. He thought that she could have just been polite with him. He knew he wouldn't know unless he asked her out some other time.

There was a message on his answering machine when he got home.

"Brandon, this is Maggie," she said in a hurried voice. "Bobby Lee was struck by a car tonight. We're at the university hospital right now. He's undergoing surgery. Bye."

Brandon charged back out the door and drove to the hospital. He found Maggie in the waiting room of the intensive care unit. Her hair was frizzy from the rain and her mascara was streaked from crying.

"Oh, Brandon," she said as she stood up. "Thank you for coming over."

Brandon put his arms around her and gave her a gentle hug.

"How's Bobby Lee?" he asked.

"He's going to be okay," she said. "He's got a broken leg and arm. They had to set some pins in his thigh. They finished about an hour ago."

"How did it happen?"

"Bobby Lee was over at a friend's house and ran in front of a car while coming home," she said, tearfully. "They said he darted between some parked cars and didn't look before crossing the street."

A nurse told Maggie that Bobby Lee was resting comfortably and they could see him for a few minutes. She led them to the recovery room.

Bobby Lee was awake but groggy when they came into the room. His right leg and arm were hoisted up. His face was cut and bruised, with stitches along his left eyebrow. He managed a soft smile for Maggie.

"How are you doing, sugar?" she said, kissing him gently on the forehead.

"Not too good," he said softly.

"Brandon came here to see you."

Bobby Lee looked at him and smiled.

"You're going to be all right, Bobby Lee," Brandon said, moving to the side of the bed and patting his hand.

Maggie ran her fingers through Bobby Lee's curly hair and wept softly. Brandon put his arm around her shoulders. Bobby Lee gazed up at her, then closed his eyes and fell asleep from all the medication.

"Oh, my poor baby," she said, turning her head to Brandon's shoulder.

"He's going to be all right," Brandon said. He patted her gently on the back.

The nurse came into the room and motioned with her hand for them to leave. Maggie bent down one more time and kissed Bobby Lee on the cheek.

"Bye, sweetie," Maggie murmured as she and Brandon returned to the waiting room.

"Is there anything I can do?" Brandon asked.

"I'm going to spend the night here," she said.

"Can I get you anything to eat?"

"I couldn't eat now."

"I understand," he said, giving her a look of reassurance.

A nurse and orderly wheeled Bobby Lee from the recovery room to a room in the pediatrics ward. Brandon and Maggie followed them to his room on the third floor.

"I appreciate you coming over," Maggie said to him as they waited outside Bobby Lee's room.

"If you need me for anything, don't hesitate to call," Brandon said. "And don't worry about work."

Brandon hugged her again and left. A tear trickled down his cheek as he stood in the elevator, thinking about Bobby Lee's broken body.

Thirteen

Graham was sitting at the front desk when Brandon walked into the office Monday morning.

"I have no idea where Maggie is," Graham said in an irritated tone. "She called my house last night but didn't leave a message. She should have been here an hour ago."

"Her son's in the hospital," Brandon said somberly. "He was struck by a car last night and had to undergo surgery."

"Really?" Graham said. "Is the boy going to be okay?"

"I believe so. They had to put steel pins in this leg. He also broke an arm and suffered a few bumps and bruises. I went by the hospital to see him last night. Maggie was pretty torn up by it all."

"I can imagine," Graham said, getting up from the desk. "What hospital is he at?"

"University."

"I'm going over there now. Can you watch the phones?"

"No problem."

"I'll be back in about an hour. Would you do me a favor?"

"Sure."

"Would you call the florist and have something sent over to the kid's room. Just charge it to the office."

"I'll take care of it," Brandon said with a nod.

Graham put on a tweed jacket and headed out the door. Before Brandon took a step toward his office, the phone rang. He picked up Maggie's phone.

"Kentucky Sports Weekly. Brandon speaking."

"Hi, Brandon. I wanted to call and thank you for last night."

Clarice's voice sounded bright and cheerful, just the tonic Brandon needed after dealing with Bobby Lee's accident.

"It's good to hear from you," he said. "I enjoyed last night, too. I hope we can do it again sometime."

"I don't know when that will be," she said. "I've got so much work to do. I can't believe how much there is after missing a week."

"Perhaps sometime for lunch then?"

"I was just kidding, Brandon," she said with a laugh. "I'm not going to be working twenty-four hours a day."

"Well, you just remember that," he said.

"I need to be getting back to work," Clarice said. "I hope you have a great day."

"You, too," he said. "Take care."

Right after he put down the receiver, the phone rang again.

"Hi, Brandon," Jenny said unpleasantly.

"Hello, Jenny. How are you?"

"Miserable."

"Why's that?"

"Because you won't call me or anything."

"I've been busy," he said. "You know how my schedule can be."

"You could've at least called."

"I was out of town over the weekend covering a football game."

"You could have called before you left and told me."

Brandon shook his head warily.

"I'll try to remember next time."

"Can we go out for lunch today?"

"I can't. We're short-staffed in the office today."

"How about if I drop by with some carryout?"

"I don't think I'd have time to eat."

"Are you trying to avoid me?"

Brandon smiled to himself. He wished that she would back off and leave him alone for awhile, but knew he couldn't tell her that because she would go ballistic with him.

"No, Jenny," he said in calmly. "Our secretary's son is in the hospital and I plan to drop by and see him during the lunch hour."

"Why can't you go after work?"

"Because I want to see him at noon."

"There you go again," she said with a pout. "Just trying to avoid me."

"I need to go now," he said firmly. "Is there anything else you want? I've got work to do."

"Well, be that way," she said, her voice rising with each word. She hung up the phone.

"Geez," Brandon said to himself as he put down the receiver.

A minute later, Debra walked through door, dressed in a tight-fitting green dress, black heels and pearls around her neck and wrist. Brandon couldn't help but admire the sight for a moment.

"Hi there, Mr. Wilkes," she said cheerfully. "Aren't you just the cutest secretary I've seen today."

"I'm just filling in here for awhile," he said, laughing. "Nothing permanent, I hope."

"Well, if you don't like it here, you can always come to my office," she said with an exaggerated wink.

"So what brings you by here this morning?"

"I was just in the neighborhood and thought I'd stop in and see how you're doing," she said. "I haven't seen you in awhile."

"I was out of town for a few days," he said. "It gets busy around here once in awhile."

"Have you been back to Hastings lately?"

"I don't think since I last saw you there."

"I was there Saturday night. It was kinda dead."

"That's the way I like it," Brandon said. "Quiet and peaceful."

"You would have had the time of your life then," she said with a giggle.

"Showing any houses today?" he asked.

"I've got one coming up in about thirty minutes," she said while glancing at her watch. "I need to be scootin'."

"It's good to see you," Brandon said.

"See ya," she said, while turning around and shaking her hips with a little more emphasis while walking to the door.

Brandon phoned in the florist order for Bobby Lee, then sorted through the mail on Maggie's desk. When Graham returned to the office about thirty minutes later, Brandon was still at her desk.

"How's Bobby Lee?" Brandon said, while Graham removed his coat.

"He seems to be fine," Graham said. "He's under a lot of medication."

"And Maggie?"

"She's worn out. I sent her home after Bobby Lee went to sleep. I think she's going to try to get cleaned up and get a bite to eat before she goes back to the hospital."

"When is she coming back to work?"

"Bobby Lee should be released from the hospital on Thursday if there aren't any complications. I told her to take her time about coming back, that we'd cover for her and may hire a temp if she needs to be with Bobby Lee."

"I don't think she's going to get much help from her deadbeat ex-husband," Brandon said.

"She mentioned about some relatives here in town to help her," Graham said. "Any messages for me while I was out?"

"Nothing," Brandon said, "but you've got some mail that I put in your box."

Brandon managed to get away from the office at noon to visit Bobby Lee, who slept the entire time. He took Maggie to the hospital cafeteria and bought her lunch.

Brandon told her to call him at any time if she needed anything. Maggie hugged him when he left.

When he returned to the office, Graham was sitting at the front desk, working at Maggie's computer.

"Anything going on?" Brandon asked.

"All quiet," Graham said. "Is the boy okay?"

"He slept the entire time I was there."

"Maggie holding up?"

"She seems to be."

Brandon went to his office, turned on his computer and checked e-mails. There were the usual news releases and spam. He nearly deleted a message from a bmcken@hotmail.com. He opened it up and it was a short note from Bev.

"Dear Brandon...I'm sorry about the other night. I guess I had too much to drink. Please forgive me? I hope to see you during basketball season...Bye, Bev."

Brandon hit the reply button and typed: "Dear Bev...Don't think anything about it. I'll see you in a few months. Take care...Brandon."

Brandon spent the remainder of the afternoon writing his column and putting together an advance story for the upcoming football game against Tulane.

"I thought I'd stop by Hastings for a beer before going home," he said to Graham. "Care to join me?"

"I can't. I've got Bernie's soccer game at six-thirty," said Graham, referring to his eleven-year-old son.

"That should be fun."

"I really didn't care for soccer until Bernie started playing," Graham said. "I thought it was boring. But it's really an exciting game once you get into it."

"Well, have a good time," Brandon said as he headed for the front door. "I hope Bernie's team wins."

"Thanks," Graham said. "See you tomorrow."

Brandon decided not to stop at Hastings and drove to the hospital instead to check on Bobby Lee.

Fourteen

Bobby Lee was released from the hospital on Thursday afternoon. Brandon helped Maggie take him home and to get situated in the house. She made a makeshift bedroom for him in the living room so that he would be able to watch television and move around easily to the bathroom and kitchen in his wheelchair.

Brandon reminded Maggie to go to the school and pick up any homework assignments so that Bobby Lee wouldn't fall too far behind in his class work. That didn't go over well with Bobby Lee, who had wanted to spend his time away from school doing as he pleased. Brandon and Graham decided to visit after work on alternating days, stopping by a restaurant to pick up carryout dinners for Maggie and Bobby Lee. It took several days for Bobby Lee to regain some strength. Maggie never ventured far from him as she took care of his every need.

After being away from the office for ten days, Maggie returned to work on a part-time basis. She called home a couple of times to make sure Bobby Lee wasn't having any problems or needed anything.

"I don't know what I would have done without you and Graham," Maggie told Brandon during a quiet moment in the office. "Bobby Lee and I really appreciate it."

"We're happy that we were able to do anything," Brandon said. "Let us know if we can do anything else."

There was a phone call for Brandon and he went to his office to answer it.

"Hello Brandon," Clarice said. "I'm sorry I haven't gotten back with you but I've been swamped at work."

"I figured you'd forgotten about me," he said with a laugh.

"You know better than that."

"So you've been busy the past couple of weeks?"

"That's an understatement. I've been putting in twelve hours a day and even working on weekends. I think I'm beginning to get my head above water."

"So much that you can go to dinner with me again?"

"Perhaps," she said, warmly.

"Will you be free Saturday?"

"I think I could squeeze you in sometime during the day," she said coyly.

"Well then, how does seven o'clock look?"

"Let me see," she said. After pausing for a moment, she added, "I think that's doable."

"I'll be at your house at seven on the dot," Brandon said with a chuckle.

Their conversation was cut short with Clarice receiving another telephone call but Brandon smiled as he put down the receiver. Although he had been busy with work and helping Maggie for two weeks, he thought that Clarice would be just a pleasant memory. He wasn't sure what was going on inside his head, but Clarice was the first woman in a long that he wanted to spend time with. He didn't feel any pressure from her to hurry the relationship. In fact, he wondered if she even wanted to take it past a friendship level.

Brandon and Graham met at Hastings after work and shared a pitcher of beer. They tried to get together every week or so to talk about work or anything that crossed their minds. Benny was behind the bar and Rosie was taking care of the tables. The bar was about one-third full. There was a dull drone from the conversation while the overhead TV was tuned to CNN with the sound turned off.

"How's the family?" Brandon asked. "I haven't seen Sheila in ages."

"She's keeping busy with work," Graham said of his wife. "She's had to work late the past few months so we often come and go with barely having time to say anything to each other. I guess we're used to it because of my job but that doesn't mean I like it."

"How is Bernie handling it?" Brandon asked about Graham's only child.

"Bernie seems to be doing okay with it," Graham said. "I think soccer helps keep him occupied. I haven't heard anything negative about school so I guess he's doing all right there. So how about you? What have you been doing?"

"Working and going over to Maggie's house," Brandon said, shrugging his shoulders slightly. "There hasn't been much time for anything else."

"I'm glad to see that Bobby Lee is getting better," Graham said. "He's a good kid."

Debra walked to their table carrying a beer. She caught the eye of Brandon and Graham, and other men sitting nearby, in her tight dark blue pant suit that accentuated her figure.

"Hi, Brandon," she said. "Long time, no see."

"Hello, Debra," he said, trying to keep his eyes on her face. "I'd like you to meet Graham. He's my boss at the magazine."

Debra extended her arm and shook hands with Graham.

"Why don't you pull up a chair and join us?" Brandon asked.

"Why, thank you," she said, flashing a big smile. "I think I'll do that."

Debra sat next to Brandon, almost too close for comfort as she occasionally bumped her shoulder against his shoulder. He remembered her husband and didn't want any encounters with him.

"I haven't seen you in awhile, Brandon," she said. "Have you been busy at work?"

"Work has been about the same," he said. "A friend's son was struck by a car a few weeks ago and Graham and I have spent a lot of time with him. Are you selling a lot of homes?"

"It's been a little slow the past few weeks," she said with a sigh. "Business usually drops off a little this time of year as the weather starts turning cooler."

"How long have you sold real estate?" Graham asked.

"About ten years or so," she said. "Are you looking for something?"

"No, I don't think so," Graham said with a chuckle, "but I'll be sure and call you when I am."

"I filed my divorce papers this past Monday," Debra said to Brandon. "It should be about six weeks before it's final."

"That was quick," Brandon said. "What brought that on?"

"I found out that he's been two-timing me. I saw him with another woman last weekend. After checking up on it, some friends told me it's been going on for several months."

"So why was he giving you such a hard time and spying on you?" Brandon asked before taking a swallow of beer.

"You got me," she said, shaking her head. "I'll just be glad when it's over with between David and me."

"Is he still following you around?" Brandon asked.

"Not after I caught him," Debra said, laughing. "At least I hope not."

"I hope everything turns out okay," Brandon said.

Debra finished her beer and wiped her mouth with a napkin.

"Well, guys, I need to be going," she said. "It was nice meeting you, Graham. Let me know when you're looking for a house."

"It was a pleasure meeting you," Graham said with a smile.

Debra pecked a kiss on Brandon's cheek and stood up.

"Bye," she said, grinning broadly. "See ya." She walked toward the front door, drawing the glances of several men along the way.

"Where did you meet her?" Graham asked after she left the bar.

"Here," Brandon said. "She's quite a looker."

"No kidding," Graham said. "Have you gone out with her?"

"We went to dinner," Brandon said. "I didn't know she was married at the time. Her husband's a cop. I don't get involved with married women. And if I were going to, it certainly wouldn't be with a cop's wife."

"I can't say I don't blame you," Graham said with a big laugh. "I guess you can go out with her again after she's divorced."

"I don't think so," Brandon said with a shrug. "She's really not my type."

"Forget that," Graham said. "I bet she's a hot one in the sack."

"I wouldn't know but I wouldn't be surprised."

"You're missing out on something if you don't go after that!"

"Boy, you sure sound horny," Brandon said with a laugh.

"Hey, like I told you, Sheila and I haven't had any time together in ages."

"You need to do something about that. Why don't you take a long weekend off or something?"

"I agree. It's just being able to juggle our schedules to do it."

Brandon looked up at the clock on the wall. It was nearly seven o'clock. They had already finished the pitcher.

"It's getting late," Brandon said. "I need to be running."

"Same here," Graham said. "Bernie will probably be getting home from soccer practice soon."

Brandon handed Rosie money and a tip for the beer when she stopped by the table. Graham led the way as they headed toward the front door. Brandon turned around and waved at Benny. Benny nodded his head while pouring a beer from the tap for another customer.

Before going home, Brandon stopped by KFC and picked up some chicken, coleslaw and biscuits for Bobby Lee and Maggie. He stayed at their house for a few minutes as Bobby Lee was engrossed in a television program.

When he got to his apartment, Jenny was sitting in her car waiting for him. She yelled at him from the parking lot as he was about to unlock the front door. He waited for her to reach the door before he turned the knob and invited her in.

"Hi Brandon," she said while catching her breath. She had already been at home and had changed into blue jeans and a casual red pullover sweater. She followed him into the kitchen, sitting at the table. She accepted his offer for a Pepsi.

"What brings you over here tonight?" he asked while handing her the soft drink.

"You," she said with pursed lips. "Don't you want to see me?"

"I've been really busy the past few weeks."

"So much that you couldn't even call?" she said, pushing out her lower lip.

"I didn't think you wanted to see me again."

"You know better than that. I get mad at you sometimes but that doesn't mean I don't want to see you."

"I've been busy. A friend's son was injured in a car accident. I've been helping them."

"That's nice but that's no excuse for not calling me," she said, brushing her hair back with her hand.

Jenny got up from her chair and straddled Brandon before he could offer any protest. She ran her hands through his hair on the sides of his head, and then kissed him softly on the mouth while pressing her breasts against his chest.

"You haven't missed me?" she asked in a soft whisper.

Brandon put his hands on her waist and looked at her.

"It's not you," he said. "I've just had a lot of things going on. Please don't take it personally."

"But I think I'm in love with you," she said, her eyes beginning to well up in tears. "Don't you love me? Just a little?"

"I like you, Jenny," he said firmly while trying to lift her off his lap.

"You just like me?" she said, standing up and backing away quickly. "That's not what I want to hear."

"You know what I mean."

"No, I don't," she said as anger mixed with tears. "We've dated for more than six months and you treat me this way."

"I'm not treating you anyway," he said, trying to speak gently to her. "Why can't we be friends?"

"Because I don't just want to be friends."

"I'm sorry then."

"Is there somebody else?"

"No," he said with an unconvincing expression.

Jenny looked him squarely in the eyes for a moment, then picked up her purse and charged toward the front door.

"Bastard!" she said before slamming the door on her way out.

Brandon shook his head in disbelief, then picked up her soft drink and poured it down the sink.

He walked to his bedroom and changed clothes, putting on gray gym shorts and a green T-shirt. He looked over at his nightstand and saw *Ulysses* next to the lamp. He hadn't read any from the book since Bobby Lee's accident. He picked it up and opened to where it was bookmarked. He had read about two-hundred pages, just a dent in the mammoth work.

Brandon took it with him to the living room. He sat down in a recliner and began reading. The next thing he knew it was five in the morning and the book was resting facedown on his lap.

Fifteen

Autumn nights were getting cooler as November approached. The leaves had already turned to their brilliant red, yellow and orange hues. Brandon noticed how some houses were decorated for Halloween as he drove to Clarice's house for their dinner date.

He rang the doorbell twice, and within a few seconds Clarice opened the door. He marveled at her appearance. She wore a dark green dress with a V-neck that revealed a little cleavage. There were no signs of the accident on her face. She looked radiant in the porch light.

"I hope I'm not too early," Brandon said with a smile.

"No, I'm just about ready," she said. "I've only got a few more things to do. Please take a seat in the den and I'll be back in a few minutes."

Brandon sat in a blue swivel rocker. On the coffee table were magazines such as *Cosmopolitan, Vanity Fair* and *New Yorker*. He also noticed a *Kentucky Sports Weekly* folded neatly in the magazine rack along with several newspapers and magazines. The den was very cozy with a black leather couch, several craft items on the walls, and a large screen television. There were two seven-shelf cherry book cases filled with books.

Clarice walked into the den carrying a light brown coat.

"I'm ready," she said with a soft smile.

"You look very nice," Brandon said as he stood next to her.

"Thank you," she said, blushing lightly.

"I thought we'd go to Romano's, that new Italian restaurant on the east side," Brandon said.

"I've never been there but I've heard it's very good," Clarice said.

The drive to the restaurant took about twenty minutes. They chatted about their work week and her recovery from the accident.

Brandon had called in a reservation to the restaurant several days earlier and they were seated at a quiet table near the back of the dining room. Soft, romantic Italian melodies played in the background and candles at each table gave off a romantic glow. Most of the customers were couples, each caught up in their own world and oblivious to those around them.

Brandon ordered a carafe of red wine, which the waiter returned in a few minutes while they were looking over the menu. Brandon selected egg plant parmigiana and a salad while Clarice decided on lasagna with a savory cream sauce and salad.

"This is very nice," Clarice said, her dark brown eyes glimmering in the candlelight.

"I'd read a review about it in the newspaper a few weeks ago," Brandon said. "The reviewer gave it high marks. I usually don't pay much attention to reviews because I seldom go to these kinds of places."

"Why not?"

"Being a bachelor, I usually pick up microwave dinners for home. I do eat out a lot, but it's usually at the low-end places on the restaurant scale."

"You'd better watch what you eat," she said. "It could come back and haunt you one of these days."

"I try to be careful with what I put in my mouth," he said before taking a sip of wine.

"I forgot to tell you that I liked the story you wrote from the news conference at the university," she said. "Very complete."

"The pressure was on because I wanted to make a favorable impression with you," he said with a wink.

Clarice smiled and drank some wine.

"Do you mind if I ask a personal question?" she asked.

"Go ahead," he said. "I'll try to answer you."

"Do you go out much?"

"Not a lot," he said. "It goes in cycles."

"Do you have someone that you see on a steady basis?"

"Hmm," Brandon said as Jenny came to mind. "Not now. I've seen a few women in the past few years but nothing serious. How about you?"

"I've gone out a few times since Howard and I divorced, but not very often. I immersed myself in work so I didn't have that much time to go out. Plus, with dinner engagements and meeting people for lunch meetings, that takes up a lot of time. Usually, when I have time off, I like to relax at home or escape to the ocean or mountains."

"I'd like to do that but my schedule is so hectic it's difficult to plan for things," he said. "I do take off to the forests and hike when I get the opportunity."

"Where do you go?"

"Just about anywhere with lots of trees and hills," he said. "I guess Red River Gorge is my favorite."

"I'd like to go there sometime."

"Would you like to go with me?" Brandon asked.

"I think that would be fun."

"This is the best time of the year because of the leaves changing colors. Could you go in the next week or so?"

"Let me check my schedule when I get to work on Monday and I'll let you know."

The waiter brought their food and a basket of warm bread. They took their time eating and drinking the wine. Brandon occasionally glanced at her, taking in her soft, delicate features and wonder how such a strong, independent woman could be inside. They finished their dinner with cappuccino.

"I'm glad you were able to squeeze me into your schedule this weekend," Brandon said with grin.

"I'm glad I was, too," she said, smiling playfully.

"And I hope that we can go hiking in the next week or so," he said.

"I'll do my best."

As they got up from their table, Brandon glanced around the room. At a table in the corner, he thought he saw Sheila. He couldn't tell who was sitting with her since his back was to him, but he knew it wasn't Graham. Brandon turned his head back around quickly, hoping that Sheila didn't notice him.

"What's the matter?" Clarice asked. "You look like you've just seen a ghost."

"Nothing," Brandon said with a puzzled look. "It was nothing."

After they got to his car, Brandon still looked distracted.

"Are you sure everything is okay?" Clarice asked. "Did I say something to offend you?"

"Of course not," Brandon said, forcing a smile. "I just thought I saw something."

"What was it?"

"I'd rather not say. I hope you don't mind."

"I understand."

Clarice invited him into her house when they pulled into her driveway. Brandon declined but walked her to the front door.

"I really had a nice time," she said. "Thank you for asking me out."

"Thank you for accepting," Brandon said. "I'll be looking forward to hearing from you on Monday about the hiking."

Brandon took her hands, leaned forward slightly and kissed her softly on the mouth.

"Good night," he said as he stepped back, nearly mesmerized by her eyes.

"Good night, Brandon," Clarice said. She turned and went inside the house and waved her hand. Brandon lifted his hand and waved and felt like he was floating back to his car.

Brandon drove slowly to his apartment as his thoughts returned to seeing Sheila at the restaurant. He was hoping that he was wrong and that it was someone who looked a lot like her. But he knew in his heart that it was Sheila. There was no denying it. But who was she with? He didn't have a clue.

It was ten-thirty when he got to his apartment. He picked up the telephone and called Graham. After three rings, Graham answered.

"What are you doing calling this time of night?"

"Did I get you out of bed?" Brandon asked.

"Nah, I was watching the Notre Dame football game. It's about over."

"How are the Irish doing?"

"Winning big."

Brandon hesitated for a few seconds, trying to think of something to say.

"I went out with Clarice tonight," he said hurriedly.

"The gal from the public relations firm?"

"Yes. I took her to Romano's. I had a very nice time."

"Good for you," he said. "I thought you might be going out with that real-estate lady."

"Debra? I don't think so," Brandon said with a laugh. "So did you have a soccer game today?"

"Only practice," Graham said. "We've got a game tomorrow afternoon."

"Sheila at home?" Brandon said, biting his tongue.

"No," Graham said. "She called and said she had a meeting and would be getting home around eleven or so. In fact, I think I just heard her car pull into the driveway."

"Well, I'd better let you go," Brandon said. "Oh, by the way, have you talked to Maggie today?"

"I dropped by to see Bobby Lee. He was watching TV. He asked about you."

"I think I'll visit him tomorrow," Brandon said. "I'd better go now."

"I'll see you Monday."

While putting down the receiver, Sheila walked into the den.

"Who were you talking to?" she asked while taking off her coat.

"Brandon."

"What did he want?" she said, her face growing pale.

"Nothing really," Graham said, his eyes on the football game. "He asked about Bobby Lee. That's about it."

"Can I get you a beer before I go upstairs?" she asked.

"Sure," he said, looking back at her and smiling. "You look nice tonight."

"I had a business meeting," Sheila said as she walked to the kitchen.

Sheila came back a minute later and handed Graham a beer. She kissed him on the cheek.

"Good night," she said.

"I'll be in bed after the game is over," he said. "Night."

Sixteen

Bobby Lee was watching an NFL game on television when Brandon knocked on the door. He heard the game blaring as he rang the doorbell three times, and then had to knock on the door. Maggie raised her voice and told Bobby Lee to turn it down moments before she opened the front door.

"Oh, hi Brandon," she said. She was wearing a pink housecoat and her hair was pulled back in a frizzy ponytail.

"I hope I'm not stopping by at a bad time?" he asked. Maggie opened the door and he stepped inside the house.

"No," she said. "I've been cleaning up around the house and was getting ready to fix some lunch. Would you care to join us?"

"No, thanks," he said. "I was just in the neighborhood and thought I'd drop in for a minute to see how Bobby Lee is doing."

"Who is it, Mom?" Bobby Lee hollered.

Maggie nodded for Brandon to go into the living room.

"Hi, Brandon," Bobby Lee said, pushing the mute button the remote. "I've been watching the Browns and Steelers play."

"Who's winning?" Brandon asked while sitting down in a rocking chair.

"The Browns are ahead fourteen to seven."

"It sounds like a good game."

"It is. The Browns are my favorite team."

"So how are you feeling?"

"Pretty good."

"Are you keeping up with you studies at school?"

"Yeah," he said with a shrug. "They send a teacher over every day to pick up my work and give me more stuff to do."

"That's good," Brandon said. "You don't want to get behind in your class work."

Bobby Lee frowned. "I guess not."

Maggie carried a tray into the living room with a tuna fish sandwich, chips and a can of Coke and set it in front of Bobby Lee.

"Are you sure you don't want something?" she asked Brandon.

"No thanks, I had a late breakfast," he said.

"We take Bobby Lee to the doctor on Wednesday for another checkup," she said.

"Do you need any help?" Brandon asked.

"I think we'll be able to manage. My friend next door has helped me a few times."

"Let me know if I can be of any assistance."

Bobby Lee turned up the volume slightly and resumed watching the game while eating his lunch.

"I need to be going," Brandon said while getting up from the rocker.

"Thanks for dropping by," Maggie said.

"Are you going, Brandon?" Bobby Lee asked.

"I've got a few things to do this afternoon," Brandon said as he walked toward Bobby Lee. "You take care of yourself and stay on top of your homework." He patted Bobby Lee gently on the head.

"Okay," Bobby Lee said with a grin. "Thanks for coming over."

"I'll see you in a few days."

Maggie walked to the front door with Brandon.

"Don't hesitate to ask if you need anything," Brandon said.

"I don't know how I'll ever be able to repay you for all you have already done," she said.

"Don't worry about that," he said while opening the door and stepping outside.

"I'll see you at work tomorrow."

Brandon drove to Raven Run park, one of his favorite spots to walk. There were several other hikers, some with their children. The sky was slightly overcast. He walked down to the cliffs overlooking the Kentucky River, sat down on a large rock and watched the water flow slowly by.

His thoughts drifted to seeing Sheila at the restaurant without Graham. Why would she be having dinner with another man at such a romantic setting? It wasn't the usual place for people to go to discuss business. Although Graham was his best friend, he decided not to say anything, at least until he learned more about what was going on between them. He hoped it wouldn't get to that point.

Brandon spent a couple of hours at the park, taking walks on several trails through the scenic area. The wind began to pick up, sending an occasional chill through his body as he returned to his car.

On the way home, he stopped by the grocery and purchased several microwave dinners and some fruit. After putting everything away, he picked up *Ulysses* from his nightstand and carried it to the living room. He sat down in the recliner, opened at the bookmarked page and began reading. Fifteen minutes later, there was a knock at the door.

Brandon peeked through the front window curtain. He frowned when he saw Jenny waiting for him to answer. He tiptoed over to his recliner and turned out the floor lamp and then retreated back to his bedroom.

There were a few more knocks.

"Brandon," she said. "Are you home?"

Brandon sat quietly on his bed, hoping that she would go away.

But the knocking continued.

"Brandon, open the door if you're at home," she said. "We need to talk."

Brandon thought about going to the door but decided he would wait her out. He wasn't in the mood for her this evening. He lay back on his bed and breathed softly.

The doorbell rang four times in quick succession. The buzzing sound grated on his skin like a dentist's drill.

"Please, Brandon," Jenny pleaded. "I know you're at home because your car is parked out front."

Brandon shook his head as he began to wonder if she was ever going to leave. Finally, there was silence. He remained in his bedroom, fearing to venture out to the living because she might be trying to peek through an opening in the curtains.

Brandon felt a little foolish avoiding her like this but he didn't feel like getting into an argument with her. He knew it would be more of a tirade against him while he stood there and took it. He was tired of the relationship. He wasn't sure if he even wanted to see Jenny again. Ever.

About ten minutes later, the phone rang. Brandon walked over to it, but wasn't sure if he should answer or not. He guessed that it would probably be Jenny, still checking to see if he was at home. But it could be Clarice. He put his hand on the receiver as it rang four more times. He decided against picking it up. It quit ringing.

Brandon looked up at the large Bavarian cuckoo clock over the bookcase. It was about to chime seven o'clock. He began to feel like a captive in his own apartment. He thought about going over to Hastings, but knew that Jenny could be waiting for him out in the parking lot. He didn't know why he was letting Jenny dictate his actions. But again, why would he want to subject himself to her rants and ravings? He knew he was going to have to tell her that it was over. Even if nothing developed with Clarice, he was sure that he didn't want Jenny as the alternative.

Brandon sat in silence the remainder of the evening, making slow progress through *Ulysses* as he read in his bedroom.

Outside in the parking lot, Jenny sat in her car until nearly nine o'clock. She kept her eyes glued to Brandon's apartment. It remained dark and quiet, not a single flicker of light or movement. She finally gave up and drove by his car as she left the parking lot.

Brandon arrived at work early the next morning, second only to Maggie. She had already taken a few messages, including one from Clarice.

After pouring a cup of coffee, Brandon called Clarice at her office. He got her voicemail but opted to talk with the receptionist rather than leaving her a message. She told him that Clarice was in a meeting that would probably last until noon. She took his name and number and said that she'd give it to Clarice.

While drinking his second cup of coffee, Maggie buzzed him to say that he had a telephone call. Thinking it would be Clarice, he quickly picked up the receiver.

"Hi," he said brightly.

"You don't normally answer the phone like that," Jenny said. "Did Maggie tell you it was me?"

Brandon's shoulders slumped at the disappointment of not hearing Clarice's voice.

"Uh, yes," he said. "How are you?"

"I'm fine, Brandon," she said. "I dropped by your apartment last night."

"You did?"

"I waited for you."

"I was out most of the day. I was over at Maggie's house to see her son and went to Raven Run."

"Your car was in the parking lot," she said tersely.

"Hmm, I wonder where I could have been?"

"That's what I want to know."

"I fell asleep while reading. I was tired after hiking."

"You must have been dead tired because I rang the doorbell and banged on the door quite a few times."

"Oh, I'm sorry," he said. "I didn't hear a thing."

"Apparently not," she said.

"Is there something you wanted?"

"I just wanted to talk. About us."

"Anything in particular?"

"Just about us."

"Want to try it again?"

"I'm sure not going to go over to your place and wait around for you," she said.

"How about lunch later in the week?"

"I'd prefer dinner."

Brandon knew that lunch would put time constraints on her while dinner was open ended. He just had to think of a time and place that would limit their time together.

"How about if I get back with you?" he asked.

"When?"

"In the next day or so. I've got work to do around here," he said, wanting to end the conversation. "We've got a magazine to finish and get to the printer."

"You do that every week."

"I need to go now," he said.

"I'll be waiting for your call."

The next thing Brandon heard was a click. He shook his head, smiled, and put down the receiver.

Maggie knocked on the side of his open door, startling him for a second.

"You had a call while you were on the phone," she said, handing him a yellow memo.

Brandon looked at the paper. It was from Clarice. The note said she would be involved in meetings the remainder of the day.

"Damn," he said.

"Any problem?" Maggie asked.

Brandon looked up at her and pursed his lips.

"It's nothing," he said. "I've been trying to reach Ms. Horton this morning on something."

"I wish I would have put her on through to you," Maggie said, apologetically.

"Don't worry about that," he said. "It's not your fault. You didn't know."

Graham walked up to his door and smiled.

"Good morning, folks," he said. "Anything going on?"

"Hi," Brandon said. "It's just a regular Monday morning."

"How was the weekend, Maggie?" Graham asked. "Is Bobby Lee doing okay?"

"He's doing fine," she said. The phone rang and she hurried to her desk to answer it.

"How was your weekend?" Graham asked Brandon.

"I went over to Raven Run yesterday. It was nice. How about you?"

"I had a soccer game," Graham said. "Other than that, I just sat in front of the television and watched football."

"You and Sheila should have gone out and done something," Brandon said.

"She went shopping at the mall for several hours."

"Oh," Brandon said as he thought about Saturday night at Romano's.

The phone rang again. A second later, Maggie told Graham the call was for him.

"I'll talk to you a little later," Graham said to Brandon as he hurried to his office.

Brandon looked down at the message from Clarice.

"Damn," he said under his breath.

Seventeen

Clarice finished her last meeting at six-thirty and returned to her office. She called Brandon's office but she got only the answering machine. She shrugged and put down the phone.

"Are you going home soon?" asked Bonnie Granger, one of her associates who'd sat through the meetings. They were good friends and shared a lot in common, both being about the same age, divorced and career-minded.

"I'm going to go through some of my mail and messages," Clarice said. "I shouldn't be here much longer."

"I think I'll stay a little longer then. I didn't want to be the last person out to leave."

"Do you want to stop and get a quick bite to eat?" Clarice asked.

"Let's do that," Bonnie said. "I don't feel like fixing anything when I get home and I don't want to mess with any carryout."

After finishing their work at seven, they drove to El Chico's for Mexican fare. They each ordered a margarita on the rocks and sat back while their sampler platters were being prepared.

"These meetings are wearing me out," Clarice said, a tiredness in her eyes. "It seems like it's just talk, talk, talk."

"I know what you mean," Bonnie said. "Sometimes I wonder if we're getting anything accomplished."

"Mr. Edwards is just so picky about what he wants in his ad campaign. You'd think he'd never done it before."

"He's probably been burned a few times and wants a little more control over how his money is spent this time. I guess I can't blame him for that."

"You're right," Clarice said, "but I think he still goes to extremes."

They ordered another margarita and nibbled on a basket of nacho chips and salsa.

"How's your love life?" Bonnie asked.

"I've actually been seeing this guy for a few weeks," Clarice said, a bright-eyed smile suddenly appearing on her face. "I wish I could see him more, but work and the automobile accident messed things up."

"Care to share his name?"

"His name is Brandon Wilkes," Clarice said. "He's a sportswriter at *Kentucky Sports Weekly*. I met him at a news conference a month or so ago at the university."

"I remember going to that news conference but don't recall meeting him."

"I only met him briefly at the time. Then he called me about something, then one thing led to another."

"What's he look like?"

"Hmm," Clarice said with a whimsical look. "He's close to six-foot tall. He's got short dark hair and brown eyes. He's rather athletic looking. I think he's good looking."

"Is it helping you get over Howard?"

"A toad would get me over Howard."

They both giggled. The waitress brought their food and they each ordered another margarita.

"Do you like this guy?" Bonnie asked.

"I think he's interesting. Only time will tell about what will happen. I hope we go out this weekend on a hike."

"Does he have any friends?" Bonnie asked with a laugh. "I could use a date."

"I'll ask him," Clarice said, grinning.

They took their time finishing their meals. They didn't order any more margaritas but each had a big glass of water to wash down the spicy food.

"I'll see you in the morning," Clarice said after they paid their bill.

"Not me," Bonnie said. "I'm meeting with a client in Frankfort. I should be back in the afternoon."

"I hope you have a good day," Clarice said as they walked out of the restaurant.

"Let's do this again soon," Bonnie said. "And don't forget to see if your friend has a friend."

"I'll do that," Clarice said with a smile. "See ya."

~ * ~

Brandon fixed rice and vegetables along with two veggie egg rolls in the microwave for dinner. He popped open a can of beer and sat down at the kitchen table for a quiet meal, flipping through the entertainment section of the newspaper as he slowly ate his dinner.

After he finished, he turned on the television and flicked through the channels with the remote. Not finding anything that interested him, he turned it off. He noticed *Ulysses* on the coffee table, but left it there. He was too restless to do any reading.

Brandon thought about calling Clarice but decided against it. He didn't want to pester her, especially like Jenny had been bothering him the past few weeks. He enjoyed Clarice's company and didn't want to run the risk of her growing tired of him. He thumbed through *Esquire, Vanity Fair,* and *Consumer Reports* magazines until he heard the cuckoo clock chime nine o'clock, and wondered what Clarice would be doing about now. He glanced at the telephone again but decided not to call her. He turned on the television, this time stopping at an *A&E*'s "Biography" about Orson Welles. His favorite movie was *Citizen Kane,* a film he had watched countless times. Although he didn't collect many movies, *Citizen Kane* was the first one he had purchased for his VCR. After the program, he skimmed the channels for about ten minutes, never staying on one for more than thirty seconds. He finally decided to turn off the TV for the night and went to bed.

His thoughts drifted back to Clarice. He hadn't felt this way for a woman for ages. He certainly didn't have these feelings for Jenny although he enjoyed her company before she started wanting commitments from him. He recalled several other women he cared a lot about. They all had given up on him when they realized he was in no hurry to get married. They all had gotten married, some even a few times, while he remained single. Before long he was asleep.

He woke at five-thirty, stepped out on the front porch, picked up his newspaper and went back to the kitchen and put on a pot of coffee. While the coffee was perking, he went to the bathroom and shaved and showered. Back in the bedroom, he put on a pair of khaki pants and blue denim shirt.

Brandon returned to the kitchen, opened a can of vanilla breakfast drink

and drank it with his daily regimen of twelve vitamin pills. He poured a cup of coffee in a large yellow cup, sat down at the table and opened the newspaper. None of the front-page headlines caught his eye, so he turned to the sports pages and perused them for a few minutes while sipping his coffee.

He arrived at work at seven-fifteen, the first person in the office. Heading to the lounge area, he prepared a pot of coffee for the staff. Maggie showed up at seven forty-five, then several of the layout and adverting representatives. Graham walked in at eight, looking a little ragged in the face.

"How was your evening?" Graham asked.

"I didn't do a thing except watch a little TV and read," Brandon said. "How about you?"

"I watched ESPN until I fell asleep in the chair," Graham said. "I didn't wake up until three. I slept awful."

"You should have slept in this morning."

"Too much to do."

"I know," Brandon said. "There's always something to do."

"I'll see you a little later," Graham said as he turned abruptly and walked to his office.

Brandon picked up the telephone and dialed Clarice's number.

"This is Clarice Horton," she answered very businesslike.

"I thought you might already be in a meeting," Brandon said with a laugh.

"Hi, Brandon," she said, cheerfully. "I tried to call you yesterday."

"And I tried to call you. You were in meetings all day."

"I didn't get out of here until seven or so, and then I went out to dinner with a friend. I didn't get home until after nine."

Brandon couldn't help wondering whom she went out with but resisted the temptation to ask her.

"Are you still game for some hiking this weekend?" he asked.

"I'd love to," she said. "When do you want to do it?"

"How about Sunday? I have a game on Saturday."

"That'd be great."

Hearing Clarice's voice brought a smile on Brandon's face.

"Are you going to be free anytime this week for lunch or dinner?" he asked.

"I'm sorry but I don't think so," she said. "I'm still trying to catch up on quite a few things from missing that week of work."

"I understand," he said.

"Would you mind if I call you and tell you if something frees up?"

"I wouldn't mind that at all," he said. "Call me anytime, day or night."

"I won't go to any extremes but I'll let you know."

"Just make sure you have Sunday marked on your calendar for us."

"I'll do that," she said. "I need to go now. I've got another meeting in about five minutes."

"I hope you have a wonderful day."

"You, too," she said sweetly.

Brandon sat back in his chair and grinned to himself. He closed his eyes.

"Did you just win the lottery?" Maggie asked, standing at his door.

"Huh?" Brandon said, momentarily lost in his thoughts about Clarice.

"Oh, nothing," Maggie said with a laugh. "The university's sports information office called and said there was going to be a news conference this afternoon. It was going to be something about naming a new coach. It's at two."

"Okay," Brandon said. "I guess that's where I'll be this afternoon. Anything else going on?"

Maggie stepped inside his office and closed the door.

"Graham seems a bit distracted," she said, slightly above a whisper.

"Do you have any idea what it could be?"

"I'm not sure," she said. "I think he and Sheila may be having some problems."

"Why do you think that?"

"You didn't hear this from me but they've had words on the phone the past couple of weeks," she said. "I don't know what it's all about but he sounds angry when he's talking to her."

"I'm sure it's nothing big," Brandon said with a smile. "Married folks get upset with each other now and then."

"I hope you're right," Maggie said. "I'd hate to see anything bad happen between them."

There was a knock on the door. Maggie opened it and Graham was standing there.

"Am I interrupting anything?" he asked.

"No, I was just leaving," Maggie said with a light blush. She smiled at Graham and returned quickly to her desk.

"What's up with her?" Graham asked.

"It's nothing," Brandon said while shuffling through some papers on his desk.

"She was telling me about Bobby Lee."

"Is everything all right at home?"

"I think so."

Eighteen

Brandon sat at the bar in Hastings sipping a frosted mug of beer. There were only a handful of customers, all of them sitting around the bar except for a couple seated at a table. Brandon left work early after putting the magazine to bed. Graham couldn't go with him because of his son's soccer match.

"How's it been going?" Benny asked, leaning against the bar during a free moment.

"I can't complain," Brandon said. "How's everything with you?"

"I ain't got no life." Benny said mournfully. "I'm down here all the time except when I'm sleeping."

"You need to make some time."

"That's easier said than done."

"I won't argue with that," Brandon said, nodding. "But sometimes you have to force yourself to do things."

"I can't find any help so that I can take time off."

"How about Rosie?"

"She's fine but she's always having boyfriend problems."

"Can't you hire someone?"

"It's hard to find good help nowadays," Benny said, frowning. "I've got a couple of college kids who work the weekends but they can't during the week because of classes."

"Is business good?" Brandon asked.

"It's never been better," Benny said, tapping his knuckles on the bar.

"Then why don't you close the place down for a week around Christmas or some other time and take a break?"

"Hell, I never thought about that," Benny said with a sheepish grin. "That's a damn good idea."

"Then do it."

"I think I will," Benny said with a hearty laugh. "I may even close for two weeks."

"Hey, let's not get carried away," Brandon said, grinning. "I need some place to go after work."

Two customers walked in and sat at the bar. Benny went over to them and took their drink orders.

"Hello stranger," Brandon heard someone say behind him. He turned around and Jenny was standing next to him.

"Hello Jenny," he said, smiling. "What brings you here?"

"I knew this was your hangout so I drove by and saw your car in the parking lot. I hope you don't mind me stopping in to see you."

"That's okay," he said. "You want to sit at the bar or do you want to get a table?"

"I'd prefer a table," she said, giving a condescending glance at the surroundings.

"What do you want to drink?"

"Do they have white wine?"

"They have everything here." Brandon looked at Benny. "Could I have a glass of white wine?"

Benny poured wine into a goblet about three-quarters full and handed it to Brandon. There was a table directly behind Brandon's spot at the bar. He placed her glass on the table and then sat down across from it.

"What brings you here?" Brandon asked.

"I just wanted to see you," Jenny said, taking a quick taste from her glass. "I didn't seem to be getting anywhere on the telephone with you."

"I've been awfully busy," he said.

"Apparently you've been too busy for me," she said solemnly. "Can I ask you something?"

"Shoot," he said, forcing a smile.

"Is it over between us?"

Momentarily startled by the question, Brandon took a slow swallow of beer and sat the mug back down, wrapping both hands around it. He cleared his throat.

"I don't think I'm going to like what you're going to say," Jenny said.

"Can't we just be friends?" Brandon asked. "Do we have to be serious?"

"We can be friends. I just wanted more between us."

"I don't know really what to say," Brandon said, lifting his shoulders slightly.

"I thought there was more between us," she said. "I guess I was wrong. Didn't those weekend trips we made to Chicago and New York mean anything?"

"I enjoyed them. I had a very good time. I thought you did, too."

"I had a very nice time," she said. "I just thought they meant something more to you than just a weekend together."

"I think we got to know each other better."

"Are you saying that you didn't like me as much after spending time with me?"

"I didn't say that."

"Then what are you saying?"

"I guess what I'm saying is that I don't think you and I have that much in common, if you don't mind me being totally honest with you," he said. "Isn't that what you want?"

Tears began welling in Jenny's eyes. She reached into her purse and pulled out a tissue and dabbed it softly under her eyes.

"It hurts to hear that," she said. "Can I ask you something else?"

"You can ask me anything, Jenny."

"Is there somebody else?"

Brandon cleared his throat again, then took a swallow of beer.

"I've been seeing someone," he said. "It's nothing serious at the moment."

"Who is she?"

"I'd rather not say."

"I guess you're not going to answer all my questions."

"I don't believe that would be fair to her."

Debra walked through the front door, wearing her trademark tight skirt and blouse. She caught Brandon's eye as she approached the bar.

"Hi Brandon," she said with a wide smile.

"Oh, hi Debra," he said.

Jenny looked at her and back at Brandon. She began to tense up.

"Hi," Debra said to Jenny.

"Hello," Jenny said, barely looking at her.

Debra flicked her eyebrows, and then looked at Brandon. She winked.

"I'll see you later," she said, then turned and sat down where Brandon had been sitting at the bar.

"Who is that?" Jenny asked with a little fire in her eyes.

"Just a friend," Brandon said. "She sells real estate. She drops in here occasionally after work."

"Perhaps I should have been doing the same."

"She's just a friend."

"Can I tell you something?"

"Feel free."

"I'm not going to give you up so easily," she said in a determined voice.

Brandon stared blankly at her as if he didn't hear what came out of her mouth.

"Why?"

"Because I love you and I think you'd love me if you would just give us a chance."

"Huh?"

Jenny got out of her chair and looked down at him.

"It's not over between us," she said. "If I can't have you, then nobody else can."

Jenny smiled demurely and walked away.

"Now wait, Jenny," Brandon said, rising from his chair. "Come back here."

Jenny ignored him and walked briskly out the front door without looking back.

"Girl problems?" Debra asked as she swiveled her stool toward Brandon and crossed her legs.

"You could say that," he said, shaking his head in disbelief.

"Anything I can do to help?"

"Buy me a beer?"

"Sure, sugar," she said. She turned around and motioned for Benny. A minute later, she slid off the bar stool and handed the mug of beer to Brandon. He took a large swallow as she sat down at his table.

"She's a pretty gal," Debra said.

"I know," Brandon acknowledged. "That's not the problem."

"So what is it?"

"I don't want to get into it now," Brandon said. "It's kinda personal."

"I respect that," she said.

"How's everything with you?"

"Hunky-dory," she said. "I sold a house today so I'm in the mood to celebrate."

"Congratulations," Brandon said half-heartedly.

"Can I treat you to dinner?" she asked.

"I don't have much of an appetite right now. Thanks any way."

"That girl really bothered you."

"You can't imagine how much," he said, running his hand through his hair.

"A good dinner might help you get over it."

"I really need to be going home," he said. "I hope you don't mind."

"That's okay," she said. "I understand hon. Perhaps some other time."

Brandon finished his beer with two quick swallows and stood up.

"I hope you have a nice evening," he said. "Don't party too hard."

"Oh, don't worry about that, sweetie," Debra said. "I may just have a quiet dinner by myself."

Brandon smiled, tapped her on the shoulder and walked over to Benny to pay his bar tab. He smiled at Debra on his way out. She looked pensively at him.

While driving home, his mind was overloaded on Jenny's remarks. He didn't think she would be possessive and refuse to let him go. She wasn't his type. She was fine as a dinner date but they shared very little else in common. He couldn't understand why she couldn't see that. He tried to be as nice to her as possible but it wasn't working. He couldn't recall ever having harsh words with a woman he was breaking up with. There always had been some disappointment, but after a short period of time, any bitterness seemed to fade away and he had been able to establish at least a civil relationship with them. But Jenny was the exception. She was always the exception. He wondered how he ever got tangled up with her to begin with.

When he got home, he picked up the telephone and called her. He wanted to reason with her about their relationship. He let the phone ring six times. There was no answer.

Brandon walked to his bedroom and changed his clothes, putting on his standard gray gym shorts and a T-shirt. After drinking three beers at Hastings, he wasn't hungry. He picked up the telephone again and dialed Jenny's number. He let it ring ten times before setting it back on the receiver.

Nineteen

Brandon awoke early the next morning. Jenny's angry words were still on his mind. He wanted to call her at home but decided against it. He thought it would be better to let the situation cool down between them before approaching her again.

Showered and dressed, he drove in a light rain to Jerry's Restaurant for breakfast. He was seated in a booth at the far end of the dining room where he had a nearly full view of the other diners. He ordered coffee, oatmeal, toast and orange juice. A newspaper had been left on the seat of a booth across from him and he reached over and picked it up and turned to the sports pages.

He kept his head buried in the newspaper while waiting for his food to arrive. When the waitress carried it over on a tray, he placed the newspaper to his side. His eyes strayed toward the dining room as his food was being placed in front of him. Walking down the right side behind the hostess was Sheila. He dropped his head for a moment. She was accompanied by a man Brandon had never seen. She sat down first, her back to Brandon, and her friend sat across from her.

Uneasiness came over Brandon. He was beginning to lose his appetite. He glanced over at the man several times, trying to place his face with a name or place or circumstance. He kept drawing blanks. A moment later, Sheila and the man got up and walked over to the breakfast bar. Brandon picked up the newspaper and held it up so that Sheila wouldn't see him. He peeked around a couple of times, finally putting it back down when they were seated again at their table.

Brandon ate about half of his oatmeal and nibbled on his toast. He wanted to leave but couldn't with Sheila sitting there. He didn't want to cause any problems because she was not only Graham's wife, but also a friend. The three of them had attended several business trips to together, and he even went on a cruise with them several years ago. Brandon had many meals in their home. To see her sitting with another man was an uncomfortable situation for Brandon.

He drank four cups of coffee, two more than his usual limit, before they finally left, waiting until he until he saw them leave the parking lot before he got up to leave. He walked past their table on the way to the counter, looking down at it and hoping to see something that would alleviate any doubts about what he saw. There was nothing but a table to be cleaned and a two dollar tip.

Brandon felt keyed up from the coffee after arriving at the office. Maggie was in the break room preparing a pot of coffee. He heard Graham shuffling through some papers in his office.

"You're here early this morning," Brandon said at the door of Graham's office.

"Yeah, Sheila had some conference to go to so I got up early with her," he said.

"Where's her conference?"

"I believe she said it was at the university. It seems like she has two or three meetings a week since she got this promotion at work."

"Anything going on with you today?" Brandon asked.

"I'm having lunch with some folks from the racetrack. Do you want to join us?"

"I think I'll pass on it. I've got some calls to make and a couple of stories I need to get out of the way."

"I'll probably be leaving early today," Graham said. "Bernie has a soccer match after school."

"Isn't the season about over?"

"Another week or so. They're in the playoffs now. If they lose, it's all over. I think they've got a good chance of winning it all."

"I hope they do well," Brandon said with a smile. "I'll talk to you later."

Brandon ambled to his office. He looked out of his window. The rain had subsided but the sky was still gray with thinning clouds. He turned on the computer and checked for e-mail. As he scrolled down the list, he came across "chorton@franklin.com." It brought a smile to his face as he clicked it open.

"Hi Brandon,

I tried unsuccessfully to call you yesterday. I was wondering if we were still on for hiking this Sunday? The weather looks terrible but perhaps it will clear up by then.

Bye,

Clarice"

Brandon clicked the reply button, and wrote back that he would try to pick her up around ten on Sunday morning and to let him know if there was a better time.

Brandon wanted to call Jenny but decided that doing it from work might not be the best idea since she was so unpredictable. He certainly didn't want to get her stirred up any more than she was about their so-called relationship.

Maggie came to his office and stood at the door. She tapped her foot on the floor.

"Do you mind if I talk to you for a minute?" she asked after glancing down the hallway.

"Certainly not," Brandon said, motioning for her to come in.

"May I close the door?"

Brandon shook his head affirmatively. She closed the door quietly, and then sat down in the chair next to his desk.

"I hate to be a gossip but have you heard anything else about Graham and Sheila?" she asked softly.

"Graham told me she got a promotion at work and has been going to several meetings a week," Brandon said. "That's all I know."

"A couple of days ago when I took Bobby Lee to the med center for a checkup, I saw her and this guy walking across the parking lot," she said. "I sat in my car and watched them from a distance. They looked a little too chummy but I didn't give it that much thought. But then they kissed. It wasn't anything romantic or anything, just a quick kiss and then they went to their cars. It was kinda like married folks. I didn't know what to think."

Silence permeated the room for a few seconds before Brandon opened his mouth.

"There may be something going on between Graham and Sheila," he said. "What you saw in the parking lot could be purely innocent."

"But kissing?" Maggie said, wide-eyed.

Brandon thought back to seeing Sheila at Romano's, then again at breakfast several hours ago. He didn't like what he had seen.

"I don't think we should be sticking our noses into their business," Brandon said, unconvincingly. What he really wanted to do was go to Graham's office and tell him what he had seen, and then visit with Sheila and find out what was going on. He knew he couldn't watch what was happening from the sidelines, but he didn't want Maggie involved in the situation.

"You're probably right," Maggie said. "It just hurts me to see what could be happening to Graham."

"Let's just wait and perhaps things will work out for the best."

"I hope so," Maggie said, getting up from the chair. "I pray everything will be all right between them."

As she opened the door, Graham was standing there about to knock.

"Sorry," he said with a laugh. "I almost bopped you on the head."

Maggie smiled with pursed lips and didn't say anything, quickly returning to her desk.

"What's the matter?" Graham asked Brandon. "More problems at home?"

"I think so," Brandon said with a shrug.

"Well, let me know if I can do anything to help her. I don't want to lose her. She's the best secretary we've ever had."

"I agree," Brandon said with a nod. "She's just a little stressed right now."

"I'm getting ready to leave for lunch. Are you sure you don't want to join us?"

"Not this time. Too much work here."

"Have you talked to that woman from the PR agency lately?"

"You mean, Clarice?" Brandon said. "We're going hiking this weekend at Red River Gorge."

"Oh, I bet it's beautiful there this time of the year," Graham said. "I wish I could go along."

"Hey, why don't you and Sheila come along with us?" Brandon said. "We could take along a picnic lunch."

"Thanks for the invitation but Sheila is going to Cincinnati this weekend for a meeting," Graham said. "She won't be back until late Sunday."

"Oh. I'm sorry to hear that."

"Aw, that's okay," Graham said. "There's football on the tube this weekend. I'll get myself a case of beer and some snacks and won't move from the recliner except to take a leak. I'll never know she's gone."

"Don't you guys ever go out anymore?" Brandon asked.

"Not much," Graham said with raised eyebrows. "Well, I need to be going or I'll be late. If I don't see you when I get back, I'll see you in the morning."

Graham raised his hand and waved, then walked away. Brandon sat quietly for a few seconds until Maggie peeked in.

"Did he say anything?" she asked.

"Nothing," Brandon said. He wanted her to quit inquiring about his friend and her boss. He wasn't going to betray his friendship to Graham with idle office gossip, even if Maggie did care a lot about him. "So you took Bobby Lee to the med center? How is he doing?"

"The doctor says he's healing just fine," she said with a smile. "They say he might be able to take his casts off by Christmas if he continues to progress like he has."

"Is he keeping up with his schoolwork?" Brandon asked.

"So far he has. I haven't heard anything differently from his teachers."

"I'll try to get over and visit him this week," Brandon said. "Is there a good day to do that?"

"Any time. We're not going anywhere."

The phone rang and Brandon picked it up.

"So we're still on for Sunday?"

Brandon smiled and nodded to Maggie that the call was for him. She smiled and returned to her desk.

"It's on my calendar."

"I hope the weather clears up," she said. "I don't want to go hiking through the mud."

"There won't be any mud but there could be some slick spots from the leaves. If it's wet, we'll plan on doing something else. Okay?"

"Whatever you want to do," she said. "How has your day been?"

"It's just a typical day around here. How about with you?"

"I just got out of a meeting with a client."

"Are you free for lunch?"

"I'm sorry but I've already got plans. Can I have a rain check on that?"

"Of course," he said. "It's an open invitation."

"I need to be going," she said. "I'll talk to you later."

After putting down the phone, Brandon walked out to the front area to Maggie's desk.

"Are you doing anything for lunch?"

"Not really," Maggie said.

"Do you want to go with me down the street to Maxwell's?" he asked. Maxwell's was an old establishment that was frequented by professionals for lunch and after work for happy hour.

"I'd like that," she said. "Give me a minute and I'll be ready to go."

"I'll get someone in advertising to watch the phones."

After Maggie returned from the restroom with fresh lipstick and several brushstrokes through her frizzy hair, they walked five blocks to Maxwell's. She ordered a cheeseburger platter and Coke while Brandon had a salad with Italian dressing and a glass of ice water.

"You make me feel bad, Brandon," Maggie said.

"Why is that?"

"You eat way too healthy."

"I have my moments when I give in to temptation," he said with a laugh.

"Really? What are they?"

"I'm not telling," he said before taking a bite from his salad.

The restaurant was buzzing with the chit-chat from every table, occasionally a burst of laughter would erupt from a group. Brandon was able to steer the conversation with Maggie about Bobby Lee's recovery and avoid any talk about Graham's marital life.

While munching on a piece of crisp lettuce, Brandon casually looked up at the entrance and saw Clarice standing there with a tall, bearded, dark-haired man. He was distinguished-looking in a tailored dark gray suit. Brandon thought she looked radiant in her soft brown skirt and blazer. But seeing her there with another man sent a chill through his body.

"What's the matter?" Maggie asked with a concerned look. "You look like you've just seen a ghost."

"Oh, it's nothing," he said. "I just remembered something from work."

"Okay," she said, then took a bite from her cheeseburger. "Was it something about Graham?"

"No," he said, shaking his head.

Brandon watched as the hostess took Clarice and her friend to a table near the rear of the dining room. She sat down with her back to Brandon.

Brandon took a small sip of water and put his fork down next to his half-eaten salad.

"Aren't you going to finish that?" Maggie asked.

"I'm really not that hungry. Go ahead and take your time and finish your lunch. I'm in no hurry."

Ten minutes later, Maggie took her last bite and took a swallow of Coke.

"Ready to go back to the office?" Brandon asked. "Or would you like some dessert?"

"No thanks, I'm full," she said.

Brandon received the check for lunch and handed the waitress a credit card. He glanced over at Clarice several times while he waiting for the waitress to return. She seemed engrossed in conversation. He could see the man smiling broadly at times. Brandon felt uncomfortable and ready to return to the office.

Brandon and Maggie left the restaurant. The skies had cleared but a cool breeze blew in their faces. They walked briskly back to the office.

"Thanks for lunch," Maggie said as she removed her coat and hung it on the coat rack.

"My pleasure," Brandon said with a smile.

"You seem a little distracted if you don't mind me saying so."

"I'm just thinking about my column and what to write."

"I know," she said. "You get all reflective and everything."

"I try."

Brandon walked to his office and closed the door. He couldn't get rid of the image of seeing Clarice with another man. He couldn't recall the last time he had this feeling.

Twenty

Brandon stopped at Hastings for a few beers after Saturday's game. Benny was working at a fast pace, trying to take care of those sitting around the bar and filling Rose's orders from the tables. He found a spot at the end of the bar that gave him a good vantage point on who else was there and the front entrance.

"How was the game?" Benny asked while preparing a Manhattan.

"It was entertaining," Brandon said. "It's a shame the Wildcats blew it late in the game."

"Isn't that typical?" Benny said before taking the drink to a customer at the other end of the counter. He stopped by the tap and poured Brandon a frosty mug.

"You guys are sure busy tonight," Brandon said.

"It's usually this way after a game. It seems like we're getting more college students."

"I've noticed that," Brandon said while gazing at a lovely young blonde sitting directly across from him.

"It's kind of a pain because I'm always having to check IDs," Benny said. "But business has been good."

Brandon felt the tap of someone's slender fingers on his shoulder and turned around. Debra was standing there, a bright smile and a bit intoxicated.

"Hi sugar," she said, then kissed him on the cheek.

"Hello Debra," Brandon said. "I didn't see you when I came in."

"I was probably back in the girls' room. There's always a line back there. I can't get Benny to add any toilets for us."

Benny overhead her and shouted, "Why don't you take up a collection and then maybe I'll do that?"

"I may just have to do that," Debra said, grinning. "How about if I find sponsors?"

They all laughed as Benny took care of another customer.

"So what are you doing here?" Debra asked while rubbing her arm against Brandon's arm

"I had a ball game this afternoon. I usually stop here to unwind a little before going home."

"The night is still young," she said before taking a sip from a Long Island iced tea.

"Not for me. I had to work today."

"When are you going to go out with me?" she blurted out loudly.

Brandon grinned and took a swallow from his beer.

"How's everything between you and your ex?" he asked.

"It's about over," she said, pressing her breasts against his arm. "I don't see him anymore."

"He doesn't follow you around?"

"I don't think so. He's still seeing this other woman."

"Do you know her?"

"Nah," Debra said, getting a little woozy on her feet. "I wouldn't know her if she came up to me and patted me on the ass."

"Why don't you take my stool?" Brandon said. "I don't mind standing."

"Why thank you, darling," she said as he eased off the stool. She braced her arm on his shoulder as she took his place, crossing her legs as her red skirt rode halfway up her thigh. She took another sip from her drink and gave him a silly smile.

"How long have you been here?" Brandon asked.

"Oh, I don't know," she said. "This is my third drink. I'm beginning to feel it."

"No kidding," Brandon said with a chuckle.

"So when are you going to go out with me?" Debra asked.

"I haven't had the time."

"So why not tonight?"

"It's late."

"We can go over to my place," she whispered in his ear. "I've got some booze and some soft, romantic music. Do you like Barry Manilow?"

"Well, thanks for the invitation but I'd better take a rain check on that," he said, trying to be diplomatic.

"I don't understand you," Debra said, with a touch of anger. "Why don't you want to go out with me?"

"Can't we be friends?" Brandon asked, forcing a smile.

"Are you afraid of me?"

"Should I be?"

"I'm not used to being turned down," she said. "I could get most of the guys in here to go home with me but not you. Am I ugly?"

"No, Debra, you're a very attractive woman."

"Then what is it? Are you seeing someone else?"

"I guess you could say that."

"Then why didn't you just tell me that?"

Brandon paused and took a big swallow from his mug.

"I guess I should have done that," he said. "My apology."

"It really pisses me off when guys act that way," she said angrily. "Do you think I'm going to be crushed because you don't want to go out with me?"

"No, Debra," he said. "You can find many guys to go out with."

"You damn straight," she said, swiveling her seat to put her back to him.

Brandon took another sip of beer.

"I'll see you," he said. "Have a nice evening and drive home safely." Debra didn't respond. He walked down the end of the bar and found a vacant stool.

Benny brought over another cold mug of beer.

"Your friend needs to sober up," Benny said about Debra. "I've already cut her off on drinks."

"Let me know if she needs a ride home," Brandon said. "I'll pay for a taxi."

"That's okay," Benny said. "That's a service I provide. I don't want any lawsuits from victims of drunken drivers."

"Why don't you pour her a cup of coffee?"

"I'm already ahead of you friend," Benny said with a smile. Brandon looked toward Debra and saw a steaming hot cup of coffee in front of her. She was sitting there motionless, staring at her near-empty drink with her hands wrapped around the glass.

Two men sitting next to Brandon recognized him from his photo in the magazine. They talked to him about the game while he finished his beer. Brandon looked down at Debra and noticed that she was drinking the coffee. He didn't want to leave the bar until he knew she was sobering up. He paid his bar tab and slipped out into the cold night air without Debra seeing him.

Brandon returned to his apartment at ten-thirty. The answering machine light was blinking. There was a message from Clarice reminding him about their hiking trip the next day. The weather had cleared, although the air was on the chilly side. Brandon went to bed early so that he would be fresh for their long walk through the forest.

He awoke around dawn, taking time reading the newspaper while drinking two cups of coffee. He put on jeans, flannel shirt, hiking boots, and a worn bomber jacket before leaving the house.

Clarice was ready when he arrived at her place, wearing jeans, hiking boots, sweater, and down jacket. Her hair was pulled back tightly and she carried a baseball cap in her hand. She fixed a picnic lunch while Brandon bought several bottles of spring water to take along with them.

"Are you ready to cover a lot of miles?" Brandon asked as they backed out of the driveway.

"I think so," she said with a grin. "I'm glad that it's not raining. I don't mind the nippy air."

"After you get out there and hike, your body will warm up and you won't even notice that."

It took an hour for them to get to the hiking area. The leaves were in full fall splendor as they started up a hiking path. They stopped about one mile over the rugged terrain and sat down on a large boulder to catch their breaths.

"I hadn't realized I was in such bad shape," Brandon said while rubbing his hands over tight muscles in his thighs.

"Me neither," she said. "My legs are really stiff."

After sitting down for five minutes, Brandon stood and stretched his legs for a few seconds. "We'd better get going or we'll never get up from here," he said.

"You're right," she said while easing to her feet. "Let's get moving."

They hiked another two miles, going up and down the side of hills as they made their way toward a scenic view on the edge of a cliff. Sitting down on a tree stump, they took in the panorama of colors before their eyes. Brandon took out the two bottles of water from his backpack and they sipped without talking, watching a squirrel scamper up the side of a tree. In the distance, a deer with her doe foraged leaves on the ground.

"This is simply beautiful," Clarice said, touching her hand on the top of Brandon's. "It makes you realize how lovely Kentucky is."

"Some folks don't realize it," Brandon said. "They feel like they have to fly off to another part of the country or world, and they really only have to look in their own backyard."

Clarice took out sandwiches and two bags of chips from her backpack and sat them on a napkin between them. They took their time eating, taking in their surroundings while talking about other places in the state.

"I saw you the other day," Brandon said.

"When?" she said, giving him a quizzical look.

"At lunch the other day after I talked to you."

"I don't remember," she said.

"I had asked you to lunch and you were busy?"

Clarice thought for a few seconds and looked at him bright-eyed.

"Oh, I remember now," she said. "Why didn't you come over and say something?"

"I didn't know who you were with."

"Silly," she said with a grin. "I was having lunch with Bill Franklin. He's my boss. I would have loved for you to meet him."

"Oh," Brandon said sheepishly. "I thought it was some guy you've been dating or something like that."

"Do I sense a trace of jealousy?" she asked with a giggle.

"Nah," he said, wishing he'd never brought it up. "Just wondering who he was."

"I'm not really dating that much," she said. "Like I told you, I really don't have that much time. In fact, you're the only person I've gone out with in the past three months."

"Really?" Brandon asked, arching his eyebrows.

"Really," she said, flashing a warm smile. "By the way, I have a friend at work who was wondering if you knew any available guys."

"I probably know a few guys but I'm not sure I'd recommend them to your friend," he said with a laugh.

"She's a lovely African-American woman with a sweet personality," Clarice said. "She's about my age, I guess."

"I'll keep that in mind but I must admit I've never played matchmaker," he said.

"Well, if someone comes to mind, let me know. She hasn't had much success in finding anyone."

"It's probably because she's in meetings all the time like you," Brandon said with a wink.

"Oh, stop it!" Clarice said, tapping him on the shoulder. "It's not that bad."

Without hesitation, she leaned over and kissed him on the cheek. Brandon blushed and cleared his throat.

"You're really a bashful guy, aren't you?" she teased.

"Sometimes," he said. "Especially when I get kissed unexpectedly by a beautiful woman."

Clarice moved the food from between them and scooted close to him. She took his hand and squeezed it lightly.

Brandon looked at her for a moment, let go of her hand and put his arm around her shoulders. He pulled her to him and kissed her long and passionately under the bright sunshine. Clarice blinked her eyes several times after their mouths parted.

"That was nice," she said softly.

Brandon kissed her again, holding her tenderly in his arms. They were oblivious to anyone or anything around them. Her kisses were warm and sweet. Brandon was aroused by the touch of her fingers on his cheeks and down his neck.

"I don't want to, but I think we need to start heading back to the car," Brandon said, pulling away from her reluctantly. "We've only got about three more hours of sunlight and I don't want to get stuck out here in the dark."

"Same here," Clarice said as they began to gather up their leftovers and put them in her backpack. They held hands or touched each other often on the trek to his car.

They returned to Lexington about six-thirty. The sun was already down. Clarice invited him into her house. She fixed hot apple cider and carried two steaming cups to the den, where he was sitting on the couch. She turned on a radio station playing soft, romantic jazz, and sat close to him. He placed his arm around her.

"I've really enjoyed today," she said while laying her head back on his arm.

"Me, too," he said. "I hope we can do it again."

They blew gently into their cups, and then took a sip of the cider before setting them down on the coffee table.

"There's something I've wanted to ask you." Clarice smiled.

"Uh oh," Brandon said. "Nothing too personal, I hope."

"Not really," she said. "But it has to do with us."

"Okay. What do you want to know?"

"Remember when I was in the hospital after the accident?"
Brandon nodded.

"Why did you come to see me that morning?" she asked.

"I wondered that while driving over there," he said with a grin. "I guess it was an impulse thing. I saw the story in the newspaper and the next thing I knew, I was on the road to the hospital."

"I must admit I was surprised at the time," she said.

"If you must know, I was attracted to you the first time I laid eyes on you," he said.

"Really?'

"Yup," he said. "I can't really explain it but you did something to me."

Brandon turned slightly and kissed her open mouth. They kissed more, each time with more passion and heat. She ran her fingers across his chest. His hand moved under her sweater, touching the soft, smooth skin of her waist.

Clarice got up slowly from the couch, took Brandon's hand and led him to her bedroom. Only the light from the gaslight by her driveway filtered into the room. She pulled back the burgundy floral comforter on the queen-size bed. They stood next to each other, softly kissing the other across the neck as they removed their clothes. They stood naked in a warm embrace, her head resting under his chin and against the soft hairs on his chest. He could feel her firm, full breasts pressing against his body.

Clarice reached over and pulled down the white satin sheet. She lay down on the bed and Brandon moved in beside her. They kissed and fondled and explored each other gently, taking their time to enjoy the moment. Finally, when they could no longer hold back their desires, Brandon entered her slowly and tenderly. When it was over, they cuddled and kissed until they fell asleep with her in his arms.

Twenty-one

"How was your weekend?" Graham asked Brandon, while pouring a cup of coffee in the break room.

"Great," Brandon said. "I went to the Gorge yesterday. A beautiful day. Simply gorgeous."

"Did you take that lady friend of yours along?"

"Yes. It was her first trip there. She loved it."

"I need to get back there one of these days," Graham said, stirring his coffee. "It's one of my favorite places."

Maggie walked into the room, took her cup from the hanger on the wall, and poured some coffee.

"So how was your weekend?" Graham asked her.

"Very uneventful," she said. "Just the way I wanted it to be. I didn't do anything and didn't want to do anything."

"How about you?" Brandon asked Graham.

"A weekend full of beer and football," he said. "I don't recall getting out of the recliner, except to go to the refrigerator or bathroom. Bernie was at a neighbor's house and Sheila didn't get back until late last night."

Brandon glanced at Maggie, who didn't make eye contact, and then looked at Graham.

"Did she have a nice trip?" Brandon asked.

"I think so. She didn't say much about it. She went to bed right after she got home."

"I think I hear the phone ringing," Maggie said as she scooted out the door. Brandon wasn't sure he heard anything but knew that she was making an excuse to leave the room.

"Anything going on today?" Graham asked.

"Not that I know of," Brandon said. "I believe most of the copy is in for the issue. I need to check on a few pieces of agate from a couple of the universities."

"I've got a few calls to make, too," Graham said as he moved toward the door. "I'll talk to you a little later."

Brandon went to his office and closed the door. He looked out the window at the trickle of falling leaves. He was glad that he made the trip to Red River Gorge when he did because he knew that the trees would start losing leaves quickly in the coming days. After checking to see if he had any important e-mails, he picked up the phone and called Clarice.

"This is Clarice," she said after answering on the second ring. "May I help you?"

"Oh, I think so," Brandon said warmly.

"Hi, Brandon," she said. "I've been thinking about you."

"I've been thinking about you, too."

"I had a wonderful time with you," she said. "I hope we can go to the Gorge again."

"We will," he said. "Let's wait until spring when it's all green. It's an entirely different experience."

"I'd love that," she said.

"So what are you doing today? Meetings?"

"That wasn't a hard guess, was it?" she said with a laugh.

"I think all those meetings would drive me nuts."

"You get used to them," she said. "Especially when you know they're bringing in revenue. It's when you don't have them that you worry."

"That's a good point," Brandon said, pausing for a moment before adding, "I enjoyed my entire time with you. Thank you for a wonderful day."

"I feel the same way, Brandon," she said, sweetly.

"How does your week look?"

"I've got meetings every day," she said with a laugh. "But I do have a few evenings free."

"Want to make a date?" he asked.

"How about Thursday night?"

"It's a date," he said quickly. "Dinner?"

"That's fine with me."

"Any place special?"

"Montana Bar and Grill."

"I'll pick you up at seven-thirty."

"Okay, Brandon," Clarice said. "I've got a meeting in a minute so I need to run."

"Have a nice great day."

"You, too," she said. "Bye."

Brandon put down the receiver. Thoughts of Clarice were running through his head. He couldn't help but smile when he recalled them sitting on the cliff in the Gorge, holding hands, and then one thing leading to another at her house.

Maggie tapped on his door and opened it up slightly.

"There's a call from Jenny on line two," she said. "Do you want to take it?"

"Not really but I will," Brandon said, puffing his cheeks with a frown.

"This is Brandon," he said.

"Hello, Brandon," Jenny said. "Remember me?"

"Of course," he said. "How are you?"

"I'm fine."

"That's good. What can I do for you?

"I miss you, Brandon," she said. Brandon could hear her weeping. He was at a loss for words on what to say.

"Really?"

"Very much so," she said. "I know I've hurt you and everything."

"It's okay."

"No it's not. I think I've said and done too much that you would ever want me back."

"Can't we just be friends?" Brandon asked, knowing he had asked her that many times before.

"That's what I mean. You only want to be friends."

"There's nothing wrong with that."

"Yes there is if I want more."

"I'm sorry, Jenny, but I can't give you any more than that."

Several seconds of silence passed by, feeling more like -minutes to Brandon. He felt uneasy as he waited for her to say something. He certainly didn't want any argument with her. He didn't want anything from her.

"Why don't you give us another chance?" she pleaded.

"Because I can't."

"Is there someone else?"

Brandon hesitated. "Yes."

"Who is it?"

"I'd rather not say," he said. "It's a woman I met several weeks ago."

"Are you serious?"

"Somewhat."

"I don't want to lose you," Jenny said, sniffling. "Give us another chance. Please."

"I'm sorry," Brandon said, coolly. "We can only be friends."

"Please."

"I need to go now," Brandon said.

"Can we talk later?"

"I don't know what else there is to say."

"Please. For me."

"I'll call you back and perhaps we can meet for lunch in the next week or two," he said.

"Thank you, Brandon," she said. "I'll be waiting to hear from you."

"Bye," he said, then put down the receiver before he could hear her voice again.

"Geez!" he said to himself. "Will that woman ever leave me alone? This is getting ridiculous!"

"Talking to yourself again?" Graham asked while standing at his door. He grinned and walked away while shaking his head. Brandon blushed and started making a few calls to universities for team statistics.

Graham came back several hours later and sat down on the chair next to Brandon's desk.

"What's up?" Brandon asked nonchalantly.

"Any plans after work?" Graham looked exasperated.

"No. Anything the matter?"

"I think Sheila is leaving me."

"What?" Brandon said, his eyes opening wide in disbelief. "Are you serious?"

"She called me this morning and said she was moving to an apartment."

"What brought this on?"

"I have no idea," Graham said, running his fingers through his thinning gray hair.

"This came out of the clear blue sky."

Maggie came into the room and tapped Graham on the shoulder and told him he had a telephone call.

"I'll see you after work," Graham said to Brandon as he got up from the chair.

"Let me know when and where."

The afternoon dragged as Brandon thought about Graham and Sheila. It really didn't surprise him that she had moved out after what he had seen the past few weeks. But they were still close friends and he hated to see this happen. He wasn't sure what he could do to help, other than be a listening post for Graham, and Sheila, if she wanted to talk.

Brandon and Graham left work early, going to Hastings. The happy hour crowd hadn't arrived as they found a table near the rear of the bar. Rosie took their order for a pitcher of beer and brought it to them in less than two minutes. She lingered for a few minutes, chitchatting about some customers who had been hitting on her the previous night, then about the weather, and then her boyfriend. Brandon didn't think she would ever leave as Graham sat quietly while sipping his beer. She finally moved to another table. Brandon waited until she was out of earshot before talking to Graham about Sheila's decision to move.

"Did you see this coming?" Brandon asked.

"Not a single clue," he said before taking a big swallow of beer. "I'm totally baffled."

"Has she been going to a lot of meetings lately?"

"Yes, but she's got a new position at work. That goes with the territory."

"You're right," Brandon said, resisting the urge to tell his friend about seeing Sheila at two restaurants. "It just seemed like you've been telling me about her being away quite a bit in the evenings."

"Like I said, that's part of her job."

"What do you think is going on then?"

"I wish I knew," Graham said, shaking his head. "I don't think she's going through the change. I don't think she has a boyfriend. I didn't think she was unhappy with me but I guess I must be wrong."

"She hasn't given you any explanation?"

"She only told me that she wanted some time to herself," Graham said, shaking his head slowly. "I told her she didn't have to leave the house and that she could have all the space she needed. I wouldn't bother her. I even told her that it might upset Bernie."

"And what did she say?"

"She said she'd talk to him. That's all."

"How long does she plan to be gone?" Brandon asked.

"I have no clue," Graham said, then chugged a half-filled mug. "I don't know a damn thing."

"Do you want me to talk to her?"

"What would you say to her?"

"I don't know. Just listen to her."

"Go ahead, but I don't think she's in the mood to say much to anybody."

"I really hate to see this," Brandon said. "I think a lot of both of you."

"Thanks, Brandon," Graham said with a weary smile. "I'm glad I have you as a friend."

Twenty-two

Brandon stopped at Maggie's house on the way home. Bobby Lee was sitting up in a chair, drinking a Mountain Dew and watching a rerun of "Seinfeld" on television. Maggie went to the basement and put clothes in the washer.

"How are you doing, Bobby Lee?" Brandon asked, sitting on the overstuffed sofa.

"All right, I guess," Bobby Lee said with a grimace. "I'll sure be glad when I can get these casts off me. They itch like crazy sometimes."

"Your mom tells me that you're doing real well and that you may have them off in the next month or so. I'm proud of you."

Bobby Lee beamed.

"I'm keeping up with my homework, too," he said. "Mom's been helping me every night."

"Are you looking forward to going back to school?"

"I guess so," said Bobby Lee, shrugging his shoulders. "It sure beats sitting here all day."

"Would you like to go to another football game?"

"When?" Bobby Lee asked excitedly.

"There's two more games on the schedule. This Saturday and two weeks after that. You pick which one."

"I think I'd rather go to the last one. Isn't it against Tennessee?"

"Yes," Brandon said with a smile. "You've studied the schedule."

"Where will I sit?"

"They've got a place for people in wheelchairs. You'll see just fine."

"I can't wait," Bobby said, his eyes wide and bright.

"But you have to promise to keep up with your class work," Brandon said.

"I promise," Bobby Lee said.

Maggie walked into the room and sat down next to Brandon.

"Guess what, Mom?" Bobby Lee said. "Brandon's taking me to another football game."

"Really?" she said, smiling at Bobby Lee and then at Brandon. "That's awfully nice of you, Brandon."

"I got a couple of tickets from a friend," Brandon said. "Would you like to go?"

"Oh, I don't think so," she said. "Thanks for asking."

Brandon stood and walked over to Bobby Lee and patted him on the back of the head.

"I need to be going," he said. "Remember our promise."

"I will," Bobby Lee said. "I'll study real hard."

Maggie walked Brandon to the front door.

"You've been very nice to us," she said. "I don't know how we'll ever repay your kindness."

"There's nothing to repay between friends," Brandon said with a soft smile. "You just let me know if there is anything I can do for you and Bobby Lee."

It took Brandon twenty minutes to drive home. The night air was cool and his car didn't get warm inside until he pulled into the parking lot. He made some hot apple cider from a mix when he got in the house. As he sat in the recliner reading a magazine, he heard someone outside his door. He placed the magazine on his lap, and then there were three hard knocks on the door.

Brandon looked through the peephole and saw a man standing with his back to the door. He opened the door. The man turned around and stared angrily at him. It was David Hatfield.

"What do you want?" Brandon asked.

"May I come in for a minute?"

Against his better judgment, Brandon unlatched the storm door and pushed it open for him to enter.

"Please have a seat," Brandon said, pointing toward the living room.

Brandon looked at him as he strode over to the couch. He must have been at least six-foot-four. He strode in erectly and sat down squarely on the couch. There was no wasted motion.

"I'd like to talk to you for just a few minutes," David said.

"Fine," Brandon said, returning to the recliner and sitting down. "Would you care for some hot apple cider?"

"No thanks. You probably know Debra filed for divorce."

"Yes," Brandon said, clearing his throat. "She mentioned it to me."

"Do you plan to marry her?"

"What?" Brandon said, quickly moving forward in the recliner. "Marry her? What are you talking about?"

"She's mentioned your name to me several times in the past few weeks."

"I have only been out with Debra that one time you saw us at the restaurant. I didn't know she was married then. If I had known that I wouldn't have gone with her then. I don't make it a habit of going out with married women."

"I still care for her," David said with little expression.

"She told me that you've been going out."

"I have, but only to get back at her."

"I can honestly tell you that there's nothing between Debra and myself."

"Then why does she keep bringing up your name?"

"I don't know," Brandon said, lifting his shoulders. "Perhaps to make you jealous."

"Why should I be jealous of you?"

"You have no reason to be jealous," Brandon said, wanting to end the conversation. "That's just something that popped into my head."

"Well, I just wanted to make sure," David said, rising from the couch. "I didn't want to do something stupid if I was wrong about something."

"Listen, why don't you just let her do what she wants to do?"

"It's none of your damn business," David said as he reached the door. "I would advise you to bug out."

David opened the door and slammed it on the way out. Brandon fell back in his recliner with a perplexed look on his face.

Brandon thought back to the last time he saw Debra at Hastings. She was half-lit and flirty but he didn't do anything to give her any ideas that he was interested in her. And what right did David have to come into his apartment and tell him what to do? Brandon got up from the recliner and went over and locked the front door. He didn't want to take any chances of David returning.

Picking up *Ulysses,* he read thirty pages before his eyes tired. He went to bed and slept soundly until awakened by a phone call at five-thirty. He answered on the third ring.

"Brandon here," he said groggily.

"This is Debra. Did I wake you up?"

"Yeah."

"Can you talk for a minute?"

"Sure." He wiped his eyes.

"I understand that David visited you last night. I want to apologize for his behavior."

"That's okay."

"What did he tell you?"

"He thought there was something between us."

Debra giggled.

"He thinks that way with every man. Didn't I tell you that?"

"Yeah."

"Don't you worry about him. His bark is bigger than his bite."

"I'll try to remember that," Brandon said, followed by a yawn.

"Are you afraid to see me again?"

"No."

"You don't feel like talking?"

"Not at this time of the morning."

"Oh, I'm sorry," she said. "I get up around five each morning and exercise. I figured you did, too."

"Sometimes but not to exercise."

"Well, I can see you don't want to talk," she said. "I'll see you later."

"Okay."

"You have a nice day," she said, cheerfully.

"You, too."

After the phone clicked, Brandon rolled over in the bed and lay for fifteen minutes before deciding to get up. He put on a pot of coffee, took a hot shower and dressed. He fixed two pieces of toast and butter for breakfast and read the newspaper while eating. Bored after spending about ten minutes flipping through the sections, he headed off to work.

Maggie was already in the office when Brandon walked through the front door. She

sipped on coffee while talking on the phone. It was probably a girlfriend since she was laughing and seemed almost oblivious to Brandon walking past her to his office. She quickly handed him a note while continuing her phone conversation. It was a message from Buck Odoms, the sportswriter at the Lexington newspaper, wanting him to call. After pouring a cup of coffee in the break room, Brandon went to his office and called him.

"What are you doing at the office so early?" Brandon asked. "You're usually a late person."

"I'm working on a feature for Sunday's paper," Buck said. "I had to make a few calls here this morning before I can could finish it."

"So what do you want from me?"

"Do you know Debra Hatfield?"

Brandon hesitated a moment. "Yeah. Why?"

"I met her the other night at Hastings," he said. "She's one sexy lady. She mentioned that she knew you."

Brandon could only imagine what she had said, but decided against asking Buck.

"Yes, I've talked to her a few times at Hastings," Brandon said. "A nice woman."

"What can you tell me about her?"

"Not much," Brandon said. "She's a real-estate agent. She's also going through a divorce. I don't know much else."

"She never mentioned the divorce to me."

"She's married to a policeman. I think it's her second or third marriage."

"Really?" Buck said. "Wow."

"That's about all I know," Brandon said.

"She gave me her card and I was thinking about asking her out."

"I think I'd wait."

"Why?"

"Her husband is kinda jealous."

"That doesn't worry me."

"Take my advice and wait until the divorce is final."

"Okay, I'll think about it," Buck said. "Thanks for the info."

"Any time."

"Are you going to the game this weekend?"

"I'll be there."

"Well, I need to make a few calls so I'd better get back to work. Thanks for getting back with me."

"Just be careful."

"I will."

Brandon put down the receiver. He began to worry if he should have told Buck about David Hatfield's visit to his apartment. He decided he'd wait and tell him at the game.

Twenty-three

"I won't be able to go out this weekend," Clarice said during lunch. "I have to go to Nashville for a meeting. I'm sorry."

Brandon couldn't hide the disappointment. He had been looking forward to a quiet, relaxing evening with her.

"Those things happen," he said with a shrug. "Perhaps the next weekend?"

"I'll have to check my calendar," she said, "but right now I don't think I have anything coming up."

They each took a sip of their ice water. They had both ordered salads and were waiting for the waitress to return with their food.

"Hi Clarice," a man said as he walked past their table.

"Hello George," she said with a smile.

"Who's that?" Brandon asked after the man was out of earshot.

"One of our clients," Clarice said. "He's with the electric company."

A few seconds later, another man smiled and said "hi" to her. Brandon gave her a quizzical look.

"That was Phillip Brasher," she said. "He's with the chamber of commerce."

"Oh," Brandon said.

During the next five minutes, four more men spoke to her. Clarice got tickled watching Brandon's expression after each greeting, especially after she told him she had dated one of the guys.

"Do you know everyone in this town?" he asked, arching an eyebrow.

"Only the movers and shakers," she teased. "That's part of my job."

"Then how did I ever fit in?" Brandon said while cutting up his salad.

"I make exceptions now and then," she said with a playful wink.

Brandon looked at her with a boyish grin, shook his head and took a bite of his salad.

"Do you enjoy meeting all these people?" he asked.

"Is this off the record?"

"Of course."

"I like some of the people but quite a few are horse's asses," she said, quietly. "Some are so full of themselves while others are really caring individuals."

"I see the same thing in my work," Brandon said. "Some of the coaches seem to think that they've been blessed by God to impart their knowledge on the rest of us poor souls. And occasionally, you run across nineteen-year-olds who think they know the meaning of life."

"I sensed some of that at the news conference we put on several months ago," Clarice said. "The coaches were full of it. Even some of the university administrators."

"They're everywhere," Brandon said.

"Even in the media?" Clarice asked with a grin.

"Believe it or not, even in the media," Brandon said with a chuckle. "And I bet you could find a few in PR."

"Oh, my goodness, do you really think so?" Clarice said, rolling her eyes.

They both laughed before drinking some more water.

"Do you think I can see you again before you go out of town?" Brandon asked.

"My schedule is really full," she said with a frown. "I'm sorry."

"I guess I need to schedule things way in advance with you," he said. "Maybe you should consider me a client."

"Now that's not fair," she said.

"I'm only kidding." He gently patted her hand.

"My work goes in cycles. I will go weeks where I'm working twelve hours a day on certain projects, and then there will be weeks where things will be relatively light. This is just a busy time for me."

"I understand," Brandon said with a warm smile. "It's the same with me at times."

Brandon picked up the restaurant bill, despite Clarice's protest, and paid the cashier. He pecked her on the cheek as they left the restaurant and they returned to their offices.

Brandon hated to admit it but he was beginning to fall for Clarice. Fall hard. He wasn't sure if it was love but it was a feeling he hadn't felt in a long time. Certainly not with Jenny. He enjoyed Clarice's company and wanted to spend more time with her. He wondered if she felt the same about him. He wasn't one of the town's movers and shakers, but he was recognizable, at least in sports circles. He didn't make the big bucks although he lived comfortably and had made some good investment choices in the past ten years.

"What are you so glum about?" Maggie asked as he removed his coat and put it on a hanger.

"Oh, nothing," he said. "Nothing's the matter."

"You look like you're depressed about something."

"Nah," he said. "I was just thinking about something. No big deal."

"Then smile."

Brandon forced a big smile and moved his head from side to side.

"Now let's not overdo it," Maggie said.

"Any messages?"

"You've got a couple here," she said while handing them to him.

"Where's Graham?"

"I think he had lunch with Sheila," Maggie said almost in a whisper. "He's been gone for nearly two hours."

"That's good," Brandon said, taking steps toward his office. "Why don't you go to lunch? I'll watch the phones."

"Oh, that's nice," she said. "I need to run a few errands."

"Go ahead. Take your time."

Maggie got up behind her desk and put on her coat.

"I'll be back in about an hour," she said as she buttoned up the coat and headed out the front door.

Brandon sat down at her desk and returned the phone calls from his messages. He called Odoms at the newspaper, wanting to tell him about David Hatfield, but he wasn't expected in the office until later. He asked for his home phone number but the news clerk wouldn't give it to him. Brandon raised his voice and tried to emphasize that he and Odoms were friends but realized that the clerk was only following company policy.

Graham came in looking haggard. He hung up his coat and turned around and looked at Brandon with dark misty eyes. He shook his head slowly after glancing at Brandon.

"She wants a divorce," Graham said without emotion. He sat down next to Brandon and ran his hands through his hair.

"A divorce?"

"I can't believe it either. We've been married for eighteen years and I've known her for more than twenty."

"Did she say why she wanted one?" Brandon asked.

"She said she was tired and bored with our marriage."

"Anything else?"

"Not really. She talked in circles."

"Did you mention counseling."

"Hell, I mentioned everything to her," Graham said, his gray eyes welling with tears. "I don't want a divorce. I don't know what in the hell has gotten into her. This makes no sense whatsoever."

"I don't know what to say," Brandon said.

"I don't either. I can't figure her out."

"Did she say anything in particular?"

"Not really," Graham said, sitting straight up in the chair. "She said she loves me but that she's not in love with me anymore. Does that make any damn sense? She loves me but doesn't love me."

"Has she said anything to Bernie?"

"She plans to stop over at the house this evening. We'll both sit down and tell him. That's her idea."

"How's he going to take it?"

"Who knows?"

"Does she want custody?"

"Would you believe that she doesn't?" Graham said, rolling his eyes. "What mother doesn't want custody of her only child? It doesn't make sense. None of this makes any damn sense whatsoever."

"Anything else?"

"Oh, I almost forgot," Graham said. "She wants to find herself. Can you believe that? She wants to have time to find herself. Now isn't that nice. I'd like to have time to find myself but I'm too god damn busy working and trying to give my family a good life."

"Perhaps she just needs a little time to think through all of this."

"Then why does she want a divorce?"

"I hate to ask this, but is there another man?"

"She said there isn't so I guess I have to believe her. She's never given me any indication that there was someone else."

"If there's anything I can do, just let me know," Brandon said. Less than a minute later, Maggie returned to the office.

"What's up, guys?" she asked with a bright smile.

"Just guy talk," Graham said, smiling with pursed lips. He got up from his seat and started walking to his office. "I need to get back to work."

"Me, too," Brandon said as he got up from Maggie's chair. "Did you take care of everything you needed to?"

"Yes," she said. "Thanks for watching the phones."

"It was quiet the entire time you were gone. Not a single phone call."

"That's the way it usually is," she said with a chuckle. "If I had stayed here the phone would have been ringing off the hook."

Brandon ambled to his office and worked on his column for the upcoming issue. It took him the remainder of the afternoon to complete it. He was the last person to leave the office and had to lock up the building.

The sky was dark and overcast as he walked to his car. A cool breeze caused him to pull his coat collar up around his neck. While fidgeting with his keys to unlock his car, a person came up behind him and pushed a sharp object into his lower back.

"Don't turn around or I'll blow your stupid head off." Brandon guessed that it was a young male because the voice had a forced gruffness.

"No problem," Brandon said, slightly holding his hands up.

"Put your goddamn hands down."

Brandon quickly dropped his hands to his side.

"What do you want?"

"Shut up and give me your wallet. And do it slowly."

Brandon reached back and removed his wallet. He held it to where his assailant could see it.

The man quickly snatched it from his hand. Brandon could hear him go through it and pull out the cash.

"Only forty-two dollars!" the man said. "You've got to be kidding!"

"I don't carry much cash."

"Didn't I tell you to shut up?"

Brandon stood quietly. The only sounds were the breeze through the trees and cars in the distance going by. A moment later, Brandon felt a hard blow against the back of his head and he fell to the pavement. The man kicked him a few times in the stomach, threw the wallet at him, and took off running around the back of the building.

Brandon rose slightly, then collapsed unconscious on the cold pavement.

Twenty-four

Flashing red lights were a blur as Brandon lay on the pavement. There was movement around him and muffled sounds. He was lifted up and placed on a stretcher. Several minutes later, a siren blared as he was being whisked to University Hospital. Brandon was in a haze as if in a dreamlike state.

It felt surreal as he was wheeled into the emergency under the bright white lights. He was taken to an X-ray room and brought back to the tiny curtained-off space. A doctor came in holding several X-rays.

"You've got a sizable concussion," the doctor said, looking at the X-rays rather than at Brandon. "You got banged on the head pretty hard."

"Really?" Brandon said groggily.

"We're going to keep you overnight for observation but I think you're going to be all right. You'll probably have a headache for several days."

"Thanks," Brandon said, closing his eyes under the glare of the lights.

An orderly came in and pushed the stretcher to a semi-private room on the fourth floor. The room's occupant was watching a game show on television with the volume turned up loud. Brandon tried to ignore it but it was beginning to make him dizzy. A nurse came in and pulled the curtains around him. She helped him remove his clothes and put on a gown.

"I'll be back in a few minutes with your medication," she said. "Is there anything else you need?"

"Could you turn down that television?" Brandon asked softly. "It's making me sick in my stomach."

"It is rather loud. We could even hear it at the nurse's station."

A moment later, the TV's sound was noticeably lower. Brandon lay on the bed, his head throbbing, eyes closed. He wanted to go to sleep but the pain was too great. The nurse returned with several pills and a glass of water.

"This should make you feel better," she said.

"Will it help me sleep?" Brandon asked after swallowing the medicine.

"No," she said. "You don't need to be going to sleep right away after getting that blow to your head. We'll be keeping you up until the swelling goes down. You're not quite out of the woods yet."

"Just what I wanted to hear," Brandon said sarcastically.

"It won't be so bad in the morning," she said with a kind smile.

Throughout the night, every two hours, the nurse returned and checked his vital signs. The pain subsided in his head to a dull throb. His eyes were heavy when sunshine began filtering through the blinds in the morning.

"Oh, Brandon. Are you all right?"

Brandon opened his eyes slowly. He thought he recognized the voice but wasn't sure. When his eyes focused on the person, it was Jenny standing next to his bed with tears in her eyes.

"Hi," he said with a sleepy half-smile.

"I heard that you were attacked in the parking lot last night," she said, taking hold of his left hand. "How are you feeling?"

"Not so hot."

"Oh, honey, you must be feeling awful," she said as she softly touched the heavy bandage behind his head.

"I'll be okay," he said. "They just kept me here for observation."

"Has the doctor been in this morning?"

"No. I don't believe so."

A member of the kitchen staff brought in breakfast of eggs, bacon, toast, coffee and orange juice on a cart. Brandon gazed down at it and turned his head.

"Do you want this?" he asked Jenny.

"No thanks," she said. "I'm not hungry. But you should eat something."

Brandon picked up the toast and took one small bite and put it back down. He reached for the coffee but had difficulty holding it. Jenny helped him put it to his mouth and then back on the tray.

"Thanks," he said.

"So this happened in the parking lot after work?" Jenny asked.

"Yes."

"How many people attacked you?"

"Only one, I think. I don't remember much."

A doctor came in and removed the bandage as Jenny stepped back toward the window. Brandon winced as the doctor moved his head to the side.

"I'm Dr. Berry," he said. "How do you feel?"

"Better than last night."

"I can keep you here another day or release you. It's up to you."

"I think I'd rather go home. I don't think I can get any sleep here."

"Well, you didn't need to sleep last night. The swelling is down. You're bruised but there are no indications of a subdural hematoma. I think you're just going to have a headache for several days. It could even be a week or so. I'll prescribe some medicine for you."

"Thanks, doc," Brandon said with a wry smile.

Dr. Berry patted him on the knee and left. Brandon took another sip of the coffee, but it had already turned cold. He looked up and two men were standing at the foot of his bed.

"Mr. Wilkes?" a black man in a gray suit said.

"Yes."

"I'm Detective Miller and this is Detective Bright," he said, nodding toward the chubby white man standing a few feet from him. "Could we ask you a few questions?"

"Go ahead," Brandon said.

The detectives went over from what Brandon did the moment he left the office to when the ambulance arrived. Brandon wasn't able to tell them much. He didn't see anything suspicious when he left the building, he didn't recognize the attacker, and didn't see any accomplices.

"Oh, by the way, here's your billfold," Miller said. "It appears that the only thing taken was money. Do you recall how much you were carrying on you?"

"I think around forty dollars," Brandon said.

"Well, you're lucky it wasn't anything worse than a headache," Bright said.

"I don't feel lucky," Brandon said, gently touching his head.

"He could have killed you," Miller said, matter-of-factly.

Brandon nodded.

"We may be getting in touch with you if we find anything or have other questions," Miller said. "Will you be at home?"

"I'll be there or at work."

The men nodded their heads and left. Jenny moved up next to his bed.

"This is really scary," she said, taking his hand again. "That man could have killed you."

"I guess my head was too hard," Brandon said, making a half-hearted joke.

"It's not funny," she said. "You could have been hurt very seriously."

"I think I was."

An elderly nurse came into the room and pushed back his tray. She took his vital signs again.

"I understand you'll be leaving us today," she said.

"That's what the doctor said."

"Do you need any help getting dressed or will you help him?" the nurse said, glancing at Jenny.

Before Brandon could open his mouth, Jenny quickly smiled and answered, "I'll help him."

The nurse pulled the curtains and left.

"I guess your clothes are in the closet," Jenny said. "I'll be right back."

Brandon slowly eased up and swung his legs over the side of the bed by the time Jenny came back with his clothes. She laid them down on the bed and took his hand while he stepped to the floor. She reached up and unsnapped his gown and it nearly fell to the floor before he realized he wasn't wearing any underwear.

"I think I can handle this," he said, wrapping the gown around his waist.

"Are you sure?" Jenny asked with a sly smile.

"Well, I think I can handle my underwear and pants," he said, slightly shaking his head.

"Let me know when you get them on and I'll help you with the rest of your clothes," Jenny said while stepping outside the curtain. "I don't know why you're being so modest. It's not like I haven't seen you before."

Brandon let the comment go by as he eased on his boxer shorts and then his khaki slacks. "You can come back in now," he said.

Jenny helped him put on his denim shirt and tuck it in his pants. He sat down while she kneeled down and slipped socks over his feet. He put on his loafers and stood up slowly.

"Thanks," he said.

An orderly came in with a wheelchair and took Brandon to the discharge area. Jenny went to the parking garage and got her car. She drove it to the back entrance, where they were waiting for her inside the glass door. Brandon walked slowly to the car.

Although he lived only fifteen minutes from the hospital, it seemed like it took her an hour to get him to his apartment. He got queasy in the stomach and dizzy in the head as she seemed to hit every stop light and drive over every bump. He felt like he was about to throw-up when she finally pulled into his parking lot.

Jenny came around and opened the passenger door, and put her arm around his waist to steady him as they walked to his apartment. He handed her the key to unlock the front door, and when they were inside, she guided him to the recliner. He sat back slowly and closed his eyes.

"What time is it?" he asked softly.

"It's about ten-thirty," she said.

"Don't you need to go to work?"

"I called in and told them that I wouldn't be in today."

"You didn't need to do that."

"Oh, yes I did," she said smiling softly and patting him gently on the shoulder. "Is there something I can get for you?"

"They gave me a prescription after you went to get the car at the hospital," he said while taking the piece of paper out of his shirt pocket. "Do you think you could take care of it for me?"

"No problem," she said. "Anything else?"

"Would you call Graham and tell him what happened?"

"I'll be happy to do that."

Jenny grabbed her purse and walked to the front door.

"I'll be back in a jiffy," she said. "I'll call Graham on my way to the drugstore. Now don't you try to do anything."

"I won't," Brandon said wearily. "Don't worry about that."

The phone rang while Jenny was away but Brandon didn't answer it although he cringed as it felt like every ring was clanking inside his head. It finally stopped after six rings.

Jenny returned in forty-five minutes with his prescription. She went to the kitchen and got a glass of water and handed it to him with a pill.

"You need to take one of these every four hours for pain," she said as he swallowed the medicine.

Brandon tried to slip off his shoes but with no success. Jenny bent down and removed them.

"Do you want to get out of these clothes?" she asked.

"I'm all right," he said. "I just want to sit here."

"Can I fix you something to eat?"

"I'm okay," he said. "I don't feel like eating anything."

Jenny sat down on the edge of the couch. She looked over and saw the light on the answering machine blinking.

"You have some messages," she said while getting up from the couch.

Before Brandon could say anything, she clicked the replay button.

"Good evening, Brandon," the woman's voice cooed. I was just thinking about you and thought I'd give you a call. I guess you had to work late. I hope you have a pleasant evening. Bye."

"Who was that?" Jenny asked.

"Just a friend," Brandon said, keeping his eyes closed and trying to keep a straight face. But the sound of Clarice's voice made him feel warm inside and momentarily made him forget about his headache. And Jenny.

Twenty-five

Graham arrived at Brandon's apartment in the middle of the afternoon. Brandon had persuaded Jenny to leave after he showed up but she told him that she'd return later in the afternoon with something for him to eat. Brandon couldn't talk her out of it.

"How're you feeling?" Graham asked "You don't look so hot."

"I still have a headache," Brandon said with a tired look. "The doctor said I'd have it for a few days."

"Don't worry about coming into work. Just stay here and get well."

"Thanks," Brandon said. "I don't plan to move from here for a while."

"I see that you've got some help."

"Yeah. Jenny showed up at the hospital this morning. She's been a big help."

"Is there anything I can do?" Graham asked.

"I think everything is okay. Thanks anyway."

"I'd better be going and let you get some rest," Graham said, getting up from the couch."

"Thanks for dropping by."

After Graham left, Brandon slowly eased out of the recliner and went to his bedroom. He pulled back the covers and lay down with his head squarely in the middle of the oversized pillow. He closed his eyes. When he opened them again, it was dark in the room. He glanced over at the clock and it was seven thirty-three. He heard the TV in the living room. He rubbed his eyes, then got out of bed and walked slowly to the doorway. Jenny was sitting in his recliner, drinking a Pepsi and watching a game show.

"Oh, hi Brandon," she said glancing up at him. "You finally wake up?"

"Yeah," he said while making his way to the couch.

"You were sleeping like a baby so I decided to let you sleep," Jenny said. "I hope you're feeling better."

"I do," he said, wincing from the chatter on the TV show. "Could you turn that down a little bit?"

Jenny picked up the remote and lowered the volume slightly.

"How's that?" she asked.

"More, please."

She gave him a flustered look before turning down the sound.

"Is it okay now?"

"Yeah, that's better. Thank you."

"Can I fix you something to eat?" she said, a smile returning to her face.

"I'm really not hungry."

"I've got some pizza over there on the counter. I could stick a piece in the microwave for you."

"Perhaps after while," he said, leaning his head on the back of the couch.

Jenny turned her attention back to the game show, increasing the volume again. Brandon didn't say anything. From experience, he knew she was going to do what she wanted to do and there was no use in trying to get her to do things any differently. And with his head still with a numbing throb, he didn't want to get her all riled up.

After the game show ended she turned the sound down and looked at him.

"You got a couple of phone calls while you were asleep," she said.

"Who was it?"

"Maggie wanted to see how you were feeling," Jenny said. "She's a real nice lady even though she dresses kind of trashy."

Brandon looked at Jenny with pursed lips and decided to let the remark go by.

"Anyone else?

"There was a woman named Clara, Carla or something like that?"

"Clarice?"

"Yes, that's it," Jenny said, her eyes lighting up a little. "Who is she?"

"A friend of mine."

"I've never heard of her."

"I'm sure I've never heard of some of your friends."

"She wanted to bring something over but I told her not to bother," Jenny said. "I told her that I have everything under control."

"Thanks," Brandon said, raising his right eyebrow.

"Anytime," she said with a curt smile.

"Why don't you go on home?" Brandon asked with a forced smile. "I think I'm going to be all right."

"I was thinking about spending the night," she said. "I don't want to leave you alone."

"No, no, you don't need to do that."

"But I already asked for a personal day off."

"Why don't you use it for something else?"

"Don't you want me to care for you?" she asked, pushing out her lower lip.

"I didn't say that. I just meant that I'm feeling much better and there's no use in you wasting a day on my account."

"I don't mind," Jenny said. She got up from the recliner and sat down on the couch next to him and patted him on the knee. "I never feel like I'm wasting anything when I'm with you."

"I think I would like that slice of pizza," Brandon said, trying to inch away from her.

Jenny put her arms around him and squeezed, then kissed him on the cheek.

"Okay, darling," she said. "How many pieces?"

"One will be fine," he said. "What kind is it?"

"Sausage and pepperoni."

"You know I don't eat meat."

"I forgot," she said. "I'll pick off the meat. How about that?"

"Okay," he said.

Jenny went back to the kitchen and took a slice out of the box. She meticulously removed all the meat and placed the slice in the microwave.

"Do you want anything to drink?" she asked.

"Ice water will be fine."

"Okay, darling."

Brandon winced slightly when she called him darling. He didn't want to get anything started back up with her. She returned with the pizza on a paper plate and a small glass of water with no ice.

"Thanks," he said before taking a bite from the pizza. "This tastes good."

Jenny stood next to him and stared at him as if she were in a trance.

"Is everything okay?" Brandon asked after a few seconds.

"Just fine," she said. "I just love to watch a man eat."

Brandon looked off for a second, and then took another bite. He wasn't going to comment on that remark.

"So why don't you go on home?" he asked with a smile.

"Are you sure you'll be all right?"

"I'm positive. You've been a big help."

"I'll stop by in the morning for breakfast."

"You don't need to do that."

"Oh, but I want to," she said. "I'll stop by McDonald's and pick us up something."

"Okay," Brandon said.

Jenny walked to the kitchen and picked up her coat that was draped over the back of a chair. She put it on and began buttoning it as she stood next to Brandon.

"And you're sure that you're going to be all right?"

"Yes," Brandon said, a bit impatiently. "I'll be all right."

"Okay, darling," She bent over and kissed him on the cheek. "I'll see you in the morning."

"Bye," Brandon said.

"See ya," she said chirpily, squinting her nose in a smile before walking out the door.

Brandon took a sip of the lukewarm water and shook his head. He got up from the couch and slowly padded back to the kitchen and fixed a large glass of ice water. He tossed the leftover pizza into the trash can under the sink, then walked to his bedroom and called Clarice. She answered on the third ring.

"Remember me?" Brandon asked.

"Oh, Brandon, how are you?" she asked with concern in her voice. "I've been worried sick."

"I'm better."

"I wanted to come over but that woman at your house told me not to."

"I've slept for most of the day."

"Who is she?"

"Who?

"The woman who answered the phone when I called earlier."

"Oh, that was Jenny. She's a friend of mine."

"She was awfully protective and not very friendly. Is she more than a friend?"

"Just a friend," Brandon said. "I swear."

"How about in the past?"

"She used to be more than a friend in the past. Can we talk about this later? I've still got a headache." Brandon was surprised by Clarice's touch of jealousy.

"I'm sorry," she said apologetically. "I didn't mean anything by it."

"That's okay. I understand."

"When are you going back to work?"

"Probably not for a day or two."

"Can I come by and see you before I leave town?"

"I'd love that," he said as smile eased across his face.

"How about after work tomorrow?"

Brandon paused for a second. He knew he had to make sure that Jenny wouldn't be around the apartment.

"I think that will be okay," he said. "Could you call first?"

"That's no problem," she said. "Can I bring some food along?"

"If it's no trouble. That would be nice."

"Chinese?"

"Sure," he said. "I love Chinese."

"I've kept you on the phone too long," she said. "I know you must be tired. I'll talk to you tomorrow."

"Thanks for calling," Brandon said, and then remembered he had placed the call to her.

"I hope you sleep well tonight," she said sweetly. "Good night."

"Good night," he said, and then put down the receiver. That warm feeling filled his chest again and he couldn't resist smiling. He definitely hadn't felt this way about someone in a long time.

~ * ~

Clarice smiled as she put down her receiver. She went to her den, poured a glass of red wine and sat down on the sofa with her legs curled under her. Picking up the current issue of *Cosmopolitan*, she slowly turned the pages. The phone rang and she hurried back to the living room to answer it.

"Hello," she said.

"Hi, Clarice."

"Hi Bart. How are you?"

"Doing just great," Bart Taylor said. "I haven't heard from you in a long time."

"I've been busy with work."

"You're always busy with work," he said. "You need to slow down."

"You're probably right," she said with a laugh.

"So what are you doing this weekend?"

"I'm going out of town on business."

"Always work and no play."

"It seems that way."

"How about dinner when you get back?"

Clarice hesitated.

"Anything the matter?" he asked.

"No," she said. "I was just trying to think ahead."

"It's been awhile since we've been out," he said. "I'd sure like to see you."

"Can I get back with you after I check my appointment book?"

"I'm surprised you don't have it with you," he said. "I've never seen you without out it."

"I left it at work," she said with a nervous laugh.

"Well, I'll call you tomorrow and we can set up a date."

"Okay," she said.

After putting down the receiver, Clarice walked back into the den and opened her oversized purse. She pulled all her appointment book and sighed.

Twenty-six

Graham was standing in front of Maggie's desk, picking up some messages from her when Brandon came in the front door.

"What are you doing here this morning?" Graham asked, surprised. "You need your rest."

"I'm fine," Brandon said. "I can't sit around home all day. That's driving me nuts."

"I understand but there's no reason for you to push things."

"If I get tired or whatever, I'll go back home. Any messages for me, Maggie?"

"The police called yesterday," she said. "And Buck Odoms called. He didn't leave a message."

"Thanks," Brandon said. "Is coffee on in the back?"

"It should be ready," Maggie said. "Do you want me to get you a cup?"

"Thanks, but I can do it."

Graham walked with Brandon to the break room.

"How's everything with you?" Brandon asked as Graham poured coffee into their cups.

"About the same," he said. "I assume you're asking about the home front."

"Yes," he said. "How is Bernie handling it?"

"He seems to be doing okay with it," Graham said. "I think he must be in some sort of denial."

"Sometimes kids pick up on things that parents don't see," Brandon said before taking a sip of coffee.

"Could be."

"Anything going on here?"

"I assigned Pete to cover the ball game this weekend. I didn't think you'd be up for it. I hope you don't mind. I can always take him off if you plan to go."

"That's okay," Brandon said. "Go ahead and let Pete cover it. He's wanted to do it for quite some time. If I decide to go, I can call the sports information office and get a credential."

"It's your call," Graham said as they left the break room and to their offices. "I'll see you later."

Brandon sifted through numerous e-mails that had accumulated while he was away from work. Maggie peeped in the door and told him he had a phone call.

"This is Brandon," he said into the receiver.

"You sound a lot better today," Jenny cooed. "Did you sleep well last night?"

"I did," he said. "Thanks for all your help the past couple of days."

"It was no problem. I'd do anything for you."

"Are you back at work, too?"

"Yes," she said. "I wish I could take a few more days off."

"You should," Brandon said. "Perhaps take a short trip somewhere. We all need breaks once in awhile."

"Only if you'd go with me," she said.

"Oh, I've got too much work to do around here," he said, leaning back in his chair.

"But wouldn't it be nice for the two of us to take off to some place for a long weekend?" she asked. "A deserted beach somewhere?"

Brandon wondered how in the world Jenny could think there was still something between them. He appreciated her help the past few days but didn't want it to lead to anything else. And he didn't want to hurt her feelings again.

"Weekend trips can be relaxing," he said. "So what are you doing today?"

"I've got some paperwork to catch up on," she said. "I need to go now. I've got a call on the other line."

Brandon breathed a sigh of relief.

After putting down the receiver, Maggie was at the door with a concerned look on her face.

"Detective Miller is here to see you," she said.

"Tell him to come on back," Brandon said. He quickly arranged papers in stacks on his desk to make it look more orderly.

"Good morning, Mr. Wilkes," Miller said, extending his arm and shaking hands with Brandon. They both sat down.

"Good morning."

"We're still investigating the attack on you," Miller said. "But I must be honest and tell you that we don't have much. There wasn't any physical evidence left at the scene that we can find. I was wondering if you could tell me anything else."

"I don't know if I can be of much help. All I remember is going out to my car after work. I was the last person to leave the office that night. I was about to unlock the door when someone came up behind me and asked for my wallet. I felt a gun in my back. I handed my wallet to him and then he hit me on the head."

"You never noticed anyone while leaving the building?"

"No," Brandon said. "This is a fairly safe area. I just walked out to my car like I've done a thousand times. The last thing I expected was to be assaulted."

"Does anyone have a grudge against you?"

"I'm sure there are some people who do. That goes with the territory of being a columnist. You're going to write things that some people don't like."

"But anyone on the personal level?" Miller asked.

Brandon thought about David Hatfield and the encounter he had with him at the restaurant. He decided not to bring it up because he was sure the attacker wasn't David.

"I really can't think of anyone," Brandon said. "I try to keep as much of a low profile as I can."

"Well, if you think of anyone, give me a call," Miller said. "I'll keep you posted if we come up with any leads."

"I appreciate all you've done. I really believe it was some punk and I ended up being the unfortunate victim."

"You may be right, but you never know about these things," Miller said while getting up from his chair. "What I can't understand is why he didn't take your money or credit cards."

"Beats me."

Brandon walked him to the front door, then stopped at Maggie's desk on the way back to his office. She handed him a note from Clarice. He walked to his office, closed the door and dialed her number.

"I just wanted to see how you're doing," she said. "I called your house and got the answering machine. I was surprised you went to work today."

"I couldn't sit around the house all day," Brandon said with a laugh. "I'd go nuts."

"How do you feel?"

"I've got a dull headache but it's not as bad as it was yesterday. It feels more like a hangover now. I take a couple of Tylenols every four hours so it's not bad. I think I'll live."

"That's good to hear," she said.

"Are you still going out of town this weekend?"

"Yes, I leave in the morning," she said. "I should be back late Sunday."

"Can we get dinner tonight?" Brandon asked.

"I'd love to but I've got stay at work tonight and go over the presentation I have to give in Nashville," she said. "We leave at six-thirty in the morning."

"I'm going to miss you," Brandon said.

"I'll miss you, too," she said sweetly. "I'll only be away for three days."

"That's three long days for me," he said.

"I need to be going," she said.

"I know," Brandon said. "You've got a meeting."

Clarice laughed. "That wasn't a difficult guess," she said. "I'll try to call you later tonight."

"Okay," Brandon said. "Have a good day."

Brandon put down the receiver and felt his heart sink a little. Talking to her made him yearn to see her even more. He was hoping they could meet before she went on her business trip. He didn't look forward to three more days without seeing her.

Brandon called Buck and they decided to meet at Hastings after work. He waited at the bar for ten minutes, chatting with Benny before Buck showed up. The music on the jukebox didn't help his headache. The bar was slowly beginning to fill up with the regular patrons, and Rosie already looked harried.

Buck came in and sat next to Brandon. Several patrons greeted Buck, recognizing him because of his thrice-weekly newspaper column. He was wearing his trademark jeans, white shirt and herringbone sports coat. Benny brought him over a bottle of Heineken.

"So what's up?" Brandon asked.

"You mean what's up with you," Buck said, wrapping his thin, long legs around the back of the stool. "I heard about you getting thumped on the head."

"I'm all right. I think it was just some punk needing some cash for drugs or whatever."

"That's happening all the time. We've had several people at the paper accosted on the way to the parking lot at night. You've really got to be careful."

"That's right," Brandon said.

"I met Debra Hatfield again the other night," Buck said, his eyes lighting up. "She's one sexy number. I was going to ask her out this weekend."

"That's your choice but I wouldn't advise it. Her soon-to-be ex is the jealous type."

"But she was really coming on strong to me," Buck said while pulling on one end of his scraggily mustache.

"You do what you want but I'd wait until she's divorced."

"I'll give that some thought. Are you seeing anyone?"

"I'm trying to but our schedules have been too hectic."

"Who is it?"

"Clarice Horton," Brandon said. "She works over at the Franklin Agency."

"I know her," Buck said.

"You do? Where?"

"A friend of mine dated her a few months ago," Buck said. "She's a nice woman. She was much too good for him."

"Who was it?" Brandon asked, arching his eyebrows.

"Bart Taylor," Buck said. "He's in the horse business."

"I think I've heard the name."

"He comes from some horse money," Buck said. "A good-looking guy. The women just fall at his feet. Well, all of them except for Clarice."

Brandon smiled faintly.

"Were they serious?" Brandon asked.

"I really don't know. I don't see Bart that often. I'm sure he's moved on to some other women. That guy scores more than anyone I've seen."

Brandon wondered if Bart had slept with Clarice. Although it was before he knew her, there was still a pang of jealousy running through his body.

"I need to be going," Brandon said, finishing his beer. "I may see you at the game this weekend."

"It was good seeing you," Buck said. "Take care of that head of yours. I think I'll stay and have one more. Who knows, Debra may show up."

"Good luck," Brandon said. "And be careful."

Brandon drove home, his thoughts consumed about Clarice and Bart. He wished that Buck had never mentioned the guy's name. He was sure that Clarice had dated quite a few different guys since her divorce. She was a beautiful woman and what man wouldn't want to ask her out?

Twenty-seven

After Brandon arrived at his apartment, he took two Tylenols to help get rid of a dull headache. The smoke and noise at Hastings didn't help any and he knew he shouldn't have gone there so soon after the injury. He sat down in the recliner and flipped on the TV set to ESPN SportsCenter. His eyes were on the screen but he didn't pay any attention to what was being said or shown.

He snapped out of it by a banging on the door. At first, he wasn't sure where it was coming from until the pounding grew louder and louder. Then he heard Jenny squeal from the other side. He eased up from the recliner and headed toward the door. Slowly.

"I'm coming, I'm coming," Brandon said, raising his voice. "Hold your horses."

He opened the door and there was Jenny with two large bags of groceries at her feet. She smiled brightly.

"Were you asleep?" she asked after he opened the door for her to step inside the living room. He picked up the groceries and she followed him to the kitchen.

"I was dozing in the recliner," he said. "I'm sorry."

"I was beginning to think you weren't home," she said. "I was about ready to take these groceries back home with me."

Brandon wished he had waited another thirty seconds before answering the door. Instead of peace and quiet, he had company and he wasn't in the mood for any. Especially Jenny.

"Do you like BLTs?" she asked.

"I like lettuce and tomato sandwiches," he said.

"Oops, forgot that you don't eat meat."

"That's okay, everybody seems to do that." He forced a smile.

Jenny took a skillet out from under the counter and put four strips of bacon on it and turned on the burner. She went over to the sink and washed the lettuce and peeled off the crispy leaves on a plate. Then she sliced a big tomato as Brandon stood to the side and watched.

"Do you have any beer?" she asked.

"I don't think so," Brandon said. "I keep forgetting to buy some. I think I have some Pepsi in the fridge."

Jenny took two glasses out of the cabinet and filled them with ice. She poured Pepsi to the top and set them on the table. She opened a bag of potato chips. The bacon was sizzling on the skillet.

"It'll be ready in a few minutes," she said. "How was your day?"

"It was okay," he said.

"Only okay? Did you do anything important?"

"I don't think so," he said with a laugh. "Detective Miller dropped by to see me this morning."

"Really?" Jenny said, turning around from the stove and looking at him. "What did he want?"

"He just asked some more questions."

"Anything in particular?"

"No, just general stuff."

"Do they have any suspects?"

"I don't believe so."

"Good."

"Good?" Brandon asked with furrowed eyebrows.

"I mean, if there were any suspects, then it would probably be someone you know," she said. "Since they don't have any suspects, then that probably means that it was some random act of violence and you won't see the guy again."

"I don't know if that makes any sense but I'm not going to argue with you," Brandon said with a chuckle.

Jenny removed the bacon from the skillet and put it on a plate. She put four pieces of bread in the toaster, and then took a jar of salad dressing from the refrigerator.

"This salad dressing looks old," she said, turning the bottle to see the expiration date. "Hmm, it's supposed to expire this month."

"It should be okay then," Brandon said.

"I think you've had this awhile," she said with a frown. "I don't know if it's safe."

"I'm sure it's fine. I used it the other day when I fixed a sandwich."

"Are you telling me the truth?" Jenny asked, raising her eyebrows.

"Don't I always?" Brandon said, grinning.

"I'm not sure."

The bread popped up from the toaster and she brought the slices and the loaf of bread to the table. They quietly fixed their sandwiches and poured some chips from a bag on their plates.

"This is good," Brandon said after taking a bite. "Thanks for going to all this trouble."

"It's not a bit of trouble," she said, flashing a smile. "I could do this all the time."

Brandon quickly took a swallow of Pepsi.

"So how was your day?" he asked.

"It wasn't bad," she said. "I took care of a few customer complaints and they turned out all right."

The telephone rang and Brandon got up to go answer it in the living room.

"This is Brandon," he said into the receiver.

"Hi," Clarice said. "I just wanted to call to see how you're doing."

"Oh hi," he said, sensing that Jenny was tuned in to every word. "I'm doing fine."

"I want you to know that I'll miss you while I'm gone,"

"Same here."

"Would you mind if I called while I'm away?"

"Sure."

"Do you have company?" Clarice asked.

"Yes."

"I guess this isn't a good time to call then." Her voice lost some of its warmth.

"No, that's okay," he said.

"I don't think so. I'll see you. Bye."

Brandon held the phone to his ear for a few seconds after she hung up.

"I want to thank you for calling," he said. "I'll be sure and take care of myself. Good bye." He put the phone down and smiled as he walked back to the kitchen.

"Who was that?" Jenny asked.

"A friend of mine."

"Well, who was it?" she asked with slight irritation in her voice.

"Uh, Ms. Horton," he said.

"Who in the hell is Ms. Horton?" Jenny said with a glare.

"She's a friend who works in PR," he said calmly. "You don't know her."

"Why didn't you just say so in the first place," Jenny said, then took a bit from her sandwich and looked away.

"Because I didn't feel like it was a big deal," Brandon said. "Can we change the subject?"

"That's fine with me."

"Did you bring any dessert?"

"No," she said with a hurt look. "I'll try to remember next time."

"That's okay," he said. "I didn't want any dessert anyway. I was just asking."

After they finished eating, Brandon offered to help her put the dishes in the dishwasher but she told him to go back to the living room. Brandon returned to the recliner. A few minutes later, Jenny sat down on the couch.

"Why don't you ever sit with me on the couch?" she asked softly while patting the cushion.

"I guess I'm just used to sitting in this recliner all the time," he said.

"Can't you do it now?" she cooed.

Brandon eased up in the recliner, and waited for a few seconds, before getting up and sitting on the couch about a foot from her. She eased over closer to him.

"You can put your arm around me if you want to," she said with a seductive smile.

"I would but when I raise my arm it creates pressure on the back of my head." He couldn't resist a smile for thinking the explanation up so quickly.

"Really?"

"Yes," he said. "It causes the back of my head to really hurt."

"Poor baby," Jenny said, moving over a little closer and kissing him on the cheek. "Does that make you feel better?"

"Yes," Brandon said with a smile.

Without warning, Jenny suddenly rose up and kissed him squarely on the mouth, forcing her tongue between his pursed lips. Brandon eased his mouth open as she continued to kiss him passionately. He kept his arms at his sides while she pressed herself closer to his body. Jenny finally released her mouth lock and Brandon let out a deep breathe.

"How does that make you feel?" she said, resting her head on shoulder.

"A bit out of breathe," he said in a raspy voice.

"We can go back to your bedroom," she said.

Brandon squirmed a little, and then cleared his throat.

"We'd better not," he said.

"How come?" Jenny said as the hurt look returned to her face.

"The medication."

"What do you mean?"

"It affects me in a certain way."

Jenny looked down at his lap.

"Oh, I'm sorry," she said. "Poor baby."

"That's okay," Brandon said, looking at her wistfully and proud of himself again for thinking of something so quickly. "The doctor said it would take a few days to wear off."

"I guess I'll just have to count the days then," Jenny said with a big smile.

"Yeah, just get back with me some other time," Brandon said, forcing a grin.

"I guess I should be going home," Jenny said. "You must be tired."

"I am. I've been going to bed really early the past few nights."

Jenny got up from the couch and picked up her purse off the coffee table. Brandon eased up slowly and walked her to the door.

"Thanks again for fixing supper," he said.

"Anytime," she said, and then kissed him softly on the cheek. "I want you to start feeling better."

A boyish grin crossed Brandon's face as he reached around and opened the door for her.

"I'll try to check on you tomorrow," she said while stepping out the door. "Bye."

"Good night," Brandon said, closing the door after he lost sight of her walking away.

Brandon looked up at the clock on the wall and saw that it was nine-thirty. He knew Clarice would be leaving early in the morning, which meant she would probably be going to bed early. After thinking about calling her for a few seconds, he picked up the receiver and dialed her number.

It rang four times before the answering machine clicked on.

"Hello Clarice," he said. "I guess you're probably in bed now. I just wanted to tell you that I'll miss you and I hope that you have a safe trip. I'll call you on Monday. Good night."

Clarice listened to the message while it was being recorded. When it was over, she picked up some papers she was reviewing and continued reading. Two hours later, after she finished packing her suitcase, she went to bed. She was up at four-thirty, showered and dressed, and at the airport at five forty-five.

Twenty-eight

Brandon sat alone in a booth at Shoney's while eating breakfast on Sunday morning. The restaurant was half-filled, mostly with elderly couples. In the next few hours, families would be showing up after church. He sipped on coffee.

He glanced up when he saw the hostess taking a woman to a table near him. When the woman sat down, and faced him, he saw that it was Sheila. She didn't notice Brandon. In a few moments, she went to the breakfast bar. Brandon watched as she sorted through the various items, finally returning with scrambled eggs, bacon, and pancakes. A waitress returned with a cup of coffee for her. As Sheila was about to take her first bite, she looked in Brandon's direction. He smiled. A slight blush came over her cheeks.

"Would you care to join me?" Brandon asked.

"That would be nice," she said, picking up her plate and coffee and carrying it over to his table. Brandon went to her table and retrieved her silverware and napkin while she settled in at his table. She was dressed casually in green slacks and light brown blouse.

"Thank you," she said as he handed her the silverware. Brandon scooted back in his seat and took another sip of coffee.

"So how have you been doing?" Brandon asked. "Long time, no see."

"I've been busy with work," she said. "That's about it."

"Graham tells me that Bernie is really doing well in soccer."

Sheila took a bite of her pancakes, and then took a swallow of water. She smiled at Brandon with pursed lips.

"I guess he is," she said. "To be honest, I haven't seen Bernie play in a couple of weeks."

"Oh, I'm sorry," Brandon said. "I figured you had."

"You know about Graham and me?" she asked. "Of course you do. That's a silly question."

"We don't have to talk about it," Brandon said.

"That's okay," she said. "It just feels a little uncomfortable."

"So what have you been up to lately?"

"Really, just work. I haven't had much time to do hardly anything. I guess Graham told you about my new position. It takes up a lot of time. I don't know why I accepted it because it wasn't that much of an increase in pay."

"That's the way those things usually work out," Brandon said. "But we all seem to get suckered in when that so-called opportunity knocks. Nice job titles but little remuneration with it."

They took a few more bites off their plates. The waitress returned and warmed their coffees as they sat in deafening silence in their small space for several moments.

"I still care about Graham," Sheila blurted out. "We just reached a crossroads in our marriage. I needed some space to think about what I want in my life."

"I know Graham cares about you very much. He doesn't understand what's happened. At least, that's the impression that I get."

"I don't know if you want to hear this or if you'll understand, being the confirmed bachelor," Sheila said quickly. "And I know that Graham is one of your closest friends."

"I've always considered you a dear friend, too, so try me."

"I hate to say this but living with Graham is so boring," she said. "All he ever wants to do is watch sports on TV and drink beer. He occasionally goes to Bernie's soccer matches but that's about it. We never go out to eat. We never go to movies. We never do anything together."

"Did you ever ask?"

"Brandon, I've been asking him to do things for years," Sheila said, her voice rising slightly. "I just got fed up with his attitude and his drinking. That's why I finally decided to pack my bags and leave."

"Any chance of you guys getting back together?"

"To be honest, I truly doubt it," she said before taking another sip of coffee. "I don't think he's going to change. He's already set in his ways."

"Can I ask you something personal?"

"I guess so," she said shyly. "I hope it's not too personal."

"Are you seeing anyone else?"

Sheila blushed. She put head back and slightly shook her short auburn hair.

"There's a man I've seen on a few occasions," she said. "It's nothing serious."

"I saw you with a man," Brandon said. "This was before you and Graham separated. I wasn't sure if it was business or what."

"I was probably with Troy," she said. "He's a guy I've been working with the past six months. I guess it's more than a business relationship. We've grown somewhat fond of each other."

"That doesn't sound too good, Sheila."

"I know it doesn't. He's married, too."

"Did he go to Cincinnati with you a few weeks ago?"

"Yes," she said quietly.

"Do you want to get back with Graham?"

"I don't know anymore."

"How about counseling?"

"I suggested it to him a long time ago and he wouldn't do it. Then he brings it up to me last month. I think it's a little too late for that."

"Is there anything I can do?"

"Not right now," Sheila said.

"I just hope you don't go so far that it will be impossible for you and Graham to get back together."

"I'm trying to be careful," she said as a tear trickled down her cheek. "I'm so confused right now."

"You know you can always come to me if you need any help. I'm not sure what I can do other than lend an ear."

"Thanks," she said while wiping her cheek with a napkin.

"And I do think you should seek some counseling, if only for yourself."

"I've been thinking about that," she said. "There's a chaplain at the hospital that I may talk to."

The restaurant was slowly filling up. Brandon looked at the clock on the wall and saw that it was nearly eleven o'clock.

"Well, I think it's time to go," he said. "I'm glad that we got to spend some time together."

"Me, too," she said with a soft smile. "You didn't get to tell me anything about you."

"We'll do that next time," he said.

Brandon left the tip and picked up both checks. They walked to the front counter and he paid the bill. When they stepped out of the building, Sheila reached over and hugged him.

"Do you mind if I tell Graham that I talked to you?" Brandon asked.

"I figured you would."

"I hope to see you again real soon," he said.

"Bye," Sheila said as she turned to walk to her car at the side of the restaurant. Brandon turned and waved as he walked to his car parked in front.

He drove by Maggie's house on the way home. There was a slight chill in the air but she was out front raking leaves from the two maples that were nearly bare. She was wearing baggy jeans and an old red sweatshirt that had "Don't Worry, Be Happy" in big letters on the front. He pulled into the driveway and she stopped for a moment and waved.

"Good morning," he said.

"Hi, Brandon," she said. "Did you come to help me rake leaves?"

"Sure," he said. "Do you have another rake?"

"I'm kidding you," she said with a hearty laugh.

"Where's Bobby Lee?

"Where you last saw him; sitting in front of the TV watching football."

"Is he doing okay?"

"I think he's getting a little restless now," she said while holding the rake in front of her. "He's also getting bored with school. Can you talk to him about it?"

"I'll see what I can do."

Brandon knocked once on the front door, and then stepped inside.

"Bobby Lee?"

"Hi Brandon!" he said excitedly. "The Browns and Packers are on TV."

"Any score yet?"

"No. They just started a few minutes ago."

"So how are you feeling?"

"I'm doing okay, I guess."

"Anything you want to tell me about?"

"Did Mom say something to you?" he asked with squinted eyes.

"Not really," Brandon said while sitting in a rocking chair.

"Ah, this is getting boring," Bobby Lee said. "I'm tired of being here all the time. All I ever do is watch TV and do homework."

"Don't you have any video games?"

"I did but the control broke."

"Why don't you get it fixed?"

"Mom says she doesn't have the money to do it."

"Oh," Brandon said, puffing his cheeks. "Well, those things do cost money."

"Are we still going to the ball game?"

"Sure," Brandon said. "You just keep doing well in school."

"I'm getting good grades," Bobby Lee said eagerly. "Don't you worry about that."

Brandon rose up from the rocking chair and walked over to Bobby Lee and placed his hand on his shoulder and patted gently.

"I need to be going now," he said. "I'll check back with you in a few days about the ball game."

Brandon stopped by Maggie in the front yard. She had three large piles of leaves under the trees. Several tiny pieces of leaves clung to her clothes and were in her frazzled hair.

"Are you sure you don't need any help?" he asked.

"No," she said. "I don't mind doing this. It's kind of relaxing and I need the exercise."

"Bobby Lee told me that his video game was broken."

"It's one of the controls. It costs forty dollars to fix it and I just don't have that on me right now."

Brandon took out his wallet and took out two twenties and handed it to her.

"Let me help," he said.

"Oh, Brandon, you don't need to do this," she said. "You've done so much for us all ready."

"I want to," he said. "And if it cost more than forty dollars let me know."

Maggie stuffed the money in her front pocket and smiled softly.

"You've been more than kind to us," she said.

"Don't worry about that," he said while gently putting his hand on her forearm. "There's nothing to pay back. You just let me know if there's anything I can do. Okay?"

"Okay," she said with a soft sigh.

"I've got to go now," he said while releasing his hand. "I'll see you at work tomorrow."

"Bye, Brandon," Maggie said. She stood with the rake in her hand until Brandon drove off. Her eyes welled with tears.

Twenty-nine

"**D**id you catch the Browns on the tube yesterday?" Graham asked Brandon in the break room Monday morning.

"For a minute while I was visiting Bobby Lee," Brandon said while pouring a cup of coffee. "How did they look?"

"Pretty good. I think they're finally getting it together. They may even make a run for the playoffs if they play like they did yesterday."

"That's good," Brandon said. "Are you going to be around this morning?"

"Sure. What's up?"

"I need to talk to you about something. It's personal. We could wait until lunch or after work."

"Can you tell me what it's about?"

"Sheila"

"Oh," Graham said with a grimace.

"It can wait."

"I'll get back with you a little later," Graham said. "I do have a few calls to make this morning."

"Any time," Brandon said. "I'll be around."

They went to their offices and closed the doors at the same time. Maggie looked up from her desk and shook her head.

Brandon checked his e-mail, hoping to find something from Clarice. No such luck. He picked up the phone and called her office but got her voicemail. He left a message, telling her he hoped she had a good trip and made it back all right. For the remainder of the morning, he sat at the computer and worked on a column.

Two soft taps on his door momentarily broke his concentration.

"Come on in," Brandon said.

Graham turned the knob and peeped in.

"Am I interrupting anything?" he asked.

"No. I'm about finished with my column."

"I can come back later."

"No," Brandon said. "I've about it wrapped up. Take a seat."

Graham closed the door and sat down next to Brandon's desk. Brandon could see an uneasy but serious look on his face.

"So what do you want to tell me about Sheila?" Graham asked. "The suspense is killing me."

"I had breakfast with her yesterday," Brandon said. "It was nothing planned. I was over at Shoney's and she showed up. I invited her to sit with me."

"So how's she doing?" Graham asked with a slight smile.

"She seems to be doing okay," Brandon said. "She's been occupied with work."

"I told you that. That's taken up a lot of her time."

"There's more."

"Well, I figured that," Graham said with a smirk.

"Do you want to talk about it here?"

"Why not?" Graham asked. "I'd rather know now than be thinking about it all day."

"We could go to lunch."

"And let it give me indigestion?" Graham said, forcing a laugh. "Let's get it over with now."

"She's unhappy with the home life," Brandon said, looking directly at Graham. "She said all you do is watch sports on television and go to Bernie's soccer games. She also mentioned your drinking."

"I don't know if it's that bad," Graham said defensively.

"I'm just relaying what she told me."

"Okay," Graham said. "Go on."

"Are you sure?" asked Brandon, beginning to feel a little ill at ease about the conversation and where it was headed.

"There's another man?" "Graham asked, arching his eyebrows.

"Yes."

"Did she tell you his name?"

"Yes."

"It must be Troy Williams. She's been putting in some long hours with him the past few months."

"She mentioned a Troy."

"He's married, too. He's got three or four children. I thought he was a nice guy."

"I don't know what else to tell you," Brandon said. "I mentioned counseling but she said it probably was too late for both of you."

"It probably is, especially after what you just told me."

"I even told her to seek some counseling for herself."

Graham lowered his head and shook it slowly.

"You know, somehow I figured this was happening but I didn't want to face it," he said, looking back at Brandon. "I'm really pissed right now."

"I'm sure you're going through all kinds of emotions."

"Sheila and I have been married eighteen years," Graham said as tears began to well up in his eyes. "Now she does this to me." His breathing became heavy and he clenched his teeth for a few seconds.

Brandon didn't respond. He thought about what Sheila had told him and knew that it wasn't entirely her fault.

"Doesn't trust mean a damn thing anymore?" Graham continued, fighting back tears. "I've made a lot of sacrifices for her. I've always been faithful although I've had my opportunities."

"I don't know what to say," Brandon said, pursing his lips. "I hope you didn't mind me telling you this."

"No," Graham said, slowly rising from the chair. "I'd rather hear it from you than anybody."

Brandon remained seated at his desk, his arms crossed on the desk.

"If there's anything I can do, please don't hesitate to ask me," Brandon said. "I'll do whatever I can do to help get the two of you back together."

"Back together?" Graham asked, his eyes beginning to show anger. "You've got to be kidding. After what she's done to me? Screwing another guy. I don't think so."

Brandon shrugged. "Well, whatever I can do."

"I've got to give this lots of thought," Graham said while opening the door. "I'll see you later."

Maggie walked into Brandon's office a few seconds later and handed him messages from Jenny and Clarice. He picked up the phone and called Clarice. He wasn't surprised to find out she was in a meeting. She was always in meetings. He called Jenny's number.

"How are you?" Brandon said after Jenny answered the phone.

"I'm fine," she said cheerfully. "Thanks for calling me back."

"What's up?"

"I was wondering if we could have dinner this week."

"Sure," Brandon said. "I'll have to get back with you though. Do you have any particular day?"

"Any day but Friday," she said. "I'm going out of town for the weekend."

"Where are you going?"

"Down to Gatlinburg."

"That should be fun."

"I hope so."

After a few more minutes, they finished their conversation and hung up. Brandon called Clarice again, this time leaving another voicemail.

Concerned about Graham, Brandon got up and walked down the hall to his office. Graham wasn't there. Brandon went back up front to Maggie's desk.

"Did Graham leave?"

"Yes," Maggie said. "He said he'd be gone the rest of the day. He seemed to be in a hurry."

"Did he say where he was going?"

"He just said he had some meetings. Is there anything wrong?"

"I hope not," Brandon said.

The phone rang and Maggie picked it up.

"It's for you Brandon," she said. "Ms. Horton."

"Thanks," Brandon said, a smile quickly covering his face. He hurried back to his office and shut the door. He picked up the phone.

"Clarice?"

"Hi Brandon," she said.

"When did you get back?"

"Very late last night."

"How was your trip?"

"All business," she said. "I'm glad I'm back home."

"I'm glad you're back, too," he said. "I missed you."

"I thought about you, too."

Brandon wasn't sure what to make about her comment but let it slide. He was happy to hear her voice.

"When can I see you?" he asked.

"This weekend?"

"That long?" he asked. "I don't know if I can go that long without seeing you."

"I've got meetings every day this week," she said, sounding apologetic.

"How about a late dinner then?"

"Can I get back with you on that?"

"Any time," he said. "I don't need any notice. How about tonight?"

"I've already got plans for this evening."

"Business?"

"Uh, not really," she said. "I'm having dinner with an old friend. He called me last week."

"Oh," Brandon said, disappointment ringing through his voice. "Perhaps some other night then?"

"Is everything all right?" she asked.

"Of course," he said with a half-hearted laugh.

"I do want to see you," Clarice said softly.

"That's good to hear."

"I need to be going now," she said.

"I know," Brandon said with a sigh. "Another meeting."

They both laughed.

After hanging up the phone, Brandon turned around in his chair and gazed out the window. The skies were overcast and a breezy wind was shaking the few remaining leaves off the trees. He decided to call Jenny again.

"What are your plans for tonight?" he asked.

"I don't have any."

"Want to go to dinner?"

"I'd love to," she said enthusiastically. "Where?

"It's your choice."

"Great," she said. "I'll try to find the most expensive."

Brandon groaned.

"What time do you want me to pick you up?" he asked.

"About seven-thirty."

"See you then."

Brandon walked back to the front lobby. Maggie was sitting at her desk eating a bologna sandwich and drinking a can of Coke.

"Have you heard from Graham?" Brandon asked.

"Not a word."

"I'm going down to Maxwell's for lunch," he said. "I'll be back in an hour."

The cool breeze whipped across Brandon's face as he walked to the restaurant. Opening the door, there was a sparse lunch crowd. He glanced around quickly, spotting Graham sitting at a booth by himself. He had a half pitcher of beer and an almost empty mug in front of him.

"May I join you?" Brandon asked.

"Why not?" Graham said with a shrug. "Get yourself a mug."

"I'm not thirsty," Brandon said with a smile. "It's too early in the day for beer."

"Not for me," said Graham, who put the mug to his mouth and finished the beer in two gulps.

"I know you're upset, but is this right thing to do?"

"Probably not," Graham said while lifting the pitcher to pour more beer into the mug, "but it sure beats sitting in the office and stewing over everything."

"Do you plan to stay here all day?"

"I thought I would."

"Why don't you come back to the office?" Brandon said. "This isn't helping you any."

"I'm not looking for any help," Graham said. "I just want to get drunk."

"Can't you do this some other time? Why don't we go out after work some evening and talk this over?"

"You're right," Graham said, a look of resignation in his eyes. "This isn't doing me any good. Let's go back to the office."

Thirty

"So where are we going?" Brandon asked Jenny inside her apartment door.

"Old Mexico," she said. "I've heard it has some of the best Mexican food in town."

"That sounds fine with me."

"How come we're going out tonight?" she said as Brandon helped her with her coat.

"I don't know what might be happening later in the week. I also owe you this for taking care of me last week."

"That was no problem," she said, opening the door and stepping into the cool night air. "I could take care of you all the time."

Brandon let her comment slip by and got her to talk about herself on the way to the restaurant. It proved to be non-stop chatter as it took up all the time it took to get to their destination nearly thirty minutes later.

They were seated in the corner of the restaurant, giving them a good vantage point of everyone around them. Mariachi music played softly in the background. Jenny ordered a pitcher of margaritas.

"Don't we have to work tomorrow?" Brandon asked.

"Oh, these things are watered down," she said. "It's almost like drinking flavored water."

"If you say so."

"How was your day?" Jenny asked while the waiter poured drinks from the pitcher.

"I wrote a column," Brandon said. "That was about it. How about you?"

"Nothing much," she said before taking a sip of the drink. "Same old stuff."

As Brandon was gazed around the restaurant, Clarice walked into the dining area with a man. She didn't see Brandon. The waiter seated them along a side row, with her back to him.

"Did you see somebody you know?" Jenny asked.

"Uh, I thought so," he said. "I'm not sure."

"Who is it?"

"Somebody I know in PR."

"That Horton woman?"

"Who?"

"Horton. The woman who called while you were home last week."

"No," Brandon said. "It's someone else." He finished the margarita in his glass and poured another one. He tried to ignore Clarice but it was difficult. The man with her looked familiar to Brandon. He was good looking with short, sandy hair and an athletic build.

"There's Bart Taylor," Jenny said with a smile. She caught his eye and waved. He waved back. He was the guy with Clarice.

Brandon felt uneasy and blushed slightly. All of the sudden he wanted to get up and leave through the back entrance so Clarice wouldn't see him.

"How do you know him?"

"We dated a long time ago," Jenny said. "He's a handsome devil and he knows it."

"Did you go out with him long?"

"A few months," Jenny said. "He's not the most faithful guy in the world."

"So you were serious with him?"

"I think every woman gets serious with Bart."

"Really?" Brandon said with a tone of resignation.

The waiter returned and brought them a basket of nacho chips and large bowl of salsa and took their orders. Brandon poured himself another drink.

"I didn't think you wanted to drink much," said Jenny, who was still on her first drink.

"Like you said, they're watered down. I'm thirsty, too."

"Well, you've got water sitting in front of you."

"Do you mind me drinking a margarita?" Brandon said, a bit irritated.

"No," Jenny said. "Just save some for me."

"I will. If not, I'll order another pitcher."

"Why are you getting angry with me?" she asked.

"I'm not angry."

"Yes, you are," she said. "You were in a good mood and then all of the sudden you're upset about something."

"I don't know what you're talking about."

"Let's just drop it," she said, a flash of anger showing in her eyes. "Okay?"

"That's fine with me."

The waiter returned with their orders. They ate quietly. Brandon offered to pour her some more margarita but she refused. He looked toward Clarice's table and noticed Bart with a big smile and laughing. Clarice seemed to be having a good time, too, from what he could tell.

When the waiter came back and asked them if they wanted desserts, Jenny quickly declined.

"I'm ready to go home," she said, looking away. "I'm tired."

The waiter placed the check on the table. Brandon took out a credit card and put it on top. A minute later, the waiter returned and took it.

"I don't know why you're acting this way," Jenny said.

"I don't know what you're talking about," Brandon said.

"I know there's something that's bothering you."

"Well, there isn't."

"Just be that way."

The waiter returned with the receipt that Brandon signed. Jenny eased out of her seat and Brandon helped her put on her coat. As they walked toward the front, Brandon looked over at Clarice's table. She looked back at him. A smile quickly melted from her face. Brandon pursed his lips and nodded. He didn't look back as he followed Jenny out of the restaurant.

~ * ~

"What's the matter?" Bart asked. "You look like you just saw a ghost."

"Nothing," Clarice said. "I was just thinking about something at work that I forgot to do."

"Well, just forget about work," he said, reaching over and placing his hands over hers. "Just think about us tonight."

Clarice forced a smile, then slipped her hands out from under his and picked up a fork and began eating.

Brandon and Jenny didn't speak as they drove back to her apartment. Brandon's thoughts were on Clarice. As soon as he pulled to a stop in a parking space, she opened the door quickly and got out.

"Let me walk you to your apartment," Brandon said, the motor still running.

"Don't bother," Jenny said as she slammed the door. She walked briskly up the sidewalk and to her apartment. Brandon waited in the car until he could see her go inside the apartment. He backed out and drove home, his thoughts still on seeing Clarice with someone else.

Brandon changed his clothes after getting home, putting on gym shorts and gray T-shirt. He was restless. He got a beer out of the refrigerator, sat in the recliner and turned on the television. After a few minutes, he got bored with the TV and turned it off. He looked around the living room. *Ulysses* was on the coffee table but he didn't pick it up. Instead, he leaned back in the recliner and closed his eyes and drifted off to sleep.

~ * ~

Bart took Clarice home in his sleek silver Corvette, going faster than the speed limit as if he was going to be rewarded by getting there quickly. He walked her to the front door. She turned and thanked him for the dinner.

"Can't I come in for a nightcap?" he asked with a wide open-mouth smile.

"Oh, Bart, I'm so tired and I've got to get to work early in the morning," she said with a sigh. "Perhaps next time."

"I was looking forward to a little more time with you this evening," he said. "We've got a lot of catching up to do."

"I don't know about that," she said.

"Please?" he said with a hurt look.

Clarice hesitated for a few seconds before answering. She glanced at her watch and saw that it was only nine forty-five.

"Okay, but for only a few minutes," she said. She turned and unlocked the door as Bart held open the storm door. She took off her coat and hung it in the hall closet after they stepped inside the living room. He removed his sports coat and followed her to the den.

"What would you like?" she asked. "Coffee or a drink."

"How about gin and tonic?"

Clarice motioned to the mini-bar in the corner.

"You know how you like it, so go to it," she said with a smile. "I'll get some ice. You can fix me one, too."

Bart had their drinks ready when she returned with the ice. He plunked down three cubes into each glass. They sat down on the sofa.

"It's been a long time," Bart said while swirling the ice in his glass. "Too long."

"I've been busy with work," she said. "I haven't had much time to do much of anything. How about you?"

"I've got the horse sales coming up next week," Bart said. "We've been getting the stable ready for it."

They each took a sip of their drink. Bart inched a little closer to Clarice.

"I can't stay up much longer," she said. "I've got a busy day tomorrow."

"I could spend the night," he said with a naughty grin.

"I don't think so," she said.

"You've always played hard to get with me," Bart said. "Why?"

"I haven't played anything."

"Oh, come on," he said. "You always seem to tighten up when things could start to get interesting."

"I think you're imagining things, Bart," she said, then sat her drink on the coffee table. "I think it's about time for you to go."

"I wish you wouldn't be this way," he said.

"I'm tired, Bart. I really need to get some rest."

Bart finished his drink and stood up.

"I was hoping for a longer evening than this," he said with an annoyed expression.

"I'm sorry to disappoint you," she said while standing up. "Let me see you to the door."

When they reached the front door, Bart turned and kissed her roughly on the mouth as she tried to push him away. Clarice finally broke loose and wiped her hand across her lips, smearing the lipstick on her cheeks.

"Now you didn't have to do that," Bart said with a sneering smile.

"Get out of my house!" Clarice demanded.

"Okay, but you'll regret it," he said while opening the door.

"I won't regret anything with you," Clarice said.

Bart shook his head slowly and walked out the door. Clarice slammed the door and locked it, then turned around and leaned against it. She began to tremble but fought back any tears.

Thirty-one

Brandon awoke at five in the morning, his neck sore from sleeping on the recliner. Easing slowly out of the chair, he ambled to the kitchen and put on a pot of coffee. While it brewed, he went to the bathroom and took a quick shower and shaved.

He put on a pair of khakis and white shirt and returned to the kitchen, poured a cup of coffee and sat down at the table. He still couldn't believe he saw Clarice at the restaurant with another man. It almost felt like a slap in the face, especially after asking her earlier in the day if she had any plans. She had plans, all right, but they didn't include him. He didn't know what to think about her now.

While putting his cup in the sink, Brandon looked out the window and noticed that it was gray and drizzling outside. He felt just as miserable as the weather outside. *How appropriate*, he thought. He almost felt like staying home but decided against it.

He was the first person at work. He went to his office and checked the e-mail on his computer. The new issue of the magazine was out and he leafed through the pages to see if there were any mistakes, glancing quickly over his column. In the break room, he could hear someone preparing coffee. A minute later, Maggie poked her head into his office.

"Good morning, Brandon," she said with a bright smile. "Coffee is brewing."

"Morning," Brandon said. "That's good. I could use a cup of coffee."

"Why the glum face?"

"I was just thinking."

"Anything you care to share?"

"Not really," Brandon said. "I was just looking over the magazine."

"Coffee should be ready in about ten minutes," Maggie said. "I'll see you later."

Brandon thought about picking up the telephone and calling Clarice, but decided against it. He didn't know what he would say to her. He didn't want to make light of the situation because he cared for her. He also didn't want to make too much of it because he didn't have the right to make any demands of her. He sat in his chair for a few minutes, shuffling through some mail, and then went back the break room. While pouring coffee, Graham walked in.

"Good morning," Graham said while getting his cup off the counter.

"Morning," Brandon said. "How's everything?"

"About the same," Graham said, holding out his cup while Brandon filled it near the top.

"You haven't heard from Sheila?"

"Nope."

"Have you tried to get in touch with her?"

"Nope. I figure the ball's on her side of the court."

"How's Bernie?"

"He seems to be doing okay," Graham said before taking a sip of coffee. "I think he's talked to her about everyday."

"That's good."

"I guess so."

"Anything going on today?" Brandon asked, wanting to change the subject.

"In the office?"

"Yes."

"Don't forget the staff meeting at ten."

"I'm glad you reminded me," Brandon said.

They refreshed their coffee and each went to his office. Brandon had a note on his desk from Clarice. He looked at it for a few seconds, then picked up the phone and called her.

"This is Brandon," he said.

"Oh, hi," she said. "How are you?"

"Okay, I guess," he said tersely.

"You don't sound that way."

"I can't imagine why."

"Brandon, we need to talk," Clarice said. "Can we meet for lunch or dinner?"

"I'll have to check my calendar," Brandon said, already knowing that it was clear all week. "I might have a meeting."

"I want to explain about last night."

"There's nothing to explain."

"Oh yes there is," Clarice said quickly.

"When do you want to meet?" he replied with a sigh.

"How about at lunch?"

"I've got a staff meeting at ten but it should be over by eleven or so."

"Could we meet at one, just to be on the safe side?"

"No problem," Brandon said. "Where?"

"How about Berringer's?" Clarice said. "That's fairly close for both of us."

"I'll see you at one."

"Bye," Clarice said, her voice bordering on sadness.

Brandon put down the receiver and looked up and saw Maggie at his door.

"I forgot to tell you that I got the video game thingy fixed for Bobby Lee," she said with a smile. "They just swapped out the control."

"That's good," Brandon said. "I hope that makes Bobby Lee's life a little more tolerable."

"Even more, it didn't cost a thing," Maggie opened her hand and returned the forty dollars to Brandon. "They said the controller shouldn't have broken that soon."

"Well, that's a nice surprise," Brandon said with a chuckle.

"Can I invite you over for dinner sometime this week?" she said, raising her eyebrows. "It's the least I can do to repay you for all you've done. And Bobby Lee loves to have you visit."

"Sure," Brandon said. "I'd like that. Give me a day."

"How about tomorrow night?

"I'll be there," Brandon said. "Time?"

"Seven o'clock?"

"I'll be there at seven."

Maggie smiled and returned to her desk. Brandon looked at the time on his computer. Nearly ten, he got up and went to the conference room. Graham was already seated. Two more employees came in after Brandon. Graham went over the story budget and made assignments. Several questions were asked during the meeting, causing it to drag until after noon. Brandon started getting a little restless but breathed a sigh of relief when the meeting broke up at twelve-fifteen.

"Any calls?" Brandon asked Maggie after leaving the conference room.

"Not a thing," she said. "It's been quiet."

Berringer's was a twenty-minute drive from Brandon's office. He waited in the front foyer until Clarice arrived at twelve-fifty. Her hair was combed back neatly, giving more notice to her soft features. She wore a tan all-weather coat and had the collar turned up.

"I thought I would get here before you," Clarice said when she saw Brandon. He helped her remove her coat. She was wearing a deep blue skirt and jacket and a strand of pearls around her neck.

"I've only been here a few minutes," he said with a smile.

The hostess took them to a table in the non-smoking section, near the front entrance.

"I haven't been here in quite a while," Brandon said after they sat down. "I'm glad you suggested it."

"I occasionally have business lunches here," Clarice said. "They have good food and the service is pretty good."

The waitress brought them tall glasses of iced water and took their orders for garden salads.

"Hi Clarice," said a tall man standing next to their table. "How are you?"

"Hello," she said with a smile. "I'm doing fine. I'd like you to meet Brandon Wilkes. Brandon, this is Howard, my former husband."

Brandon rose from his seat, extended his arm and they shook hands.

"A pleasure to meet you," Brandon said.

"Likewise," Howard said. "So what have you been up to, Clarice?

"Work," she said. "That's about it."

"Still the same, huh?" he said in a tone that tinged on arrogance.

"Yes, Howard," Clarice said. "Work, work, work."

"Well, I'd better go," he said. "I saw you sitting here and thought I'd stop by for a second. It was nice meeting you, Mr. Wilkes."

"Same here," Brandon said.

Howard tipped his head slightly at Clarice and went to his table on the other side of the dining room. Brandon watched him walked away, trying to figure out what Clarice ever saw in him. He was a gangly-looking man with tight, curly hair and a beak nose. He had envisioned her with a suave, debonair man, like Cary Grant.

"Now you've met Howard," Clarice said. "Pretty unimpressive, huh?"

"Well, I didn't want to say anything but I would have never imagined you married to him," Brandon said with a slight chuckle.

"He hasn't always looked so dorky," she said with a laugh. "Perhaps he's always looked this way but I just didn't notice."

"He looks older than you."

"He's about forty-five," Clarice said. "I met him in college. He seemed like the mature type that I needed back then. He's also very intelligent, probably an intellectual, so I was attracted to that as well."

"Anything else?"

"That was about it and that didn't last too long," she said. "He never liked to do anything. He was content to sit around the house and read or go outside and work in the yard. It drove me nuts."

"And he wanted children?"

"Yes," Clarice said with a sigh. "I had my career. I didn't want to have kids right from the start. And after being married to him for several years, I was sure that I didn't want him to be the father to my children. Isn't that an awful thing to say?"

"Not really," Brandon said. "It's probably good that you didn't have any kids."

The waitress returned and set their salads on the table. There was a few seconds of silence as they took a few bites and a drink of water.

"About last night," Clarice said after clearing her throat.

"You don't need to explain anything," Brandon said.

"Yes, I do," she said. "It wasn't what it appeared to be."

"What do you mean?"

"Bart had asked me out last week and I accepted," she said. "I used to date him a long time ago."

"I know about him," Brandon said while picking at his salad with the fork.

"I won't be going out with him again," Clarice said.

"Why?"

"Because I don't want to," she said. "There is someone else I'm interested in."

"Really?"

"Yes, silly," she said as a warm smile crossed her face. "You."

"Me?"

"I really enjoy being with you," she said. "I hope you feel the same about me."

"Well, I do," he said. "I just wasn't sure about your feelings toward me."

"I've wondered about you, too," she said. "When I called your house last week and that woman answered. And then last night when I saw you with someone else."

"That was Jenny," Brandon said. "She came over and helped me after I got out of the hospital. I was just paying her back last night."

"Have you ever been close to her," Clarice asked.

"Uh, yes, a while back," Brandon said, "but there's really nothing between us. How about you and Bart?"

"A long time ago," Clarice said, blushing slightly. "We've never been serious. I don't think Bart couldn't be serious about anything except himself."

"That's what I've heard," Brandon said.

"You know him?"

"I know of him through mutual friends."

"He's really a creep."

"I know," Brandon said dryly. "That's why I was surprised to see you with him."

"It will never happen again," Clarice said, reaching over and putting her hand on top of Brandon's hand.

"How does your schedule look for the next few weeks?" Brandon asked, turning his hand over and touching her fingertips.

"If it's possible, it will be free for you," Clarice said with a soft smile. "I don't have any weekend trips for awhile."

"That's good to hear."

They finished their salads. Howard waved to them on his way out of the restaurant, and they both nodded and smiled.

Thirty-two

"That was a nice column you wrote this week," Buck Odoms said to Brandon over a pitcher of beer at Hastings after work. "The university should provide more parking if they continue to expand their facilities."

"The university is going to do what it wants to do," Brandon said.

"Sometimes they listen to the voice of reason," Buck said with a laugh.

"It seems that voice of reason is money. Money talks and they listen."

"You've got that right."

Rosie came over with another pitcher of beer and put it on their table without saying a word.

"That girl needs a vacation," Brandon said after she left. "She's worked so hard that she's lost her sense of humor."

"She didn't have much of one to begin with," Buck said, "but I know what you mean. She's even getting a little grumpy lately."

"Anything going on with you these days?" Brandon asked while Buck poured beer into their mugs.

"Not much," Buck said. "I took your advice on Debra. I don't believe I'll ask her out until she's divorced. I've got enough problems in my life without adding an irate cop to the list."

"Are you seeing anyone else?"

"I talked to Graham's wife the other night at a Shoney's," Buck said. "She was by herself. I didn't pry or anything but are they separated?"

"For several weeks," Brandon said.

"Wow. I'm sorry to hear that," Buck said. "I like Graham and Sheila."

"I hope they can reconcile. They've been married for eighteen years or so."

"I've known people married longer than that who split."

"I do, too," Brandon said. "That still doesn't make it any easier."

Debra walked in and spotted Brandon and Buck almost immediately. She smiled and waved and strolled over to their table.

"How are you guys?" she asked with a bright smile.

"Doing okay," Brandon said. "How about you?"

"I closed on another house today," she said. "I came here to celebrate. Can I buy you guys another pitcher?"

"Sure," Buck said with a grin. "But only if you'll help us drink it."

"How about if I buy a pitcher for you and a glass of red wine for myself?" she asked coyly.

"You've got a deal," Buck said.

Debra stepped over to the bar and told Benny what she wanted. A few minutes later, he came over with the pitcher and wine.

"Where's Rosie?" Brandon asked. "Anything the matter?"

"Nah," Benny grumbled. "She's taking a smoke break in the women's john. She told me she's entitled to a fifteen-minute break after working for four hours."

"You need some more help," Buck said.

"You wanna put on an apron and start serving?" Benny asked sarcastically.

"Not really," Buck said with a chuckle.

"You can't find help these days," Benny said. "I mean you can't find good help. I go through waitresses all the time. Rosie has been the exception. I need to get back over to the bar."

"Don't work too hard," Brandon said.

"Smartass!" Benny said with a grin.

Debra pulled out a chair across from Buck and Brandon and sat down. She tugged at her short brown skirt.

"How's married life?" Buck asked.

"Almost over," Debra said. "I finally got David to sign the papers."

"Let's have a toast to that," Buck said, raising his mug. Brandon and Debra lifted their glasses and tapped them together.

"Has he bothered you anymore?" Brandon asked.

"Not since he found his little sweetie," Debra said, shrugging her shoulders.

"Does that bother you any?" Buck asked.

"Hell no!" she said. "The quicker I can rid myself of him, the better. She's a godsend."

"Have you been going out any?" Brandon asked.

"I wish," Debra said, shaking her head. "I think most guys are turned off about me being married to a cop."

"I'm sure you'll get flooded with offers after the divorce is final," Buck said.

"Let's hope so," she said. "I sure don't want to be an old maid now. I do like to have fun."

They all laughed. Buck excused himself for a few minutes and went to the restroom.

"I think Buck wants to ask you out," Brandon said to Debra.

"That's nice," she said.

"Would you go out with him?"

"Probably," she said, "but I'd rather go out with you."

"Buck's a great guy," Brandon said.

"I think you're a great guy," she said with a sexy gaze.

"Well, thanks," Brandon said, nervously.

"I'd go out with you on a moment's notice."

"That's very nice of you."

"So why don't you ask me out?"

Brandon took a swallow of beer and cleared his throat. He was beginning to feel uneasy in her presence.

"I'm seeing someone," Brandon said.

"Oh, I'm sorry," Debra said, her voice returning to its normal pitch. "I didn't know you had someone else."

"That's okay," he said with a quick smile.

"Do I know her?"

"I don't believe so," Brandon said. "Her name is Clarice Horton. She works in PR."

"I don't know her," Debra said. "She's a lucky gal."

"I feel like the fortunate one."

Buck returned to the table and picked up the pitcher and refilled his and Brandon's mugs.

"Did I miss anything?" Buck asked.

"Only the meaning of life," Debra said with a giggle.

"Damn," Buck said. "I'm always a day late and dollar short."

"You need to stick around, sugar," Debra said, turning her attention to Buck.

Rosie brought over another glass of wine for Rosie. The bar was getting more crowded and noisier. Someone dropped some money in the jukebox and John Mellencamp's "Authority Song" began to mix with the bar chatter.

Brandon was looking at the front entrance when Jenny came. She was with David Hatfield.

"I don't believe it," Brandon said to himself.

"What is it?" Buck asked.

"Look who's with Jenny," Brandon said, nodding toward the front of the bar. Buck angled over and saw Jenny talking to David.

"I don't know the guy," Buck said. "Who is he?"

Debra turned around in her chair.

"Oh, my god!" she blurted. "It's David and his little sweetie."

David and Jenny walked toward them. David noticed Debra while Jenny saw Brandon. They smiled at each other but didn't say a word as they eased past the table to the rear of the bar.

"Who was that?" Buck asked.

"That's my soon-to-be ex," Debra said. "And that's his bimbo."

"That bimbo is a lady I used to go out with," Brandon said.

"Oh, I'm sorry," Debra said. "I didn't mean it to come out like that."

"That's okay," Brandon said with a short laugh. "I'm just amazed that she's with your hubby."

"It's a small world," Buck said.

"No kidding," Debra said before taking a big sip of wine.

"Does it bother you to see him with another woman?" Buck asked.

"Hell, no," Debra said. "The quicker I get him out of my life the better. I don't need him following me around all over the place."

"They should make a good couple," Brandon said. "She likes to have a lot of attention."

"She'll damn well get it from him," Debra said. "She'll be smothered with attention."

"How long have they been going out?" Brandon asked Debra.

"A week or two," she said. "I'm really not sure. I had some friends tell me they saw him with a woman last week. Have you known her long?"

"Several years," Brandon said. "We've dated off and on for awhile. Nothing serious."

"I can't imagine you getting serious about any woman," Debra teased.

"Some guys get serious about women," Buck said with a grin.

"Yeah, some guys get too serious," Debra said, laughing.

"Well folks, I hate to leave good company but I need to be going home," Brandon said.

"Why don't we all go out to dinner and celebrate some more?" Debra asked, raising her glass.

"I'll have to take a rain check on that," Brandon said. "Why don't the two of you go on?" Brandon looked over at Buck and wriggled his eyebrows.

"I don't know," Debra said, glancing down at her watch. "It's getting a little late."

"You were the one who brought it up," Brandon said. "Are you getting cold feet now?"

"No," she said on the defensive. "Do you want to go out for dinner, Buck?"

Buck knocked his leg against Brandon's leg and grinned.

"Only if you don't keep me out too late," Buck said.

Rosie came by the table and Debra picked up the tab.

"My treat guys," she said. "It's almost Thanksgiving."

They got up from the table. Brandon looked to the rear and saw David and Jenny in deep conversation. He thought that Debra wasn't the only person to be thankful to see them together.

Debra and Buck left in their own cars to the restaurant while Brandon drove home, stopping at a Chinese carryout on the way. He would have gone with Debra and Buck but he wanted to get home and call Clarice.

He quickly ate his meal and washed it down with a large glass of ice water. After changing into gym shorts and T-shirt, he brushed his teeth and went to the living room and dialed Clarice's number.

"Am I calling too late?" Brandon asked, noticing it was eight thirty-five on the wall clock.

"No," she said warmly. "I've only been home for about thirty minutes. I had to stay late in the office as usual. I just finished eating some Chinese carryout."

"Me, too," Brandon said with a laugh. "I guess we should have met at a Chinese restaurant."

"Did you work late, too?"

"No," Brandon said. "I went over to Hastings and had a few beers with Buck Odoms from the newspaper and a woman who sells real estate."

"What's her name?" Clarice asked.

"Debra Hatfield."

"I think I've seen her name in some real-estate ads in the paper."

"Probably so," Brandon said. "She and Buck went out to dinner and I came home so I could call you."

Clarice smiled.

"What plans do you have for tomorrow?" she asked.

"Nothing much," Brandon said. "I've got some copy to edit and I need to start thinking about next week's column. How about you?"

"I've got a meeting in the morning," she said. "The afternoon looks fairly open."

"Want to do something?"

"I was hoping you'd take the hint," Clarice said with a laugh.

"What would you like to do?"

"Is it too cold to do something outdoors?"

"I don't think so," Brandon said. "We just need to wear some warm clothes."

"Have you ever been to Raven Run?"

"A few times," he said. "How about you?"

"I never have but I've heard it's really nice," Clarice said.

"That's where we'll go then. How about two o'clock?"

"I'll be ready," she said.

"I'll call you in the morning to make sure nothing comes up," Brandon said.

"And I'll cross my fingers," Clarice said with a soft laugh.

Thirty-three

Brandon and Clarice got through the morning without any unexpected problems for their hike. He left work at noon to go home and change clothes. Clarice rescheduled a meeting for the following day and left her office at one o'clock.

Brandon put on a green flannel shirt, jeans and ankle-high hiking boots as soon as he got home. He fixed himself a peanut butter-and-jelly sandwich and glass of milk and sat down at the kitchen table. He was anxious to leave but he didn't want to arrive at her house too soon. The phone rang and it startled him for a moment. He prayed that it wasn't Clarice canceling out on the hike.

"This is Brandon," he said.

"Hi Brandon," said a soft voice on the other end. It was Jenny.

"Good afternoon," Brandon said.

"Do you forgive me?"

"For what?"

"For last night," Jenny said, sounding like she was on the edge of tears.

"What happened last night?"

"You know," she said. "Me and that other guy."

"I don't mind."

"I swear there's nothing going on between us. He's going through a divorce and just wanted some company. We're only friends."

"Jenny, I really don't mind," Brandon said. "I don't care who you go out with."

"Don't you care about us anymore?" Jenny asked.

"We're just friends. Okay?"

"I thought we were more than that," she said.

"I'm sorry but...."

Brandon heard a click.

"Jenny?" he said. After a moment Brandon realized that she had hung up. He felt relieved the conversation was over. Now if she would finally get it in her head that it's really over between them, everything would be great, he thought.

He looked up at the clock and saw that it was one-thirty. He put on a lightly-lined brown corduroy jacket. The temperatures were in the low fifties and the sun was shining.

Clarice was ready when he arrived. She was wearing jeans and a blue denim shirt with a turtleneck and pink Nike walking shoes. She put on a light tan jacket as they left her house.

"Did you have much trouble getting away from work?" Brandon asked as they pulled out of her driveway.

"I thought I might have a meeting but I was able to move it to tomorrow," she said.

"I figured you'd have a close call," Brandon said with a chuckle.

"I know you tease me about meetings but they're really an important part of my job," she said. "That's the only way we can really understand a client and their needs."

"I know," he said. "I guess I'm just not a meeting person."

"They're really not that bad," Clarice said. "Every meeting is a little different so that makes it interesting."

"I just know I'd go nuts if I sat around a table every day in a meeting to talk and listen and then talk and listen some more," Brandon said. "I'm too much of a free spirit."

"Hey," she said with a smile. "You make it sound like we're a bunch of robots or something."

"I didn't mean it that way," Brandon said, glancing over at her. "I guess that I'm not disciplined enough to sit in meetings. Does that sound better?"

"I'm not so sure but that's okay," Clarice said. She glanced out the passenger window. "It's sure a beautiful day."

"I'm glad we're able to get out and enjoy it. Before too long it will be too cold to do it."

"Don't you like to hike in the winter?"

"Nope," he said. "I'm a warm-weather person. Sometimes I wish I could migrate with the birds every winter."

"I like the cold weather," Clarice said. "The air feels so fresh."

"And cold. Brrrr!," Brandon said with a laugh.

Brandon pulled into the parking lot at Raven Run. He had hoped there wouldn't be many people but there were several cars and a mini-bus from a retirement home. He knew they'd have company on the hiking trails. They got out of the car and started walking through a field that led to the wooded area. He took her hand and held it as they walked briskly along a path. She squeezed his hand lightly. When they reached the woods, they could hear chatter in the distance. Before long, they came up on several older women walking slowly and carefully on the jagged path strewn with broken limbs and decaying leaves. They smiled and exchanged greetings.

Brandon and Clarice reached an overlook to the Kentucky River and sat down on a large rock. When they were sure that nobody was watching, they shared a long kiss.

"I love it out here," Clarice said. "One of these days I would like to move out to the country. It's so peaceful and relaxing."

"I know what you mean," Brandon said. "I've been thinking about doing that myself."

"And give up your bachelor pad?" Clarice asked with a grin. "How would you ever manage out in the country?"

"I may live in the city but I'm still a country boy at heart," Brandon said. "I used to live in Campbellsville when I was a kid."

"Really?" Clarice said. "I thought you always lived in big towns."

"I didn't go to the city until I went to college," he said. "I always said that I'd never return to a small town but I've changed my thinking somewhat the past few years."

"Are you thinking about moving back to Campbellsville?" Clarice said, lowering her brows.

"No," Brandon said, "but I wouldn't mind moving to one of the towns around Lexington."

"I think I'd rather stay in Fayette County," Clarice said. "I just want to get out of the city."

"The city is growing so fast that if you moved out in the country, I bet in five years you'd be surrounded by subdivisions."

"You're probably right," Clarice said. "I may as well stay where I'm at."

They heard a crackle that sounded like someone stepping on a limb and turned around. An older couple was approaching them. The woman looked almost out of breath as the man held her hand tightly.

Brandon and Clarice stood up as the couple got closer to them.

"Why don't you sit here," Brandon said to the man.

"Thank you," he said in a raspy voice. "Mildred is getting a little winded."

The old lady smiled at Brandon and Clarice as her husband led her to the rock. She eased down slowly and took a deep breath.

"Are you going to be all right?" Clarice asked the woman.

"Oh, I'm fine," she said in a squeaky voice. "I just need to rest for a few minutes."

"We'll be happy to stay and help you back to your car," Brandon said. "It would be no trouble at all."

"That's kind of you to offer but we'll get back," the man said. "This is always our resting point. We'll be back up in fifteen minutes or so."

"We'll leave you then," Brandon said. "I hope you have a nice day."

"Thank you," the woman said.

Brandon and Clarice started back through the woods with Brandon leading the way.

"I hope she's going to be okay," Clarice said after they were out of earshot from them.

"I do, too," Brandon said. "But they seemed confident that there weren't any problems. I guess if anything happens we'll read about it in the newspaper tomorrow or see it on TV tonight."

"That's a terrible thought," Clarice said, shaking her head.

"Well, I'm right. I'm not wishing for anything to happen."

"Okay, I see what you mean."

When they reached the Raven Run office, they went in and told a park assistant about the couple. The assistant said she would go back down the path and make sure they made it back safely.

"Hungry?" Brandon asked as they got into his car.

"A little bit," Clarice said.

"Would you like to come over to my place?" he said. "I was thinking about ordering a pizza."

"Okay," Clarice said with a smile. "I was afraid you'd want to go to some restaurant with these clothes on."

"Now you look just great," Brandon said, tapping her on the hand.

"Let's not get carried away," she said. "My hair's a mess and I need lipstick."

"Don't be so hard on yourself. I wouldn't turn you away."

It took about forty-five minutes to get to Brandon's apartment after getting caught in the five o'clock rush hour. When they got there, he was glad he'd made up the bed and straightened the living room and kitchen.

"Nice place," she said while stepping into the living room. "Very cozy."

Brandon took their jackets and hung them in the closet at the front door.

"Have a seat," Brandon said. "Can I get you anything to drink? Coke? Beer? Water?"

"I think I'd like to have a beer," she said as she sat on the couch.

Brandon took two Miller Lites out of the refrigerator and handed her one. He sat on the couch next to her.

"My legs are a little sore," he said. "How about you?"

"Mine are too, now that you mentioned it," she said. "I need to get out and do this more often."

"Same here," Brandon said. "I'm on my rear end too much."

Brandon got up and turned on the stereo. He put on a CD by Mary Chapin Carpenter.

"Do you like her?" Brandon asked.

"I really like her," Clarice said. "I saw her in concert a few years back. She's a wonderful songwriter and singer."

"I'm going to order the pizza," he said. "What do you like on yours?"

"I'm not really particular," Clarice said. "I'll eat about anything."

"Is a veggie all right?"

"Sure," she said, and then took a swallow of beer.

Brandon called in the pizza while Clarice sat on the couch. While the apartment was clean and orderly, it was evident to her that it still needed a woman's touch as some of the furniture needed dusting and the carpet had a few soiled spots.

"Want to see the rest of the apartment?" Brandon asked.

"Sure," she said, easing up slowly from the couch.

She walked over to Brandon and he led her to the utility room, bath room and then the bedroom.

"It's not much but it's home," Brandon said while sitting on the corner of the queen-sized bed.

"I think it's nice," she said while standing a few feet from him. "Are you reading *Ulysses*?"

The book was on the nightstand with a bookmark about midway through the pages.

"I've been reading it off and on for the past few months," Brandon said. "It's heady stuff."

"I read it back in college," she said. "I think it's great. In fact, I've read it several times. I find new things every time I read it."

"I'll be lucky to get through it one time," Brandon said. "I hardly remember what I've already read."

"Give it a chance. You'll see what I mean."

"I'll try."

Brandon got up from the bed and they walked into the living room. A few minutes later the doorbell rang. Brandon paid for the pizza and put it on the coffee table.

"Do you need another beer?" he asked Clarice.

"Yes please," she said. "I'm about finished with this one."

Brandon grabbed two more beers from the refrigerator and returned to the living room. He sat beside her on the couch. Clarice had already opened the box and had taken out a slice.

"This is good," Clarice said after taking her first bite.

They ate half of the pizza. Brandon closed the box and put it in the refrigerator.

"Are you in any hurry to go home?" Brandon asked. He noticed that it was nearly eight o'clock.

"I probably need to get back by ten or so," she said. "I have a few papers I need to go over before I go to work tomorrow."

Brandon put his arm around her on the couch and she eased next to him. He looked into her soft brown eyes and could feel his heart began to patter. He wasn't sure of the scent she was wearing, but it was subtle and sexy. Clarice rested her head on his shoulder for a few seconds, and then rose up. Brandon met her mouth with his and they kissed passionately as they embraced each other warmly and tenderly.

After several minutes, Brandon whispered to her, "Do you want to get more comfortable?"

With her eyes half closed, Clarice softly said, "Yes."

Brandon led her to the bedroom, their fingertips interlocked as they reached the foot of his bed. They stood facing each other, the only light coming from a floor lamp in the living room. He slowly began to unbutton her shirt while her fingers worked their way down the buttons on his shirt. He slid the shirt off of her shoulders. Clarice removed her turtleneck and reached behind and removed her bra. Brandon touched her breasts softly and left wet kisses on her neck.

After a few intense moments, they removed the remainder of their clothes. Clarice pulled back part of the covers and got in the bed and Brandon followed her. She cuddled up close to him as they continue to kiss and explore each other's bodies with their hands. Clarice moved on top of Brandon, smothering him with hot kisses as he entered her. Their passion built to a fiery climax and she collapsed in his arms. They lay under the covers for another hour, kissing and touching in a tender embrace.

Clarice noticed that it was after ten on the clock on the nightstand.

"Honey, I hate to tell you this but I need to be going home," she said.

"You're welcome to spend the night," Brandon said, kissing her on the cheek.

"I'd loved to but I do have some papers to read," she said, raising up from the bed while covering her breasts with the sheet.

Brandon eased out of the bed and put on his clothes. While he went to the bathroom, she got dressed.

Brandon took her home. He walked her to the front door and kissed her in the cold night air.

"I enjoyed today very much," she said under the moonlight.

"I did, too," he said. "Can we talk tomorrow?"

"We can talk everyday," she said with a smile. She turned and unlocked the front door.

"Good night, Brandon," she said, turning around and facing him. She kissed him gently on the lips.

"Good night," Brandon said, and then walked to his car with a wide smile on his face.

Thirty-four

"There's sure a glow about you this morning," Rachel Townsend told Clarice in the women's lounge area at work. "I need to take an afternoon off."

"We all need it once in awhile," Clarice said with a bright smile.

"So what did you do?"

"A friend of mine took me to Raven Run," Clarice said. "We spent a couple hours out there hiking. It's really beautiful even though most of the leaves have fallen."

"I've been there a couple of times with the kids," said Rachel, who worked in accounting office. "Who is this friend of yours if you don't mind me asking?"

"I don't mind," Clarice said. "His name is Brandon Wilkes. He's a sportswriter. I met him several months ago. We've gone out a few times."

"Is it getting serious?" Rachel said with a playful grin.

"I believe it's going in that direction," Clarice said, lifting her eyebrows. "He's really a nice guy."

"Good looking?"

"I think so," Clarice said while combing her hair.

"I hope all goes well," Rachel said. "Let me know if you have wedding plans."

"I think that may be a long way off," Clarice said with a laugh.

Clarice touched up her lipstick and went to her office. There was already a message on her desk from Brandon. She picked up her phone and dialed his number.

"I think you beat me to work this morning," she said.

"I guess because I had such a relaxing sleep," he said. "Plus, I was tired after the afternoon."

"Me, too," Clarice said. "My legs are still a little achy."

"What's going on today?" Brandon asked.

"I've got a dinner meeting with a client after work," Clarice said. "I hope to be home by eight-thirty or so."

"Can I call you?"

"I hope you do," Clarice said softly. "What are you going to do today?"

"I may go visit Bobby Lee after work."

"That's nice."

"I enjoy it. I plan to take him to a football game next week."

"I bet he'll enjoy that."

"I took him to a game earlier this season and we had a good time together."

"I need to go now," Clarice said. "It was nice hearing your voice this morning."

"Same here," Brandon said. "I'll talk to you later."

After hanging up the phone, Brandon walked out to the front lobby. Maggie was on the phone. Graham stormed through the front door and rushed to his office without saying a word. Brandon and Maggie looked at each other with their eyes opened wide. She quickly finished her conversation and put down the telephone.

"What's up with him?" Maggie asked quietly.

"I don't have any idea," Brandon said. "I think we'd better let him cool down a little before we say anything."

"I think you're right."

"I was wondering if Bobby Lee will be at home tonight. I was thinking about stopping by for a little while and seeing him."

"He's where you last saw him," Maggie said. "The poor kid is really getting tired of being cooped up all the time."

"I would imagine so. Haven't you been able to take him anywhere?"

"Not as much as I would like to," Maggie said.

"How about if I take him to Baskin & Robbins for some ice cream?"

"That's fine but don't you think it's a little too cold outside for ice cream?"

"I thought kids liked ice cream no matter what time of the year."

"Probably so," Maggie said. "I'm sure he would enjoy getting out. He's also got some crutches now and he needs to get out and use them."

"He must be coming along real well."

"His arm is about healed," Maggie said. "It's going to take a little while longer for the leg."

"That's great. He's getting there though," Brandon said with a smile.

Graham stepped out of his office and to the hallway.

"Can I see you in a few minutes?" he asked Brandon, grimly.

"Just a minute," Brandon said. He turned toward Maggie and said, "I'll be over at your house around seven. Is that okay?"

"That's fine," she said. "I'll have him ready."

Brandon, with pursed lips, walked to Graham's office. He stepped inside and closed the door behind him. He sat down in a wooden chair facing Graham's desk.

"What's up?" Brandon asked.

"Sheila has filed for divorce."

"What?" Brandon said with a look of surprise. "I can't believe it."

"It's true. I'm still in shock. I was hoping we could work something out. She didn't even give me a chance."

"Have you been able to talk to her?"

"Only briefly on the phone a few times," Graham said. "She won't let me say anything. Every time I tried to talk about us getting together, she'd end the conversation."

"Do you want me to talk to her?"

"Do what you want but I don't think it's going to do any good," Graham said glumly. "I think she's already made up her mind to go ahead with the divorce."

"Is she making any demands?"

"Not really," Graham said. "She wants visitation rights with Bernie. That's about it. She doesn't even want the house. She said that Bernie needs a home and that making him leave the house would be too disruptive for him on top of the divorce."

"How is Bernie taking it?"

"He doesn't know about the divorce yet," Graham said. "I guess I'll tell him tonight."

"Damn," Brandon said, shaking his head. "This is really hard to believe. I can't imagine you and Sheila divorced."

"I can't either but it's going to happen," Graham said. "Probably by the end of the year. Isn't that a great way to start a new year?"

"I feel for you friend," Brandon said. "If there's anything I can do, anything, let me know."

"Thanks, pal," Graham said. "I would appreciate it if you wouldn't tell anybody about what's going on."

"Maggie already suspects something," Brandon said. "She's going to ask me."

"Well, you can tell her. I guess it doesn't hurt."

Brandon stood up and opened the door.

"I'll see you later," Graham said.

Brandon walked to his office and sat down at his desk. A few seconds later, Maggie was standing at the door. Brandon wasn't surprised by her presence.

"What is it?" she whispered.

Brandon motioned for her to close the door.

"Sheila filed for divorce," Brandon said.

"Oh, poor Graham," Maggie said sorrowfully. "How is he?"

"Naturally, he's upset about it all."

"I don't know what to say to him."

"You don't need to say anything. I'm sure he understands your feelings about this."

"I hope you'll tell him I'll do whatever it takes to help him get through it. I know what it's like."

Maggie returned to her desk. Brandon spent the remainder of the day copyediting and making phone calls. He went home after work and changed clothes, putting on jeans and a sweater before going to pick up Bobby Lee. He cleaned out the back seat of his car so that Bobby Lee would have room to sit.

The front porch was brightly lit when Brandon pulled into Maggie's driveway. Bobby Lee was standing at the front door, crutches under each arm and his broken leg cocked back with a brace. A big smile was on his face.

"Hi Brandon," he said as Brandon opened the front door. "I've got crutches."

"Hey, Bobby Lee," Brandon said, brushing his hand over the top of Bobby Lee's hair. "I bet they beat using a wheelchair."

"They're kinda hard to use right now."

"They won't be after you get used to them."

"Are we going to get some ice cream?"

"Yes," Brandon said. "Is that okay?"

"Yeah," Bobby Lee said, grinning.

"Where's your mom?"

"She's downstairs in the basement washing clothes."

"Let me go down and tell her we're about to leave."

"Okay," Bobby Lee said.

Brandon walked to the steps and headed down into the basement. He could hear the washing machine churning and the dryer humming. Maggie was under a light folding clothes.

"We're getting ready to leave," Brandon said.

Maggie jumped back.

"Oh!" she said, putting her hand to her chest. "You startled me for a moment."

"Oops," Brandon said. "Sorry about that."

"That's okay," she said with a laugh. "I was just caught up in my thoughts. I've been thinking about poor Graham."

"He's going to be all right."

"I know, but I know he'll be going through a very difficult time the next couple of months," Maggie said as her eyes began to water.

"Are you ready?" Bobby Lee shouted from the top of the stairs.

"I guess I'd better be going," Brandon said. "Someone upstairs seems a bit anxious. We'll be back by eight-thirty or so."

"Have a good time," Maggie said.

Brandon went back up the stairs. He helped Bobby Lee put on a green car coat that was a little big on him. Brandon rolled up the sleeves. He opened the door and Bobby Lee gingerly moved outside to Brandon's car. Brandon pulled open the back door and Bobby Lee backed in to the seat.

"Good job," Brandon said after Bobby Lee got settled.

"That was easier than I thought it would be," Bobby Lee said.

Brandon drove to Regal Park Shopping Center and parked in front of the Baskin & Robbins. He opened the back door and helped Bobby Lee work his way out of the car. Bobby Lee got across the parking lot with no problem as if he'd been using them for a long time.

He ordered a banana split while Brandon got a small cup of fat-free banana yogurt. They sat down at a booth and each ate a few bites before saying anything.

"Are you ready to go back to school?" Brandon asked.

"I think so," Bobby Lee said. "I'm tired of doing all that school stuff at home. It's boring."

"Do you like your teacher?"

"She's nice," Bobby Lee said after taking a bite. "She helps me a lot."

"Are you getting good grades?"

"Yep," he said. "All A's and B's."

"That's great," Brandon said with a warm smile. "Do you still want to go to the football game next week?"

"Yeah. I can't wait."

Brandon didn't ask any more questions as he watched Bobby Lee devour the banana split. He thought about what he had missed by not having any children. Bobby Lee had opened his eyes about the joys of being around a child. At least he knew he could show attention to kids and find ways to enjoy their company.

After they finished, Brandon drove Bobby Lee around town. He figured the boy liked being out of the house after spending so much time in the house.

Maggie was sitting in the living room when they returned to the house. Brandon could see her silhouette move across the curtain on the front window as she walked to the front door. Bobby Lee slid out of the back seat easily and moved quickly to the house as Maggie opened the door.

"Aren't I doing good with the crutches?" he said with a toothy grin.

"You sure are," she said, pressing his head against her bosom and hugging him.

Brandon walked into the house behind Bobby Lee and closed the door. Maggie helped Bobby Lee remove his coat and hung it in the front closet. Bobby Lee hopped over to the hide-a-bed and sat down on the side.

"How was the ice cream?" Maggie asked Bobby Lee.

"Delicious," Bobby Lee said. "I had a banana split."

"Sounds yummy," she said.

"I should have brought something back for you," Brandon said.

"I don't need any ice cream," Maggie said, patting the sides of her hips. "That's the last thing this body needs."

"I need to be going," Brandon said.

"Can't I make you a cup of coffee?" Maggie asked.

"Thanks but it's getting late for me."

"Thanks again for taking Bobby Lee out for ice cream. What do you say, Bobby Lee?" Maggie said.

"Thanks, Brandon," he said.

"You're welcome. We'll do it again soon. Keep up with the good grades."

"I will," Bobby Lee said.

"I'll see you all later," Brandon said as he opened the door.

"See you in the morning," Maggie said as she walked toward him. "Have a nice evening."

Brandon was home by nine o'clock. He took out two slices of pizza from the refrigerator, put them in the microwave, and poured a tall glass of ice water. After he finished, he called Clarice.

"How was your dinner?" he asked.

"It was okay," she said. "It didn't last as long as I thought it would. I got home before eight."

"I just finished eating some pizza," he said. "You sound tired."

"I am," she said. "It was a long and busy day."

"I'll let you go," Brandon said. "You need to get some rest."

"Do you mind?" Clarice asked. "I'm really tired."

"I don't mind," he said. "I'll probably retire early tonight after I read."

"*Ulysses*?"

"Yeah, I think I'll try to read a few more pages," Brandon said. "You talk about long days, Joyce really stretched it out to a long one."

Clarice laughed softly.

"Will you call me in the morning?" she asked.

"Of course," Brandon said. "I look forward to it."

"Good night," she said.

"Good night, Clarice," Brandon said warmly. "Sweet dreams."

After putting down the telephone, Brandon cleaned up his mess in the kitchen. He went back to the bedroom, put on gym shorts and a T-shirt, picked up *Ulysses* on the nightstand and opened it to the bookmark. He read ten pages before deciding to turn off the light and go to sleep.

Thirty-five

"Why don't we go over to Churchill Downs this afternoon?" Graham said in the break room. "There's only three more days left in the meet. It might be nice get out for the afternoon."

"Sounds okay with me," Brandon said. "When do you want to head over there?"

"Around eleven-thirty or so. I've got a few calls to make."

"Same here."

They went back to their offices carrying a steaming cup of coffee. Brandon picked up the phone and called Clarice.

"Good morning," he said brightly when she answered.

"Hi," Clarice said cheerfully.

"Did you get a good night's sleep?

"I slept like a baby."

"That's good," Brandon said. "You've been working too hard lately."

"Maybe so," she said. "What are you doing today?"

"Graham and I are going out to Churchill Down a little later this morning. I haven't been there this meet."

"I love Churchill Downs," she said. "I wish I could find the time to go."

"You're welcome to join us."

"Thanks but I've got too much work to do. I've got a report I need to finish by this weekend."

"If you change your mind, I'll be around here until eleven-thirty," Brandon said.

"Don't be waiting by the phone," Clarice said with a laugh.

"What are you doing this evening?"

"I'll probably work late."

"Would you like to go out for some pizza after work?"

"Why don't you call me first?" Clarice said. "Sometimes we call out for pizza when we're working late."

"Okay," Brandon said. "I've got to go now. I hope you have nice day."

"You, too," Clarice said. "I'll be thinking about you."

Brandon made a few more calls and answered several e-mails before Graham knocked on his door.

"Ready?" Graham asked.

"Sure," Brandon said, getting up from his chair.

They walked to the lobby where Maggie was tidying the waiting area.

"We're going to Churchill Downs," Graham said. "We probably won't be back until late."

"Any horses you want us to bet on?" Brandon asked.

"I don't gamble," she said. "I work too hard for my money to throw it away on horses."

"Just inquiring," Brandon said with a laugh. "I didn't ask for a sermon."

"I didn't mean it that way," Maggie said, a little red in the face.

"I'm just teasing you," Brandon said.

"I know," she said. "I hope you have a good time."

Graham drove to the track. Along the way they discussed ways to improve the publication. Brandon thought Graham would bring up his marital problems but that never surfaced. Graham used his parking sticker to park next to the grandstand. Cars were steadily coming in to the parking lot as patrons were hoping to examine the horses in the paddock before the first race. Graham and Brandon went to the press box and spoke to some of the track's officials. Buck

Odoms was seated at one of the tables studying *The Daily Racing Form* and making scribbles next to some of the entries.

"Found a winner?" Brandon asked as they approached Buck.

"Hey guys!" Buck said. "What's up?"

"We thought we'd get out of the office for the afternoon," Graham said.

"Well, you couldn't have picked a nicer day," Buck said, looking toward the window and the clear blue sky in the distance. "I think it's supposed to get up into the sixties today."

"We may go down with the railbirds a little later," Graham said. "It is too nice to be in here."

"Have you guys had lunch yet?" Buck asked.

"No," Brandon said. "I could use a bite to eat."

"Same here," Graham said.

"They've got a great buffet," Buck said. "Want to go with me?"

"That's sounds fine with me," Graham said. "When are you going?"

"Now," Buck said as he stood and rolled the paper in his hand.

Buck led the way to the buffet area. It was half full as a waitress led them to a table. They went through the food line and filled their plates. After they sat down, they ate and talked about the meet.

"Hi, Buck," a tall, slender man standing behind Brandon said. "How's the food?"

"Great, as usual," Buck said. "Care to join us?"

"If you don't mind."

Brandon turned his head around and saw that it was Bart Taylor. He forced a small smile, turned back around and continued eating.

Bart went to the food line and brought back a plate full of food. He sat down opposite Brandon at the four-seat table.

"Bart, I'd like you to meet Graham Jones and Brandon Wilkes," Buck said.

"A pleasure to meet you," Graham said, nodding his head.

"Good to meet you," Brandon said.

"Same here, guys," Bart said. "Are you regulars here?"

"Hardly," Graham said. "We're with *Kentucky Sports Weekly*."

"I've read it a time or two," Bart said while cutting roast beef into small pieces.

"Bart's in the horse business," Buck said.

"I think I've heard the name," Brandon said. "Somewhere."

Buck gave Brandon an amused look as if everyone should know who he is.

"Any tips on the races?" Buck asked Bart.

"Hmm, I've heard number two looks good in the third race and number six in the fifth," Bart said. "Don't bet your retirement on it though."

"Don't worry about that," Buck said with a laugh. "I've used your tips in the past so I know better."

"You're finally wising up," Bart said.

"Bart has more babes than anyone in the state," Buck said to Graham and Brandon.

"Really?" Graham said with a grin. "Care to share any tips on that?"

"I've had a few," Bart said with a smirk. "It's pretty easy."

"Why don't you set me up with someone?" Buck asked. "I've seen some of your discards."

"These ladies have standards," Bart said with a laugh.

"Thanks a lot," Buck said. "How's your woman doing, Brandon?"

"She's fine," Brandon said, suddenly beginning to feel uneasy. "How was your dinner with Debra?"

"The lady sure likes to talk," Buck said. "She even talked about you. I had to remind her that she was with me."

"Who's this Debra?" Bart asked Buck.

"Debra Hatfield," Buck said. "She sells real-estate. A good-looking blonde with a nice rack."

"You need to introduce me sometime," Bart said before picking up a glass of ice water and taking a big swallow. "I'm sure she could use some class."

"Isn't the name of the woman you date Clarice?" Buck said to Brandon.

Brandon choked lightly on some food and cleared his throat.

"Yes," he said. He took a sip of water.

"I know a Clarice," Bart said. "What's her last name?

"Horton," Brandon said. "Clarice Horton."

"Hey, she's something else," Bart said with a knowing grin.

"I think she's something else, too," Brandon said, trying to control his emotions. He wanted to get up from the table and leave but knew that would send off signals to the others about his feelings for her.

"I went out with her a few weeks ago," Bart said.

"I know," Brandon said, glaring at Bart.

"Isn't it about time to go out to the track?" Buck said, seeming to pick up on the hostility between Brandon and Bart.

"I'm ready," Graham said quickly while pushing his chair from the table.

"You guys go ahead," Bart said. "I've still got a ways to go. Nice meeting you."

Brandon, Graham and Buck stood and sliding their chairs under the table.

"Same here," Graham said to Bart. Brandon simply nodded as they walked away toward the elevator.

"Is he really your friend?" Brandon asked Buck.

"I've known him for a few years," Buck said. "He can be kind of arrogant at times but he's harmless."

"He's certainly got an attitude," Brandon said as the elevator trudged slowly down to the first floor.

"Don't give him any thought," Graham said. "He's a shithead."

"I'm not," Brandon said, still feeling a little hot under the collar as the elevator door opened. They stepped out and walked out in front of the green grandstand.

Brandon turned around and looked up into the grandstand. On the third row, wearing a bright red hat, was Sheila sitting with a man in a dark gray suit. They were looking at the program.

"Why don't we go up to the press box?" Brandon asked.

"What's wrong with this?" Graham said.

"I think it might be too crowded," Brandon said.

"It doesn't make any difference with me," Buck said.

"Let's go then," Brandon said, walking toward the elevator. He glanced up to the grandstand and caught Sheila's eye. She had a frozen look on her face for a moment. Brandon nodded and smiled as he and his friends walked past her. Graham never looked in her direction.

Brandon and Graham left after the sixth race to beat the crowd leaving the track. Brandon won more than three hundred dollars, most of it off Bart's tips, while Graham had two hundred and fifty in winnings.

"We need to come back here more often," Graham said as they slowly drove off in his car. After stopping for gas, Graham returned to the office building at five-thirty. Brandon's car was the only vehicle in the parking lot. Graham dropped him off at the curb and Brandon walked over to his car.

While unlocking the vehicle, he heard footsteps coming up quickly behind him. He felt a blunt object pushed against his back.

"Give me you wallet!" the man demanded. Brandon recognized the voice as the person who robbed him before. Without hesitation, Brandon rammed his elbow into the man's stomach. The man bent over, his hands against his belly, and Brandon kicked him across the head. The man fell over, dropping a folded pocket knife to the ground.

A moment later, a car swerved into the parking lot with its lights shining brightly on Brandon standing over the man. Graham stopped the car a few yards away, jumped out and ran to Brandon as he dialed 911 on his cell phone. Brandon kneeled over the man with his knee lodged against his back and hand pushing his head against the cold pavement.

"Something told me to come back," Graham finally said after talking to the 911 dispatcher. "I don't know why in the world I left you at a dark parking lot after what happened a few weeks ago."

"I'm glad you came back when you did," Brandon said with a grin.

"The cops will be here in a few minutes," Graham said.

Moments later, they could hear a siren in the distance. Brandon kept a firm hold on the man.

"Hey, let me up," the man moaned. "I wasn't going to hurt you bad."

"You were just going to take my money and run?" Brandon asked sarcastically.

"Some chick paid me to do this," the man said.

"What?"

"Yeah, she wanted me to rob you and rough you up a little."

Brandon looked at Graham and shook his head.

"What in the hell are you talking about?" Brandon asked.

"Let me go and I'll tell you," the man pleaded.

"No such luck," Brandon said.

"I didn't plan to hurt you that bad last time," the man said.

"You were the person who mugged me here?" Brandon demanded.

A police car pulled quickly into the parking lot with its blue lights flashing. Two policemen got out of the car and hurried over to Brandon.

"What's going on?" an older cop asked sternly.

"This man assaulted me," Brandon said.

The other policemen motioned for Brandon to get off the man. He pulled the man up and put his arms behind his back and handcuffed him. He read him the Miranda rights and hauled him over to the police car while the policeman questioned Brandon about the incident.

"Can you come down to headquarters for more questioning?" the policeman asked.

"No problem, officer," Brandon said. "I'll be right behind you."

Thirty-six

Detective Miller was sitting in the squad room drinking a cup of coffee when Brandon and Graham walked in.

"They've got your man back in the interrogation room," Miller said after offering them a seat next to his desk. "His name is Johnny Powers. He has no prior criminal record. Do you know him?"

"No," Brandon said. "I've never seen him before in my life. Is he the person who attacked me the last time?"

"We think so," Miller said. "We'll know a little bit more when we're through with him."

"Any information on what he does?"

"From what it appears, he works at a bank."

"A bank?"

"Yeah, I think he pushes paper over at Bankers Trust. He's worked there for about four years."

"I have a friend who works there."

"What's her name?"

"Jenny Thomas."

"Do I know her?"

"She was with me at the hospital last time," Brandon said.

"I remember," Miller said, nodding slowly.

"Is anything the matter?" Brandon said, glancing over at Graham.

"Powers said a few things," Miller said. "We're going to have to bring her in for questioning."

"Jenny?" Brandon asked with a puzzled look.

"I'm afraid so," Miller said. "I can't give you any details right now other than it could be serious."

A few minutes later, a plainclothes policeman brought Powers out of a small room. Powers looked over at Brandon with a blank stare on his face. Another policeman walked out of the room and came over to Miller's desk.

"Are you Mr. Wilkes?" he asked Brandon.

"Yes, I am," Brandon said. "What can you tell me?"

"Well, if you want to believe young Mr. Powers, it seems that he was paid to assault you," the policeman said.

"What?" Brandon asked, incredulously.

"He said a Ms. Jenny Thomas paid him five hundred dollars to attack you. He was supposed to hurt you enough to send you to the hospital and make it look like a mugging."

"You've got to be kidding," Graham interjected. "It was a damn mugging."

"I can't believe she'd do something like that," Brandon said.

"We'll find out in a little while," Miller said. "We're sending someone over to her address at this minute."

"Did he mention a motive?" Brandon asked.

"He wasn't really sure," the policeman said. "He did say he hadn't planned to hurt you as bad as he did last time."

"That's comforting," Brandon said with a wry grin.

"I'd like for you to hang around here when we question Ms. Thomas," Miller said.

"Sure," Brandon said. "I'm curious to know what's going on."

The policeman returned to the interrogation room. Miller offered Brandon and Graham something to drink but they declined.

"You know, thinking back on the last time, Jenny sure got to the hospital awfully quick," Brandon said. "I don't know how she knew about it."

"I guess we may find out in an hour or so," Miller said.

A double-wide glass door to the squad room opened. Brandon looked over and saw David Hatfield. He walked over to his desk near the front of the room but didn't notice Brandon.

"Oh boy," Brandon said to himself.

"What's the matter?" Miller asked, looking up from a report he was reading.

"Oh, this may get interesting," Brandon said. "That policeman over there has been going out with Jenny."

"Hatfield?" Miller asked.

"Yes," Brandon. said.

"I thought he was married," Miller said. "Of course, I guess that doesn't make much of a difference anymore."

"I think he's in the process of a divorce," Brandon said.

Miller got up from his desk and walked over to speak to Hatfield. After a few seconds, Hatfield turned and looked in Brandon's direction and nodded unsmiling. As Miller returned to his desk, Hatfield stood for a moment and left the room.

"I told him what was going on and suggested that he leave," Miller said.

A few minutes later, Jenny walked in to the squad room with a uniformed policeman. She immediately caught Brandon's eye.

"Oh, Brandon," she said, breaking loose from the policeman's hold and rushing over to Brandon. "I hope you're okay."

Brandon and Graham stood up. Jenny wrapped her arms around Brandon and rested her head against his shoulder. The policeman took a hold of her arm but released it after Miller nodded for him back off from her.

"I'm all right," Brandon said, standing stiffly.

"He attacked you in the parking lot again?" Jenny asked, her eyes filled with tears.

Brandon nodded.

"Ma'am, we need to ask you a few questions," Miller said. "It shouldn't take very long."

"Of course, officer," she said while brushing away her tears. "I'll do whatever I can to help Brandon."

The policeman escorted her to the interrogation room and closed the door.

"She puts on quite an act," Graham said to no one in particular.

"We'll see if it's an act when they're through with her," Miller said. "Powers could be lying through his teeth."

Brandon and Graham got up from their chairs and walked to the corner of the room and poured themselves a cup of coffee. The coffee was lukewarm and bitter.

"Damn, if any coffee will put hair on your chest, this will," Graham said after making a face as if he'd bit into a lemon.

"Or it'll take it off," Brandon said with a chuckle.

"What do you think about all of this?" Graham said of the assaults.

"It's almost unbelievable," Brandon said. "I don't know what to think right now."

"Could she do something like that?"

"I hate to say it but she could," Brandon said. "She's awfully jealous and possessive."

"But to have someone attack you?" Graham asked.

"That's what I can't understand. I guess we'll find out in a little while."

They tossed their nearly full paper cups into the trash and returned to Miller's desk and sat down. A few minutes later, a door clicked and a policeman came out of the questioning room followed by Jenny. She glanced quickly at Brandon, then turned her head away.

The policeman who questioned Powers walked over to Miller's desk with several sheets of paper in his hand.

"She told us quite a bit and then asked for an attorney," the policeman said to Brandon.

"What did she say?"

"She admitted having Mr. Powers assault you in the parking lot," the policeman said grimly. "She said she wanted to take care of you."

"What?" Brandon said, squinting his eyes. "Take care of me?"

"She said she cared for you and that the only way for you to let her show you any attention was for her to have someone harm you. She did say that she hadn't planned for Mr. Powers to hurt you as much as he did."

"And I'm sure that she hadn't planned for Mr. Wilkes to take out Mr. Powers like he did this time," Miller said with a half-laugh.

"What's going to happen?" Brandon asked.

"She's being booked right now as an accessory to an assault," the policeman said. "She'll be taken over to the detention center and appear before a district judge in the morning."

"I can't believe this," Brandon said, shaking his head.

"Well, you'd better believe it," Miller said. "This lady apparently had one of those so-called fatal attractions for you."

"At least it wasn't fatal," Graham said.

Brandon looked up at the clock on the middle of the wall. It was eight forty-five and he wanted to get out of there.

"Can we go now?" Brandon asked impatiently.

"Go ahead," Miller said. "I may drop by your office in the morning for more questioning."

"I'll be there," Brandon said while standing up. "Thanks for all your help."

Brandon shook hands with Miller and the policeman as Graham headed toward the door.

"Feel like a beer?" Graham asked Brandon outside the building.

"I need to get on home," Brandon said. "It's been a long day."

"That's a good idea. I'm a bit frazzled myself."

They walked to their cars parked on the street.

"Did you notice that she said that *he* attacked you *again* in the parking lot?" Graham asked. "I thought that was a bit odd. Like she already knew who had done it."

"I picked up on that as well," Brandon said. "I wonder if Miller and the others did?"

"I'm sure it didn't go over their heads. She did put on quite a show for them."

"It was heart-warming," Brandon said, rolling his eyes. "Well, I'm going home. I'll see you at work."

"Be safe in the parking lot after you get home," Graham said with a laugh.

Brandon had a message from Clarice on his answering machine. He picked up the phone and called her.

"Hi Brandon," Clarice said. "Did you just get home?"

"I just got here," he said. "You wouldn't believe what happened."

Brandon proceeded to give her the details of the assault and Jenny being arrested in connection with the crime.

"That's so unreal," she said. "I'm glad you're all right."

"How was your day?" Brandon asked.

"Certainly not as exciting as yours," she said. "I got home shortly after seven. How was your day at the track?"

"I won about three hundred dollars," Brandon said.

"That's great," she said.

"I also met one of your old friends."

"Who was that?"

"Bart Taylor."

There was momentary silence on the Clarice's end of the phone.

"And what did he have to say?"

"Nothing, really," Brandon said. "He's kinda arrogant."

"That's putting it mildly. He's full of himself," Clarice said.

"I got that impression." Brandon sensed that she was uncomfortable talking about Taylor. "So, are you going to help me spend my winnings?"

"Sure," she said with a laugh. "I always enjoy helping people spend their money."

"How about dinner this weekend?

"You name the time and place."

"I'll give that some thought," Brandon said with a chuckle. "I'm already looking forward to it."

"Me, too," Clarice said sweetly.

Thirty-seven

Detective Miller was waiting in the front lobby for Brandon when he arrived at work the following morning. Maggie had poured him a cup of black coffee and kept him company by talking about the football season.

"Good morning," Brandon said. "I didn't expect to see you this early."

"I just want this taken care of and out of the way," Miller said while easing up from his chair and shaking Brandon's hand. "I don't think we're going to have any more problems from your friend."

"I hope not," Brandon said. "Come on back to my office."

Miller followed Brandon and sat down in a chair next to his desk. Brandon excused himself for a minute to go get a cup of coffee.

"So what's the scoop?" Brandon asked after he sat down behind his desk.

"It seems that Ms. Thomas and Mr. Powers didn't mean to give you much bodily harm," Miller said. "As strange as it may sound, she paid him to rough you up a little so she could care for you. She felt that was the only way she could be with you. Had you been involved in a close relationship with her?"

"I guess it depends on a person's perspective," Brandon said.

"How so?"

"She wanted a commitment from me for marriage or whatever," Brandon said. "I didn't want that kind of involvement with her. I was happy to keep it as a friendship. She wanted a lot more."

"Apparently," Miller said.

"So what's going to happen?"

"Well, they're scheduled to be arraigned this morning over at district court," Miller said. "They'll probably be released on bail. A lot of this depends on you. I would hope you would press charges for assault and battery."

"I really don't want to," Brandon said. "I'd rather put this behind me."

"I don't know how you can say that after what happened the first time."

"Can I do something to minimize the charges, especially against Jenny?" Brandon asked.

"We can talk to the Fayette County attorney's office and see if they can work something out," Miller said.

"I'd like to see Jenny get some counseling," Brandon said. "As for Powers, I don't think a week or two in jail would hurt him. Perhaps they could give him shock probation after serving some time."

"I'll see what I can do but that's up to the prosecutor and judge," Miller said. "You're too nice of a guy."

Brandon shrugged his shoulders. "Is there anything else you need from me?"

"Not for now," Miller said as he began to get out of the chair. "The only thing I can tell you is to be careful when walking in dark parking lots."

"Thanks a lot," Brandon said with a grin. "I'll try to remember that. Can I ask you something?"

"I guess," Miller said. "What is it"

"I was wondering if you're married."

"For nearly thirteen years. Same woman. We have three children. Why do you ask?"

"Just curious. I guess it's difficult mixing police work and family."

"At times, but I try to put family first."

They shook hands and Miller left the office. Maggie was standing at the doorway less than a minute after Miller left.

"I can't believe that story about Jenny," Maggie said, shaking her head. "It's really weird."

"I agree," Brandon said with his hand on the telephone. He was about to call Clarice when Maggie appeared.

"What are they going to do to her?" Maggie asked.

"I hope she receives some counseling," Brandon said.

"I do, too," Maggie said. "She always seemed a little different to me."

"Why do you say that?"

"It's just something a woman can pick up," Maggie said. "There was just something about the way she talked about you. You could tell she was the jealous type."

"How are the others?" Brandon asked. "I don't want to encounter someone else like her."

"Oh, the others are fine," she said. "This Ms. Horton seems awfully nice and pleasant."

"That's good to hear," Brandon said. "I don't want to make the same mistake twice."

Maggie turned and returned to her desk when the phone rang. Brandon punched in the other line and dialed Clarice's number. He got her voice mail. Maggie buzzed Brandon's line and told him the call was for him.

"This is Officer Hatfield," the man said.

"Hi," Brandon said. "What can I do for you?"

"I just want to tell you that I misjudged you," he said. "I hadn't realized the problems you were having with Jenny. I've seen her the past few weeks and all she seemed to talk about was you."

"It's difficult to understand what she did," Brandon said. "I only considered her as a friend."

"She's really been a confused woman," Hatfield said. "I shouldn't say this so pardon me if I'm out of line, but I hope you won't be too hard on her."

"I wouldn't do that," Brandon said. "I hope she can receive some counseling."

"Well, that's what she needs. She's not a bad person."

"I know that," Brandon said. "I hope to help her in any way I can."

"Do you plan to see her again?"

"What do you mean?"

"Do you plan to go out with her again?

"No," Brandon said. "If I see her it will only be at social functions. Or, unfortunately, in court."

"I was just wondering," Hatfield said. "Again, I hope everything turns out right for you."

"Thanks," Brandon said. "And I hope the same for you."

After he put down the receiver, Brandon shook his head. He wasn't sure what the conversation was all about. He hoped that talking to Hatfield didn't jeopardize the investigation.

Brandon picked up the phone again and called Clarice. This time she answered.

"I thought I'd get your voice mail," Brandon said with a chuckle.

"I'm not always in meetings," she said. "And sometimes I actually take a break and get away from the phone."

"So what are your plans for the evening?

"Would you mind coming over to my house?" she asked. "I'd love to fix dinner for you."

"That's an invitation I can't refuse," he said. "What time?

"How about seven-thirty?"

"I'll be there," Brandon said. "Can I bring anything?"

"Just yourself," Clarice said.

After they finished talking, Graham tapped on his door and came in carrying a cup of coffee.

"What's up?" Brandon asked.

"I think that's my question," Graham said while sitting down.

Brandon gave him a rundown of what the police told him about the assaults and what he had recommended.

"I think I would throw her sorry ass behind bars for six months," Graham said.

Brandon figured Graham's bitterness toward Jenny stemmed from his unhappiness in his failing marriage and didn't respond to the comment.

"Is soccer season over?" Brandon asked.

"We have our last game this weekend," Graham said. "It's for the city championship."

"Where?"

"It's going to be over at Shillito Park at two on Sunday."

"I may try to make it over there if I can."

"You should," Graham said. "Bernie would like that."

"Any other plans for the weekend?"

"Not really," Graham said. "I'll probably watch football on TV."

"I'm taking Maggie's boy to the game on Saturday. Why don't you and Bernie join us?"

"I'd like that but Bernie has practice on Saturday afternoon."

"Well, perhaps the four of us can go to a basketball game this season."

"That'd be nice," Graham said. "The boys would love to do that. Let's try to work something out."

Graham received a telephone call and returned to his office to answer his phone. Brandon checked his e-mail and worked on his weekly column.

~ * ~

Clarice went to lunch with Rachel at a neighborhood bar and grill. While waiting for their order, Bart Taylor strolled over to her table.

"Good afternoon, Clarice," he said.

"Hello, Bart," she said with a forced smile. "How are you?"

"I'm doing fine," he said. "We've got the horse sales going on this week so I've been somewhat busy."

"I'd like you to meet Rachel," Clarice said.

Bart nodded and smiled at Rachel, and she smiled back at him.

"Can I call you sometime?" Bart asked Clarice.

Clarice twisted slightly in her seat and paused a moment.

"I don't think so, Bart," she said. "I'm seeing someone now."

"Oh, I think I met him at the track this week," Bart said. "His name is Wilkes or something like that. A sportswriter."

"Yes," Clarice said with a stiff smile.

"Can't you do better than that?" Bart asked smugly.

"I beg your pardon?"

The waitress returned with their food order. Clarice glared at Bart. He smirked.

"I think I'd better move on," Bart said. "I hope you have a nice lunch."

Clarice didn't reply.

"It was nice meeting you, Rachel," Bart said, nodding his head.

"It was nice to meet you, too," Rachel said.

Bart turned and returned to his table.

"You used to date him?" Rachel asked.

"A long time ago," Clarice said. "He's a bad memory."

"He's sure good looking," Rachel said while blending her salad.

"That's about all," Clarice said with a look of disdain.

"Is he rich?"

"Probably. He was born into money. He didn't work for it."

"Oh."

"You should feel fortunate that you married someone like Eddie," Clarice said. "He's a hard-working guy who cares a lot for you. Bart only cares for himself."

"I guess you're right," Rachel said. "He's still good looking."

Clarice laughed softly and shook her head.

"Can't we change the subject?"

Thirty-eight

Brandon arrived at Clarice's house with a bottle of red and a bottle of white wine.

"I wasn't sure what you were going to fix so I got a bottle of both," Brandon said as he followed her into the kitchen. He looked around for a moment, marveling at all the gadgets, pans, skillets, and appliances on the counters and hanging from the wall.

"What's the matter?" Clarice asked.

"I feel like I'm in Julia Child's kitchen," Brandon said. "This place makes my kitchen look primitive."

"Your kitchen is just fine," Clarice said with a grin. "I wouldn't expect much more from a bachelor unless he was really into cooking."

"You must enjoy it," Brandon said.

"I really do," she said. "It's my escape. I wish I had more time to conjure up different meals in here."

"Conjure?"

"I like to fool around with different recipes and put my own little stamp on something," she said. "A lot of cooks do that."

"Interesting," Brandon said. "I prefer not to mess with my microwave dinners."

They laughed.

"Why don't you go into the den while I finish a few things in here?" Clarice said. "I've got a few CDs that you may like. And feel free to turn on the TV."

Brandon went through her modest CD collection and picked out a Jim Brickman album of love songs and put it in the player. He kept the volume low and sat down on the couch. A few minutes later, Clarice joined him.

"Dinner should be ready in about twenty minutes," she said, slipping a leg under her. "Can I get you anything to drink?"

"Perhaps later," Brandon said. "How was your day?"

"Rather uneventful. I worked on a few reports. How was yours?"

"No reports here except from the police," Brandon said. "Detective Miller showed up."

"I still can't believe someone would do something like that to a person they supposedly cared about," Clarice said.

"I still have trouble believing it. But she had been bothering me lately. She's very possessive."

"She sounds desperate."

"She just couldn't accept no for an answer. She just didn't want to be friends. She wanted more."

"Amazing," Clarice said, shaking her head.

"Well, she did take good care of me after I got popped on the head," Brandon said with a laugh. "By the way, I thought I had found a nice guy for your friend but he's happily married with three kids."

"We don't want to break up a good marriage," Clarice said. "She'll find someone."

"You have a nice collection of music," Brandon said.

"Do you like Jim Brickman, too?" Clarice asked.

"I think he's a good composer," Brandon said. "Nice, mellow sounds."

"He's one of my favorites," Clarice said.

"Who else do you like?"

"Oh, I guess Barbra Streisand, Celine Dion, Vince Gill. People like that."

"People who sing love songs," Brandon said with a soft smile.

"I guess you could say that," she said. "Who do you like?"

"Linda Ronstadt, James Taylor, Justin Hayward, George Strait, Patty Loveless, and of course, the Beatles," Brandon said. "I like classic rock."

"Do you like disco?"

"Nope," he said with a laugh. "Don't tell me that you do."

"I hate to disappoint you but I do because I like to dance," she said. "But don't worry, I don't have any disco music here."

"Thank goodness," Brandon said, wiping his hand over his forehead.

"I think dinner is about ready," Clarice said while getting up from the couch.

"Can I help?"

"Just sit here and relax," she said. "I've already set the table. I'll let you pour the wine in a few minutes."

Brandon skimmed through a magazine while Clarice was taking food out of the oven. The telephone rang and she answered it.

"Hi Clarice."

"Hello," she said coldly, recognizing Bart's voice.

"Am I calling at a bad time?"

"Yes."

"Do you have company?"

"Yes."

"Who is it?"

"None of your business."

"It must be the Wilkes guy."

"What do you want?" she asked. "I've only got a minute."

"How about dinner some evening?"

"No thank you."

"Don't you want to see me again?"

"No," she said. "I need to go now."

Clarice hung up the telephone and went back to the dishes. She put food on their plates, an egg plant casserole, sliced carrots and peas and carried it out to the table.

"You can pour the wine now," Clarice said.

Brandon went to the kitchen, where Clarice handed him two wine glasses. He poured a half a glass of white wine in each and carried them to the table. She brought along the bottle of wine, turned down the dining room light with the dimmer switch and lit two blue long-stemmed candles on the table.

"Everything looks and smells delicious," Brandon said as he pulled out her chair for her to sit down.

"I hope everything tastes good," she said.

"I'm sure that you've conjured up something that will be great," Brandon said with a smile.

Brandon sat down and picked up his fork and took a bite of the vegetarian lasagna.

"Hmm, this is very good," he said.

"Thank you," Clarice said with a slight blush in her cheeks.

"Was that a call from work?" Brandon asked.

"No," she said. "It was one of those unsolicited phone calls."

"I get them occasionally," Brandon said. "They usually come at dinner time."

"You're right about that," she said. "I hope this one will cease."

"Good luck," Brandon said. "Those folks sometimes can't take no for an answer."

Clarice smiled with pursed lips.

After finishing their meal, Clarice went back to the kitchen and returned with a red velvet cake.

"I don't know if I need that," Brandon said with a laugh. "But it does look delicious."

"I'll only give you a small slice," Clarice said. "I really don't need it either."

"When did you have time to bake this?"

"Well, I baked it last night," she said, smiling. "I was expecting company tonight."

"You're a little sure of yourself, aren't you?" Brandon said with a grin.

"I take my chances once in a while when I feel the odds are good," she said.

"I'm glad you do," Brandon said. She placed a slice of cake on a small dish and handed it to Brandon and took their dinner plates back to the kitchen. He waited until she sat down and sliced a piece of cake for herself before taking a bite.

"This is delicious," Brandon said. "I love red velvet cake."

"Thank you," she said, again with a slight brush. "I'll give you some to take home with you."

After finishing dessert, Brandon helped Clarice clear the table. She put the dirty dishes in the dishwasher and covered the leftovers with plastic wrap and put them in the refrigerator. He blew out the candles.

Brandon took her hand and led her back to the den. The CD had finished playing on the stereo. The only light was from a lamp on an end table on a low setting. They sat down on the couch and Clarice snuggled close to him as he put his arm around her.

"That was a wonderful meal," Brandon said softly. "Thank you for inviting me over."

"You're welcome," Clarice said, her head resting against his shoulder. "I'm happy you enjoyed it."

Brandon turned his head slightly and kissed her gently on the forehead. Clarice titled her head back and gazed up at him with soft, warm eyes. He could feel his heart skip a beat as he gazed at her inviting mouth. He closed his eyes and kissed her long and passionately as he put his arm across her waist. With his other arm around her back, he put his hands on the back of her head and ran his fingers slowly through her hair. Their lips parted for a moment and he ran his tongue under her chin. He could feel her shiver and moan slightly as he left a trail of wet kisses across her neck.

Clarice moved back from him and slowly got up from the couch. She took his hands and tugged slightly as he stood up next to her. She smiled and held his hand while leading him to the bedroom. The dark blue curtains were pulled together and the only light came from a night light just outside the bedroom door. Clarice pulled back the bedspread and covers and turned back around to face Brandon. He took her into his arms in a secure embrace and kissed her hard and passionately.

Moments later, they were in the bed, under the white satin sheets. He kissed her body tenderly, across her breasts and soft belly. Her hands dug gently into his arms and shoulders, sending sensations throughout his body. He touched her warm softness. She cooed in delight. Their lovemaking reached a peak to where he could no longer resist being inside her, and she needed all of him as he pulled over on top of her. She wrapped her legs and arms tightly around him while they devoured each other with hot kisses. When it was over, he rolled over on his back and she cuddled up to him, her arm across his chest and a leg over his leg. He kissed her lightly on the forehead and squeezed her gently. They savored the moment for several minutes in silence.

"Clarice?" Brandon whispered.

"Yes," she responded as her head was nestled between his neck and shoulder.

"Can I tell you something?"

"I guess so."

"I think I'm falling in love."

"You do?" she said, then raised her head back and looked at him.

"I think so," he said. "Is that okay?"

"I think so," she said softly. "Can I tell you something?"

"Will it hurt my feelings?"

"No, silly," she said with a soft laugh.

"What is it then?"

"I think I'm falling in love with you, too."

Brandon kissed her gently on the mouth and smiled. Her face glowed with soft reflections of light in her dark eyes.

"It's getting late," Brandon said. "I think I'd better be going home soon."

"You don't have to go home tonight," Clarice said. "You can stay here."

"Are you sure?"

"Yes, I'm sure," she said. "Unless you don't want to."

"I want to," Brandon said, kissing her again on the forehead.

"Can I ask you something personal?" Clarice asked, raising up and looking at him.

"Uh, oh," Brandon said a laugh. "I guess so."

"Why haven't you ever been married?"

"I never had the time," he said. "I was so wrapped up in work when I was younger that I never had time to develop any kind of meaningful relationship with someone. After awhile, I began to enjoy my freedom."

Clarice laid back and put her head on a pillow. Brandon rested his head on a pillow as they lay next to each other, looking up at the ceiling with the covers pulled up to their shoulders.

"Has there ever been anyone you thought about marrying?"

"I guess there were a couple of women when I was younger," Brandon said. "There was a girl I worked with on the newspaper staff in college. We dated for a few years but after we graduated we went out separate ways."

"Did you think you'd marry her?"

"At the time I did, but after being apart from her I realized that it wouldn't happen."

"What happened to her?

"Let's see, I think Susan got married a few years later and started having babies. The last I heard she was living on a farm in Oregon."

"Anyone else?"

"There was a woman I worked with in Georgia," Brandon said. "We never became engaged but she talked about marriage a lot."

"What happened?"

"I think I just got cold feet," Brandon said with a laugh. "I was in my late twenties and wasn't ready to settle down."

"And what happened to her?"

"She went to Central America on an assignment and was killed by some rebels."

"Oh, Brandon, that's sad," Clarice said, turning her head toward him.

"Brenda was a free spirit," Brandon said. "She loved dangerous situations. She thrived on them. Even if I didn't get cold feet, I couldn't keep up with her."

"And that's all the women?"

"I think so."

"How about Jenny?"

"There was nothing between Jenny and myself," Brandon said. "She was basically a friend to do things with."

"Did you ever sleep with her?"

"Aren't we getting a little too personal here?"

"You don't have to answer," Clarice said. "By not answering you've given me an answer."

"You shouldn't be so hasty to read between the lines."

"So you didn't sleep with her?"

"I didn't say that either," Brandon said with a laugh. "I'm just saying that you shouldn't assume things."

"It doesn't matter anyway."

"I could use a glass of wine," Brandon said. "How about you?"

"How about a glass of wine while sitting in a hot bubble bath?"

"Hmm, that sounds even better," Brandon said. "I'll go get the wine while you run the water."

In the darkness, Brandon walked nude to the kitchen and turned on the light. He found two wine glasses and poured them nearly full with red wine. Clarice was in the bathroom, running water into an oversized garden tub that was surrounded on three sides with mirrors. She lit four rose-scented candles and placed them around the tub. Clarice had a large red towel wrapped around her when Brandon returned with the wine. He handed her a glass and picked up a towel and wrapped it around his waist. The tub slowly filled up with bubbles. Clarice swirled her hand in the water, then turned off the faucet. She modestly removed the towel with her back to Brandon and stepped in the tub. Brandon waited until she was settled and took off his towel and got in facing her.

"This feels great," Brandon said as he gradually lowered his body in the swirling water. Clarice was reclined, the bubbles coming up to her neck.

"It is relaxing," she said with her eyes closed.

"Can I ask you a personal question?" Brandon asked.

"How personal?" Clarice said with a shy grin.

"You asked me some personal questions," Brandon said. "Do you think turnabout is fair play?"

"Sometimes," she said with a giggle.

"Is Howard the only person you've been intimate with?" Brandon asked before taking a sip of wine.

"No."

"Have there been many others?"

"Hardly," she said with a laugh. "Like you, I've been too wrapped up in a career."

"How about Bart?" Brandon blurted out.

"Bart?" Clarice said as she squirmed slightly in the water.

"Were you ever close to him?"

"Not really," Clarice said. "We dated for awhile but it never amounted to anything."

"Why?"

"Bart can be quite the charmer," Clarice said. "He can sweep you off your feet until you realize that Bart is looking out for Bart. He's quite egotistical."

"So he swept you off your feet?"

"I guess so," Clarice said. "But it didn't take long before I realized what a shallow person he is."

"Did you get serious?"

"I think I got serious," Clarice said. "I think he was playing along with me."

"How long did it last?"

"Six months or so."

"Did you sleep with him?"

"Unfortunately, I did," Clarice said. Sadness enveloped her face.

"I didn't expect you to answer that," Brandon said.

"You shouldn't have asked then," Clarice said with a forced smile. "Does that bother you?"

"No," Brandon said, although feeling a small pang of jealousy. "Adults do those things in relationships."

"Like you and Jenny?"

"Are you fishing again?" Brandon asked with a laugh.

"Just setting a trap," she said with a sly grin.

"Has there been anyone else?"

"I've met a few guys here and there but nothing really serious," Clarice said.

"No one?"

"Until you," Clarice said with a smile.

Brandon moved up beside her and put his arm behind her head. They kissed long and tenderly.

"I love you," Brandon whispered.

"And I love you."

Thirty-nine

Clarice woke Brandon up at six the next morning with a several soft kisses around his ear. He turned over and held her in his arms for a few seconds while kissing her lightly across her face.

"It's too bad we have to work today," Brandon said.

"Why don't we call in sick and play hooky" Clarice said.

"Don't tempt me."

"I'm kidding," she said. "I've got a ton of work at the office."

"You always have a ton of work. I've never met a person in PR who wasn't always swamped with work."

"What's that supposed to mean?" Clarice asked before playfully jabbing him in the side.

"You guys always seem busy."

"Because we are. It's a simple fact."

"I believe you," Brandon said, arching his eyebrows. "I really do."

"Smarty," Clarice said, poking him again.

Brandon pulled her against him and kissed her long and passionately. His hand slowly and gently massaged her back. When their mouths parted, she tucked her head under his chin and put her hand on his chest. They lay silently for several minutes, feeling their heartbeats against the other.

"It's getting late," Clarice said with a sigh. "We should be getting up. Can I fix you some breakfast?"

"How about coffee?"

"No problem," she said. "You can take a shower while I make the coffee."

Clarice slipped out of bed and went over to the closet and took out an oversized pink robe and put it on. She smiled at Brandon as she walked to the kitchen. Brandon got up and went to the bathroom and turned on the shower faucet. He finished by the time Clarice returned with a tray holding the coffee, creamer and sugar.

"That was quick," she said while watching him put on his clothes. She sat down on the side of the bed and stirred sugar and creamer into her coffee.

"I need to hurry," Brandon said. "I have to go home and change clothes. I also need to get out of your hair because I know you have to get ready for work."

"Take your time," Clarice said. "It won't take me that long."

Brandon took a cup of coffee from the tray and stirred in a teaspoon of creamer.

"What are you doing this weekend?" Brandon asked.

"Nothing," she said.

"How would you like to go to a football game?"

"That would be fun but aren't you taking your secretary's son?"

"Yes," Brandon said.

"Don't you think he would mind?"

"I don't think so. He's a good kid."

"Why don't you just take him?" Clarice asked. "I think it's important for him to be with you. He may resent me being there."

"Are you sure?"

"Yes," Clarice said with a soft smile. "Perhaps we can do something Sunday."

"Okay," Brandon said. "We have a date on Sunday."

Brandon finished his coffee and put the cup back on the tray.

"I need to run," he said. "I'll call you later this morning."

"Better make it around noon," she said.

"I know, you've got a meeting," Brandon said as walked over to her. He kissed her softly on the mouth. "Bye."

"Good bye," she said while rising from the bed. "Talk to you later."

Brandon locked the front door on the way out to his car. The sky was overcast and gray and there was a cool dampness in the air. He turned the ignition on his car. The clock on the console read five past seven. He let the engine idle for a minute before backing out of the driveway. He thought of the evening with Clarice and how the words, "I love you" came from his mouth so naturally. He had never felt this way for a woman in his life.

After he got to his apartment, he checked to see if there were any messages on his answering machine. There was one from Graham saying that it wasn't urgent and that he'd see him in the morning. Brandon went back to the bedroom and changed clothes, putting on brown slacks and soft yellow shirt. He quickly brushed his teeth and headed out the door to work.

Maggie and Graham were in the break room, chatting about their sons when Brandon strolled in with his empty coffee cup.

"Where were you last night?" Graham asked. "I called around eleven."

"I had a dinner date," Brandon said, slightly blushing.

"That must have been some meal," Graham teased.

"It was delicious, if you need to know," Brandon said, grinning.

"What was it?" Maggie asked.

"A vegetarian lasagna," Brandon said.

"Hmm, that does sound good," she said. "I had a grilled cheese and tomato soup last night."

"And I had beer and pretzels," Graham said.

"I guess I must be living right," Brandon said with a laugh.

The phone rang out front and Maggie left to answer it. Graham and Brandon stood silently for a few seconds to see if the call was for them. They could hear Maggie engaged in a conversation.

"You must like this new woman," Graham said.

"We have seemed to hit it off just right," Brandon said. "I enjoy her company. What did you do last night?"

"Sheila dropped by and picked up some more clothes," Graham said. "I tried to talk to her but she would hardly acknowledge me."

"I'm sorry to hear that," Brandon said. "Did she talk to Bernie?"

"She went to his room for a few minutes and they talked. After that, she was out the door with a suitcase of clothes."

"That just doesn't sound like her."

"I know," Graham said while shaking his head. "I can't figure out what's going on inside her head. She's almost hostile toward me and I don't know why."

"Do you think it's over?"

"Hell yes. I don't want it to be but I don't see anything I can do to change things," Graham said sadly.

"Well, if there's anything I can do, don't hesitate to ask," Brandon said.

"I only ask that if you see her to try to find out what's going on," Graham said. "It's apparent that she's not going to tell me."

"I'll see what I can do," Brandon said.

"Let's get to work," Graham said as he stepped toward the door.

Brandon warmed his coffee and went to his office. He turned on his computer and read e-mail. Maggie buzzed him with a telephone call.

"Brandon, I want to apologize for everything," Jenny said from the start.

"Really?" Brandon said.

"I don't know why I did what I did," she said in a weeping voice. "I wasn't thinking. It was stupid."

"I really don't know what to say," Brandon said after clearing his throat.

"I've lost my job," Jenny said. "I'll be moving after this is all over."

"I'm sorry to hear about your job but perhaps you need a fresh start."

"I want you to know that I did what I did because I cared for you. I know that doesn't make any sense. Looking back, it doesn't make any sense to me."

"We all do crazy things once in awhile that we end up regretting."

"But to hurt someone like I did to you is not right. I hope that someday you'll find room in your heart to forgive me."

"I forgive you already," Brandon said. "I only want the best for you. I hope you realize that."

"You are such a special man," Jenny said while crying. "If only..."

"Let's not go there," Brandon said quickly. "That's all behind us now. I want you to get on with your life."

"I'll try," she said.

"I know you will."

"Good bye, Brandon," she said sorrowfully.

"Good bye."

After putting down the telephone, Brandon rested his head in his hands for a few seconds. As much as he couldn't understand Jenny's actions in having him attacked, he didn't have it in his heart to hate her for it. He hoped that she would receive the kind of counseling that would help her develop healthy relationships. And to get over him.

Brandon looked at the time on his computer and saw that it was close to noon. He picked up the telephone and called Clarice. He got her voice mail.

"I guess you're still in a meeting," Brandon said. "I'll be in the office for most of the day if you get a chance to call. I hope you have a great day. Love ya."

Brandon smiled after putting down the telephone. He was lost in his thoughts for a moment before he realized Maggie standing at the door.

"Are you love sick or something?" she asked with a smile.

"Could be," Brandon said.

"I just wanted to make sure that you're still taking Bobby Lee to the game on Saturday," she said.

"As far as I know," Brandon said. "I've got the tickets and everything."

"Bobby Lee is excited about it," she said. "I may go to a movie or something while you're out."

"Go ahead and make plans," Brandon said. "Bobby Lee and I will be gone all afternoon."

"Was that Jenny who called?" Maggie asked.

"Yeah," Brandon said. "She was saying good bye."

"I hope that woman gets her head on straight."

"Same here," Brandon said with a nod. "She's really not a bad person."

"You know her better than I do," Maggie said with a shrug.

"I think she'll be okay after some counseling. It's going to take some time."

"I hope so for your sake," Maggie said.

"Me, too."

Forty

Brandon pulled into Maggie's driveway at eleven-thirty on Saturday morning. The football game started at one-thirty and he wanted to make sure that he got there in plenty of time to find a parking space close to the stadium. Bobby Lee was wearing a Kentucky sweatshirt and ball cap and was watching the coach's show on television when Brandon knocked on the front door.

"Good morning," Maggie said. "I believe Bobby Lee is about ready to leave."

Brandon stepped inside the house and glanced over to the living room where Bobby Lee was on the couch.

"Have you made plans?" Brandon asked Maggie.

"I'm going to a movie," she said. "There's a new movie with Tom Hanks that I've wanted to see. After that I may stop over at Wal-Mart and do a little shopping."

"We should be back by six," Brandon said.

"That gives me plenty of time," she said.

"Are you ready?" Brandon asked Bobby Lee. "You'd better wear a heavy coat. It's cold and a little windy outside."

Maggie opened the closet door and took out a heavy blue-and-white winter coat. Bobby Lee got up from the couch and she helped him put it on.

"Who do you think is going to win, Brandon?" Bobby Lee asked.

"Since it's Tennessee, I think I'll go with the Volunteers," Brandon said.

"I think Kentucky will win," Bobby Lee said while placing the crutches under his arms and moving to the front door.

"You guys have a good time," Maggie said. She gave Bobby Lee a kiss on the cheek. "And you behave and do everything Brandon says."

"I will mom," Bobby Lee said. "Bye."

Brandon arrived at the stadium at noon and found a parking space about five hundred feet from the entrance. Bobby Lee had mastered using the crutches and didn't have any problem keeping up with Brandon or negotiating around tailgaters in the parking lot. They took an elevator to the upper level. Their seats were located near the forty-yard line on the lower part of the upper level. Some of the players were already out on the field, passing and kicking footballs.

"I hope I can play football when I get bigger," Bobby Lee said. "I think it would be fun."

"It's a lot of hard work, too," Brandon said. "And you can get hurt."

"I don't care," Bobby Lee said. "I think it would be fun running into people and tackling them."

"Have you ever played?"

"Mom won't let me," Bobby Lee said. "She said she's afraid I'd get hurt."

"Well, you can get hurt," Brandon said. "I can understand why she feels that way. Have you ever played soccer?"

"I think that's a sissy game."

"Now, you shouldn't say that until you've played it," Brandon said.

"It doesn't look like that much fun."

"I bet your mom would let you play soccer."

"Probably," Brandon said with a shrug, "but I'd rather play football."

Brandon smiled and laughed to himself. Bobby Lee's remarks reminded him of trying to convince his mother to let him play football a long time ago. When she finally relented, he went out on the first day of practice and broke his arm while tackling a player.

While the band was playing, Brandon walked to the concession stand and bought a hot dog, chips and hot chocolate for Bobby Lee and coffee for himself. The wind had picked up a little in the stadium, making it feel even colder than the forties.

The stadium was nearly packed at kickoff. Kentucky played the Volunteers close for most of the game, but lost in the final minute on a long touchdown pass. Brandon watched as Bobby Lee's shoulders slumped when the player in the orange and white jersey crossed the goal line for the winning score.

Brandon didn't get out of the stadium parking lot until five-fifteen. They stopped at White Castle and Bobby Lee ordered six hamburgers, fries and milkshake while Brandon had a large cup of coffee. They got back to Bobby Lee's house shortly after six. Maggie was already at home, sitting in the living room watching TV.

"I hope you guys had a great time," Maggie said.

"It was fun but we lost," Bobby said dejectedly.

"Did you have a nice afternoon?' Brandon asked. "How was the movie?"

"It was wonderful," Maggie said. "You should see it."

After spending a few minutes in the house listening to Bobby Lee describe the game to Maggie, Brandon went over to Hastings. It was nearly seven. He found a spot at the bar.

"Where have you been stranger?" Benny said while setting a draft beer on a napkin in front of Brandon. "I haven't seen you in awhile."

"I've been busy with work," Brandon said before taking a sip from the mug. "How's everything been with you?"

"I can't complain," Benny said. "Busy as usual."

Benny went to the end of the bar and took care of another customer while two others were trying to get his attention. Rosie was intently working the tables for drink orders.

"Hello handsome," Brandon turned around in his stool and Debra standing behind him in a tight blue sweater and tight blue pants.

"Hi, Debra," Brandon said. "Do you want my seat?"

"Thanks but I think I'll stand," she said. "I need to get my blood circulating after sitting out in the cold at the game. I froze my behind off."

"I was there," Brandon said. "It was a good game."

"I'm told it was," Debra said with a laugh. "We had a couple of flasks of bourbon with us. I don't remember much of it."

"Tennessee won."

"I know that," she said emphatically. "Don't they always?"

"Most of the time," Brandon said.

"So what are you doing here?" Debra asked. "Don't you have anything better to do on a Saturday night?"

"I thought I'd stop here for a few beers before going home."

"Buck may be here a little later," she said.

"How are things with him?" Brandon asked.

"Buck's a lot of fun," Debra said. "We've gone out a few times."

"How's everything with your marriage?"

"It's about over," Debra said. "I think David is going to be leaving."

"Quitting the police force?"

"He's fallen in love with some woman who's going to be moving and I think he's going with her."

Brandon thought about seeing David with Jenny and wondered if he was leaving because of her. Nothing would surprise him anymore.

"So how's your love life?" Brandon said after taking a swallow of beer.

"Kinda boring," she said, leaning up against him with her breasts. "Want to do something about it?"

Brandon eased toward the bar to put some distance from her. He motioned to Benny for another beer.

"Do you want something to drink?" Brandon asked Debra.

"Yeah, give me a Coors," she said. "And I think you're trying to change the subject."

Brandon asked Benny for a Coors when he brought over the draft beer. Benny turned around and took one out of the cooler, unscrewed the top, and handed it to Brandon.

"Change the subject?" Brandon asked while giving the Coors to Debra.

"Yeah," she said with a sexy smile. "Do you want to do something about my love life?"

"I'll leave that up to Buck," Brandon said with a grin.

"Buck is too easy," she said. "He's one horny guy. He can't keep his hands off me."

Brandon laughed. He could see that Debra was feeling the effects of the alcohol. A couple sitting next to him got up and Debra took a stool next to him.

"He's just lonesome," Brandon said. "He works long hours and probably needs a little companionship."

"All Buck wants is to get in my pants," she said with a loud laugh.

"Well, he has good taste," Brandon said.

"Then why don't you?" she asked, leaning toward him. "Don't you have good taste?"

"I have good taste," Brandon said. "I'm seeing someone."

"Then why don't you say that?" Debra asked.

"I was just having a little fun with you," Brandon said.

"I know you were, honey," Debra said. "I was playing along with you, too. You're much too nice of a guy to sleep with every woman he meets."

"I take that as a compliment," Brandon said, tipping his head.

"It is," Debra said. "It seems like all men want to sleep around. It's rare to find someone like you. Your lady friend is very lucky."

"Thank you, again," Brandon said with a smile. "I'm sure you'll find Mr. Right one of these days."

"I'm not counting on it," Debra said after taking a long swallow from the bottle. "But I'm not sweating it either. Life is too short."

Brandon turned around and glanced at the clock on the wall behind him. It was almost eight forty-five.

"I need to be going," Brandon said. "It's getting late."

"Late?" Debra said. "Are you serious?"

"It's been a long day for me," Brandon said.

"The night is still young," she said, holding up the bottle in front of her.

"For you, perhaps," Brandon said while motioning to Benny to bring over his tab.

"Are you going home?" Debra asked.

"Yes," Brandon said with a chuckle.

"Take me home with you," she said.

Brandon noticed that she was getting more intoxicated.

"Are you going to be all right?" Brandon asked. "Can I get a taxi for you?"

"I'm fine, sweetheart," she said loudly. "Why don't you take me home with you?"

Several patrons sitting close to them turned around and stared at her momentarily, then went back to their conversations. Brandon felt embarrassed by her remarks.

"Hey guys!"

Brandon turned and saw Buck approaching them. He breathed a sign of relief.

"Hi Buck," Brandon said. "I'm getting ready to leave."

"Don't rush off," Buck said.

"I'm tired," Brandon said. "I need to be going home."

"And he won't take me with him," Debra blurted out. Her eyes were half closed and she was beginning to slur her words.

"Buck will take care of you," Brandon said.

"I know what Buck will want to take care of," she said. "And it rhymes with his name."

Brandon looked at Buck and shook his head in amusement. Buck flickered his eyebrows and grinned.

Brandon eased out of his stool and nodded for Buck to take it.

"You'd better order her some coffee," Brandon whispered in Buck's ear. "She's had way too much. She's going downhill fast."

"I'll take care of her," Buck said.

Brandon handed Benny ten dollars and walked away without saying anything to Debra. She was sitting motionless at the bar with her eyes closed.

After getting home, Brandon called Clarice on the phone.

"How was the game?" she asked.

"I had a good time," Brandon said. "Bobby Lee seemed to enjoy it even though Kentucky lost. What have you done today?"

"Nothing," Clarice said with a light laugh. "I watched *Bridges of Madison County* on the DVD and cried, and then I've been reading."

"Do you have any plans for tomorrow?"

"Only with you," Clarice said. "Did you forget?"

"I don't take things for granted," Brandon said with a chuckle. "What do you want to do?"

"How about a movie and dinner?

"That sounds like fun," Clarice said.

"Maggie said there's a new Tom Hanks movie out," Brandon said. "She saw it today and really liked it."

"Let's go see it then," Clarice said.

"I'll be over around one. Is that okay?"

"I'll be ready."

Forty-one

Brandon and Clarice remained seated in the theater watching the credits after the movie as others made their way to the exits. After the auditorium emptied, they put on their coats and headed toward the front lobby.

"I'm glad your friend recommended the movie," Clarice said while leaving the theater. "Tom Hanks and Meg Ryan are really good together. I've always liked their chemistry on screen."

"They're very good together," Brandon said. "I wonder how they are away from the cameras?"

"They both seem like warm people," Clarice said. "I bet they're good friends."

"Probably so. They probably wouldn't have that chemistry on screen if they didn't like each other. That would be too difficult to fake."

Brandon opened the passenger side of the car for her and she got in and reached over to unlock his door as he walked around to the other side. They waited in the parking lot for a few minutes as the traffic thinned out.

"Hungry?" Brandon asked.

"A little," Clarice said.

"Any special cravings?"

"I wouldn't mind some Mexican food," she said.

"Is Old Mexico all right with you?"

"That's one of my favorite places."

Old Mexico was a ten-minute drive from the theater. They discussed the movie all the way to the restaurant.

After they were seated, Brandon remembered the last time he was there. It was with Jenny. He also remembered Clarice there with Bart. He almost wished he had selected another place.

"Is anything the matter?" Clarice asked, smiling.

"Oh nothing," Brandon said.

"You seemed lost in thought there for a few seconds," she said.

"You should have captured that on film because it doesn't happen that often," Brandon said with a laugh.

"I think you're a very serious-minded person," Clarice said. "And I think you have a great sense of humor."

"Why, thank you," Brandon said.

The waiter came by with salsa and chips and they ordered a pitcher of margaritas and an appetizer plate of quesadillas.

"Do you have a busy week ahead of you?" Clarice asked.

"Not really," Brandon said. "We get into a routine and it's pretty much the same way week after week. About the only change is when we have special sections but those are planned months in advance."

"I think you have a good publication," Clarice said. "I'm not really that interested in sports but I do think your magazine is visually appealing."

"Thank you. Are you going to have a busy week?"

"About the same as the past few weeks," Clarice said. "We don't have any major campaigns coming up, which is fine with me. I think everything will begin to pick up at the beginning of the year."

The waiter came back with the margaritas and two glasses. He salted the top of each glass and poured the drink to the top. They took a sip from their drinks and savored the taste for a few seconds.

"Are you the jealous type?" Brandon asked

"I've never really thought about it," Clarice said. "I guess I can be somewhat. How about you?"

"A little," he said. "I really haven't been that close with someone to get really jealous over anything."

"Are you jealous over me?" Clarice asked.

"Hmm, a little I guess," Brandon said.

"Who are you jealous over?"

"I'd rather not say," Brandon said, squirming slightly in his chair from uneasiness.

"Go ahead and tell me," she said. "I'd like to know."

"You probably know the person."

"It couldn't be Howard," she said.

"No, it's not Howie," Brandon said. "And to be honest, I still can't believe you were married to him."

"That was another life," Clarice said. "Sometimes I can't believe I was married to him either."

"It's Bart Taylor," Brandon said.

"Bart Taylor?" Clarice said, squinching her nose. "You've got to be kidding."

"The last time I was in here you were with him," Brandon said. "Remember?"

Clarice took a sip of her margarita and paused a moment to think.

"That was a long time ago," she said.

"But you and he were an item at one time."

"I guess we were but that was another time, too," she said. "There's nothing there between us anymore."

"That's good to hear," Brandon said, letting out a deep breathe and smiling.

"You shouldn't worry about things like that," she said. "You're the only man in my life."

Brandon wanted to reach over and kiss her but the waiter came back with their food. He refilled their glasses.

"So you're not jealous?"

Clarice blushed slightly.

"I must admit that I got a little upset when I called your apartment that time and Jenny answered," she said. "But after I thought about it, I knew it was silly because I had no right to be that way."

"But you had feelings for me back then?"

"I guess that was the first time I realized that I did," Clarice said, smiling.

"I've met Bart a couple of times," Brandon said.

"Really?" Clarice asked. "You never told me about it."

"I haven't?" Brandon said sheepishly.

"No, you haven't," Clarice said. "And where did these occur?"

"I met him at Churchill Downs a few weeks ago and then at Hastings," Brandon said. "He's a friend of Buck Odoms, a buddy of mine from the newspaper. He's a handsome dude."

"There's nothing much under those good looks," Clarice said. "I think a lot of women find that out early."

"And he has money."

"Money that he didn't earn," Clarice said. "He's never had to work for anything in his life."

"That doesn't surprise me," Brandon said. "He seems to want everyone to bow down around him."

Clarice laughed.

"You really don't like him, do you?" she asked.

"To be honest, I wouldn't care for him even if he hadn't been involved with you at one time," Brandon said, a touch of anger flaring in his eyes. "Can we change the subject?"

"Sure," Clarice said while reaching over and gently touching his hand. "I didn't want to talk about him to begin with."

After they began eating their quesadillas, Brandon looked around the restaurant and saw Bart and a woman being seated at the far end.

"You've got to be kidding me," Brandon said incredulously.

"What's the matter?" Clarice asked.

"Speaking of the devil, look at who just arrived?" Brandon said while nodding in Bart's direction.

"I guess I should have told you that this is one of Bart's favorite restaurants," Clarice said.

"I wish you had," Brandon said before taking a big swallow from the glass.

"Just relax," Clarice said. "We're about finished. We'll be leaving in a few minutes."

Brandon ate another quesadilla and avoided looking toward Bart. He smiled at Clarice with pursed lips, not wanting her to sense his uneasiness but realizing that it was showing like a neon light.

"Are you ready to go?" he asked.

"Yes," Clarice said. "I'm full. The food was really good."

"I hope so. This will probably be the last time we eat here together."

"Oh Brandon, don't be that way." A tender smile crossed her face.

What seemed like an hour for Brandon, but was only minutes, the waiter returned with the check. Rather than use his credit card, Brandon paid with cash and left a large tip so he could leave the place immediately.

While walking toward to the front entrance, Bart seemed to instinctively turn around in his seat and look at Brandon and Clarice. He flashed a big grin at them and waved. Brandon felt like it was in slow motion as they walked past his table. Clarice smiled curtly. Brandon didn't acknowledge him.

"He gives me the creeps," Clarice said as they stepped outside the restaurant and into the cold air and walked across the parking lot to Brandon's car.

"I know exactly what you mean," Brandon said.

Clarice wrapped her arm inside his and squeezed as they walked toward his car.

Brandon drove Clarice back to her house with neither of them hardly saying a word to each other. He had the radio on a station that was playing forgettable love songs that all sounded the same.

"Would you like to come in?" Clarice asked when they pulled into her driveway.

"I don't know," Brandon said with a slight shrug.

"Bart really upsets you, doesn't he," she asked, touching his arm gently.

"I guess he does."

"You shouldn't let him bother you like that, sweetheart. He's not worth it."

"I know you're right," Brandon said, shaking his head. "I'll get over it. I guess it's just that jealous bone in my body."

Clarice kissed him softly on the cheek.

"Why don't you come in for an hour or so and we can watch some TV and relax?" Clarice said.

"Okay, I'll come in for a little while," Brandon said. "But run me out by ten because we both have to work tomorrow."

"I'm not going to make that promise," she said, seductively.

Brandon grinned.

"Well, run me off when you've had enough of me," he said with a laugh.

After they got into the house, Clarice turned on the television and went to the kitchen and made cappuccino. Brandon fooled with the remote while she went to her bedroom to put on jeans and a T-shirt. She came back with the drinks and sat down next to him.

They watched television until ten, then Clarice took the remote and turned it off. Without saying anything, she took his hand and led him to the bedroom. They made tender love before falling asleep in each other's arms.

Forty-two

"Have you heard from Graham this morning?" Brandon asked Maggie at ten forty-five on Monday morning.

"No I haven't and it's not like him not to call or something," Maggie said with a look of concern. "I called his house about thirty minutes ago and didn't get an answer."

"I think I may drive over there and see if there's anything wrong," Brandon said.

"Oh, please do," Maggie said. "I'm really worried about him."

Brandon returned to his office and put on his coat. As he was about to walk out the front door, he received a phone call. He told Maggie to take a message and went on to his car.

~ * ~

Graham's car was parked in the driveway and Brandon pulled in behind it. He walked briskly to the front door and banged on it a few times. He didn't get a response and then he walked around the side to the den window. He could see Graham motionless in the recliner. Brandon ran around to the backdoor and found it locked. He picked up a piece of a branch in the back yard, broke a small window panel in the door and reached in and unlocked it. Brandon hurried to the den. He noticed that Graham was breathing lightly. On the side of the recliner was an empty fifth of whiskey.

Brandon shook Graham from the shoulders. Graham moaned and barely opened his eyes. His breath reeked of bourbon.

"Oh," Graham slurred. "What time is it?"

"It's after eleven," Brandon said. "What in the hell is going on?"

"I guess I got drunk last night," Graham said with a silly grin.

"Let me fix a pot of coffee."

"That would be nice my good friend."

Brandon went to the kitchen and shuffled through the cabinets until he found a can of coffee. He made a big pot in the Mr. Coffee and went back to the den while it was brewing.

"Why did you get drunk last night?" Brandon asked.

"Because I felt like it," Graham said.

"You don't get tanked for no reason at all."

"I just felt like it. Can't a guy get drunk because he just wants to?"

"What's going on, Graham?" Brandon asked sternly.

Graham put his forearm over his eyes and began sobbing.

"What is it?" Brandon asked again.

"Sheila came and took Bernie last night," Graham said.

"Why?"

"Bernie said he wanted to live with his mom, so I told him to go on," Graham said. "He called her and she came over last night and got him."

"I wish you would have called me," Brandon said. "You don't need to be going through all of this alone."

"I don't want to lay my problems on anyone."

"We're friends, Graham," Brandon said. "You're not laying troubles on me."

"I don't know what I'm going to do," Graham said after a sniffle. "I lose Sheila and now my son. It's almost getting to be too much."

"You're not going to find any answers in a bottle of whiskey."

"I know that," Graham said. "But at least I can escape with a few drinks."

"How long has this been going on?"

"What?"

"The drinking."

"I don't drink that much," Graham said. "I usually have a few beers in the evening when I'm watching TV. I don't get drunk or anything."

"How long has it been going on?"

"I don't know," Graham said, sounding a bit irritated. "I just drink to relax."

"Okay," Brandon said. "Let me go fix you a big cup of coffee."

Brandon returned to the kitchen and took two cups from the cupboard. Graham staggered in a minute later and sat down at the kitchen table.

"Do you want me to call Sheila?" Brandon asked as he handed Graham his coffee.

"It's too late," Graham said. "It's too damn late for anything."

"Maybe it's not," Brandon said. "Do you have her phone number?"

"I think it's over by the phone book."

Brandon saw the phone book on the counter with Sheila's number written on the cover. He took a piece of paper out of his pocket and wrote it down, then went back and sat down at the table.

"Would you do something for me?" Brandon asked.

"What?"

"If I can set up some counseling, would you go?"

"I don't need any damn counseling."

"What are you afraid of?"

"I'm not afraid of a damn thing," Graham said, raising his voice. "There's nothing wrong with me."

"I didn't say there was anything wrong with you. But there is something wrong. You know that. Why are you denying it?"

"Because I don't see any hope."

"That's because you're being so bullheaded," Brandon said. "What's it going to hurt?"

"Will Sheila be there?"

"I was going to find something for you. I'll ask around and see what we can do."

"Are you going to tell anyone?"

"No," Brandon said, shaking his head. "Why would I do that? We're friends, aren't we? This will be between you and me for the time being."

"Go ahead then," Graham said before taking a sip of coffee.

"Can I suggest something else?"

"What?"

"Would you go to an AA meeting?"

"I'm not an alcoholic," Graham said.

"I didn't say you were. But when someone drowns his misery with booze, that's not a good sign."

"I'll think about it."

"I've got a few friends who are members," Brandon said. "It turned their lives around. It even saved a couple of marriages."

"Like I said, let me give it some thought," Graham said. He took a slow sip of coffee.

"Why don't you stay home the rest of the day?" Brandon asked. "There's nothing going on back at the office. I'll tell Maggie that you've got some kind of stomach virus."

"I think I'll do that," Graham said. "The first thing I'm going to do is take a hot shower."

"I'm going to head back to the office. Will you be all right?"

"I'm fine. I'll feel better after a shower. Thanks for coming over."

"Call me if you need anything," Brandon said while getting up from the chair.

"Will do," Graham said, giving a short salute.

"You might want to call someone to replace the glass in the backdoor," Brandon said while turning the knob.

"What happened there?" Graham asked.

"It was the only way I could get in," Brandon said, shrugging his shoulders slightly. "Sorry about that."

Graham laughed and shook his head. "Don't worry about it. I'll see you tomorrow."

Brandon drove back to the office. Maggie was on the phone as he walked back to his office. He sat down and took Sheila's number from his shirt pocket and dialed it. There was no answer. He remembered that she was probably at work.

"Is he okay?" Maggie said at the doorway.

"He's fine," Brandon said. "I think he has some kind of stomach virus."

"Are you telling me the truth?" Maggie said.

"His stomach was really upset," Brandon said.

"I know you're not telling me everything but that's okay," Maggie said. "I'm just glad that he's all right."

"He'll be at work tomorrow morning."

"Ms. Horton called as you were leaving. She said she'd be in meetings for most of the day."

"That woman has more meetings than the president of the United States," Brandon said with a laugh. "Did anyone else call?"

"That's it," Maggie said. She smiled and walked back to her desk. Brandon spent the remainder of the day working on a column and arranging coverage of games. He drove home after work, stopping only at a Chinese carryout for a vegetarian dish and two egg rolls. After he finished eating, he picked up the telephone and called Clarice. She wasn't home so he left her a message on her answering machine. He dialed Sheila's number. Bernie answered.

"Hi Brandon," Bernie said cheerfully.

"How are you, Bernie?" Brandon asked.

"I'm staying with Mom now," he said. "I came over last night."

"Is everything okay?"

"I miss Mom."

Brandon hesitated before asking Bernie about his family since he knew that it was a difficult time for him.

"Is your mom at home?"

"No. She called and said she'd be here around eight or so. She had someplace to go after work."

"I'll call back later," Brandon said. "Let me know if you need anything."

"Okay," Bernie said. "Bye."

Brandon dialed Graham's phone number, and after five rings, Graham answered in a groggy voice.

"How are you?" Brandon asked.

"Doin' fine."

"Do you want me to come over?"

"I'm okay," Graham said slowly.

"Have you been drinking again?"

"Only a couple of beers. Monday Night Football is coming on in an hour so. I just had a few beers to get ready for it."

"Beers to get ready to watch TV?"

"I always have a few beers for football."

"Who's playing tonight?" Brandon asked.

"The Cowboys and Redskins."

"Can I come over and watch it with you?" Brandon asked, wanting an excuse to go over to Graham's house.

"Hey, that would be great," Graham said. "We haven't done that in a long time."

"Can I bring over something for you to eat?"

"Nah, but you can pick up a couple of six packs. I only have two beers left in the fridge."

"Have you had anything to eat today?"

"I'm not hungry."

"I'll stop by KFC and pick up some chicken wings for you."

"That would be great."

"I'll be over in about forty-five minutes," Brandon said. "Don't start the game without me."

"I won't." Graham slurred a chuckle.

Graham opened the front door holding a beer when Brandon arrived. Brandon stepped inside carrying the chicken wings.

"Where's the beer?" Graham asked. "We only have one left in the fridge."

"I don't care for any beer," Brandon said. "You can have it."

"Are you sure?"

"I'll drink a soda or something," Brandon said as they walked back to the kitchen.

"Can we go back out for some more beer?"

"We don't need any beer."

Graham sighed and ran his hand over the top of his head.

"If you say so."

Brandon stayed until nearly one in the morning. He didn't bring up Graham's faltering marriage or Bernie. They talked about the game on television and sports in general. He didn't leave until Graham was in bed.

When he got home, there was a message from Clarice on the answering machine. He wanted to return her call, but knew it was too late. He went on to bed, falling asleep almost the moment he put his head on the pillow.

Forty-three

"**G**ood morning," Maggie said to Graham as he walked into the office the next morning. "We missed you yesterday."

"I had some things to do around the house," Graham said, avoiding eye contact. "Any messages for me?"

Maggie handed him several phone memos and a small stack of mail.

"What are you doing on Thursday?" Maggie asked.

"What's Thursday?"

"It's Thanksgiving."

"Really?" Graham said, raising his eyebrows. "I'll probably go out to eat."

"Why don't you and Bernie come over to the house and have dinner with Bobby Lee and me?" Maggie asked with a smile. "I plan to ask Brandon when he comes in."

A pained expression came over Graham's tired face.

"Uh, let me think about it," he said, and walked away to his office without saying another word.

Brandon came in while Maggie was on the phone. He took off his overcoat and hung it on the hooks against the wall, smiling at Maggie as he walked down the hall. He noticed Graham's door open and looked in.

"Morning," Brandon said. "How's everything?"

"I'm doing okay," Graham said, sitting behind his cluttered desk and holding a cup of coffee. "Thanks for coming over last night."

"We need to do it more often," Brandon said. "It's been a long time since I stayed up and watched Monday Night Football. I had a good time."

"I know why you came over and I appreciate it," Graham said.

"Well, Graham, not to sound corny but that's what friends are for," Brandon said. "I would hope that you would do the same for me in a similar circumstance."

"You know I would," Graham said. "I've given some thought about the counseling you mentioned. Do you think you can find someone for me to see?"

Brandon stepped inside the office and closed the door.

"No problem. I'll make a few calls this morning. Have you thought anymore about AA?"

"That scares me," Graham said, looking away from Brandon for a moment. "Do you really think I have a drinking problem?"

"I don't know your drinking habits, but seeing you yesterday morning on the recliner made me wonder if you aren't using it as an escape for some of your problems."

"I'll give AA some more thought," Graham said.

"Just let me know and I'll put you in contact with someone," Brandon opened the door.

"Thanks for everything," Graham said quietly.

"Just let me know if there's anything else I can do."

Brandon walked to the break room and poured a cup of coffee. Maggie came in while he was stirring in creamer.

"Hi, Brandon," she said. "What are you doing Thanksgiving?"

"When is it?"

"You're as bad as Graham," she said with a laugh. "It's this Thursday."

"I really don't know," Brandon said. "Clarice hasn't mentioned anything to me."

"I'd like to invite you and Clarice over to the house to have dinner with Bobby Lee and me. I've also asked Graham to come over with Bernie."

"What did he say?" Brandon asked.

"He gave me a funny expression and said he'd let me know."

"Let me get with Clarice and see if she has made any plans," Brandon said. "I'll let you know after I talk to her."

"Is everything okay with Graham?" she whispered.

"Things are getting better," Brandon said with a smile. "I'd rather not say anything else right now. I'll let Graham tell you when he's ready to."

They went to their desks. Brandon checked his e-mails while Maggie filed her nails when the phone rang.

"I missed you last night," Clarice said.

"I had some things I needed to take care of," Brandon said. "By the time I got home last night it was too late to call. I hope you forgive me."

"Don't be silly," she said.

"Do you have any plans for Thanksgiving?"

"Not really," she said. "I was kind of hoping that we could go out to eat."

"We've been invited by Maggie to come over to her house for Thanksgiving dinner. She's also invited Graham. Would you like to go?"

"I think that would be very nice," Clarice said. "Maggie sounds like a pleasant person on the phone. I'd like to meet her. And you've talked about Bobby Joe so much that it would be nice to meet him, too."

"It's Bobby Lee," Brandon said with a laugh. "I'll tell Maggie that we'll be over."

"What did you do last night if you don't mind me asking?" Clarice said.

"I went over to Graham's house and watched Monday Night Football," Brandon said. "Well, it was more than that. He's got some personal problems and I went over there in case he needed me."

"Is everything going to be okay?"

"I hope so," Brandon said. "I need to find a marriage counselor for him to meet with. Do you know of anyone I can recommend?"

"My minister is a certified marriage counselor," Clarice said. "He helped me when Howard and I were going through our divorce."

"You needed a counselor to help you get over Howard?" Brandon said with a laugh.

"There's more to a divorce than a man and woman going their separate ways," Clarice said. "But being a lifelong bachelor, you wouldn't understand."

"Oops, I think I touched a sensitive nerve," Brandon said. "Sorry."

"That's okay," Clarice said. "I'm just telling you that there's more to a divorce than signing on the dotted line."

"What's your minister's name?"

"John Beard," Clarice said. "He's at the First Christian Church. He's in the phone directory."

"And you think he can help Graham?"

"I don't know the particulars of Graham's marriage but I assume that he can," Clarice said. "And if he can't, I'm sure he would recommend someone else to your friend."

"I'll tell Graham then," Brandon said. "Thanks."

"Are you busy today?" Clarice asked.

"I'm not busy at all. We're between football and basketball seasons so it's kind of slow around here. How about with you?"

"About the same," Clarice said.

"So if you're not that busy, what are you doing this evening?"

"I thought you were never going to ask," Clarice said with a laugh. "I don't have any plans."

"Do you want to go out to eat after work?"

"I'd love to," she said.

"Do you want me to pick you up at your house?"

"We could meet somewhere."

"How about Olive Garden?"

"Seven o'clock?"

"I'll see you there at seven," Brandon said.

After hanging up the phone, Brandon picked up the Yellow Pages and found the number of the marriage counselor that Clarice recommended and wrote it on a piece of paper. He also got the number for AA. Graham was on the phone when Brandon walked into his office. Brandon handed him the paper and Graham glanced at it and nodded.

Brandon walked out to the front lobby and told Maggie that he and Clarice had accepted her invitation for Thanksgiving dinner.

"Oh, that's great!" Maggie said as a bright smile came over her face. "Bobby Lee will be so excited. Is there anything special you'd like me to cook?"

"I like the traditional things like cranberry sauce, dressing, sweet potatoes and pumpkin pie," Brandon said. "But it's all up to you. I know that it will be delicious, no matter what you make."

"I hope Graham can come over," Maggie said.

"I'll talk to him about it and see what I can do," Brandon said.

Brandon returned to his office and began working on his weekly column. He was about halfway through with it when Graham peeked his head inside the office.

"Thanks for the numbers," Graham said. "I've got an appointment next Monday."

"Good," Brandon said. "Clarice recommended him. He helped her through her divorce."

"I'm still hopeful that I won't have to go that far," Graham said.

"Me, too."

"I didn't call AA," Graham said. "I'd rather wait."

"That's a choice you'll have to make," Brandon said. "All I can say is if it's a problem, don't let it linger. Get some help."

"I'll think about it," Graham said.

"Maggie wanted me to ask you about Thanksgiving."

"I don't know," Graham said, shaking his head. "It won't seem right without Sheila and Bernie."

"But you don't need to spend it alone," Brandon said. "Why don't you go? It might get your mind off some things. And I know that Maggie would be so happy for you to show up."

"Okay," Graham said. "It's been awhile since I had a decent meal. I'll go tell her now."

Brandon was the last person to leave the office. It was cold and dark outside as he walked to the parking lot. Although his attacker was behind bars, Brandon couldn't help being cautious as he went to his car. He arrived at Olive Garden before Clarice and stood in the front foyer, watching for her car. When she arrived, he went to the front door and opened it for her as she came in with her coat collar pulled up around her neck.

"Brrr, it's cold out there," Clarice said as he closed the door. She gave Brandon a quick peck on the lips as she began to unbutton her coat. They were seated at a candlelit table where they ordered their meals along with a carafe of white wine.

"Graham has an appointment with your counselor next week," Brandon said.

"That's good," Clarice said. "I think he will like him."

"Graham is still hoping that he and his wife can get back together."

"Dr. Beard is a good person to see then because he believes a marriage is important and that couples should work through their problems," she said.

"Did he try the same for you and Howard?" Brandon asked.

"I think he could sense that Howard and I were a total mismatch from the start," Clarice said. "Dr. Beard helped me deal with the stigma of divorce. My parents have been married for nearly fifty years. Although they were supportive, it was still difficult for me to handle it. I felt like a failure."

"Why?" Brandon asked. "Don't half of the marriages today end in divorce?"

"That doesn't make it any easier," Clarice said. "It's still a traumatic experience. Fortunately, Howard and I didn't have any children. We had an amicable divorce so it wasn't as bad as what a lot of people go through."

"You're probably right," Brandon said. "Sometimes I'm glad I never got married."

"Really?" Clarice asked with a surprised look on her face.

"I don't mean it the way it sounds," Brandon said. "I've just known so many people who have gone through a divorce. Even my parents."

"So you know what it's like on a family," Clarice said.

"But that doesn't mean I'll never get married," Brandon said with a nervous smile.

"That's good to hear," Clarice said, grinning. "I'd hate to think that you'd go through the rest of your life breaking women's hearts."

"Funny, funny," Brandon said with a laugh. He reached over and put his hand over the top of her hand.

"A woman just wants to make sure," Clarice said as the candlelight cast a glow over her soft features.

The waiter brought their dinners. They ate while Italian melodies played in the background over the sound system. After they finished, Brandon walked her out to her car. He put his arm on her waist and pulled her gently toward him and kissed her tenderly. She opened the door to get into her car, when he bent down and kissed her again. Clarice closed the door and backed out. She smiled and waved as she drove away. Brandon felt warmth over his body as he watched her car until it was out of sight.

Forty-four

Brandon got Sheila's work number from Graham the following morning and called her to set up a meeting place and time. They met after work at a coffee shop near the campus. She was already sitting at a table near the front when he arrived shortly after six.

"I hope you haven't waited very long," Brandon said. "I ran into a little traffic on the way over here."

"I've only been here a few minutes," she said. "It's nice to see you, Brandon. I hope all is going well with you."

"I can't complain," he said while sitting down across from her. "How's everything with you?"

"Work is great," she said. "I'm staying busy. I can't complain."

"That's good," Brandon said. "I know so many folks who don't enjoy their work. It's always nice to run into people who truly love what they're doing."

"How is Graham?" Sheila asked solemnly.

"As you might expect, he's kinda tore up about Bernie leaving," he said.

"That wasn't my idea," Shelia said. "I know how much Graham loves that boy. His life practically revolves around Bernie. But I had no choice."

A waitress came to their table and they each ordered a cup of coffee.

"I've talked to Graham about some counseling," Brandon said. "He meets with a counselor next Monday."

"That's good to hear," she said. "I wish he had seen a counselor several years ago when I asked him to."

"Is there something I don't know?" Brandon asked.

"There's probably lots of things you don't know." she said. "What you see at the office isn't necessarily what you see at home."

"I know that," Brandon said. "Can you tell me something? Anything? Perhaps I can help."

"I think it's probably a little too late to help," she said. Her eyes began to well with tears. She took a tissue from her purse and dabbed them softly.

"Well, maybe I can help Graham," Brandon said. "Why did you leave him?"

"Do you really want to know?"

"Yes, I do, Sheila. He's my friend and I want to help him. And you know that I care very much for you. We've known each other for a long time."

As she was about to speak, the waitress returned with a mocha blend for Sheila and cinnamon flavor for Brandon. They stirred their coffees for a few seconds while Sheila collected her thoughts.

"Graham is an alcoholic," Sheila said. "For the past few years, he sits on the recliner after he gets home and gets looped. Many nights he sleeps there. We haven't had a social life to speak of."

"I've talked to him about attending AA," Brandon said.

"Good luck," Sheila said. "I've pleaded with him time and time again to go to AA. He's in denial. He doesn't think he has a drinking problem."

"I hate to ask you this, and you don't have to answer, but what about the affair you're having?" Brandon asked softly.

"That's over," Sheila said. "That was a fling. Troy's married. He was having some marital problems and we just happened to fill a void with each other for a month or so. He's back with his wife now."

"Do you want to get back with Graham?"

"I don't know anymore," Sheila said before taking a sip of coffee. "My life has certainly been more peaceful since I left him."

"Why did you file for divorce?"

"Because that may be the best thing for both of us."

"Do you still love him?"

"Brandon, I've known Graham for more than twenty years," she said. "There will always be a part of me that loves him, no matter what happens with our marriage. We've had a child together. We've had some wonderful moments. But to be honest, the past couple of years have been pure hell."

"I wish you'd told me about it," Brandon said.

"When these things happen, you pray each night that it won't last long," Sheila said. "But each day passes and nothing changes, and before long it's out of control."

"Has Graham ever hurt you?"

"Graham has never physically harmed me," Sheila said. "He would never do that. He's a gentle man."

"How about verbally?"

"Not really," she said. "He would raise his voice now and then when I mentioned the drinking but more than anything there was silence between us. We've hardly talked the past year. And if you're wondering about our sex life, it's been practically non-existent, too. He's hardly ever touched me in the past year or so."

"I hadn't planned to get that personal," Brandon said with a shy smile.

"You wanted to know what's been wrong so I told you about everything," she said.

"Would you give him a second chance if he goes through counseling?" Brandon asked.

"I've already given him second, third, fourth...a hundred chances," Sheila said. "Don't you know that?"

"I understand," Brandon said. "But what if he cleans up his act?"

"That's asking an awful lot of him," Sheila said. "I would expect him to quit drinking and I don't know if he's ready to do that. And I don't know if he's ready to forgive me for my affair."

"Would you consider counseling with him?"

"Perhaps after he's been in it for awhile," she said. "I want to see that he's committed to getting his life in order."

"How's Bernie?"

"He seems to be handling this okay," Sheila said. "But I've seen kids who seem to be dealing with things well on the outside but are torn up on the inside. I want to give him as much support as I can. The reason he came to live with me is because he's tired of seeing Graham drunk. He loves his dad very much but there's only so much he could take. Speaking of Bernie, I need to be getting home."

"I'm glad we got to talk," Brandon said. "Regardless of what happens between you and Graham, I want you to know that I consider you a very good friend and I want the best for you."

"I know that Brandon," she said as tears came to her pale green eyes again. "You've been a very good friend to both of us."

Brandon paid for the coffee and they walked outside into a breezy cold night air. Brandon walked Sheila to her car along the street and hugged her.

"Good night," he said. "Call me if you need anything."

"I will," Sheila said. "Thanks again. I hope you have a happy Thanksgiving tomorrow."

"You, too," Brandon said as he walked away toward his car in the side parking lot.

Brandon stopped by a phone booth several blocks away and called Clarice.

"Have you had supper tonight?" he asked.

"Where have you been?" Clarice asked. "I've been worried about you."

"I met Graham's wife after work and we talked about their marriage," Brandon said.

"How did it go?"

"I see some hope. We'll have to wait and see."

"Did you mention something about supper?" Clarice asked with a laugh.

"I think I did before you snapped at me," Brandon teased.

"What did you have in mind?"

"I could pick you up and we could go out to eat or I could stop and get some carryout and take it to your place."

"How about coming over?" she said. "Actually, I haven't been home very long."

"Let me guess," Brandon said. "You had a meeting."

"Smarty," Clarice said.

"How about if I stop by Subway and pick up a couple sandwiches and chips?"

"That sounds good," she said. "I'll take whatever you get."

"A veggie?"

"Yep," she said. "I like whatever you like."

"Let's not get carried away," Brandon said.

"Okay, I try to like what you like," she said, giggling.

After hanging up the phone, Brandon stopped by a Subway on the way to her house. She was waiting at the door with the porch light on when he pulled into her driveway. Clarice pecked him on the mouth as he stepped inside the house and he followed her to the kitchen. She had already poured tall glasses of iced tea and set the table with paper plates and napkins.

"We should have gone on a picnic," Brandon said.

"Don't you think it might be a little too cold for that?" she said with a grin.

"I'd keep you warm," he said, flicking his eyebrows up and down.

"You really think so?" she said coyly.

"Want to go outside?"

"No," Clarice said as she wrapped her arms around him. "I believe you." She squeezed him and kissed him on the cheek before sitting down.

"How was your day?" Brandon asked.

"Do I really need to answer that?" she said.

"Not really," he said.

"How is Graham's wife?"

"She seemed to be handling everything very well," Brandon said. "She's always been a very strong person."

"Do you mind telling me what the problem is between them?"

"I guess Graham has a drinking problem," Brandon said before taking a bite from his sandwich. "In fact, he may have a serious drinking problem."

"You never knew?"

"Not really," Brandon said. "When we go over to Hastings he usually has a beer or two like me. But apparently he chugged a few at home."

"So he's a closet alcoholic?"

"I guess you could say that except that he was parked in his recliner most of the time."

"I've known a few alcoholics," Clarice said. "You never knew they had a drinking problem because they were doing most of it at home. It destroyed one marriage I know of and wrecked the health of a couple of friends."

"I hope Graham shows up at Maggie's house tomorrow," Brandon said. "I think you'll like him."

"I'm looking forward to meeting him," Clarice said. "What time are we going over there?"

"Maggie said to come over around two or so."

"Should I bring anything?"

"No," Brandon said. "She'll have everything."

They finished their sandwiches and Brandon picked up the trash while Clarice wiped off the table. In the den, Clarice turned on the radio to a soft rock station and sat down next to Brandon on the couch. She put her hand in his hand.

"I'm so glad that I've gotten to know you," she said softly while resting her head on his shoulder.

"Me, too," he said.

"Does it bother you that I've fallen in love with you?" she asked, looking up at him.

"Only if it bothers you that I'm in love with you," he said before kissing her on the forehead.

"Not in the least," she said with a glowing smile. "I don't know how long it's been since I've been this happy and content."

"I don't know if I've ever felt that way before knowing you," Brandon said, gently squeezing her hand.

They sat in the dark room and listened to the music without saying a word. Brandon put his arm around her and she put her arm across his chest and snuggled up closer. She dozed off with a soft smile on her face. Brandon savored the peaceful moment with her. He had never experienced this kind of relationship with another woman. It could only be one thing. He knew he was truly in love with Clarice. And each day he was with her, he could feel it grow deeper and deeper. While thinking about the other women he had known, there was no other that compared to Clarice in the way she made him feel.

Forty-five

Maggie took Brandon's and Clarice's coats and carried them to the front bedroom and placed them neatly across a bed. Maggie was wearing a dark green dress and an apron decorated with smiling turkeys and "Happy Thanksgiving!" emblazoned across the front. Brandon couldn't remember the last time he saw her in a dress because she always wore slacks to the office or blue jeans around her house.

"Everything sure smells delicious," Brandon said to Maggie after he introduced her to Clarice inside the front door. Maggie had a large turkey cutout on the front door and several small Pilgrim figurines sitting on end tables.

"I've got a few things in the oven but it shouldn't be much longer," Maggie said.

"Can I help?" Clarice asked.

"You can help me set the table," Maggie said.

While Clarice followed Maggie to the kitchen, Brandon went to the living room and sat down on the couch with Bobby Lee, whose leg was propped up on an ottoman.

"Hi Brandon," Bobby Lee said cheerfully.

"How's it going, Bobby Lee?"

"I'll sure be glad when I can get this thing off my leg."

"What does the doctor say?"

"He said it may be another six weeks. That means I'll still be wearing this durn thing at Christmas."

"That'll be here before you know it."

"I guess," Bobby Lee said with a shrug.

The door bell rang and Maggie opened the door. Graham stood smiling.

"Oh, Graham, come on in," Maggie said, giving him a hug as he stepped inside. "I'm so happy you could make it."

"How could I miss a Thanksgiving dinner?" he said.

"Where's Bernie?"

"He's with his mother today," Graham said.

"Well, Brandon and Bobby Lee are in the living room," Maggie said while taking his coat. "Why don't you join them while Clarice and I finish getting dinner ready."

Graham walked into the living and sat down on a rocking chair.

"Hi, Mr. Jones," Bobby Lee said.

"Hi, Bobby Lee," Graham said. "How are you feeling?"

"I've got to wear this cast for six more weeks."

"Bobby Lee isn't very happy about that," Brandon said. "I told him it would go by in no time."

"That's right," Graham said. "It'll be off before too long."

"The Lions play the Packers this afternoon," Bobby Lee said.

"The Lions play every Thanksgiving day," Graham said.

"Really?" Bobby Lee asked. "I bet that's not much fun for the players."

"It's probably not but they get paid for it," Brandon said with a laugh. "And I'm sure they get turkey after the game."

"That's good," Bobby Lee said with a grin.

"I talked to Sheila last night," Brandon said to Graham. "I'll tell you about it later today or tomorrow."

Graham nodded.

"Dinner is ready," Maggie said at the doorway.

Brandon and Graham waited until Bobby Lee got up from the couch and placed his crutches on the floor. They followed him to the dining room.

A large turkey with dressing was in the middle of the table, sliced in thin pieces. Maggie had already removed a leg and put it on Bobby Lee's plate. Sweet potatoes with marshmallows on top, corn on the cob, and bowls of broccoli, cranberry sauce, peas, mashed potatoes, and green beans surrounded the turkey.

Brandon introduced Clarice to Graham as they stood next to the table.

"It's a pleasure to meet you," Graham said politely. "Brandon has said nice things about you."

"It's nice to finally meet you, too," Clarice said, smiling. "I've heard so much about you."

Clarice caught Graham making a quick glance at Brandon.

"I mean, I really like your publication and what you do," Clarice added quickly. "I think you and Brandon do an excellent job."

"Thank you," Graham said with a modest smile. "We try to do our best."

Maggie helped Bobby Lee get situated in his chair, with a leg on a hassock. Maggie sat at one head of the table, next to Bobby Lee, while Graham sat at the other end. Brandon sat next to Bobby Lee and Clarice sat across from him.

"Would you say a prayer, Graham?" Maggie asked with a smile.

"Uh, sure," Graham said. He paused a moment and cleared his throat. "Lord, we thank you for this meal and the hands that prepared it. We ask your blessings each day. Please be with those who are less fortunate. We thank you for everything. Amen."

"Let's dig in," Bobby Lee said wide-eyed.

They all laughed and began passing the food around. Within a few minutes, everyone's plate was full and they were eating with hardly any talk.

"This is simply delicious," Clarice said, breaking the silence.

"You're a very good cook," Graham said. "I never realized you had this talent."

"We need to have you fixing lunch at work each day," Brandon teased.

"Thank you but let's not get carried away," Maggie said with a slight blush. "I enjoy cooking but it's kind of hard to fix a lot when it's only for Bobby Lee and I."

"We'll take care of that," Graham said with a chuckle. "We'll all come over for dinner every night then."

"That's fine by me," Maggie said, "if you pay for the groceries."

"There's always a catch," Brandon said, shaking his head.

After they finished their dinner, Maggie went to the kitchen and brought out pumpkin and mincemeat pies. She had a bowl of whipped cream to put on top of the pumpkin pie. Bobby Lee wanted an extra scoop on his and Maggie obliged. She poured coffee for the adults to have with their desserts.

"I don't believe I can move," Graham said, patting his belly after he finished eating. "I'm stuffed."

"Same here," Brandon said. "I may have to take a nap."

"Why don't you guys go relax in the living room while Maggie and I clean up here?" Clarice said.

"You don't have to do that," Maggie said. "I can do it."

"I don't mind," she said with a smile.

Brandon and Graham got up and followed Bobby Lee back to the living room. The Lions-Packers game was already in the second quarter. They took the places they had before going to the dining room.

"Have you ever gone to an NFL game?" Bobby Lee asked Brandon.

"Quite a few," he said.

"I'd like to see one someday," Bobby Lee said.

"Perhaps next season we can go to see a Bengals' game," Brandon said.

"That'd be great," Bobby Lee said.

Clarice and Maggie joined them thirty minutes later. Clarice sat down next to Brandon on the couch while Maggie sat in a recliner.

"I don't know if I told you but you don't need to come in tomorrow," Graham said to Maggie. "Most places are closed."

"Actually, you did tell me yesterday that I could stay at home," Maggie said.

"I did?" Graham said with a perplexed look. "If so, I'm just reminding you."

"Do you work tomorrow?" Maggie asked Clarice.

"Unfortunately, I have a meeting with a client," Clarice said, then grinning at Brandon. "Don't you say anything."

"Me?" Brandon said with an exaggerated look of surprise. "Why would I say anything?"

"Brandon likes to give me a hard time about all the meetings I have," Clarice said, looking first at Maggie and then Graham.

"Meetings are the bane of modern society," Brandon said. "People can't get things accomplished because of meetings."

"Some people do," Clarice said, playfully sticking out her tongue at Brandon.

"Well folks, I hate to leave good company but I'd better be going," Graham said, rising from the rocking chair. "If I sit here too long I'll never get up."

"Thanks for coming over," Maggie said, getting up to go get his coat.

"It was a wonderful dinner," Graham said warmly. "And it was nice meeting you, Clarice. I hope to see you again."

"I hope so, too," Clarice said.

"You take care of yourself, Bobby Lee," Graham said after walking over and patting the boy on the shoulder.

"Thanks, Mr. Jones," Bobby Lee said, taking his eyes off the TV for only a few seconds to smile at Graham.

"You don't need to come to work tomorrow either," Graham said to Brandon.

"I've got a few things to take care of," Brandon said. "I'll see you in the morning."

Graham raised his hand and waved to everyone and left.

"I'm sure happy that Graham showed up," Maggie said after sitting back down in the living room. "He has seemed so down lately."

"There's a lot going on in his life right now," Brandon said. "I was glad to see him here, too. I think that's a good sign."

"Is there anything I can do to help him?" Maggie asked.

"I think by inviting him here helped him a lot," Brandon said. "I guess we'd better be going, too,"

"You don't need to rush off so soon," Maggie said. "I can put on another pot of coffee."

"Thanks, but we need to be running," Brandon said. "You need your rest too after that feast."

Maggie went to the bedroom and retrieved their coats.

"I'll see you next week," Brandon said to Bobby Lee.

"Okay," Bobby Lee said. "Were you serious about that Bengals' game?"

"Of course I was. Just remind me next summer."

"I will," Bobby Lee said. "I won't let you forget."

"Thanks again for inviting us," Clarice said. "Everything was delicious and I'm glad we finally got to meet."

"Thank you and it was nice to meet you as well," Maggie said.

Brandon hugged Maggie at the front door. "I'll see you on Monday."

Brandon drove Clarice to her house. It was late in the afternoon as the sun was setting in the cloudless purple horizon. He accepted her offer to come in.

"Can I get you anything to eat?" Clarice asked.

"I don't think so," Brandon said. "I don't think I'll be able to eat for a week. I'm still full."

Clarice excused herself to go back to her bedroom and change clothes. She returned barefoot and wearing jeans and a large, red sweatshirt and plopped down on the couch next to Brandon.

"Want to watch TV?" she asked.

"Sure," he said. "Where's the remote?"

"Right there," she said, pointing to it on the coffee table.

Brandon reached down and picked it up and turned on the TV. He surfed through the channels, never staying on one for more than a minute.

"Anything you care to see?" he asked.

"Any movies?"

Brandon clicked until he found *It's A Wonderful Life* on a channel.

"I guess this is the first of a thousand times this movie will be shown between now and Christmas," Brandon said sarcastically.

"It's a great movie," Clarice said. "I love it."

"It's okay."

"It's one of my favorite movies," Clarice said. "I cry every time I see it."

"I know what you mean," Brandon said. "I cry every time when I see it's on TV."

"That's not nice," she said with a pronounced pout.

"We'll watch it," Brandon said.

"No, we don't have to if you don't want to," she said.

Brandon kept it on the channel. Clarice snuggled up next to him as he put his arm around her. She watched the movie, teary-eyed at times, while Brandon dozed off. Before long, he let out a long snore. Clarice giggled.

"What's the matter?" Brandon asked, shaking his head from his light slumber

"Oh, nothing," Clarice said, her head resting against his chest. "It was just a humorous scene."

"I know," Brandon said with a sleepy smile. "It is funny in parts."

Forty-six

Brandon sat down at his desk and read e-mails while sipping a cup of coffee. He was still full from Thanksgiving dinner at Maggie's. It was quiet around the office as he was the only person there and traffic was light outside. He wanted to call Clarice but she told him before he left her house that she had an early meeting that would probably last a couple of hours.

Brandon heard a click from the door out front, and a few seconds later Graham was standing at his door.

"Morning," Graham said while removing his green barn jacket. He was wearing a gray flannel shirt, jeans and work boots since no one would be coming around to the office.

"How are you doing?" Brandon asked as he stood to go warm his coffee in the break room.

"I still feel stuffed," Graham said as he followed Brandon down the hall.

"Same here. I don't normally eat that much."

While Brandon poured his coffee, Graham took a cup from the counter. He held it out and Brandon filled it near the rim.

"So tell me what Sheila had to say," Graham said while stirring his coffee.

"Want to go back to your office?"

After sitting down in Graham's office, Brandon paused for a few seconds while gathering his thoughts. Graham sat intently across from him, sipping from the coffee cup.

"Well," Brandon said, then taking a short breath, "she's glad that you're going to have some counseling."

"That doesn't surprise me. I'm sure she told you that she's wanted me to do it for some time now."

Brandon nodded and took a sip of coffee.

"What else did she say?" Graham asked. "I'm sure there was more to it than that."

"Some of this is difficult to say," Brandon said.

"Go ahead and spit it out," Graham said. "We're friends. I don't think you're going to hurt my feelings or tell me something I don't know. And what you say I won't hold against you."

"Sheila talked about your drinking," Brandon said, clearing his throat. "She says it's been a problem for a few years."

"I think she's exaggerating."

"I'm only telling you what she told me," Brandon said.

"Okay," Graham said with a sigh, keep going."

"She said that your relationship with her has deteriorated because of the drinking. She said you and her haven't communicated with each other very much."

"She's probably right," Graham said. "But I think it's partly due to her job."

"That could be," Brandon said. "I just heard her side of the story so that's what I'm relating. There're always at least two sides to every story."

"What else?"

"She said you parked yourself in front of the TV every night and would drink," Brandon said.

"I like my beer," Graham said. "I don't deny that. But that doesn't mean I have a drinking problem."

"As for this affair," Brandon said slowly, "Sheila said it was over. She said that this guy was married and they were filling a void in each other's lives."

A pained expression came over Graham's face as he slightly turned his head.

"I don't know if I can ever forgive her for that," Graham said quietly, almost as if to himself.

"I'm sure it would be difficult," Brandon said. "That's why it's good that you're going to go through some counseling."

"That's not going to be easy for me either," Graham said, looking back at Brandon. "I'm very private. I don't open up to many people."

"I understand," Brandon said. "I'm probably the same way. But perhaps you need to open up with someone."

"I'll admit that I probably drink too much," Graham said, "but it's not something I can't control. I haven't had hardly anything to drink since you came over on Monday night. Only a few beers."

"Do you think you could go several days or weeks without drinking?"

"I think so," Graham said, "but what's the purpose? I'm not trying to drown in my sorrows when I drink." He shrugged his shoulders.

"Maybe you're doing it more than you think," Brandon said.

"I don't think so. I just like to drink a beer now and then."

Brandon realized that he wasn't getting anywhere with him about the drinking. Graham was adamant that there wasn't a drinking problem and there was no way of opening his eyes to it.

"How about Sheila?"

"What do you mean?" Graham said.

"Do you want to get back with her?"

"I'm not sure," Graham said.

"How about Bernie?"

"Of course, I want Bernie back home," Graham said. "That's tearing me apart. I can't believe that he wants to live with her after what she's done to me."

"Does he know about her affair?"

"I haven't said anything to him but I think kids are wise at picking up things going on between a father and mother. They may not say anything but they know something is going on."

Brandon wanted to bring up the drinking again but figured Graham would deny that Bernie was concerned about the drinking.

"Do you still love Sheila?"

"I think I always will," Graham said. "We've been together for a long time."

"She told me the same thing about you."

"She did?"

"I think she still cares very much for you," Brandon said. "I know she feels bad about the affair."

"She should," Graham said. "I've never screwed around on her although I had the opportunities."

"I know that. You've been very dedicated to her."

"So why couldn't she have been that way with me?"

"She was troubled," Brandon said. "People do crazy things when they're emotionally distraught. Perhaps you would do the same if the tables were turned?"

"What do you mean?"

"Well, if you perceived that she had a drinking problem and there was little communication between you and her, maybe you would turn to another woman," Brandon said.

"I don't think so," Graham said. "I have more will power than to do that."

"That's about all we talked about," Brandon said. "I hope that helps."

"I guess it does," Graham said. "I'll have to give it a lot of thought."

"I know it's difficult," Brandon said, solemnly. "I wish we weren't even having this conversation. And I hope you don't mind me saying this, but I hope you and Sheila can work things out because I care a lot about both of you. If I can say one more thing, it's that I wouldn't give up on her. I think you and she can make things work again."

Graham didn't reply. He looked pensively at Brandon, then rose from his chair.

"I need to warm up my coffee," he said. "And then I've got some work to do."

Brandon smiled with pursed lips and stood. He didn't say anything and walked to his office. A few minutes later, Graham stood at his doorway.

"Brandon, I want you to know that I appreciate everything you've done," Graham said. "I hate it that you're caught in the middle of this mess. And I want you to know that I want to get through it all."

"I know you will," Brandon said. "And I know it's not easy."

Graham nodded and returned to his office.

The phone rang to break the silence in the office and Brandon answered it.

"Do you guys need me down there today?" Maggie asked pertly.

"No, we've got everything under control," Brandon said. "It's relatively quiet around here."

"I was just checking before Bobby Lee and I went to the mall," she said. "I could drop off some turkey sandwiches and some other leftovers for you guys."

"Thanks for the offer but we're still stuffed," Brandon said with a laugh. "We probably won't be here all day either. Most of the places around town are closed so we can't get a whole lot accomplished."

"Okay then," she said. "I'll see you Monday."

"You and Bobby Lee have a nice weekend," Brandon said.

After hanging up the phone, it rang again and Brandon picked it up on the first ring.

"Busy today?" Clarice asked.

"Nope," Brandon said. "It's dead around here. How about with you?"

"It is now," she said. "We had our meeting and most everyone has gone home for the rest of the day."

"How much longer are you staying there?"

"Not much longer," Clarice said. "I've got to proofread a report and that shouldn't take more than an hour."

"Want to meet somewhere later?"

"Sure," she said. "Any place in particular?"

"Have you ever been to Hastings?"

"It's been awhile."

"That's my watering hole," Brandon said. "Would you like to meet there around two or so."

"I should be finished by then," Clarice said. "I'll see you at two."

<h1 align="center">Forty-seven</h1>

Clarice left work earlier than she expected and arrived at Hastings around one forty-five. She found a table near the front of the pub and sat down. Glancing around, she noticed that the TV was on with no sound, the daily food specials written on a chalk board.

"What can I get for you, hon?" Rosie asked.

"I'd like a wine spritzer," Clarice said.

"A wine spritzer?" Rosie asked with a perplexed look.

"Yes, please," Clarice said with a pleasant smile.

"Okay," Rosie said and went to the bar to give the order to Benny.

Clarice opened her purse and took out a compact mirror. She looked at herself and flipped back her hair with her hand.

"What's a nice girl like you doing in a place like this?" a man said.

Clarice looked to her side. Bart stood there with a wide grin on his face, holding a half-full mug of beer.

"That's sure an original line," Clarice said.

"I figured you'd appreciate the humor in it," Bart said. "Do you mind if I join you?"

"I'm sorry, Bart, but I'm expecting someone," Clarice said.

Rosie returned and placed the wine spritzer in front of Clarice on a napkin.

"Put it on my tab," Bart said to Rosie.

"I'll pay for it," Clarice said quickly while giving Bart an irritated look. "How much is it?"

"Three dollars," Rosie said.

Clarice took a five dollar bill from a pocketbook and handed it to Rosie. "Please keep the change," she said with a smile. Rosie took the money and returned to the bar.

"So who's your company?" Bart asked.

"A good friend," Clarice said. She took a sip of her drink and looked toward the front entrance.

Bart sat down across from her and grinned.

"I'll sit here until your friend arrives," he said. "I haven't seen you in awhile and you don't return my phone calls."

"Shouldn't that tell you something?" Clarice said curtly

"I guess that it should but I don't give up so easily. I thought we had a good thing going between us."

"You thought wrong."

"Why don't you give me a second chance?"

"Because I wish I hadn't given you a chance in the first place."

"I must have hurt you real bad," Bart said with a smirk.

"Hardly," Clarice said. "It just took me some time to wise up about you."

Clarice glanced at her watch and saw that it was five minutes until two.

"Expecting your friend soon?" Bart asked.

"In about five minutes. So why don't you go?"

Bart pushed back his chair from the table. He took a big swallow from his mug and glared at Clarice.

"I'll go," he said. "But you'll regret it."

"I don't think so," Clarice said, looking away.

Bart stood and walked to the bar. He sat down with his back to her, looked around one time and shook his head. A moment later, Brandon walked into the bar and spotted Clarice to his left. She turned and smiled as he kissed her on the cheek before sitting down across from her.

"I hope you haven't had to wait very long," Brandon said.

Clarice looked at her watch.

"Actually, you're two minutes early," she said. "I got here about fifteen minutes ago."

"I see you've already ordered a drink," Brandon. "Would you like an appetizer?"

"What do you recommend?" Clarice asked.

"Mozzarella sticks aren't bad."

"That would be fine," Clarice said.

Brandon waved his hand to catch Rosie's attention. Benny poured him a frosty mug and handed it to Rosie to take with her to his table. Brandon ordered the appetizer. He sensed that Clarice was distracted about something by the look on her face.

"What's the matter?" Brandon asked.

"Oh, it's nothing," she said. "Someone came over before you got here."

"Hitting on you?" Brandon asked.

"I guess you could say so."

"Is he still here?"

"Yes, but that's okay,"

"Who is it?" Brandon asked, feeling his nerves tighten a little as he looked toward the bar.

"Bart is here," Clarice said.

"Oh," Brandon said. "He comes in here occasionally."

Brandon noticed Bart sitting with his back to them, talking to one of the regulars.

"I told him to go fly a kite," Clarice said with a slight laugh.

"Apparently, he took your advice," Brandon said.

"I hope so," she said with a sigh. "I really can't stand to be around the man."

"We can leave if you want to."

"No way," Clarice said. "I'm not going to let him run me off."

Rosie came back with the mozzarella sticks and a saucer of salsa. Brandon ordered another beer. Clarice had barely touched her wine.

Bart turned around and looked at them for a few seconds and swiveled back facing the counter. Brandon noticed him shaking his head.

"Are you doing anything tonight?" Brandon asked Clarice as she dipped a mozzarella stick into the sauce.

"I was thinking about renting a video and popping some popcorn," she said. "Would you like to come over?"

Brandon grinned. "What time?"

"Hmm, how about six?" Clarice said with a smile.

"Isn't that a little early for a movie and popcorn?" Brandon said.

"I supposed it is but we might be able to find something to do before movie," Clarice said coyly.

"I'll be there at six on the dot," Brandon said.

Before they realized it, Bart was standing next to their table.

"So you chose this guy over me?" Bart said to Clarice. His words slurred a little from having too much to drink.

"I would choose anyone over you," Clarice said. "Would you please leave?"

Brandon sat silently but kept his eyes focused sharply on Bart.

"That's not nice," Bart said sarcastically.

"I don't feel like being nice to you."

"You were nice to me a few months ago," Bart said with a chuckle. "Don't you want to be nice to me again?"

"Why don't you go on," Brandon said as politely as he could.

"Why don't you kiss my ass?" Bart said, raising his voice. "I wasn't talking to you."

"Well, she doesn't want to talk to you and I don't want to hear what you're saying to her," Brandon said. "Understand?"

Benny heard Bart and moved over to the edge of the counter. "Is everything okay?" he said in their direction as he wiped his hands on a dish cloth.

"No problem," Bart said, backing away from the table. "I was just talking to my good friends here."

"Then why don't you come over here and leave your good friends alone for awhile," Benny said forcefully.

"Sure thing," Bart said while looking at Clarice and Brandon. "I'll see you folks later."

Brandon quickly finished his beer.

"Ready to go?" he asked Clarice.

"Yes," she said as she took her coat off the back of the chair and over her shoulders.

"I'm sorry about this," he said. "It's usually very laid-back here."

"That's okay," Clarice said with an understanding smile.

Rosie came over and Brandon paid the bill. As he and Clarice stood up, Bart turned around in his stool.

"Leaving so soon?" he asked

Brandon and Clarice looked at him for a moment and left without saying a word.

"I'm sorry about all of this," Brandon said as he walked Clarice to her car in front of the pub. "This is usually a great place to unwind after work."

"He's just a jerk," Clarice said as they walked to the parking lot. "Don't worry about it."

"Let me know if he ever bothers you again."

"I will but I don't believe that's going to happen."

Brandon kissed her softly on the mouth after she got into her car. He closed the door and watched her drive away. He walked to his car parked on the side of the building. As he put the key into the door, he heard someone shout at him.

"You're not good enough for Clarice."

Brandon turned around. Bart was approaching quickly.

"I don't doubt that," Brandon said, trying to remain calm. "She's a very special woman and I don't feel deserving of her."

Bart stood about a foot from Brandon with his fists clenched.

"Don't get smart with me," Bart said angrily. "Unless you want me to kick your ass."

"Listen, Bart," Brandon said coolly. "I don't want to fight you but if you insist, I won't be backing off."

"I don't know what in the hell Clarice sees in you. You're just a damn newspaper hack."

"At least I work for a living," Brandon said with a smile.

"What in the hell is that supposed to mean?" Bart asked.

"What I said," Brandon said. "I didn't stutter."

"Don't mess with me asshole. Like I said, I'll kick your ass all over this parking lot."

"Start kicking."

Bart took a wild swing and missed Brandon's head by six inches. The momentum of the swing carried him past Brandon and against the car. Brandon backed off and grinned. Bart glared at him and took another swing, missing again as he nearly fell to the pavement.

"You sonofabitch!" Bart said as he lunged toward Brandon.

Brandon greeted Bart with a sharp fist to the belly, causing Bart to keel over. Brandon followed with an uppercut that sent Bart to the paving with blood streaming from his mouth and nose.

"Had enough?" Brandon asked as he raised a fist. "I've got more where that came from."

Bart held a bloody hand over his mouth and looked at Brandon as if he was going to charge at him again. After a few seconds, Bart shook his head and slithered away with his head down. Brandon watched until he saw Bart fool with his keys before opening the door to his Jaguar convertible.

Brandon rubbed his fingers on his left hand over his right-hand knuckles and smiled.

"Not bad," he said to himself. "Not bad at all."

Forty-eight

The phone was ringing when Brandon opened the door to his apartment. He hurried over and answered it.

"This is Brandon," he said while slipping his coat off.

"I'm sorry about today," Clarice said.

"There's nothing to be sorry about. It wasn't your fault that he showed up."

"Still, I wish I could have made him leave before you showed up. He can be such an ass."

"I don't think you're going to hear from him again."

"I don't know about that," Clarice said. "I've turned him down over and over again and he won't take no for an answer."

"Perhaps he will this time."

"Why do you say that?"

"After we left Hastings he came out to the parking lot," Brandon said.

"Oh no, Brandon," Clarice said with alarm in her voice. "What happened?"

"He took a couple of swings at me."

"Oh, honey, are you hurt?"

"Hurt?"

"Did he hit you?"

"Let's just say that my knuckles are a little sore from popping him."

"Is he hurt?"

"There was some blood coming from his mouth and nose, but I don't think it was anything serious," Brandon said. "He made it to his car and left."

"I'm glad that you're okay but I wish you didn't have to get into a fight," Clarice said.

"But he started it."

"That still doesn't make it right for two grown men to fight."

"Whose side are you on?" Brandon asked.

"I'm sorry," Clarice said. "I'm glad you didn't get hurt. It just upsets me that it happened."

"I didn't want it to happen either but that's all I could do when he attacked me."

"Well, I must admit that he probably deserved it," Clarice said with a light laugh.

"Let's get off this," Brandon said. "Do you still want me to come over?"

"Of course."

"Why don't we go out to a movie instead of renting a video?"

"I'm not really dressed for a movie," she said.

"We can go to one of the discount movies," Brandon said. "You don't have to get dressed up for them."

"Let's see," Clarice said. "It's almost five. Do you want to catch a seven o'clock movie?"

"Sure," Brandon said with a laugh. "Just let me change out of these bloody clothes."

"Oh, Brandon," Clarice said. "Are you telling me everything?"

"Just kidding," he said. "I'm going to put on some jeans and a sweater. It's a little nippy outside tonight. I'll be over around six-thirty."

"I'll see you then," she said.

Brandon quickly showered, brushed his teeth and changed clothes. He pulled into her driveway at six-thirty. Clarice was standing inside the front door. She motioned at him to stay in his car, then locked the door and walked briskly to his car. After getting into the car, she eased over and they kissed.

As Brandon backed out of the driveway, she noticed the redness on his right hand.

"Does your hand hurt?" Clarice asked.

"Nah," Brandon said. "I'm sure that Bart received most of the pain."

Clarice shook her head and smiled. Brandon gave her a pesky look.

Clarice picked a Patrick Swayze movie at the cinema. Brandon bought a large tub of popcorn and two large Cokes. They sat near the middle in the sparsely-filled theater. When it was over, they stopped at a pizza restaurant to eat. Brandon ordered a pitcher of beer and a large veggie pizza.

"I really enjoy evenings like this," Clarice said. "Just doing spur of the moment things. I find it relaxing."

"Same here," Brandon said. "And it does get a little lonely around the apartment during the evening."

"You don't like being alone?"

"It depends," Brandon said. "I enjoy quiet time, too."

"I must admit that I don't mind being alone at times," Clarice said. "I can come and go as I please. I don't have to answer to anyone except myself. Freedom."

"Was your ex-hubby controlling?" Brandon asked.

"Not in a bad sense," Clarice said. "I'd rather say he was more protective than controlling. But after awhile, it seems like the same thing."

"I would imagine that it does," Brandon said. "Is that a reason why you haven't remarried?"

"I haven't remarried because I haven't found the person I want to marry," Clarice said. She noticed a dour expression on Brandon's face and reached over and touched his hand. "I mean until I met you."

"I understand what you're saying," Brandon said. "If I were in your shoes, I wouldn't want to rush into anything either."

"I'm still involved in my career and I don't believe it would be right to get married at this time," she said. "It wouldn't be fair to the other person."

"I know where you're coming from," Brandon said. "My career always seemed to take a higher priority with me."

"Will that always be the case?" Clarice asked.

"It's not the case anymore," Brandon said with a grin.

A waitress came to their table with the pitcher and two mugs. She poured their beer and left silverware.

"How is Graham doing?" Clarice asked. "He seems like an awfully nice man."

"He has his first counseling session on Monday," Brandon said. "I hope that he and Sheila can get back together. I really believe she wants to."

"Perhaps they will, but it will probably take some time."

"I think she wants me to get some help on his drinking. He doesn't believe he has a problem."

"Isn't that usually the case?"

"Probably so," Brandon said. "To be honest, Graham and I have been friends for a long time and I've never suspected him of having a drinking problem."

"I guess that only shows that we don't know people as much as we think we do."

Brandon lifted up his mug. "I'll drink to that," he said with a laugh.

"That's mean," Clarice said.

"I didn't mean it that way," Brandon said. "Graham is my best friend."

"I just hope that you can help him."

"I can only do so much," Brandon said. "I think the counseling is a good first step."

"It is," Clarice said. "Friends just have to be supportive."

"I'd like for you to meet Sheila one of these days," Brandon said.

"I'd like that," Clarice said. "Perhaps after they're back together."

The waitress returned with the pizza and sat it between them. She took two slices and put it in their plates.

"I don't know if we can eat all of this," Clarice said. "That popcorn pretty much filled me up."

"We can always take the leftovers home with us," Brandon said before taking a bite.

They quietly ate for a few minutes while the jukebox played some hip-hop music that some teen-agers had selected. They ate half of the pizza and had the waitress bring them a carryout box.

"Any plans for tomorrow?" Brandon asked while they waited for the waitress to return with their change.

"Not really," she said. "I have a report that I need to go over this weekend but that's about it. I'll probably sleep in."

"Would you like to sleep in at my place?" Brandon asked and puckered his lips.

"Do you have anything I can sleep in?" Clarice asked coyly.

"I may have a T-shirt somewhere," he said. "But at my place, clothes are optional."

"Oh, really?" Clarice said with a grin.

"Any objections?"

"Hmm, we'll see," she said. "Can I tell you after we get there?"

"No problem," Brandon said.

The waitress returned with their change. Brandon left a tip while Clarice picked up the container of pizza. He put his arm around her shoulder as they walked to his car in the cold night air. He kissed her softly on the mouth after opening her door.

"Don't worry about the clothes," he said with a smile. "I'll keep you warm tonight."

Forty-Nine

Clarice awoke up the next morning with her head resting on Brandon's chest, his arm around her, and the sheet pulled over her shoulder. The sun was peeping through the window blinds, casting a soft glow across the bed. Brandon began gently massaging the middle of her back.

"Keep that up and I don't think I'll be getting out of bed this morning," Clarice said softly.

"That's the idea," Brandon said before gently kissing the top of her head.

"I think this is going to be a lazy day for me," she said. "I don't feel like doing anything."

"Can I be lazy with you?" Brandon asked.

"Certainly. What don't you want to do today?"

"I don't want to do any work," Brandon said. "I don't want to exert any extra effort into anything. How about you?"

"Hmm, I don't want to get dressed and go anywhere," she said. "I don't want to put on any makeup."

"Then what do you want?" Brandon asked.

"I just want to be with you today," she said as she reached up and kissed him on the cheek. "And what do you want?"

"Well, besides breakfast, I want to make love to you again this morning," he said.

Clarice rolled over on her back and Brandon put his arm around her. He began leaving soft, wet kisses across her the neck and chest. Clarice arched her back slightly and sighed from his tender touches. They began to kiss long and passionately as their hands explored each other bodies. Her fingers squeezed tightly into his back as they worked to a climax. They relaxed in each other's arms for a few minutes without saying anything, savoring the moment as sunlight began to fill the room.

"I know what I want to do now," Brandon said.

"Eat breakfast?"

"I want to take a hot shower," he said. "Do you want to join me?"

"Only if you let me set the temperature."

"That's a deal," Brandon said as he got out of bed and tiptoed to the bathroom. He took two oversized towels out of the closet and tossed one to her on the bed. While he turned on the shower faucet, Clarice got out of the bed and wrapped the towel around her. Brandon had the shower running when she got to the bathroom.

"How's the temperature?" Brandon asked.

Clarice put her hand under the spray.

"Just a tad too hot," she said.

Brandon made a slight adjustment and she put her hand back under.

"How's that?"

"Just right," Clarice said. She unwrapped the towel and stepped under the shower. Brandon followed her inside and handed her a washcloth and bar of soap. Clarice noticed a generic brand of shampoo on the railing.

"This isn't my regular shampoo, but I guess it will work," she said with a laugh.

"It's all the same," Brandon said.

"Don't you believe that," Clarice said as she began to lather up her hair. "All shampoos are not created equal."

"Perhaps in a woman's view," Brandon said.

As Clarice began to rinse the shampoo out of her hair, Brandon took a soapy washcloth and ran it slowly over her back and shoulders. After a minute, she turned around and he moved it gently over her breasts and stomach and around her neck. She kissed him softly on the mouth as the soap rinsed off her body. As Brandon stepped under the shower and washed his hair, she stepped out and began to dry off, went into the bedroom and put on her clothes. She was combing her hair when Brandon walked up behind her at the dresser mirror and kissed her on the neck.

"Ready for breakfast?" Clarice turned around and asked.

"I guess so," Brandon said. "What are you going to fix?"

"How about coffee and toast?" she said. "Somehow, I don't think I'm going to find a lot of different things to make in the kitchen."

"I'm sure there's some French toast in the freezer," Brandon said. "I think there're some Pop Tarts in the cabinet. And I think I have some eggs in the refrigerator. There might even be some cereal in the cabinet."

"I'm impressed," Clarice said.

"Hey, I'm a self-sufficient bachelor," he said, ginning.

"How about toast and eggs then?"

"That's fine with me as long as you make the coffee first."

As Clarice went to the kitchen, Brandon put on a pair of jeans and blue flannel shirt. He sat on the side of the bed as he buttoned his shirt and put on a pair of house shoes. He could hear Clarice taking a skillet out from under the cabinet.

Brandon sat quietly for a moment, thinking about how much he was beginning to care for Clarice. For the first time he was with a woman who he felt comfortable with all the time. He never felt that way with any other woman. He wondered if she felt as strongly about him.

"Is something the matter?" Clarice asked from the bedroom door. "It got awfully quiet in here."

Brandon looked at her and smiled. He rose from the bed.

"No," he said. "I was just thinking."

"Thinking about what?"

"It was nothing," he said as he walked over to her. He clasped her head in his hands and kissed her on the mouth.

Clarice looked at him and smiled softly. The gaze from her soft eyes made him feel slightly light-headed as they walked to the kitchen. He sat down and she poured him a cup of coffee for him.

"The eggs will be ready in few minutes," Clarice said. "Scrambled okay?"

"That's fine," Brandon said as he stirred creamer into his coffee. He took a sip from the mug and watched her beat the eggs in bowl and put them in the skillet. As she spooned the eggs onto their plates, the toast popped up from the toaster. Brandon got up and took the four pieces and put them on a saucer. He got the margarine out the refrigerator and put it on the table with the toast.

"How are the eggs?" Clarice asked.

"Delicious," Brandon said. "I don't eat them that often but it's nice to have them on a weekend."

"Same here," she said. "I usually have a bowl of cereal and a cup of coffee in the mornings."

The telephone rang as Brandon put a bite of eggs in his mouth.

"I wonder who that could be?" he said after quickly swallowing the eggs.

He hurried to the living room and picked up the phone on the fourth ring. It was Graham on the other end.

"Brandon, I need your help," Graham said wearily.

"What's up?"

"I'm at the jail."

"Jail? What happened?" Brandon asked with a frown.

"I got arrested last night?"

"Arrested? What for?"

"DUI," Graham said glumly.

"Oh shit," Brandon said. "What can I do?"

"I need you to post bail for me and drive me home."

"I'll be there in thirty minutes," Brandon said.

"I'd appreciate that," Graham said wearily. "I'd like to go home."

After putting down the receiver, Brandon told Clarice what happened to Graham.

"You go ahead and leave and I'll clean up here," she said. "I'll watch TV or do something while you're gone."

Brandon took a big sip of his coffee and walked over to the closet and got out his coat. He took off his slippers and put on brown hiking boots.

"Can you believe this? After everything that has happened, he ends up in jail."

"I know, honey," Clarice said. "But why don't you see what Graham has to say?"

"I'll try not to be gone for very long," he said as he opened the front door.

~ * ~

Graham's eyes were sunken and dark and his clothes were wrinkled from sleeping in them when the jailer brought him out to the waiting area. Brandon signed him out and they walked to Brandon's car in the chilly autumn air. They didn't say anything to each other until Brandon pulled out of the parking lot.

"Thanks for doing this," Graham said while looking straight ahead.

"So what happened?" Brandon asked while glancing over at Graham.

"I went over to Hastings after work and saw Buck," Graham said. "We started drinking and I guess I had too many."

"I'm surprised Benny would let you leave in that condition."

"I went somewhere else after Hastings," Graham said quietly. "I stopped off at another bar on the west side and had a few more beers."

"Really?"

"And then I drove over by Sheila's place. That's when the cops stopped me."

"Did you go up to her door?"

"No," Graham said. "I didn't make it that far. I got stopped a few blocks away."

"What for?"

"They said I was driving the wrong way down a one-way street."

Brandon looked over at Graham again and shook his head.

"Is there anything I can do?" Brandon asked.

"You've done enough already," Graham said as sadness crossed his face. "I just need to go home and do a lot of thinking. I'm embarrassed."

"Do you want me to stay with you?

"No, I need to be alone for awhile."

Brandon pulled into Graham's driveway and stopped the car.

"It won't be any problem for me to stay awhile if you want to talk about some things."

"That's okay," Graham said, forcing a smile. "I'll be fine. I'll give you a call later today or tomorrow."

"Just don't hesitate to call me for anything."

Graham unlatched the door and got out of the car. He walked slowly up to his house, turning once for a half-hearted wave, and disappeared into his home. Brandon backed out of the driveway and drove back to his apartment.

Clarice was sitting in the recliner watching television when he opened the front door.

"How's Graham?" Clarice asked after turning down the volume on the TV.

"He's a bit down as you can imagine," Brandon said as he removed his coat and placed it on a hanger in the closet. "I offered to stay with him but he wanted some time alone."

"Is he going to be all right?"

"I think so," Brandon said as he sat down on the couch. "He's the kind of person who needs to be alone to think things over."

"Has he done this before?"

"Not to my knowledge," Brandon said. "He usually confines his drinking to home. I think he's close to hitting rock bottom now. At least I hope so. He was going over to Sheila's house when the police pulled him over."

"Don't you think she should know?"

"I may tell her," Brandon said. "I think she needs to realize how much he thinks about her."

"What do you think she'll do?"

"I'm not sure," Brandon said. "I really don't think she'll do anything until he does something about the drinking."

Fifty

After spending the afternoon going to antique stores around town, Brandon and Clarice stopped at a Chinese carryout on the way to her house. Clarice purchased several Victorian figurines while Brandon found some early edition F. Scott Fitzgerald and William Faulkner novels.

"I really had fun today," Clarice said as they sat in the kitchen. "I haven't done this in a long time."

"I like to go out and look for so-called treasures about once a month," Brandon said.

"We'll have to do it again at the first of the year," Clarice said. "Have you ever gone to other towns to look for things?"

"I've been to Louisville a few times," Brandon said. "I also go to Danville, Georgetown, Winchester, Versailles, and Frankfort. They've got some nice shops in those towns."

"Have you given much more thought about Graham?" Clarice asked.

"I guess I've thought about him off and on most of the day," Brandon said. "I still can't believe that he got jailed. I guess you really don't know people as much as you think you do."

"You always hear office gossip but I try to ignore it," Clarice said.

"We don't have much gossip where I work," Brandon said. "We're pretty much in the open about everything. At least I thought we were."

"A drinking problem isn't something a person tells everyone," Clarice said. "And you know as well as I do that most people won't acknowledge a drinking problem until it's almost too late."

"I just hope that Graham will finally see that he has problem with it. I hope this was a wakeup call for him."

"Only time will tell," Clarice said, pursing her lips.

After they finished eating, Brandon helped her clean the kitchen before they went to the den. They sat down together on the couch. Brandon picked up the remote and turned on the television news. Near the end of the program, there was a brief mention of Graham's arrest.

"I can't believe this," Brandon said, keeping his eyes on the TV set.

"I can't either," Clarice said.

"I guess they consider Graham a public figure because of his position at the magazine," Brandon said. "I wonder how many people are going to see this?"

"Since it's Saturday night, probably not as many people as would see it during the week."

"Can I use your telephone?"

"It's on the end table."

Brandon picked up the telephone and called Graham. He tapped his fingers on the table as the phone rang. Graham finally answered on the sixth ring.

"How are you?" Brandon asked.

"I could be doing better," Graham said unemotionally.

"Did you see the news tonight?"

"No. Did I miss something?"

"Damnit! There was something about your arrest."

"You've got to be kidding me," Graham said, his voice raising. "What did it say?"

"They only said you were arrested on DUI and that was about it," Brandon said. "It was at the end of the newscast so perhaps a lot of people didn't see it."

"I wonder if Sheila and Bernie saw it?"

"Do you want me to call her and find out?"

"No," Graham said quietly. "That's okay. I'll probably call her later this evening or tomorrow. She may even call me if she heard it."

"Are you going to be all right?" Brandon asked. "I can come over if you want me to."

"I'm okay," Graham said. "I've been watching TV this afternoon."

"Well, if you need me for anything, don't hesitate to ask."

"Thanks," Graham said.

After putting down the phone, Brandon sat down on the couch next to Clarice.

"He hadn't heard it?" she asked.

"No," Brandon said, slowly shaking his head. "I broke the news to him."

"How did he take it?"

"He was surprised but I think he's going to be all right. He was more concerned about his family finding out."

"I can't blame him."

"He said he may call Sheila a little later and tell her."

"That's a good idea."

Clarice moved closer to Brandon and rested her head on his shoulder and closed her eyes. He reached down and held her hand. They sat quietly for a few minutes, oblivious to the television.

"I may visit my parents for Christmas," Clarice said, breaking the silence. "I want you to meet them."

"I'd like that," Brandon said while gently squeezing her hand. "Do they know about me?"

"I told Mom about you a long time ago," Clarice said.

"What did you tell her?"

"I told her that I met this really nice guy," Clarice said.

"Is that all?"

"I'm not going to tell you everything," Clarice said with a laugh. "That's between Mom and I."

"But it took you awhile to tell your dad?"

"Dads are more particular," Clarice said. "I told him a month or so ago after we had dated a few times. I think Mom had mentioned something to him, though."

"So what was his response?"

"Dad only wants me to be happy," she said.

"Are you happy?"

"What do you think?" she said while looking up at him with a bright smile. She pecked him on the cheek.

"You've made me very happy," Brandon said. "I hope I've done the same for you."

"You have," she said. "Very much so."

Brandon let go of her hand and put his arm around her and gave her a long and lingering kiss.

"I love you," Brandon said as he continued to hold her closely.

"I love you, too," she said as tears began to fill her eyes.

"I've never felt this way about a woman as I do you," Brandon said. "I can't get enough of you."

Clarice snuggled closer to him with her face against his neck. He could feel the wetness of her tears against his skin and pulled back to look at her face.

"What's the matter?" Brandon asked tenderly. "Why are you crying?"

"Because I love you so much," she said. "I didn't think I would ever find someone I cared about as much as I do you."

"I'm glad we found each other," Brandon said before kissing her softly on the tip of her nose.

Clarice closed her eyes and put her mouth against Brandon's mouth in a long passionate kiss. They held each other warmly and securely while savoring the moment.

They stayed on the couch until Clarice dozed off to sleep. Brandon nudged her gently and told her to go on to bed.

"I am tired," she said drowsily. "This was a long day."

"Get your rest," Brandon said. "I'll call you tomorrow."

"Do you have to leave?" she asked. "Can't you stay over?"

"I need to go to the apartment and see if I've received any messages on my answering machine and check my mail."

"Will you promise to call tomorrow?" she asked.

"I'll call in the afternoon," he said. "I'll let you sleep in."

Clarice walked with Brandon to the front door and kissed him before he went to his car.

After he got home, Brandon played back his answering machine. There were messages from Maggie, Sheila, and Buck about the news story on television.

He picked up his phone and called Graham. This time he answered on the second ring.

"How's it going?" Brandon said.

"Everything's cool," Graham said. "I talked to Sheila."

"What did she say?"

"She said she wasn't surprised it happened," Graham said dryly.

"Is that all?"

"She said she wouldn't see me until I did something about the drinking."

"What did you tell her?"

"I told her that I'd think about it."

"Is that all?"

"That's basically it."

"Don't you think you should do something?"

"About what?"

"The drinking."

"I'll think about it."

"Don't wait too long."

"I need to go now, Brandon," Graham said quickly. "Thanks for calling. Good bye."

Graham hung up the phone before Brandon could say anything else. Graham sat on the recliner for a minute, then got up and went to the refrigerator and took out a can of beer. Before the night was over, he drank eight cans and was passed out in his chair.

Fifty-one

Brandon banged on the front door of Graham's house several times before he finally saw a figure through the curtains stumbling toward the door. The door opened and Graham stood groggily.

"I wasn't expecting you," Graham said before a long yawn. He shook his head and ran his hand over his head.

"Are you okay?" Brandon asked. "You look like shit."

"Thanks friend," Graham said. "Come on in."

Brandon followed Graham into the den. There were several empty beer cans on the floor.

"What's going on?" Brandon asked angrily

"What do you mean?"

"The drinking."

"I didn't say I was going to quit drinking or anything," Graham said defensively while falling back hard into the recliner. "I don't know what gave you that idea."

"I figured that after what happened Friday night that you would have opened your eyes," Brandon said as he sat down on the corner of the couch.

"Drinking isn't a problem of mine."

"Then what is?" Brandon asked forcefully.

"Sheila's my problem."

"It still hasn't sunk in that the drinking drove her away?"

"That's just a damn excuse," Graham said. "She was having an affair."

"That was because of the drinking."

"Whose side are you on anyway?" Graham said.

"I think you know the answer to that," Brandon said. "I want what's best for you."

"Then why don't you just leave me alone for awhile?"

"Because we're friends," Brandon said, lowering his voice. "I don't want to see you wreck everything."

"That crap on TV last night," Graham said. "Could you believe it?"

"I know but it's over and done with," Brandon said.

"Have you seen the paper this morning?"

"No," Brandon said.

Graham picked up the local section and opened it to the third page and handed it to Brandon. A small headline read: Local Editor Arrested for DUI.

"I'm sorry to see this," Brandon said, "but it's not the end of the world. Wouldn't we be doing the same if something similar happened to a person in the news?"

"Yeah, probably," Graham said, shrugging his shoulders.

"Are you going to the counseling tomorrow?" Brandon said.

"I plan to."

"Have you given any more thought to AA?"

"I don't need that," Graham said. "I'm not a drunk."

"You don't have to be a drunk," Brandon said. "But you have a problem with it."

"I'll think about it," Graham said with his head down. "Okay?"

"Can I fix you some breakfast or anything?"

"No thanks, I'm fine," Graham said. "I'll put on a pot of coffee a little later."

Brandon stood and walked over to Graham. He tapped him on the shoulder.

"Call me anytime you need me," Brandon said. "You've got a lot of friends out there who support you. Don't let all of this get you down."

"I'll try not to," Graham said.

Brandon drove to Maggie's house. Maggie and Bobby Lee were eating breakfast when he arrived. She came to the door wearing a loose bathrobe that she kept pulling together at the top to cover her ample cleavage.

"I came at a bad time," Brandon said.

"No, come on in," Maggie said as she opened the door wide for him to come in. "We're just eating breakfast. Care for some eggs and bacon?"

"No thanks," Brandon said. "Coffee would be great though."

Maggie led the way back to the kitchen. Bobby Lee looked up and grinned as Brandon appeared.

"Hi Brandon!" he said between bites.

"Hey, Bobby Lee," Brandon said as he walked over and patted him on the back. "How are you doing?"

"The doctor says that I'm getting better real fast," Bobby Lee said excitedly.

"That's good news," Brandon said. "You'll be out on your bicycle before you know it."

"I don't have a bicycle," Bobby Lee said.

"Oh, you'll be out and running then," Brandon said, giving a furtive glance toward Maggie.

Brandon sat down across from Bobby Lee. Maggie set a hot cup of coffee in front of him with a spoon and creamer. Brandon put a teaspoon of creamer in his coffee and stirred it slowly.

"I guess you know about Graham," Brandon said.

"Yes," Maggie said. "I couldn't believe it. Is he doing okay?"

"I just stopped by house before I came over," Brandon said. "He's taking it pretty hard."

"Is there anything I can do?" Maggie asked.

"Just give him a lot of support. He'll need that when he returns to work tomorrow."

"I'll do whatever I can."

"I'm going to try to get in touch with Sheila this afternoon. He really needs her support."

"Do you think she'll help him?"

"I hope so," Brandon said after sipping some coffee. "I know she'll want him to be doing something to help himself."

"I'm sure there's a reason behind that," Maggie said.

"There is. She's been through a lot the past few years. There's a lot that we didn't know about."

"Are you going to watch any games on TV today?" Bobby Lee interjected. "The Browns are going to play the Rams."

"I may try to watch it if I get enough time," Brandon said with a smile.

"You can come over here and watch it with me," Bobby Lee said. "Mom wouldn't mind."

"Thanks for the offer," Brandon said with a light laugh. "I'll think about that. But I need to go now. I've got some other things to do."

"Don't forget about the game," Bobby Lee said as Brandon pushed back his chair and stood. He took the last swallow from his cup and set it back down on the table.

"I won't," Brandon said warmly.

Maggie followed Brandon to the front door clutching the front of her robe.

"You know you're welcome to come back," Maggie said.

"I know but I've got a lot of things to do," Brandon said. "I hope you explain that to Bobby Lee."

"I will," she said. "And if there is anything you need me to do for Graham, just let me know."

"Okay," Brandon said as he stepped outside. "I'll see you tomorrow."

Brandon drove to his apartment. After pouring himself a glass of ice water, he sat down on the couch and picked up the telephone and called Sheila. Bernie answered the phone.

"Hi Bernie," Brandon said. "Is your mother at home?"

"No," he said. "She went to the supermarket."

"Do you know when she'll be back home?"

"She didn't say but I guess in an hour," Bernie said.

"Could you have her give me a call?"

"Sure, Brandon," Bernie said.

There was a momentary silence on the line. Brandon sensed that Bernie wanted to say something else to him.

"Is something the matter?" Brandon asked.

"Uh, I was wondering about Dad," Bernie said.

"I saw him this morning," Brandon said. "He's doing just fine. He misses you."

"I miss him, too," Bernie said. "I wish Mom and him would quit fighting and everything."

"I hope so, too," Brandon said calmly.

"I'll tell Mom you called," Bernie said. "Good bye."

Brandon put down the phone and took a drink of water. He picked up the newspaper on the coffee table and turned to the story about Graham. He read it again and shook his head. The phone rang and startled him for a moment before he picked it up.

"Hello darling."

"Hi Clarice," Brandon said as a smile came to his face.

"What have you been doing today?"

"I went over to see Graham and Maggie," Brandon said. "I just got off the phone with Graham's son."

"How is Graham?"

"He's not doing too well," Brandon said. "Did you see the story in the newspaper this morning?"

"No, I didn't," Clarice said. "I must have overlooked it."

"I hope a lot of people do," Brandon said. "It said basically the same thing that we heard on TV."

"Poor Graham," Clarice said.

"He was drinking again last night," Brandon said. "At least he wasn't behind the wheel."

"I don't know what to say," Clarice said. "Is he ever going to learn that he has a problem?"

"He's going to have to make some decisions about it," Brandon said. "He's on the verge of losing his wife and son."

"Doesn't he realize that?"

"I don't think he realizes that he has a chance of getting them back. I think he believes it's a lost cause right now. I want Sheila to call him and give him some support."

"Do you think she'll do it?"

"I hope so," Brandon said. "They've been together for a long time. I would hate to think she would turn completely cold with him."

"Let me know what happens," Clarice said.

"What are you doing today?" Brandon asked.

"I've got that report to read," she said. "It'll take most of the day."

"I won't bother you then," Brandon said.

"You never bother me," she said. "I want you to know that."

"I'll call you later tonight or in the morning," Brandon said. "If you get a chance, you can call me when you're finished. I should be here all day."

"I love you," Clarice said sweetly.

"I love you, too," Brandon said. "Talk to you later."

Brandon went to his kitchen and fixed a bowl of canned vegetable soup. He poured a large glass of milk and crumbled some crackers in his soup. He read the book reviews in the newspaper while eating his lunch. He was about finished when he heard two knocks on the front door. Wiping his mouth with a paper towel, he walked over and opened the door. Sheila stood at the doorway with a weary smile.

"Come on in," Brandon said as he stepped aside for her to enter. "It's cold out there. Let me take your coat."

Sheila removed her winter jacket and handed it to Brandon. He hung it up in the closet.

"Can I get you something to drink?" Brandon asked.

"No, thank you," Sheila said while sitting down on the couch. Brandon sat down on the recliner.

"I think I know why you're here," he said.

"Bernie told me you called the house a little while ago," Sheila said. "I wanted to talk to you in person rather than on the phone with him listening."

"I understand," Brandon said. "I'm sure it's been very difficult on Bernie."

"It has been," Sheila said. "And with this DUI, he's dreading going to school tomorrow because he's afraid all the kids will tease him."

"I don't think that will happen," Brandon said. "At least I hope not."

"Have you talked to Graham?" Sheila asked.

"I did this morning. He's taking it very hard. He really needs you."

Sheila put her face in her hands and sobbed. Brandon got up from the recliner and walked back to the bathroom and came back with a box of tissues and handed it to her. He sat back down in the recliner and waited until she felt like talking.

"I don't know if I can help him," Sheila said after wiping the tears from her cheeks.

"He's going to start counseling tomorrow," Brandon said. "He's making an effort."

"He needs to do more than that," Sheila said. "He needs to quit drinking."

"I've talked to him about attending an AA meeting. He's kind of reluctant. He's in denial about a drinking problem."

"He's been that way for years, Brandon. I could only take so much."

"I think it might help him if you give him some hope for reconciliation if he goes to AA."

"Do you really think that would help?" Sheila asked.

"I do," Brandon said. "He needs all the support he can get now. Can you help him?"

"I still care very much for him," Sheila said. "I guess I still love him despite all that's happened between us. I'll talk to him."

"He really needs you and Bernie," Brandon said. "You know how empty his life is without the two of you."

"I know," she said. "My life is somewhat empty without him."

"Why don't you go over and see him this afternoon?" Brandon said.

"If you think that will help, then I will," Sheila said. "Do you mind if I use your phone and call him?"

"Of course not," Brandon said. He got the cordless phone from the kitchen table and brought it back to her. He went back to the bedroom as she made the call, waiting until he heard the hang-up click on the phone before going back to her.

"How did everything go?" Brandon asked.

"I'm going over there now," Sheila said while getting up from the couch.

Brandon walked over and took her coat from the closet. He held it and she slipped her arms into the sleeves. When she turned around, he put his arms around her and gave her a gentle hug.

"Please let me know if there is anything more I can do for you both," Brandon said.

"I will," Sheila said. "You're a very good friend to both of us."

Fifty-two

Brandon arrived at the office early on Monday morning and fixed a pot of coffee. Maggie showed up a few minutes later and joined him in the break room.

"Do you think we'll see Graham this morning?" Maggie asked as Brandon poured coffee into her cup.

"I sure hope so," Brandon said. "It's still early."

"What time is his appointment with the counselor?"

"I think it's around eleven or so."

"Is there anything I can do?" Maggie asked while clutching the cup in two hands.

"Just treat him like nothing has happened," Brandon said. "He's already got enough on his mind without wondering what people are thinking when they see him. But if you want to offer him some support, go ahead because he thinks a lot of you."

"I'll do what I can," she said with a forced smile.

A minute later, Graham came through the front door and went into his office. He called the counselor to confirm the appointment. A minute later, he went to the break room with his cup.

"Good morning," he said smiling.

"Hi Graham," Maggie said, and then blurted out, "I want you to know that I'll help you in any way I can."

Graham poured his coffee in silence and turned around and faced her.

"I appreciate that," he said. "I've done a lot of thinking the past twenty-four hours. I need all the help and support I can get from my friends."

"Don't hesitate to ask for anything," Brandon said.

The phone rang in the lobby and Maggie hurried to answer it. Graham motioned for Brandon to follow him to his office. He closed the door as Brandon sat down in front of his desk. Graham stood next to the window and gazed outside for a moment.

"Sheila came by yesterday," Graham said. "She said she'd talked to you."

"Was it a good meeting?"

"I think so," Graham said. "She said she'd give me a second chance if I do several things."

"Such as?"

"The counseling and AA," Graham said as he turned around and looked at Brandon.

"And?"

"I told her I would do it," Graham said. "After she left, I thought about our past few years together and realized that she was right about my drinking. I wasn't a drunk or anything but I parked my butt in front of the TV each night and drank. Other than Bernie's soccer matches and work, I had no time for anyone or anything."

"Do you want me to help line you up with an AA chapter?"

"I've already made a call to a friend of ours. I'll be going to my first meeting tonight."

"Good for you," Brandon said with a smile. "I know it had to be a difficult decision."

"After I gave it some thought it wasn't," Graham said. "It was just getting past the denial and realizing that I have been drinking too much."

"When will Sheila be coming back?"

"Well, she wants me to go through meetings for a month or so and show her that I'm determined to get better," Graham said. "She also said that she was willing to join me in counseling."

"Are you able to forgive her?"

"I think so," Graham said. "I think I'm the reason she did what she did."

Maggie knocked on Graham's door and told him that he had a telephone call.

"As I've told you, if there is anything I can do to help, please don't hesitate to let me know," Brandon said as he got up from the chair.

"Thanks again," Graham said as he picked up the phone.

Brandon walked over to his office and closed the door. He leaned back in his chair and looked out the window. A light snow was beginning to fall. He smiled as he thought about Graham and Sheila getting back together. He knew it would be difficult at times for Graham, but felt that being back with Sheila was the motivation needed to turn his life around. Brandon picked up the telephone and called Clarice but she was already in a meeting. He couldn't help but grin as he put the phone back down.

Maggie tapped on his door and opened it.

"Is everything going to be okay?" she whispered with arched eyebrows.

"I believe so," Brandon said. "I wanted to tell you that Bobby Lee seems to be doing well. He's making a quick recovery."

"He'll be so glad to get the cast off his leg so he can get around," Maggie said. "He can't wait to get back to school."

"Couldn't he go back now?"

"Probably but the school decided it would be best for him to return after Christmas break," Maggie said.

"That's a good idea. It would give him a fresh start."

Graham came out of his office with his coat on.

"I've got an eleven o'clock appointment," he said sheepishly. "I'll be back around one or so. Hold down the fort while I'm away."

"Will do," Brandon said.

The phone rang and Brandon answered before Maggie could dart to her desk. It was Clarice.

"Good morning," she said brightly.

"I see you've already been in a meeting," Brandon said. "What a way to start the week."

"It's not that bad," she said with a laugh. "I got a few minutes and thought I'd see how everything went with Graham."

"He just left for a meeting a few minutes ago," Brandon said. "And he's got AA tonight."

"Really?" Clarice asked. "Good for him."

"He seemed very upbeat this morning," Brandon said. "A total reversal from the weekend."

"Let's hope he stays that way."

"So what are you doing today, other than meetings?" Brandon asked.

"I've got to complete that report I read yesterday," she said.

"Any plans for the evening?"

"Perhaps," she said coyly.

"Hmm, with whom?"

"I'm just waiting for him to ask," Clarice said.

"Do you want to go out for dinner?"

"Yes," Clarice said. "Do you want to meet somewhere?"

"Sure," Brandon said. "How about El Cajuns at six-thirty? Will that give you enough time?"

"That's fine. I'll just go over there from work."

"I'll do the same."

"See you then," Clarice said. "Bye."

"Bye."

Graham returned to the office shortly after one. He came to Brandon's office. Brandon was sitting at his desk eating a veggie sandwich for lunch.

"How did it go?" Brandon said, swallowing a bite.

"It was very preliminary stuff," Graham said as he sat down. "I think he wanted us to get acquainted."

"Do you feel comfortable with him?"

"I guess," Graham said, shrugging his shoulders. "It's kind of difficult to open up about things in your life to a stranger."

"I know it is," Brandon said. "I think you just have to give it time."

"That's what the counselor said. We're going to meet three times a week for the first couple of months. He wants to schedule Sheila for a few individual sessions before he gets us together."

"Just don't get discouraged," Brandon said.

"I don't plan to," Graham said. "It's something I need. It's something I've needed for a long time."

"That's the right attitude."

Graham stood and stepped to the doorway.

"I'll let you finish your sandwich," Graham said. "I'll talk to you later."

"No need to rush off," Brandon said.

"I've got some things to do."

Brandon spent the afternoon writing his column and laying out several pages. He left the office at six and got to El Cajuns about twenty minutes later. Clarice was waiting in the lobby when he walked through the front door. They smiled at each other and quickly kissed.

"You wouldn't believe who is here," Clarice said as they waited for the hostess to take them to their table.

"Who?" Brandon asked.

"Bart," she said. "And he's with Sheryl, a woman I work with at the agency. He must be fifteen years older than her."

"Did they speak?"

"Yes," Clarice said. "In fact, Bart was quite cordial."

"He'd better be or I'll punch him in the nose again," Brandon joked.

The hostess guided them to a table that was several tables away from Bart. Bart's back was to them but Sheryl smiled timidly as they were being seated.

"Don't they make a nice couple?" Brandon asked with a grin.

"Better her than me," Clarice said. "I wonder how long that will last?"

"Who knows?" Brandon said. "She may be his soul mate."

"I don't think so," Clarice said. "She's rather shallow."

"And Bart's deep?"

"Well, I guess you have a point," Clarice said.

They ordered a carafe of red wine to go with their New Orleans-style dinners of wild rice, peppers, and vegetables. Clarice excused herself to go to the women's room. A minute later, Sheryl was there with her.

"I hope you don't mind me being with Bart," Sheryl said.

"Why should I mind?" Clarice asked.

"Well, you used to go with him."

"Honey, it was never anything serious and it didn't take much to get over him."

"I just want to make sure."

"I hope you're careful," Clarice said, looking at Sheryl from the mirror. "He's got quite a reputation."

"I know but he's been nice to me."

"I hope it remains that way," Clarice said, turning around and patting Sheryl on the hand.

"Thanks," Sheryl said with a smile.

They left the women's room together. When Sheryl reached her table, Bart turned around for a moment and smiled. Brandon nodded back.

"Sheryl wanted my approval," Clarice said after taking a sip of wine.

"And did you give it?"

"With a caveat," Clarice said. "I hope he doesn't hurt her."

"She's a woman," Brandon said. "She can take care of herself."

"I'm sure she can but that still doesn't mean I don't worry about her. She's a nice girl."

"Do you want me to go bop him in the nose?" Brandon said with a grin.

"No!" Clarice said. "Keep out of it."

"Just kidding."

"I know," Clarice said. "Let's talk about us."

"Us?"

"Yes," she said softly while reaching over and touching his hand. "What are you doing for Christmas?"

"I don't have any plans," he said.

"Would you like to meet my parents?"

"Don't they live in Florida?"

"Yes," Clarice said. "Would you like to fly down there and spend a few days with them?"

"How would they feel about that?"

"They want to meet you," Clarice said.

"Really?"

"Believe it or not, but I've told them some good things about you," Clarice said with a grin. "It was difficult but I found a few nice things to say."

"Gee, thanks," Brandon said with a chuckle. "It's nice to know that I've made a good impression on you. I guess you can fool some of the people some of the time."

"I don't think you've fooled me about anything," she said, looking over her wine glass before taking another swallow. Brandon felt like he was getting lost in her dark eyes as he looked into them.

"All you see is me," he said.

"And I love what I've seen," Clarice said while putting down her glass. They smiled at each other for a few seconds. Brandon could feel his heart pumping as he gazed at her soft features.

"I don't feel like eating anymore," he said.

"Why not?" she asked.

"I've got other things on my mind now."

"Such as?"

"You."

"Me?" Clarice said while opening her eyes wide. "What do you want with me?"

"What do you think?" Brandon said, then winked.

Clarice looked seductively at Brandon.

"My place or yours?" she asked.

"Your choice," he said before picking up his glass of wine and taking another sip.

"How about my place?"

"Sounds good to me."

Clarice took a few more bites from her dinner. Brandon paid for their meal and they left without Bart and Sheryl noticing they were gone. Brandon followed Clarice to her house, and within a few minutes after arriving, they were under the sheets making passionate love.

Fifty-three

Snow covered the ground the week before Christmas. Cars were moving cautiously and slowly through the downtown streets as Brandon headed to the office. Pedestrians were bundled up in heavy coats as winter had finally arrived. Brandon stomped his feet on the pavement before going inside the building.

"Good morning," he said to Maggie as he took off his coat. "It's sure nasty outside."

"I wish I were going to Florida like some people I know," Maggie said.

Brandon grinned. He and Clarice had planned to leave December twenty-third, only five days away. He was somewhat reluctant after thinking about but as it got closer, he was looking forward to meeting her parents and spending some time with her away from Lexington.

"I don't think I'll be missing a white Christmas," Brandon said. "I've already had enough of the white stuff."

"You've got company in your office," Maggie said.

"Who is it?" Brandon asked.

Maggie mouthed J-E-N-N-Y slowly and arched her eyebrows.

"Can I get you some coffee?" Maggie asked.

"Yes, please," Brandon said. "Two cups."

"She already has a cup," Maggie said softly.

"Okay," Brandon said as he walked back to his office.

Jenny was seated in the chair facing his desk and looking through the current issue of the magazine. She was wearing a green sweater with a Christmas reindeer embroidered across the front and red slacks.

"Hello," Brandon said as he walked to his desk.

"Good morning, Brandon," Jenny said, then placing the magazine on the table next to her. "I hope you don't mind me dropping by."

"That's fine," Brandon said. "Is there something you want?"

Maggie stepped quietly into the office and handed the coffee to Brandon. She looked at both of them, smiled tightly, and backed out while closing the door.

"I don't think she likes me," Jenny said.

"I don't know why you'd say that," Brandon said.

"She's never very friendly to me."

"She hardly knows you," Brandon said, wondering where the conversation was going. "So what do you want?"

"I came by to say goodbye," Jenny said.

"Where are you going?"

"I'm moving to Oklahoma City in two days," Jenny said. "I wanted to tell you how sorry I am for everything that happened between us."

"We had some good times," Brandon said with a smile. "And the rest is forgiven."

"I'm going to get married, too," she said with a bright smile.

"Married?" Brandon said. "Who's the lucky man?"

"David Hatfield," Jenny said. "He's a police officer."

Brandon was thinking that this was an early Christmas present for him, knowing that Jenny was going to be out of his life along with Hatfield. He smiled to himself for a moment.

"That's just wonderful," Brandon said gleefully. "I wish the best for the both of you."

Jenny got up from her chair and took a step toward Brandon. He wasn't sure what was happening and flinched. He pushed back his chair and stood. Jenny gave him a long hug.

"I'm going to miss you, Brandon," Jenny said as tears began to fill her eyes.

"I'll miss you, too," Brandon said, patting her gently on the back. Jenny kissed him softly on the cheek and backed away. She put on her fur-lined, knee-length coat, smiled and walked quickly out the door without saying another word. Brandon didn't move for a second, then sat down in his chair.

A few seconds later Maggie poked her head inside his office.

"What was that all about?" Maggie asked. "She was crying."

"She just dropped by to say good bye," Brandon said.

"She's leaving?"

"Yep, moving to Oklahoma City in two days."

"Good riddance," Maggie said. "I never liked that woman."

A look of disdain came over Maggie's face as she returned to her desk. Brandon shook his head and smiled, then turned on his computer and skimmed through his e-mails. He wrote down on his calendar any news conferences and meetings that were announced.

"Busy?"

Brandon looked over to the door and Graham was standing there.

"No, just checking e-mails and what-not," Brandon said. "Come on in."

Graham stepped inside, holding a cup of coffee, and sat down across from Brandon.

"Sheila and Bernie are moving back in," Graham said with a huge smile.

"Great!" Brandon said. "That's the best news I've heard in ages."

"She told me last night."

"Did she give you any reasons?"

"She thought the family should be together at Christmas," Graham said.

"That's a good reason."

"We've also had a few sessions together in counseling and she feels that we're beginning to overcome some of the problems."

"I've always been confident that you and Sheila would be able to work things out," Brandon said.

"I haven't had a drink for three weeks," Graham said. "I've been going to meetings about every day."

"Has it been difficult?"

"Not really," Graham said. "It's made me realize that I am an alcoholic and how much I sacrificed because of my drinking. It's good to know that I'm getting some of it back."

"Let me know if there's anything I can do," Brandon said.

"I will," Graham said as he got up from his chair. "You've already been a big help."

After Graham left his office, Brandon picked up the telephone and called Clarice. She answered on the second ring.

"I've had an eventful morning," Brandon said, then told her about Jenny's visit and Graham getting back with Sheila.

"I've got our reservations for Florida," Clarice said. "You're not going to get cold feet on me now are you?"

"No way," Brandon said. "I was telling Maggie this morning that I couldn't wait to get away from this snow and cold."

"I talked to Mom last night and she and Dad are really excited about finally getting to meet you."

"I'm looking forward to meeting them," Brandon said. "I can't wait to see the couple that produced such a lovely woman."

"And they can't wait to meet the man who has made their daughter such a happy woman."

"What are you doing today?"

"Rachel and I are going over to a public relations society meeting after work for a Christmas party."

"I remember you telling me that," Brandon said. "I hope you have a good time."

"What are you going to do?"

"I think I'll stop by Hastings for a little while."

Fifty-four

A two-foot tall artificial Christmas tree with one strand of white lights and silver icicles draped unevenly stood in the corner of Hastings bar. A string of multi-colored lights wrapped around the front window as Benny took a minimalist approach to holiday decorations.

"Merry Christmas," Brandon said as he sat down at the bar.

"Merry Christmas," Benny said, setting down a frosty mug of beer in front of Brandon. "I haven't seen you in awhile. Busy with the magazine?"

"Pretty much so," Brandon said, and then took a swallow from the mug.

"How's Graham? I haven't seen him in ages."

"About the same," Brandon said. "He has lots of things going on right now."

Benny walked away to take care of a customer. Brandon sat quietly at the bar, thinking about the upcoming trip to Florida in a few days. He wasn't going to miss the cold weather that had enveloped Kentucky. He wondered what Clarice's parents would think of him and what he would think of them. He didn't recall ever making a special trip to visit a friend's parents. Again, he had never been involved with a woman like he was with Clarice.

"Hello stranger."

Brandon turned to his side. Buck was standing there wearing a heavy coat.

"Hey," Brandon said smiling. "What's up?"

"I haven't seen you in awhile," Buck said while removing his coat and placing it on the back of the stool. "I heard about Graham. Is he doing okay?"

"Much better," Brandon said. "His life is back on course."

"That's great to hear."

Benny came over and set a mug of beer on a napkin in front of Buck.

"So what's been going on?" Brandon asked Buck.

"I've just been covering lots of basketball."

"The Cats look pretty good."

"They've got a lot of talent," Buck said. "They should a tough team to beat by March."

"How's the woman you've been dating?"

"Debra?"

"Yeah. Are you still going out with her?"

"No," Buck said. "I thought we were doing okay but she doesn't want to be tied down to one guy right now. I found that out when I went to a bar on the south end one night."

"Huh?"

"She was there with another guy."

"I'm sorry to hear that."

"It's no big deal," Buck said. "She's gone through that divorce and I don't think she wants to get involved in a deep relationship. I'll survive. How about you?"

"I must admit that things are pretty serious," Brandon said. "At least I hope so. I'm going down to Florida with her in a few days to spend Christmas with her parents."

"That sounds serious to me."

"I'm going to pop the big question before we leave."

"Marriage?"

"Yeah," Brandon said with a shy smile. "I bought a ring last week and I plan to give it to her before we leave for Florida."

"Congratulations," Buck said with a wide grin. "Hey Benny, bring us over another round of beer. Our buddy is planning on getting married."

Brandon blushed as several patrons turned their heads and looked at him.

"You didn't have to broadcast it," Brandon said to Buck. "She might tell me no."

"I don't think so," Buck said. "For you to go this far, that means she must feel close to you."

"I hope I'm reading her correctly," Brandon said as Benny set beers in front of them.

"You need a second opinion," Benny said, unsmiling and leaning on the counter. "Don't do it."

"Don't do it?" Brandon asked with a perplexed look.

"You've been a bachelor for a long time," Benny said. "You're giving up too much freedom."

"Maybe I'm ready to," Brandon said with a grin.

"I'm just kidding you," Benny said as a smile crossed his face. "I saw her that night you brought her in here. She's a fine lady."

"Thanks, Benny," Brandon said. "That's why I want to marry her."

Another patron got Benny's attention for a drink and he walked over to him.

"So when do you think you'll get married?" Buck said.

"Probably next summer," Brandon said. "I'll leave it up to her. You know how women like June weddings."

"You're right," Buck said.

"I'm sure she won't be in a rush."

"This is kind of sad," Buck said, pursing his lips.

"Why is that?"

"I don't know," Buck said, shrugging his shoulders. "We've been friends for several years and now you're going to get married. Things won't be the same."

"Perhaps you need to find a woman and get settled down?"

"I don't think so," Buck said. "I'm on the road too much and enjoy it. I like it too much."

"Ah, one of these days some gal may sweep you off your feet."

"I doubt it but it could happen," Buck said. "I'll just have to wait."

"It happened to me."

Brandon finished the rest of his beer and put some money down on the counter. He waved at Benny and got down from the stool.

"I need to be running now," Brandon said to Buck. "I've got to finish up on some Christmas shopping."

"Well, if I don't see you in the next few days, I hope you have a safe trip and merry Christmas," Buck said.

"Thanks," Brandon said. "Merry Christmas to you."

After leaving Hastings, Brandon stopped by a toy store. It was crowded with shoppers scurrying up and down the aisles. There were long lines at the registers.

Brandon walked over to the bicycle racks and began looking at the different models. He found a metallic blue 26-inch, 10-speed that glistened under the fluorescent lights. Another man walked up to him and glanced at the bicycle. Brandon put his hands on it and pulled it to the aisle.

"I'm buying it," Brandon said pleasantly.

"Sure," the man said nonchalantly and walked away.

Brandon pushed the bicycle to one of the lines leading to the register. It took him nearly an hour to get through the line and pay for it, then he picked it up and carried it out to the snow-covered parking lot and put it in the trunk of his car. He tied down the trunk since the bike was too big for it to close.

Back at his apartment he set the bike in the corner of the living room. He sat down on the couch and called Clarice but only got the answering machine. He figured she was still at the Christmas party.

After putting on gym shorts, T-shirt and a large flannel bathrobe, he went back to the kitchen and boiled some water on the stove to make green tea.

While the tea was brewing in his cup, the phone rang and he answered it on the second ring.

"This is Brandon Wilkes," he said.

"Mr. Wilkes," the voice said. "I'm Sergeant Elliott with the police department."

"Is something wrong?" Brandon asked.

"Clarice Horton gave me your number to call," he said. "She was involved in an accident on Richmond Road."

"Is she all right?" Brandon asked hurriedly.

"I believe so," the policeman said. "She's at the med center."

"I'll be right over," Brandon said and put down the phone without waiting for the policeman to respond. He ran back to his bedroom and put on the clothes he wore to work. Within five minutes, he was in his car and driving to the med center.

Brandon found a space on the first level of the parking garage and pulled in. He ran to the information desk. It was unmanned but there was a phone he used to find out where she was. He found her on the fourth floor in a semi-private room. The television was on. Clarice was sitting up in bed while a nurse was taking her vital signs.

"Clarice!" Brandon said hurrying over to her side. "What happened?"

"Someone skidded into the back of my car," Clarice said. Her cheek was bruised and her mouth was swollen.

"Are you okay?" Brandon said as he held her hand.

"I think so," she said. "They want to keep me here overnight for observation."

"No broken bones or anything?"

"I just hit my head on the steering wheel," she said. "My neck is a little sore, too."

"Oh, honey," Brandon said while gently squeezing her hand. "I'm so glad you're all right." He bent over and kissed her on the cheek.

"I'm feeling better already," she said with a soft smile.

Fifty-five

Brandon was at the hospital early the next morning. Clarice was already dressed when he walked into her room. There were some blood stains on her blouse and pants and her face was puffy but she was in good spirits because she was going home.

"Good morning," Brandon said smiling. "I see that you're ready to leave."

"I should have asked you to bring me some clothes," Clarice said as she got up from a chair in the corner. "These look awful."

"You look fine," he said, giving her a quick hug. "And you'll bounce back fast after a few days in Florida."

"I hate going to Florida looking like this," Clarice said with a frown. "I looked this way the last time I went down there."

They went to the discharge desk and she paid her bill, then they walked arm-in-arm across the slushy snow in the parking lot to his car.

"Where's your car?" Brandon asked as he opened the passenger door for her.

"The police took it," she said. "They said it'll be impounded until I pick it up."

"We can go get it before we leave for Florida," Brandon said.

"That's fine with me," she said. "I'm in no hurry. I won't be going anywhere until I go to the airport in two days."

Brandon pulled out of the parking lot slowly and headed toward her house.

"Do you want something to eat?" he asked.

"Not really," Clarice said. "I'll eat something later after I get home. I really want to go back to bed. Those nurses kept me up all night coming into my room."

"I can imagine," Brandon said.

Brandon stayed at her house while she took a shower and put on a nightgown. He called the office and told Maggie why he wasn't at work. After Clarice went to bed, he returned to the office.

"How is she feeling?" Maggie asked as he removed his coat in the lobby.

"She's a little sore but other than that she'll be all right," Brandon said.

"That's good to hear. I heard on the news this morning that there were fender-benders all over town last night. I hate to drive in the snow."

"Where's Graham?" Brandon asked.

"Sheila was moving a few of their things over this morning so he's helping her. He said he'd been in around one or so. He has a meeting at eleven so he's probably on the way over there right now."

"Do you and Bobby Lee have any plans for Christmas?" Brandon asked.

"Are you inviting us to Florida?" Maggie kidded.

"You're not packed already?" Brandon said with a grin.

"I wish," Maggie said. "We're probably going to visit my parents in Maysville if the roads clear up. We always get the family together for Christmas."

"That sounds like a good time. Have you finished your shopping?"

"I think so," she said.

"What did you buy for Bobby Lee?"

"Mostly clothes," Maggie said. "I also bought him a couple video games that he's been wanting."

"Do you mind if I come over tomorrow night and wish him Merry Christmas before I leave town?"

"Please do," Maggie said. "I'll fix some eggnog for us."

"Don't go to any trouble," Brandon said.

"It's no trouble at all. I fix eggnog, cookies and candy every Christmas."

Brandon walked to his office and opened his mail and checked his e-mails. He overcame the urge to call Clarice because he knew she was probably sound asleep. A few minutes later he had a phone call and it was her.

"What are you doing up?" Brandon asked.

"I couldn't sleep," she said.

"Can I bring you anything?"

"I'm fine," she said with tiredness in her voice. "I've made a pot of coffee and have been watching TV."

"You need your rest," Brandon said.

"I'll go back and lay down in a little while," she said. "I'm just a little restless."

"Is there anything I can bring you this evening?" he asked.

"How about my car?"

"Your car?"

"It has my folders in it," she said.

"I guess I can get Graham to go over there with me and pick it up. You'll have to call the police and give us permission to do it."

"I'll do that and call you back later," she said. "I hope it's not too much trouble for you and Graham."

"It's no problem at all," he said. "Just call me back after you've spoken with the police."

"Okay," she said. "Bye."

"See you later," Brandon said.

Brandon and Graham picked up her car in the afternoon. Brandon drove it to her house while Graham followed in Brandon's car. Graham waited in the driveway as Brandon took the keys to the front door and handed them to Clarice along with her briefcase.

She looked out the door and smiled and waved at Graham and he waved back at her.

"Thanks so much," Clarice said to Brandon. "You wouldn't believe it but I've actually fretted over this."

"I believe it," Brandon said with a laugh. "You're a workaholic."

"Probably so," she said with a sigh.

Brandon kissed her softly on the mouth and walked carefully back to his car and got in on the passenger side. Clarice waved again as they backed out of the driveway.

"She's really a lovely woman," Graham said. "You're a lucky guy."

"I think so," Brandon said, smiling proudly.

"I was beginning to think that you'd never find the right woman. You always seemed so particular."

"I was just too busy to get tied down," Brandon said.

"Another one bites the dust," Graham said with a laugh.

"How did things go this morning with Sheila?"

"The move?"

"Yes," Brandon said.

"Oh, we got all of their clothes back in," Graham said. "There are a few other things but we can get them after Christmas."

"How did the session go?"

"It was pretty intense," Graham said. "She really opened up today and started crying and all. She even had me crying."

"Is everything okay now?"

"I believe so," Graham said, taking a deep breath. "She didn't say anything about moving back out."

"What came up at the session?"

"Her affair."

"I guess it was good to get it out in the open?"

"I think so," Graham said. "I think she feels as bad about it as I do."

"I'm sure she does," Brandon said. "I got that feeling from her a month or so ago."

"The funny thing is that she didn't want to put the blame on me," Graham said. "She said she was accountable for her own actions."

"I guess we all are in the long run to some extent," Brandon said.

Graham pulled into the parking lot next to the office. It had been cleared of snow by a road crew while they were away.

"Any calls while we were away?" Graham asked Maggie.

"Nothing urgent," she said. "It's been kind of quiet around here."

"That's good," Graham said. "We don't want anymore bad news to spoil the holiday season."

Fifty-six

Brandon stopped by a Chinese carryout restaurant on the way to Clarice's home and bought an egg foo yong dinner and two egg rolls. Clarice was sitting in the den in her night gown and bathrobe, going over work from office when he got to her house.

"How are you feeling?" Brandon asked, kissing her on the cheek inside the front door.

"I'm still a little sore," she said, taking the food from him and carrying it to the kitchen. He removed his coat and placed it in a chair. She got plates and silverware from the cabinet.

"Can I help?" Brandon asked.

"You can fix our drinks," she said. "I'll have ice water."

Clarice set the silverware while Brandon got ice from the refrigerator and put them in tall glasses and poured water from the tap. He looked over at her after she sat down and was dividing up the carryout on their plates. The swelling had reduced somewhat but the bruises were still a deep blue around her eyes. She glanced up at him.

"I don't look very pretty, do I?" she said, pursing her lips.

"You look like you've been in an accident," he said with a soft smile. "In a few days it will be cleared up. It's just going to take some time."

"I know but I didn't want to look this way for our trip," she said as he sat down next to her.

"Being in the Florida sun will make you feel better," Brandon said.

"I know it will," she said.

After they finished eating, Brandon helped her clean the dishes. He followed her into the den and waited while she cleared the papers off the couch and put them on the coffee table. They sat down and he put his arm around her as she rested her head on his shoulder.

"Since we're leaving in two days, would you mind if I give you your Christmas present tomorrow night?" Brandon asked.

"I wouldn't mind," she said. "Can I guess what it is?"

"I'd rather you wouldn't," he said with a chuckle, "although I don't believe you could guess what it is."

"Could I try anyway?" she said, looking up at him with a grin.

"No," he said emphatically.

"But I like to guess," she said in a teasing pout.

"I'm sure you do," he said. "But you'll be receiving it tomorrow night so what's the hurry?"

"It's just fun to do," he said.

"Perhaps you can guess tomorrow when I call you on the phone," Brandon said. "That way, if you don't guess what it is then I'll have time to go out and buy you something that you thought you'd get."

"That's no fun," she said while sitting up straight.

"So let's just wait until tomorrow night," he said.

"Do you want to guess what I bought you?"

"You didn't need to buy me anything," he said.

"If that's the case then you didn't have to buy me anything," Clarice said, arching her eyebrows.

"Good point," he said, patting her on the leg. "I guess I can return it then."

"No you don't!"

"If you say so."

Clarice reached up and kissed him on the cheek.

"Do you know that I love you?" she said sweetly.

"I think so," he said. "And do you know that I love you?"

"I kinda figured that out," Clarice said as she put her hand in his hand.

Brandon gave her a long and lingering kiss on the mouth. She tucked her head under his chin and they sat in silence for a few minutes.

"I'm going over to Maggie's tomorrow night after work," Brandon said. "I don't think I told you but I bought Bobby Lee a bicycle for Christmas. It's a 10-speed."

"That was sweet of you," Clarice said. "Will he be able to ride it soon?"

"I think he'll be getting the cast off any day now," Brandon said. "I'm sure it will take awhile for him to build strength back in leg."

"Did you buy anything for Maggie?"

"No," Brandon said. "Graham and I usually give her two hundred dollars in a card"

"That sounds like a couple of men," Clarice said with a light laugh. "But I guess you'd find it difficult to buy anything personal."

"She seems to appreciate the money," Brandon said in mock protest. "She's never complained."

"Did you buy anything for Graham?"

"Not yet," Brandon said. "I usually get him a fifth of good whiskey. I won't be doing that this year. Any ideas?"

"If it's not too late why don't you have a fruit and nut tray delivered to his house as a family gift?" Clarice said.

"That's not a bad idea," Brandon said. "I'll do that first thing in the morning. Any other ideas?"

"You could give them a gift certificate to a good restaurant."

"That's another great idea. You're full of them tonight."

"Smarty," she said playfully.

"Do you buy gifts for people in your office?"

"We draw names and then I buy Rachel and a few more people some small gifts."

"Have you started buying them?"

"I finished that a month ago," Clarice said with a giggle.

"You're much too efficient," Brandon said.

"You have to be in my business," She said.

"I guess it's all those meetings," Brandon said.

"You're really trying to push my buttons," she said, then poked him in the rib with her finger. He jumped back.

"Yo!" Brandon said with a laugh. "Don't be so rough."

Clarice reached over and pulled him back close to her. He put his arms around her and kissed her long and passionately.

"Do you have any plans for the evening?" Clarice asked.

"Not really," he said. "How about you?"

"I've finished going over the papers from work."

"Do you want to watch TV?"

"No," she said. "Do you?"

"No."

"Do you want to read?"

"No," Brandon said. "I left *Ulysses* at home."

Clarice laughed lightly.

"So what would you like to do?"

"I think I'd like to pick you up in my arms and carry you to the bedroom."

"And then what?"

"I'd pull back the covers and lay you down gently on the sheet."

"And what would you do then?"

"I'd take off your robe and nightgown."

"Oh my," she said coyly. "And what would you do then?"

"I'd take off my clothes and get in bed with you," he said with a naughty grin.

"And then what?"

"We'd make wonderful and passionate love."

"Then what's keeping you?"

Brandon rose up from the couch and pulled her up gently by the hand. He lifted her off the floor and carried her to the bedroom in his arms. As her dark eyes sparkled from the light coming through the window and a knowing smile spread over her face, he pulled back the covers and lay her down on the bed. He slowly removed her clothes and put them on the dresser. He took off his clothes and got in bed beside her and pulled her to him. They kissed passionately.

And they made wonderful and passionate love.

Fifty-seven

Bobby Lee was watching television when Brandon arrived at his house. Maggie knew beforehand that Brandon would be dropping by with a gift so she intentionally waited in the kitchen when the doorbell rang.

"Bobby Lee, would you answer the front door?" she said. "My hands are in dishwater."

"Aw Mom," Bobby Lee said. "I'm getting to a good part in this show."

"Please Bobby Lee," she said.

"All right," Bobby Lee said as he reached for a crutch and stood up from the couch. He went to the front door while catching a few glimpses of the TV program. When he opened the front door, he saw Brandon and smiled. Then he saw the bicycle glistening behind him. Bobby Lee stood transfixed for a few seconds, looking first at the bike and then at Brandon without knowing what to say.

"A bike!" Bobby Lee finally blurted as pushed open the door. "Mom! Mom! Brandon brought over a bike!"

A few seconds later, Maggie stood at the doorway. She knew Brandon would have a present but had no idea that it would be an expensive bicycle. She began to sob.

"Oh, Brandon," she said. "You shouldn't have."

Bobby Lee stood outside in the cold, night air with Brandon and marveled at his Christmas present. Finally, Maggie opened the door wide.

"You guys are going to freeze out there," she said with a laugh. "Bring the bike in and put it next to the Christmas tree."

Bobby Lee came in first, then Brandon took the bike and guided it inside to the living room. He set it to the side of the tree. Bobby Lee went straight to the bike and began examining it closely while Brandon took off his coat and sat down on the couch.

"Can I get you something to eat?" Maggie asked. "I have some eggnog."

"I'm not hungry but a small glass of eggnog would be nice," Brandon said.

Maggie went back to the kitchen to get the eggnog. Bobby Lee was running his hands over the bike almost as if he was in a dream and couldn't believe it was real.

"This is my best Christmas ever," Bobby Lee said. "Thanks, Brandon."

"You're welcome," Brandon said. "I figured that you'd be getting that cast off soon and you'd need something to exercise that leg."

Maggie returned from the kitchen and handed a glass of eggnog to Brandon.

"Are you ready to go to Florida tomorrow?" Maggie asked while sitting in an easy chair.

"I still have some packing to do but not that much," Brandon said. "I don't plan to take that much with me. We won't be gone that long."

"How is the weather there?"

"It's been in the seventies so I just hope it stays that way. And I hope this stuff here melts away by the time we return on Sunday night."

"I do, too," Maggie said. "I've had enough of it."

"I want it to go away so I can ride my bike," Bobby Lee said.

"You need to get that cast taken off first," Maggie said.

"Can we go to the doctor tomorrow?" Bobby Lee asked with a pleading look on his face.

"Sorry, but your appointment isn't until next Monday," Maggie said. "The doctor is probably out of the office now for vacation."

"Shucks," Bobby Lee said while puckering up his cheeks.

"Well, I need to be going," Brandon said after taking the final swallow of coffee. "I have another errand to run before going home."

Brandon stood and put on his coat. Bobby Lee moved over to him and wrapped his arms tightly around his waist.

"Thanks, Brandon," Bobby Lee said as a tear trickled down his cheek.

"You're welcome," Brandon said, rubbing Bobby Lee on the back of the head. "I'm glad you like it."

Bobby Lee took a step over to the tree and bent down and took out a red package with green ribbons. He handed it to Brandon.

"This is for you," he said with a big smile.

"You didn't need to buy me anything," Brandon said.

"Open it," Bobby Lee said excitedly.

Brandon sat back down on the couch and slowly unwrapped the package. He opened it and there was a deep blue cardigan sweater. He held it up in front of him and smiled.

"Looks like it will be a perfect fit," Brandon said, looking at Bobby Lee and then at Maggie. "Thank you very much."

"You probably won't have any need for it in Florida but you may be able to wear it when you come back," Maggie said.

"I'm sure I will," Brandon said. He neatly folded the sweater and placed it back in the box.

"Thanks again," Brandon said to Bobby Lee. "I needed a sweater."

"I figured you did," Bobby Lee said with a smile. "You never seem to wear one."

"Oh, hush, Bobby Lee," Maggie said, blushing.

Brandon laughed. "You're right, Bobby Lee. I don't own many sweaters."

Maggie walked Brandon to the door and hugged him.

"You've been awfully good to us," she said. "I hope you have a nice trip. Tell Clarice Merry Christmas from us."

"I will," Brandon said. "I hope you enjoy the holiday."

"Merry Christmas!" Bobby Lee shouted from the living room as Brandon opened the front door.

"Merry Christmas," Brandon said. He smiled at Maggie and went to his car. She waited at the door until he backed out in the street and began to drive away, then she waved and closed the door.

Brandon drove slowly to Clarice's house. There were still many shoppers out and a lot of traffic on the streets. As he pulled into her driveway, he looked up to her house and saw a tiny Christmas tree in the front window. The white lights twinkled and the silver garland glistened through the darkness. A moment later, the porch light came on and Clarice stood at the doorway wearing a long red, velvet gown with white lace on the neckline and sleeves.

Brandon sat in the car for a few seconds after turning off the ignition, looking at her from the distance and thinking how lovely and regal she appeared. He reached inside his coat pocket and felt a small box. He took a deep breathe, opened the door and ambled to the house.

Fifty-eight

Clarice smiled and kissed Brandon softly on the mouth when he reached the door. He stepped inside and removed his coat, before following her into the den and sitting on the couch.

"It's been a long day without you," Clarice said, cuddling up next to him on the couch. "I missed you."

"I missed you, too," Brandon said before kissing her on the cheek.

"What did Bobby Lee think of his bicycle?" Clarice asked.

"I believe he liked it a lot," Brandon said. "I think if Maggie would've allowed it, he would have taken it outside for a spin if he didn't have the cast."

"That was awfully sweet of you to buy him that."

"He's a good kid," Brandon said. "He's been through a lot the past few months. They gave me a sweater."

"Really? Why didn't you bring it in?

"I forgot. It's a blue cardigan. It's very nice."

"Are you ready to go to Florida tomorrow?"

"Almost," Brandon said. "I've still got some packing to do."

"You're not finished yet?" Clarice asked.

"I've been working," he said.

"I'm packed and ready to go."

"Why doesn't surprise me? You're very organized. Do you think I should bring along *Ulysses* to read while I'm down there?'"

"Haven't you finished that book?" she asked, shaking her head in mock amazement.

"Only a few more chapters."

"Maybe you can finish it before we leave."

"I'll try."

"How do I look?"

"Gorgeous," Brandon smiled. "The gown is lovely."

"I mean my face," Clarice said. "Does it look like the swelling is going down and the bruises are fading?"

Brandon looked at her intently for a few seconds.

"I hardly noticed anything when I came in," he said. "I think you're beautiful."

"I should have known I wouldn't get a straight answer from you," Clarice said with a grin.

"Don't you like to be told that you're beautiful?"

"Well, yes, but I didn't feel beautiful after the accident."

"You're much too hard on yourself."

"I talked to Sheryl today," Clarice said. "She's no longer seeing Bart."

"Is that a surprise?"

"No," Clarice said. "I just wish I could have said something to her before she got so wrapped up in him. He got what he wanted."

"She probably wouldn't have listened,"

"You're right," Clarice said, shaking her head. "She was blind to it all."

"Is she going to be all right?"

"I think so," Clarice said. "She's a little disappointed but she'll find someone else. I guess it was the timing more than anyone, just before Christmas."

"Bart is such a classy guy," Brandon said sarcastically.

"Is there a bigger jerk in town?"

"Is there a bigger jerk anywhere?"

"Have you had anything to eat?" Clarice asked.

"I had a cup of coffee at Maggie's house," Brandon said. "I'm really not hungry. Go ahead and eat if you want to."

"I had a late lunch," Clarice said.

Brandon reached into the coat pocket and fidgeted with the small package. He had a distant look in his eyes as he gazed across the room.

"Is something the matter?" Clarice asked.

"Huh?" Brandon said. "What do you mean?"

"You're acting like something is on your mind."

"I'm fine," he said with a sheepish grin. "I just thought of something."

"Do you care to share?" Clarice said, raising her eyebrows and smiling.

"I was just thinking how much I love you," he said.

Clarice was silent for a few seconds as tears welled up in her eyes.

"How long have we known each other?" Brandon asked. "About four months?"

"I think so," Clarice said.

"That's not very long, is it?" Brandon asked.

"It all depends," Clarice said. "In terms of time, I guess it isn't. But I feel like I've known you for a very long time."

"I feel the same way about you," Brandon said while putting his hand back into the coat pocket. "I really enjoy being with you."

"I love being with you," she said softly. "I feel a little empty when you're not around."

Brandon took the package out of his coat and handed it to Clarice.

"I have a little something for you for Christmas," he said with a smile. "I hope you don't mind me giving it to you a couple of days early."

The box had a tiny red ribbon wrapped around it and a white bow. She looked at it for a few seconds and then at Brandon.

"I don't know what to say," she said. "I sent your presents down to Florida to open on Christmas morning."

"I've got a couple more for you but I thought this one was a little too personal," he said. "Aren't you going to open it?"

Clarice carefully removed the bow and untied the ribbon. She opened the box and removed the small container inside. She flipped it open and diamond engagement ring dazzled before her eyes.

"It's beautiful," Clarice said as her eyes began to fill with tears.

"I was wondering if you'd marry me?" Brandon asked nervously as he looked into her eyes. "If you think it's too soon, I'll understand."

Clarice smiled softly at him. Brandon could feel his heart beating almost uncontrollably during the brief silence.

"Yes, Brandon, I would love to be your wife," Clarice said as she wrapped her arms around him. "I'm so much in love with you."

Brandon held her for a few seconds, smelling the sweet, seductive scent of her perfume and the feel of her soft hair against the side of his face.

"I love you very much," he whispered into her ear. "I want to be with you the rest of my life."

"And I want to spend the rest of my life with you."

Clarice looked at him with tear-filled eyes and a tender smile. Brandon looked at her contentedly. And their mouths came together in a long passionate kiss.

Meet Michael Embry

Michael Embry, a native of Kentucky, is the author of three nonfiction sports books and three novels. Among his Kentucky "hometowns" are Frankfort, Louisville, Lexington, Richmond, Jeffersontown, Campbellsville, Madisonville, Morehead, and Hopkinsville. He is a graduate of Eastern Kentucky University and a veteran of the Air Force, spending most of his time at Whiteman AFB in Missouri.

Embry has worked for Kentucky newspapers in Madisonville and Lexington and a national news service, making stops in Louisville, New York, Milwaukee and Lexington. He retired as editor of *Kentucky Monthly* magazine in Frankfort in 2006 to return to school to become a special education teacher. Among the organizations he is involved in are the Honorable Order of Kentucky Colonels, Golden Key International Honour Society, National Sportscasters and Sportswriters Association, U.S. Basketball Writers Association, Sierra Club, and The Friends of the Paul Sawyier Public Library in Frankfort.

Embry and his wife, Mary, live in Frankfort with their two Yorkshire Terriers, Bucky and Baxter.

**VISIT OUR WEBSITE
FOR THE FULL INVENTORY
OF QUALITY BOOKS**:

http://www.wings-press.com

**Quality trade paperbacks and downloads
in multiple formats,
in genres ranging from light romantic
comedy to general fiction and horror.
Wings has something
for every reader's taste.
Visit the website, then bookmark it.
We add new titles each month!**

www.ingramcontent.com/pod-product-compliance
Lightning Source LLC
Chambersburg PA
CBHW072010110726

47910CB00005B/1703